HOUND DUNNIT

Edited by Isaac Asimov
Martin Harry Greenberg
and Carol-Lynn Rössel Waugh

Carroll & Graf Publishers, Inc.
New York

Collection copyright © 1987 by Carroll & Graf Publishers, Inc.

First Carroll & Graf edition, 1987

Carroll & Graf Publishers, Inc.
260 Fifth Avenue
New York, NY 10001

Library of Congress Cataloging-in-Publication Data

Hound dunnit.

   1. Detective and mystery stories, American.
2. Detective and mystery stories, English.   3. Dogs—
Fiction.   I. Asimov, Isaac, 1920-   II. Greenberg,
Martin Harry.   III. Waugh, Carol-Lynn Rössel.
PS648.D4H68   1987   813'.0872'08   87-15765
ISBN: 0-88184-353-9

Manufactured in the United States of America
The stories are copyrighted respectively:
The Sleeping Dog Copyright © 1965 by Ross Macdonald. Reprinted by
permission of Harold Ober Associates, Inc.
The Enemy copyright © 1951 by Charlotte Armstrong. Copyright renewed ©
1977 by Charlotte Armstrong. Reprinted by permission of Brandt &
Brandt Literary Agents, Inc.
The Dog Who Hated Jazz copyright © 1983 by William Bankier. First
published in *Prime Crimes*. Reprinted by permission of Curtis Brown,
Ltd.
The Dark Road Home copyright © 1960 by Paul Fairman. Reprinted by
permission of Virginia Fairman.
The Emergency Exit Affair copyright © 1970 by Davis Publications, Inc.
First published in *Ellery Queen's Mystery Magazine*. Reprinted by
permission of the author.

Table of Contents

DOGS

BY ISAAC ASIMOV

The Bible hasn't a good word to say for dogs. Thus, Jesus is quoted as saying in the Sermon on the Mount: "Give not that which is holy unto the dogs . . ." (Matthew 7:6) where dogs symbolize anyone who is totally unworthy of divine blessing.

This is perhaps understandable, for in the Middle East in Biblical times (and now, too, perhaps) the dog was a scavenger and carrion-eater, a source of fleas and disease, very useful in the absence of a sanitation department but not much good otherwise.

In this respect, however, the Biblical point of view does not represent the attitude of our Western world. In Homer's *Odyssey*, the Grecian war-hero, Odysseus, returns from a long war under the walls of Troy and long years of wandering since. He comes home after a lapse of twenty years to find his wife still faithful, but besieged by arrogant suitors who are trying to succeed to the kingdom by marrying her.

The returning king is in the guise of a beggar and, of course, no one recognizes him (except his old nurse who sees a distinctive scar on his leg, which he received while hunting a boar in his youth.) However, Odysseus had a dog whom he had bred before leaving for Troy and who had been a famous hunter. He was left behind when Odysseus left and now, twenty years older, he barely retained life. He was lying on a dunghill, covered with fleas, but as Odysseus approached, the dog, Argus, wagged his tail and tried to stand up, but couldn't—and he died even as he carried through this feat of recognition.

Odysseus wept at this and who knows how many millions have read the *Odyssey* and felt a suspicious moistness about their own eyes. I myself feel it now, having just reread the passage, even though I seriously doubt that a dog would have recognized its master after twenty years.

The loyalty and utter fidelity of a dog has come down as an article of faith to most people of our Western culture. In 1884, Senator George G. Vest gave a speech in the Senate (a speech which, as far as I know, is the only deed for which he is remembered) and spoke highly of dogs. He said, in part: "The one absolutely unselfish friend that man can have in this selfish world, the one that never deserts him, the one that never proves ungrateful or treacherous, is his dog . . . He will kiss the hand that has no food to offer . . . When all other friends desert, he remains."

Again, my sense of cynicism, keeps me from ignoring the fact that there are such things as conditioned reflexes and that a dog may be following this rather than any high moral sense of loyalty. In any case, Vest's encomium struck a chord in millions and it may have given rise to the common expression: "A man's best friend is his dog."

Mark Twain, ten years later, said much the same thing in his book *The Tragedy of Pudd'nhead Wilson,* but did so in the bitter, epigrammatic way of which he was a master. He said: "If you pick up a starving dog and make him prosperous, he will not bite you. That is the principal difference between a dog and a man." I suspect, however, that Mark said that not because he loved dogs so much as because he loved men so little.

Whether the dog is man's best friend, or not, he seems certainly to be man's oldest animal friend. The dog has been domesticated since 8000 B.C. at least, and he is the one animal that has followed human beings over all the world. The American Indians had very few domesticated animals, but they had the dog. Even the Australian aborigines had the half-wild dingo.

Why is that? Dogs were useful, for one thing, since they are hunting carnivores and could therefore hunt along with human beings. Dogs were also intelligent enough to see that if they actually helped human beings with the hunting they would be rewarded with a share of the carcass. It was a symbiotic relationship that helped both. Dogs could locate the prey, pursue it, worry it, and wear it out, while men with spears and arrows could do the actual killing.

Dogs may have descended from some variety of wolf or, perhaps, jackal—we can't be sure which—and the association with man must have arisen because some early dogs would sniff around a campfire to see if they could scavenge any left-over food.

Human beings may not have felt very fond of dogs at first. Running off with a precious gobbet of meat is an action unlikely to win the hearts of human beings about to eat it themselves. There would surely have been wild shouting and rock-throwing.

However, my own theory is that we have to consider the young of the species. Every once in a while, a human child would come across a doggish child (a puppy, in other words) and they might have enjoyed each other. When it came time for the parents to drive the dog away (or, perhaps, to consider it as an article of diet) the child would object vociferously—and children often have their way in such matters.

As a dog grows older and more dangerous, however, the pressure to get rid of it or kill it grows stronger. Those dogs escape this fate that show themselves to be particularly friendly and amiable, or particularly adept at hunting. In other words, without knowing exactly what they were doing, human beings would discard some dogs and keep others, thereby breeding friendliness and hunting ability into the animals.

It helps in this respect that dogs are pack animals, and have the instinct of following their leader, that is, whichever of their group can either beat the others physically, or browbeat them psychologically. If a puppy is brought up by human beings, one human being or another becomes the leader as far as that puppy (and, later, dog) is concerned and his fidelity is, again, a matter of instinct rather than some high moral virtue.

But what is the use of talking of instinct and conditioned reflexes? That means something only if we can retain some sort of cool and aloof attitude towards dogs, and that is a difficult thing to do.

Whatever the cause, the dog acts toward human beings *as if* it is filled with love and affection for them, and that appearance of love is taken as fact; and the love is usually returned in full.

Man has many domestic animals, kept for food or for work. Love has nothing to do with it. Chickens, geese, cattle, sheep show no love. They are docile at best, and do what is expected of them, yielding eggs or milk or wool.

Even the hardworking horse, perhaps the most beautiful of animals, which can inspire the affection of its owner, can show only a nuzzling affection of its own, one that is quiet and subdued.

The only animals that are kept as pets *only*, kept solely out of affection even when they do no work and have no use, are dogs and cats, and, of these, cats show no affection and rarely inspire the deep love lavished on dogs.

But why do I say no use? To experience a steady, unwavering, constantly expressed love—is that no use? To have a companionship that does not fail—is that no use? Psychologists have recently discovered that the possession of a pet contributes enormously to mental health and to emotional stability. They are probably the last to have made the discovery. Everyone else knows it.

Why not, then, combine two great loves: that for dogs and that for mysteries, and present the readers with mysteries that in one way or another involve dogs? In this book, "Hound Dunnit," you have a collection of such mysteries.

Ross Macdonald

Born in Los Gatos, California, raised in Canada, Kenneth Millar (aka Ross Macdonald) is known for his semi-autobiographical mysteries featuring detective Lew Archer ("I'm not Archer, exactly, but Archer is me"), which appeared in 1949. He wrote under a pseudonym to avoid confusing his work with that of his successful wife, Margaret Millar, who published her first mystery novel in 1941)

Famous for his complicated plots and his Southern California settings, Millar's books often explore psychological themes, especially children's search for lost fathers and/or their search for identity by running away from affluence. He describes Archer as "a socially mobile man who knows all levels of Southern California life and takes a peculiarly wry pleasure in exploring its secret passages. Archer tends to live through other people, as a novelist lives through his characters."

The Crime Writers' Association selected *The Chill* as runner-up for best novel of 1964, and *The Far Side of the Dollar* as best of 1965.

THE SLEEPING DOG

BY ROSS MACDONALD

The day after her dog disappeared, Fay Hooper called me early. Her normal voice was like waltzing violins, but this morning the violins were out of tune. She sounded as though she'd been crying.

"Otto's gone."

Otto was her one-year-old German shepherd.

"He jumped the fence yesterday afternoon and ran away. Or else he was kidnaped—dognaped, I suppose is the right word to use."

"What makes you think that?"

"You know, Otto, Mr. Archer—how loyal he was. He wouldn't deliberately stay away from me overnight, not under his own power. There must be thieves involved."

She caught her breath. "I realize searching for stolen dogs isn't your métier. But you *are* a detective, and I thought, since we knew one another . . ."

She allowed her voice to suggest, ever so chastely, that we might get to know one another better.

I liked the woman. I liked the dog, I liked the breed. I was taking my own German shepherd pup to obedience school, which is where I met Fay Hooper. Otto and she were the handsomest and most expensive members of the class.

"How do I get to your place?"

She lived in the hills north of Malibu, she said, on the far side of the county line. If she wasn't home when I got there, her husband would be.

On my way out I stopped at the dog school in Pacific Palisades to talk to the man who ran it, Fernando Rambeau. The kennels behind the house burst into clamor when I knocked on the front door. Rambeau boarded dogs as well as trained them.

A dark-haired girl looked out and informed me that her

2

husband was feeding the animals. "Maybe I can help," she added doubtfully, and then she let me into a small living room.

I told her about the missing dog. "It would help if you called the vets and animal shelters and gave them a description," I said.

"We've already been doing that. Mrs. Hooper was on the phone to Fernando last night." She sounded vaguely resentful. "I'll get him."

Setting her face against the continuing noise, she went out the back door. Rambeau came in with her, wiping his hands on a rag. He was a square-shouldered Canadian with a curly black beard that failed to conceal his youth. Over the beard, his intense dark eyes peered at me warily, like an animal's sensing trouble.

Rambeau handled dogs as if he loved them. He wasn't quite so patient with human beings. His current class was only in its third week, but he was already having dropouts. The man was loaded with explosive feeling, and it was close to the surface now.

"I'm sorry about Mrs. Hooper and her dog. They were my best pupils. He was, anyway. But I can't drop everything and spend the next week looking for him."

"Nobody expects that. I take it you've had no luck with your contacts."

"I don't have such good contacts. Marie and I, we just moved down here last year, from British Columbia."

"That was a mistake," his wife said from the doorway.

Rambeau pretended not to hear her. "Anyway, I know nothing about dog thieves." With both hands he pushed the possibility away from him. "If I hear any word of the dog I'll let you know, naturally. I've got nothing against Mrs. Hooper."

His wife gave him a quick look. It was one of those revealing looks which said, among other things, that she loved him but didn't know if he loved her, and she was worried about him. She caught me watching her and lowered her eyes. Then she burst out, "Do you think somebody killed the dog?"

"I have no reason to think so."

"Some people shoot dogs, don't they?"

"Not around here," Rambeau said. "Maybe back in the bush someplace." He turned to me with a sweeping explanatory gesture. "These things make her nervous and she gets wild ideas. You know Marie is a country girl—"

"I am not. I was born in Chilliwack." Flinging a bitter look at him, she left the room.

"Was Otto shot?" I asked Rambeau.

"Not that I know of. Listen, Mr. Archer, you're a good customer, but I can't stand here talking all day. I've got twenty dogs to feed."

They were still barking when I drove up the coast highway out of hearing. It was nearly 40 miles to the Hoopers' mailbox, and another mile up a black-top lane which climbed the side of a canyon to the gate. On both sides of the heavy wire gate, which had a new combination padlock on it, a hurricane fence, eight feet high and topped with barbed wire, extended out of sight. Otto would have to be quite a jumper to clear it. So would I.

The house beyond the gate was low and massive, made of fieldstone and steel and glass. I honked at it and waited. A man in blue bathing trunks came out of the house with a shotgun. The sun glinted on its twin barrels and on the man's bald head and round, brown, burnished belly. He walked quite slowly, a short heavy man in his sixties, scuffling along in huaraches. The flabby brown shell of fat on him jiggled lugubriously.

When he approached the gate, I could see the stiff gray pallor under his tan, like stone showing under varnish. He was sick, or afraid, or both. His mouth was profoundly discouraged.

"What do you want?" he said over the shotgun.

"Mrs. Hooper asked me to help find her dog. My name is Lew Archer."

He was not impressed. "My wife isn't here, and I'm busy. I happen to be following soy-bean futures rather closely."

"Look here, I've come quite a distance to lend a hand. I met Mrs. Hooper at dog school and—"

Hooper uttered a short savage laugh. "That hardly constitutes an introduction to either of us. You'd better be on your way right now."

"I think I'll wait for your wife."

"I think you won't." He raised the shotgun and let me look into its close-set, hollow, round eyes. "This is my property all the way down to the road, and you're trespassing. That means I can shoot you if I have to.''

"What sense would that make? I came out here to help you.''

"You can't help me.'' He looked at me through the wire gate with a kind of pathetic arrogance, like a lion that had grown old in captivity. "Go away.''

I drove back down to the road and waited for Fay Hooper. The sun slid up the sky. The inside of my car turned oven-hot. I went for a walk down the canyon. The brown September grass crunched under my feet. Away up on the far side of the canyon an earth mover that looked like a crazy red insect was cutting the ridge to pieces.

A very fast black car came up the canyon and stopped abruptly beside me. A gaunt man in a wrinkled brown suit climbed out, with his hand on his holster, told me that he was Sheriff Carlson, and asked me what I was doing there. I told him.

He pushed back his wide cream-colored hat and scratched at his hairline. The pale eyes in his sun-fired face were like clouded glass inserts in a brick wall.

"I'm surprised Mr. Hooper takes that attitude. Mrs. Hooper just came to see me in the courthouse. But I can't take you up there with me if Mr. Hooper says no.''

"Why not?''

"He owns most of the county and holds the mortgage on the rest of it. Besides,'' he added with careful logic, "Mr. Hooper is a friend of mine.''

"Then you better get him a keeper.''

The sheriff glanced around uneasily, as if the Hoopers' mailbox might be bugged. "I'm surprised he has a gun, let alone threatening you with it. He must be upset about the dog.''

"He didn't seem to care about the dog.''

"He does, though. *She* cares, so *he* cares,'' Carlson said.

"What did she have to tell you?''

"She can talk to you herself. She should be along any minute. She told me that she was going to follow me out of town.''

He drove his black car up the lane. A few minutes later Fay Hooper stopped her Mercedes at the mailbox. She must have seen the impatience on my face. She got out and came toward me in a little run, making noises of dismayed regret.

Fay was in her late thirties and fading slightly, as if a light frost had touched her pale gold head, but she was still a beautiful woman. She turned the gentle force of her charm on me.

"I'm dreadfully sorry," she said. "Have I kept you waiting long?"

"Your husband did. He ran me off with a shotgun."

Her gloved hand lighted on my arm, and stayed. She had an electric touch, even through layers of cloth.

"That's terrible. I had no idea that Allan still had a gun."

Her mouth was blue behind her lipstick, as if the information had chilled her to the marrow. She took me up the hill in the Mercedes. The gate was standing open, but she didn't drive in right away.

"I might as well be perfectly frank," she said without looking at me. "Ever since Otto disappeared yesterday, there's been a nagging question in my mind. What you've just told me raises the question again. I was in town all day yesterday so that Otto was alone here with Allan when—when it happened."

The values her voice gave to the two names made it sound as if Allan were the dog and Otto the husband.

"When what happened, Mrs. Hooper?" I wanted to know.

Her voice sank lower. "I can't help suspecting that Allan shot him. He's never liked any of my dogs. The only dogs he appreciates are hunting dogs—and he was particularly jealous of Otto. Besides, when I got back from town, Allan was getting the ground ready to plant some roses. He's never enjoyed gardening, particularly in the heat. We have professionals to do our work. And this really isn't the time of year to put in a bed of roses."

"You think your husband was planting a dog?" I asked.

"If he was, I have to know." She turned toward me, and the leather seat squeaked softly under her movement. "Find out for me, Mr. Archer. If Allan killed my beautiful big old dog, I couldn't stay with him."

"Something you said implied that Allan used to have a gun or guns, but gave them up. Is that right?"

"He had a small arsenal when I married him. He was an infantry officer in the war and a big-game hunter in peacetime. But he swore off hunting years ago."

"Why?"

"I don't really know. We came home from a hunting trip one fall and Allan sold all his guns. He never said a word about it to me but it was the fall after the war ended, and I always thought that it must have had something to do with the war."

"Have you been married so long?"

"Thank you for that question." She produced a rueful smile. "I met Allan during the war, the year I came out, and I knew I'd met my fate. He was a very powerful person."

"And a very wealthy one."

She gave me a flashing, haughty look and stepped so hard on the accelerator that she almost ran into the sheriff's car parked in front of the house. We walked around to the back, past a freeform swimming pool that looked inviting, into a walled garden. A few Greek statues stood around in elegant disrepair. Bees murmured like distant bombers among the flowers.

The bed where Allan Hooper had been digging was about five feet long and three feet wide, and it reminded me of graves.

"Get me a spade," I said.

"Are you going to dig him up?"

"You're pretty sure he's in there, aren't you, Mrs. Hooper?"

"I guess I am."

From a lath house at the end of the garden she fetched a square-edged spade. I asked her to stick around.

I took off my jacket and hung it on a marble torso where it didn't look too bad. It was easy digging in the newly worked soil. In a few minutes I was two feet below the surface, and the ground was still soft and penetrable.

The edge of my spade struck something soft but not so penetrable. Fay Hooper heard the peculiar dull sound it made. She made a dull sound of her own. I scooped away more earth. Dog fur sprouted like stiff black grass at the bottom of the grave.

Fay got down on her knees and began to dig with her lacquered fingernails. Once she cried out in a loud harsh voice, "Dirty murderer!"

Her husband must have heard her. He came out of the house and looked over the stone wall. His head seemed poised on top of the wall, hairless and bodiless, like Humpty-Dumpty. He had that look on his face, of not being able to be put together again.

"I didn't kill your dog, Fay. Honest to God, I didn't."

She didn't hear him. She was talking to Otto. "Poor boy, poor boy," she said. "Poor, beautiful boy."

Sheriff Carlson came into the garden. He reached down into the grave and freed the dog's head from the earth. His large hands moved gently on the great wedge of the skull.

Fay knelt beside him in torn and dirty stockings. "What are you doing?"

Carlson held up a red-tipped finger. "Your dog was shot through the head, Mrs. Hooper, but it's no shotgun wound. Looks to me more like a deer rifle."

"I don't even own a rifle," Hooper said over the wall. "I haven't owned one for nearly twenty years. Anyway, I wouldn't shoot your dog."

Fay scrambled to her feet. She looked ready to climb the wall. "Then why did you bury him?"

His mouth opened and closed.

"Why did you buy a shotgun without telling me?"

"For protection."

"Against my dog?"

Hooper shook his head. He edged along the wall and came in tentatively through the gate. He had on slacks and a short-sleeved yellow jersey which somehow emphasized his shortness and his fatness and his age.

"Mr. Hooper had some threatening calls," the sheriff said. "Somebody got hold of his unlisted number. He was just telling me about it now."

"Why didn't you tell me, Allan?"

"I didn't want to alarm you. You weren't the one they were after, anyway. I bought a shotgun and kept it in my study."

"Do you know who they are?"

"No. I make enemies in the course of business, especially the farming operations. Some crackpot shot your dog, gunning for me. I heard a shot and found him dead in the driveway."

"But how could you bury him without telling me?"

Hooper spread his hands in front of him. "I wasn't thinking too well. I felt guilty, I suppose, because whoever got him was after me. And I didn't want you to see him dead. I guess I wanted to break it to you gently."

"This is gently?"

"It's not the way I planned it. I thought if I had a chance to get you another pup—"

"No one will ever take Otto's place."

Allan Hooper stood and looked at her wistfully across the open grave, as if he would have liked to take Otto's place. After a while the two of them went into the house.

Carlson and I finished digging Otto up and carried him out to the sheriff's car. His inert blackness filled the trunk from side to side.

"What are you going to do with him, Sheriff?" I asked.

"Get a vet I know to recover the slug in him. Then if we nab the sniper we can use ballistics to convict him."

"You're taking this just as seriously as a real murder, aren't you?" I observed.

"They want me to," he said with a respectful look toward the house.

Mrs. Hooper came out carrying a white leather suitcase which she deposited in the back seat of her Mercedes.

"Are you going someplace?" I asked her.

"Yes, I am." She didn't say where.

Her husband, who was watching her from the doorway, didn't speak. The Mercedes went away. He closed the door. Both of them had looked sick.

"She doesn't seem to believe he didn't do it. Do you, Sheriff?"

Carlson jabbed me with his forefinger. "Mr. Hooper is no liar. If you want to get along with me, get that through your head. I've known Mr. Hooper for over twenty years—served under him in the war—and I never heard him twist the truth."

"I'll have to take your word for it. What about those threatening phone calls? Did he report them to you before today?"

"No."

"What was said on the phone?"

"He didn't tell me."

"Does Hooper have any idea who shot the dog?"

"Well, he did say he saw a man slinking around outside the fence. He didn't get close enough to the guy to give me a good description, but he did make out that he had a black beard."

"There's a dog trainer in Pacific Palisades named Rambeau who fits the description. Mrs. Hooper has been taking Otto to his school."

"Rambeau?" Carlson said with interest.

"Fernando Rambeau. He seemed pretty upset when I talked to him this morning."

"What did he say?"

"A good deal less than he knows, I think. I'll talk to him again."

Rambeau was not at home. My repeated knocking was answered only by the barking of the dogs. I retreated up the highway to a drive-in where I ate a torpedo sandwich. When I was on my second cup of coffee, Marie Rambeau drove by in a pickup truck. I followed her home.

"Where's Fernando?" I asked.

"I don't know. I've been out looking for him."

"Is he in a bad way?"

"I don't know how you mean."

"Emotionally upset."

"He has been ever since that woman came into the class."

"Mrs. Hooper?"

Her head bobbed slightly.

"Are they having an affair?"

"They better not be." Her small red mouth looked quite implacable. "He was out with her night before last. I heard him make the date. He was gone all night, and when he came home he was on one of his black drunks and he wouldn't go to bed. He sat in the kitchen and drank himself glassy-eyed." She got out of the pickup facing me. "Is shooting a dog a very serious crime?"

"It is to me, but not to the law. It's not like shooting a human being."

"It would be to Fernando. He loves dogs the way other people love human beings. That included Otto."

"But he shot him."

Her head drooped. I could see the straight white part dividing her black hair. "I'm afraid he did. He's got a crazy streak and it comes out in him when he drinks. You should have heard him in the kitchen yesterday. He was moaning and groaning about his brother."

"His brother?"

"Fernando had an older brother, George, who died back in Canada after the war. Fernando was just a kid when it happened and it was a big loss to him. His parents were dead, too, and they put him in a foster home in Chilliwack. He still has nightmares about it."

'What did his brother die of?"

"He never told me exactly, but I think he was shot in some kind of hunting accident. George was a guide and packer in the Fraser River valley below Mount Robson. That's where Fernando comes from, the Mount Robson country. He won't go back, on account of what happened to his brother."

"What did he say about his brother yesterday?" I asked.

"That he was going to get his revenge for George. I got so scared I couldn't listen to him. I went out and fed the dogs. When I came back in, Fernando was loading his deer rifle. I asked him what he was planning to do, but he walked right out and drove away."

"May I see the rifle?"

"It isn't in the house. I looked for it after he left today. He must have taken it with him again. I'm so afraid that he'll kill somebody."

"What's he driving?"

"Our car. It's an old blue Meteor sedan."

Keeping an eye out for it, I drove up the highway to the Hoopers' canyon. Everything there was very peaceful. Too peaceful. Just inside the locked gate, Allan Hooper was lying face down on his shotgun. I could see small ants in single file trekking across the crown of his bald head.

I got a hammer out of the trunk of my car and used it to break the padlock. I lifted his head. His skin was hot in the sun, as if death had fallen on him like a fever. But he had been shot neatly between the eyes. There was no exit wound; the bullet was still in his head. Now the ants were crawling on my hands.

I found my way into the Hoopers' study, turned off the stuttering teletype, and sat down under an elk head to telephone the courthouse. Carlson was in his office.

"I have bad news, Sheriff. Allan Hooper's been shot."

I heard him draw in his breath quickly. "Is he dead?"

"Extremely dead. You better put out a general alarm for Rambeau."

Carlson said with gloomy satisfaction, "I already have him."

"You have him?"

"That's correct. I picked him up in the Hoopers' canyon and brought him in just a few minutes ago." Carlson's voice sank to a mournful mumble. "I picked him up a little too late, I guess."

"Did Rambeau do any talking?"

"He hasn't had a chance to yet. When I stopped his car, he piled out and threatened me with a rifle. I clobbered him one good."

I went outside to wait for Carlson and his men. A very pale afternoon moon hung like a ghost in the sky. For some reason it made me think of Fay. She ought to be here. It occurred to me that possibly she had been.

I went and looked at Hooper's body again. He had nothing to tell me. He lay as if he had fallen from a height, perhaps all the way from the moon.

They came in a black county wagon and took him away. I followed them inland to the county seat, which rose like a dusty island in a dark green lake of orange groves. We parked in the courthouse parking lot, and the sheriff and I went inside.

Rambeau was under guard in a second-floor room with barred windows. Carlson said it was used for interrogation. There was nothing in the room but an old deal table and some wooden chairs. Rambeau sat hunched forward on one of them, his hands hanging limp between his knees. part of his head had been shaved and plastered with bandages.

"I had to cool him with my gun butt," Carlson said. "You're lucky I didn't shoot you—you know that, Fernando?"

Rambeau made no response. His black eyes were set and dull.

"Had his rifle been fired?"

"Yeah. Chet Scott is working on it now. Chet's my identification lieutenant and he's a bear on ballistics." The sheriff turned back to Rambeau. "You might as well give us a full confession, boy. If you shot Mr. Hooper and his dog, we can link the bullets to your gun. You know that."

Rambeau didn't speak or move.

"What did you have against Mrs. Hooper?" Carlson said.

No answer. Rambeau's mouth was set like a trap in the thicket of his beard.

"Your older brother," I said to him, "was killed in a hunting accident in British Columbia. Was Hooper at the other end of the gun that killed George?"

Rambeau didn't answer me, but Carlson's head came up. "Where did you get that, Archer?"

"From a couple of things I was told. According to Rambeau's wife, he was talking yesterday about revenge for his brother's death. According to Fay Hooper, her husband swore off guns when he came back from a hunting trip after the war. Would you know if that trip was to British Columbia?"

"Yeah. Mr. Hooper took me and the wife with him."

"Whose wife?"

"Both our wives."

"To the Mount Robson area?"

"That's correct. We went up after elk."

"And did he shoot somebody accidentally?"

"Not that I know of. I wasn't with him all the time, understand. He often went out alone, or with Mrs. Hooper," Carlson replied.

"Did he use a packer named George Rambeau?"

"I wouldn't know. Ask Fernando here."

I asked Fernando. He didn't speak or move. Only his eyes had changed. They were wet and glistening-black, visible parts of a grief that filled his head like a dark underground river.

The questioning went on and produced nothing. It was night when I went outside. The moon was slipping down behind the dark hills. I took a room in a hotel and checked in with my answering service in Hollywood.

About an hour before, Fay Hooper had called me from a Las Vegas hotel. When I tried to return the call, she wasn't in her room and didn't respond to paging. I left a message for her to come home, that her husband was dead.

Next, I called R.C.M.P. headquarters in Vancouver to ask some questions about George Rambeau. The answers came over the line in clipped Canadian tones. George and his dog had disappeared from his cabin below Red Pass in the fall of 1945. Their bodies hadn't been discovered until the following May, and by that time they consisted of parts of the two skeletons. These included George Rambeau's skull, which had been pierced in the right front and left rear quadrants by a heavy-caliber bullet. The bullet had not been recovered. Who fired it, or when, or why, had never been determined. The dog, a husky, had also been shot through the head.

I walked over to the courthouse to pass the word to Carlson. He was in the basement shooting gallery with Lieutenant Scott, who was firing test rounds from Fernando Rambeau's .30/30 repeater.

I gave them the official account of the accident. "But since George Rambeau's dog was shot, too, it probably wasn't an accident," I said.

"I see what you mean," Carlson said. "It's going to be rough, spreading all this stuff out in court about Mr. Hooper. We have to nail it down, though."

I went back to my hotel and to bed, but the process of nailing down the case against Rambeau continued through the night. By morning Lieutenant Scott had detailed comparisons set up between the test-fired slugs and the ones dug out of Hooper and the dog.

I looked at his evidence through a comparison microscope. It left no doubt in my mind that the slugs that killed Allan Hooper and the dog, Otto, had come from Rambeau's gun.

But Rambeau still wouldn't talk, even to phone his wife or ask for a lawyer.

"We'll take you out to the scene of the crime," Carlson said. "I've cracked tougher nuts than you, boy."

We rode in the back seat of his car with Fernando handcuffed between us. Lieutenant Scott did the driving. Rambeau groaned and pulled against his handcuffs. He was very close to the breaking point, I thought.

It came a few minutes later when the car turned up the lane past the Hoopers' mailbox. He burst into sudden fierce tears as if a pressure gauge in his head had broken. It was strange to see a bearded man crying like a boy. "I don't want to go up there."

"Because you shot him?" Carlson said.

"I shot the dog. I confess I shot the dog," Rambeau said.

"And the man?"

"No!" he cried. "I never killed a man. Mr. Hooper was the one who did. He followed my brother out in the woods and shot him."

"If you knew that," I said, "why didn't you tell the Mounties years ago?"

"I didn't know it then. I was seven years old. How would I understand? When Mrs. Hooper came to our cabin to be with my brother, how would I know it was a serious thing? Or when Mr. Hooper asked me if she had been there? I didn't know he was her husband. I thought he was her father checking up. I knew I shouldn't have told him—I could see it in his face the minute after—but I didn't understand the situation till the other night, when I talked to Mrs. Hooper."

"Did she know that her husband had shot George?"

"She didn't even know George had been killed. They never went back to the Fraser River after nineteen forty-five. But when we put our facts together, we agreed he must have done it. I came out here next morning to get even. The dog came out to the gate. It wasn't real to me—I'd been drinking most of the night—it wasn't real to me until the dog went down. I shot him. Mr. Hooper shot *my* dog. But when he came out of the house himself, I couldn't pull the trigger. I yelled at him and ran away."

"What did you yell?" I said.

"The same thing I told him on the telephone: 'Remember Mount Robson.' "

A yellow cab, which looked out of place in the canyon, came over the ridge above us. Lieutenant Scott waved it to a stop. The driver said he'd just brought Mrs. Hooper home from the airport and wanted to know if that constituted a felony. Scott waved him on.

"I wonder what she was doing at the airport," Carlson said.

"Coming home from Vegas. She tried to call me from there last night. I forgot to tell you."

"You don't forget important things like that," Carlson said.

"I suppose I wanted her to come home under her own power."

"In case she shot her husband?"

"More or less."

"She didn't. Fernando shot him, didn't you, boy?"

"I shot the dog. I am innocent of the man." He turned to me. "Tell her that. Tell her I am sorry about the dog. I came out here to surrender the gun and tell her yesterday. I don't trust myself with guns."

"With darn good reason," Carlson said. "We know you shot Mr. Hooper. Ballistic evidence doesn't lie."

Rambeau screeched in his ear, "You're a liar! You're all liars!"

Carlson swung his open hand against the side of Rambeau's face. "Don't call me names, little man."

Lieutenant Scott spoke without taking his eyes from the road. "I wouldn't hit him, Chief. You wouldn't want to damage our case."

Carlson subsided, and we drove on up to the house. Carlson went in without knocking. The guard at the door discouraged me from following him.

I couldn't hear Fay's voice on the other side of the door, too low to be understood. Carlson said something to her.

"Get out! Get out of my house, you killer!" Fay cried out sharply.

Carlson didn't come out. I went in instead. One of his arms was wrapped around her body, the other hand was covering her mouth. I got his Adam's apple in the crook of my left arm, pulled him away from her, and threw him over my left hip. He went down clanking and got up holding his revolver.

He should have shot me right away. But he gave Fay Hooper time to save my life.

She stepped in front of me. "Shoot me, Mr. Carlson. You might as well. You shot the one man I ever cared for."

"Your husband shot George Rambeau, if that's who you mean. I ought to know. I was there." Carlson scowled down at his gun and replaced it in his holster.

Lieutenant Scott was watching him from the doorway.

"You were there?" I said to Carlson. "Yesterday you told me Hooper was alone when he shot Rambeau."

"He was. When I said I was there, I meant in the general neighborhood."

"Don't believe him," Fay said. "He fired the gun that killed George, and it was no accident. The two of them hunted George down in the woods. My husband planned to shoot him himself, but George's dog came at him and he had to dispose of it. By that time George had drawn a bead on Allan. Mr. Carlson shot him. It was hardly a coincidence that the next spring Allan financed his campaign for sheriff."

"She's making it up," Carlson said. "She wasn't within ten miles of the place."

"But you were, Mr. Carlson, and so was Allan. He told me the whole story yesterday, after we found Otto. Once that happened, he knew that everything was bound to come out. I already suspected him, of course, after I talked to Fernando. Allan filled in the details himself. He thought, since he hadn't killed George personally, I would be able to forgive him. But I couldn't. I left him and flew to Nevada, intending to divorce him. I've been intending to for twenty years."

Carlson said, "Are you sure you didn't shoot him before you left?"

"How could she have?" I said. "Ballistics don't lie, and the ballistic evidence says he was shot with Fernando's rifle. Nobody had access to it but Fernando—and you. You stopped him on the road and knocked him out, took his rifle, and used it to kill Hooper. You killed him for the same reason that Hooper buried the dog—to keep the past buried. You thought Hooper was the only witness to the murder of George Rambeau. But by that time, Mrs. Hooper knew about it, too."

"It wasn't murder. It was self-defense, just like in the war. Anyway, you'll never hang it on me."

"We don't have to. We'll hang Hooper on you. How about it, Lieutenant?"

Scott nodded grimly, not looking at his chief. I relieved Carlson of his gun. He winced, as if I were amputating part of his body. He offered no resistance when Scott took him out to the car.

I stayed behind for a final word with Fay. "Fernando asked me to tell you he's sorry for shooting your dog."

"We're both sorry." She stood with her eyes down, as if the

past was swirling visibly around her feet. "I'll talk to Fernando later. Much later."

"There's one coincidence that bothers me. How did you happen to take your dog to his school?"

"I happened to see his sign, and Fernando Rambeau isn't a common name. I couldn't resist going there. I had to know what had happened to George. I think perhaps Fernando came to California for the same reason."

"Now you both know," I said.

Charlotte Armstrong

Born May 2, 1905 in Vulcan, Michigan, Charlotte Armstrong was a novelist, playwright, poet and short-story writer. Several of her television scripts were produced by Alfred Hitchcock; hallmarks of her work are suspense and peril.

Her novels have enjoyed enormous popularity: *A Dram of Poison* won the Edgar for Best Mystery Novel of 1956 from the Mystery Writers of America. "The Enemy" won first prize in the 1951 *Ellery Queen's Mystery Magazine* short-story contest. She died in California in 1969.

THE ENEMY

BY CHARLOTTE ARMSTRONG

They sat late at the lunch table and afterwards moved through the dim, cool, high-ceilinged rooms to the Judge's library where, in their quiet talk, the old man's past and the young man's future seemed to telescope and touch. But at twenty minutes after three, on that hot, bright, June Saturday afternoon, the present tense erupted. Out in the quiet street arose the sound of trouble.

Judge Kittinger adjusted his pince-nez, rose, and led the way to his old-fashioned veranda from which they could overlook the tree-roofed intersection of Greenwood Lane and Hannibal Street. Near the steps to the corner house, opposite, there was a surging knot of children and one man. Now, from the house on the Judge's left, a woman in a blue house dress ran diagonally toward the excitement. And a police car slipped up Hannibal Street, gliding to the curb. One tall officer plunged into the group and threw restraining arms around a screaming boy.

Mike Russell, saying to his host, "Excuse me, sir," went rapidly across the street. Trouble's center was the boy, ten or eleven years old, a towheaded boy, with tawny-lashed blue eyes, a straight nose, a fine brow. He was beside himself, writhing in the policeman's grasp. The woman in the blue dress was yammering at him. "Freddy! Freddy! Freddy!" Her voice simply did not reach his ears.

"You ole stinker! You rotten ole stinker! You ole nut!" All the boy's heart was in the epithets.

"Now, listen . . ." The cop shook the boy who, helpless in those powerful hands, yet blazed. His fury had stung to crimson the face of the grown man at whom it was directed.

This man, who stood with his back to the house as one besieged, was plump, half-bald, with eyes much magnified by

20

glasses. "Attacked me!" he cried in a high whine. "Rang my bell and absolutely leaped on me!"

Out of the seven or eight small boys clustered around them came overlapping fragments of shrill sentences. It was clear only that they opposed the man. A small woman in a print dress, a man in shorts, whose bare chest was winter-white, stood a little apart, hesitant and distressed. Up on the veranda of the house the screen door was half open, and a woman seated in a wheel chair peered forth anxiously.

On the green grass, in the shade, perhaps thirty feet away, there lay in death a small brown-and-white dog.

The Judge's luncheon guest observed all this. When the Judge drew near, there was a lessening of the noise. Judge Kittinger said, "This is Freddy Titus, isn't it? Mr. Matlin? What's happened?"

The man's head jerked. "I," he said, "did nothing to the dog. Why would I trouble to hurt the boy's dog? I try—you know this, Judge—I try to live in peace here. But these kids are terrors! They've made this block a perfect hell for me and my family." The man's voice shook. "My wife, who is not strong . . . My stepdaughter, who is a cripple . . . These kids are no better than a slum gang. They are vicious! That boy rang my bell and *attacked* . . . *!* I'll have him up for assault! I . . . ."

The Judge's face was old ivory and he was aloof behind it.

On the porch a girl pushed past the woman in the chair, a girl who walked with a lurching gait.

Mike Russell asked, quietly, "Why do the boys say it was you, Mr. Matlin, who hurt the dog?"

The kids chorused. "He's an ole mean . . ." "He's a nut . . ." "Just because . . ." ". . . took Clive's bat and . . ." ". . . chases us . . ." ". . . tries to put everything on us . . ." ". . . told my mother lies . . ." ". . . just because . . ."

He is our enemy, they were saying; *he is our enemy.*

"They . . . " began Matlin, his throat thick with anger.

"Hold it a minute." The second cop, the thin one, walked toward where the dog was lying.

"Somebody," said Mike Russell in a low voice, "must do something for the boy."

The Judge looked down at the frantic child. He said, gently, "I am as sorry as I can be, Freddy . . ." But in his old heart there was too much known, and too many little dogs he remembered that had already died, and even if he were as sorry as he could be, he couldn't be sorry enough. The boy's eyes turned, rejected, returned. To the enemy.

Russell moved near the woman in blue, who pertained to this boy somehow. "His mother?"

"His folks are away. I'm there to take care of him," she snapped, as if she felt herself put upon by a crisis she had not contracted to face.

"Can they be reached?"

"No," she said decisively.

The young man put his stranger's hand on the boy's rigid little shoulder. But he too was rejected. Freddy's eyes, brilliant with hatred, clung to the enemy. Hatred doesn't cry.

"Listen," said the tall cop, "if you could hang onto him for a minute . . ."

"Not I . . ." said Russell.

The thin cop came back. "Looks like the dog got poison. When was he found?"

"Just now," the kids said.

"Where? There?"

"Up Hannibal Street. Right on the edge of ole Matlin's back lot."

"Edge of *my* lot!" Matlin's color freshened again. "On the sidewalk, why don't you say? Why don't you tell the truth?"

"We are! *We* don't tell lies!"

"Quiet, you guys," the cop said. "Pipe down, now."

"Heaven's my witness, I wasn't even here!" cried Matlin. "I played nine holes of golf today. I didn't get home until . . . May?" he called over his shoulder. "What time did I come in?"

The girl on the porch came slowly down, moving awkwardly on her uneven legs. She was in her twenties, no child. Nor was she a woman. She said in a blurting manner, "About three o'clock, Daddy Earl. But the dog was dead."

"What's that, Miss?"

"This is my stepdaughter . . ."

"The dog was dead," the girl said, "before he came home. I saw it from upstairs, before three o'clock. Lying by the sidewalk."

"You drove in from Hannibal Street, Mr. Matlin? Looks like you'd have seen the dog."

Matlin said with nervous thoughtfulness, "I don't know. My mind . . . Yes, I . . ."

"He's telling a lie!"

"Freddy!"

"Listen to that," said May Matlin, "will you?"

"She's a liar, too!"

The cop shook Freddy. Mr. Matlin made a sound of helpless exasperation. He said to the girl, "Go keep your mother inside, May." He raised his arm as if to wave. "It's all right, honey," he called to the woman in the chair, with a false cheeriness that grated on the ear. "There's nothing to worry about, now."

Freddy's jaw shifted and young Russell's watching eyes winced. The girl began to lurch back to the house.

"It was my wife who put in the call," Matlin said. "After all, they were on me like a pack of wolves. Now, I . . . I *understand* that the boy's upset. But all the same, he cannot . . . He must learn . . . I will not have . . . I have enough to contend with, without this malice, this unwarranted antagonism, this persecution . . ."

Freddy's eyes were unwinking.

"It has got to stop!" said Matlin almost hysterically.

"Yes," murmured Mike Russell, "I should think so." Judge Kittinger's white head, nodding, agreed.

"We've heard about quite a few dog-poisoning cases over the line in Redfern," said the thin cop with professional calm. "None here."

The man in the shorts hitched them up, looking shocked. "Who'd do a thing like that?"

A boy said, boldly, "Ole Matlin would." He had an underslung jaw and wore spectacles on his snub nose. "I'm Phil Bourchard," he said to the cop. He had courage.

"We jist know," said another. "I'm Ernie Allen." Partisanship radiated from his whole thin body. "Ole Matlin doesn't want anybody on his ole property."

"Sure." "He doesn't want anybody on his ole property." "It was ole Matlin."

"It was. It was," said Freddy Titus.

"Freddy," said the housekeeper in blue, "now, you better be

still. I'll tell your Dad.'' It was a meaningless fumble for control. The boy didn't even hear it.

Judge Kittinger tried, patiently. "You can't accuse without cause, Freddy.''

"Bones didn't hurt his ole property. Bones wouldn't hurt anything. Ole Matlin did it.''

"You lying little devil!''

"*He's* a liar!''

The cop gave Freddy another shake. "You kids found him, eh?''

"We were up at Bourchard's and were going down to the Titus house.''

"And he was dead,'' said Freddy.

"*I* know nothing about it,'' said Matlin icily. "Nothing at all.''

The cop, standing between, said wearily, "Any of you people see what coulda happened?''

"I was sitting in my backyard,'' said the man in shorts. "I'm Daughterty, next door, up Hannibal Street. Didn't see a thing.''

The small woman in a print dress spoke up. "I am Mrs. Page. I live across on the corner, Officer. I believe I did see a strange man go into Mr. Matlin's driveway this morning.''

"When was this, Ma'am?''

"About eleven o'clock. He was poorly dressed. He walked up the drive and around the garage.''

"Didn't go to the house?''

"No. He was only there a minute. I believe he was carrying something. He was rather furtive. And very poorly dressed, almost like a tramp.''

There was a certain relaxing, among the elders. "Ah, the tramp,'' said Mike Russell. "The good old reliable tramp. Are you sure, Mrs. Page? It's very unlikely . . .''

But she bristled. "Do you think I am lying?''

Russell's lips parted, but he felt the Judge's hand on his arm. "This is my guest, Mr. Russell . . . Freddy.'' The Judge's voice was gentle. "Let him go, Officer. I'm sure he understands, now. Mr. Matlin was not even at home, Freddy. It's possible that this . . . er . . . stranger . . . Or it may have been an accident . . .''

"Wasn't a tramp. Wasn't an accident.''

"You can't know that, boy," said the Judge, somewhat sharply. Freddy said nothing. As the officer slowly released his grasp, the boy took a free step, backwards, and the other boys surged to surround him. There stood the enemy, the monster who killed and lied, and the grown-ups with their reasonable doubts were on the monster's side. But the boys knew what Freddy knew. They stood together.

"Somebody," murmured the Judge's guest, "somebody's got to help the boy." And the Judge sighed.

The cops went up Hannibal Street, towards Matlin's back lot, with Mr. Daugherty. Matlin lingered at the corner talking to Mrs. Page. In the front window of Matlin's house the curtain fell across the glass.

Mike Russell sidled up to the housekeeper. "Any uncles or aunts here in town? A grandmother?"

"No," she said, shortly.

"Brothers or sisters, Mrs. . . . ?"

"Miz Somers. No, he's the only one. Only reason they didn't take him along was it's the last week of school and he didn't want to miss."

Mike Russell's brown eyes suggested the soft texture of velvet, and they were deeply distressed. She slid away from their appeal. "He'll just have to take it, I guess, like everybody else," Mrs. Somers said. "These things happen."

He was listening intently. "Don't you care for dogs?"

"I don't mind a dog," she said. She arched her neck. She was going to call to the boy.

"Wait. Tell me, does the family go to church? Is there a pastor or a priest who knows the boy?"

"They don't go, far as I ever saw." She looked at him as if he were an eccentric.

"Then school. He has a teacher. What grade?"

"Sixth grade," she said. "Miss Dana. Oh, he'll be O.K." Her voice grew loud, to reach the boy and to hint to him. "He's a big boy."

Russell said, desperately, "Is there no way to telephone his parents?"

"They're on the road. They'll be in some time tomorrow. That's all I know." She was annoyed. "I'll take care of him. That's why I'm here." She raised her voice and this time it was arch and seductive. "Freddy, better come wash your face. I know where there's some chocolate cookies."

The velvet left the young man's eyes. Hard as buttons, they gazed for a moment at the woman. Then he whipped around and left her. He walked over to where the kids had drifted, near the little dead creature on the grass. He said softly, "Bones had his own doctor, Freddy? Tell me his name?" The boy's eyes flickered. "We must know what it was that he took. A doctor can tell. I think his own doctor would be best, don't you?"

The boy nodded, mumbled a name, an address. That Russell mastered the name and the numbers, asking for no repetition, was a sign of his concern. Besides, it was this young man's quality—that he listened. "May I take him, Freddy? I have a car. We ought to have a blanket," he added softly, "a soft, clean blanket."

"I got one, Freddy . . ." "My mother'd let me . . ."

"I can get one," Freddy said brusquely. They wheeled, almost in formation.

Mrs. Somers frowned. "You must let them take a blanket," Russell warned her, and his eyes were cold.

"I will explain to Mrs. Titus," said the Judge quickly.

"Quite a fuss," she said, and tossed her head and crossed the road.

Russell gave the Judge a quick nervous grin. He walked to the returning cops. "You'll want to run tests, I suppose? Can the dog's own vet do it?"

"Certainly. Humane officer will have to be in charge. But that's what the vet'll want."

"I'll take the dog, then. Any traces up there?"

"Not a thing."

"Will you explain to the boy that you are investigating?"

"Well, you know how these things go." The cop's feet shuffled. "Humane officer does what he can. Probably, Monday, after we identify the poison, he'll check the drug stores. Usually, if it *is* a cranky neighbor, he has already put in a complaint about the dog. This Matlin says he never did. The humane officer will get on it, Monday. He's out of town today. The devil of these cases, we can't prove a thing, usually. You get an idea who it was, maybe you can scare him. It's a misdemeanor, all right. Never heard of a conviction, myself."

"But will you explain to the boy . . . ?" Russell stopped, chewed his lips, and the Judge sighed.

"Yeah, it's tough on a kid," the cop said.

When the Judge's guest came back, it was nearly five o'clock. He said, "I came to say goodbye, sir, and to thank you for the . . ." But his mind wasn't on the sentence and he lost it and looked up.

The Judge's eyes were affectionate. "Worried?"

"Judge, sir," the young man said, "*must* they feed him? Where, sir, in this classy neighborhood is there an understanding woman's heart? I herded them to that Mrs. Allen. But she winced, sir, and she diverted them. She didn't want to deal with tragedy, didn't want to think about it. She offered cakes and 'Cokes' and games."

"But my dear boy . . ."

"What do they teach the kids these days, Judge? To turn away? Put something in your stomach. Take a drink. Play a game. Don't weep for your dead. Just skip it, think about something else."

"I'm afraid the boy's alone," the Judge said gently, "but it's only for the night." His voice was melodious. "Can't be sheltered from grief when it comes. None of us can."

"Excuse me, sir, but I wish he *would* grieve. I wish he would bawl his heart out. Wash out that black hate. I ought to go home. None of my concern. It's a woman's job." He moved and his hand went toward the phone. "He has a teacher. I can't help feeling concerned, sir. May I try?"

The Judge said, "Of course, Mike," and he put his brittle old bones into a chair.

Mike Russell pried the number out of the Board of Education. "Miss Lillian Dana? My name is Russell. You know a boy named Freddy Titus?"

"Oh, yes. He's in my class." The voice was pleasing.

"Miss Dana, there is trouble. You know Judge Kittinger's house? Could you come there?"

"What is the trouble?"

"Freddy's little dog is dead of poison. I'm afraid Freddy is in a bad state. There is no one to help him. His folks are away. The woman taking care of him," Mike's careful explanatory sentences burst into indignation, "has no more sympathetic

imagination than a broken clothes-pole." He heard a little gasp.
"I'd like to help him, Miss Dana, but I'm a man and a stranger,
and the Judge . . ." He paused.

". . . is old," said the Judge in his chair.

"I'm terribly sorry," the voice on the phone said slowly.
"Freddy's a wonderful boy."

"You are his friend?"

"Yes, we are friends."

"Then, could you come? You see, we've got to get a terrible
idea out of his head. He thinks a man across the street poisoned
his dog on purpose. Miss Dana, *he has no doubt!* And he
doesn't cry." She gasped again. "Greenwood Lane," he said,
"and Hannibal Street—the southeast corner."

She said, "I'll come. I have a car. I'll come as soon as I
can."

Russell turned and caught the Judge biting his lips. "Am I
making too much of this, sir?" he inquired humbly.

"I don't like the boy's stubborn conviction." The Judge's
voice was dry and clear. "Any more than you do. I agree that
he must be brought to understand. But . . ." the old man
shifted in the chair. "Of course, the man, Matlin, is a fool,
Mike. There is something solemn and silly about him that makes
him fair game. He's unfortunate. He married a widow with a
crippled child, and no sooner were they married than *she* col-
lapsed. And he's not well off. He's encumbered with that
enormous house."

"What does he do, sir?"

"He's a photographer. Oh, he struggles, tries his best, and all
that. But with such tension, Mike. That poor misshapen girl
over there tries to keep the house, devoted to her mother. Matlin
works hard, is devoted, too. And yet the sum comes out in petty
strife, nerves, quarrels, uproar. And certainly it cannot be necessary to feud with children."

"The kids have done their share of that, I'll bet," mused
Mike. "The kids are delighted—a neighborhood ogre, to add
the fine flavor of menace. A focus for mischief. An enemy."

"True enough." The Judge sighed.

"So the myth is made. No rumor about ole Matlin loses
anything in the telling. I can see it's been built up. You don't
knock it down in a day."

"No," said the Judge uneasily. He got up from the chair.

The young man rubbed his dark head. "I don't like it, sir. We don't know what's in the kids' minds, or who their heroes are. There is only the gang. What do you suppose it advises?"

"What could it advise, after all?" said the Judge crisply. "This isn't the slums, whatever Matlin says." He went nervously to the window. He fiddled with the shade pull. He said, suddenly, "From my little summer house in the backyard you can overhear the gang. They congregate under that oak. Go and eavesdrop, Mike."

The young man snapped to attention. "Yes, sir."

"I . . . think we had better know," said the Judge, a trifle sheepishly.

The kids sat under the oak, in a grassy hollow. Freddy was the core. His face was tight. His eyes never left off watching the house of the enemy. The others watched him, or hung their heads, or watched their own brown hands play with the grass.

They were not chattering. There hung about them a heavy, sullen silence, heavy with a sense of tragedy, sullen with a sense of wrong, and from time to time one voice or another would fling out a pronouncement, which would sink into the silence, thickening its ugliness . . .

The Judge looked up from his paper. "Could you . . . ?"

"I could hear," said Mike in a quiet voice. "They are condemning the law, sir. They call it corrupt. They are quite certain that Matlin killed the dog. They see themselves as Robin Hoods, vigilantes, defending the weak, the wronged, the dog. They think they are discussing justice. They are waiting for dark. They speak of weapons, sir—the only ones they have. B.B. guns, after dark."

"Great heavens!"

"Don't worry. Nothing's going to happen."

"What are you going to do?"

"I'm going to stop it."

Mrs. Somers was cooking supper when he tapped on the screen. "Oh, it's you. What do you want?"

"I want your help, Mrs. Somers. For Freddy."

"Freddy," she interrupted loudly, with her nose high, "is going to have his supper and go to bed his regular time, and that's all about Freddy. Now, what did you want?"

He said, "I want you to let me take the boy to my apartment for the night."

"I couldn't do that!" She was scandalized.

"The Judge will vouch . . ."

"Now, see here, Mr. What'syourname—Russell. This isn't my house and Freddy's not my boy. I'm responsible to Mr. and Mrs. Titus. You're a stranger to me. As far as I can see, Freddy is no business of yours whatsoever."

"Which is his room?" asked Mike sharply.

"Why do you want to know?" She was hostile and suspicious.

"Where does he keep his B.B. gun?"

She was startled to an answer. "In the shed out back. Why?"

He told her.

"Kid's talk," she scoffed. "You don't know much about kids, do you, young man? Freddy will go to sleep. First thing he'll know, it's morning. That's about the size of it."

"You may be right. I hope so."

Mrs. Somers slapped potatoes into the pan. Her lips quivered indignantly. She felt annoyed because she was a little shaken. The strange young man really had hoped so.

Russell scanned the street, went across to Matlin's house. The man himself answered the bell. The air in this house was stale, and bore the faint smell of old grease. There was over everything an atmosphere of struggle and despair. Many things ought to have been repaired and had not been repaired. The place was too big. There wasn't enough money, or strength. It was too much.

Mrs. Matlin could not walk. Otherwise, one saw, she struggled and did the best she could. She had a lost look, as if some anxiety, ever present, took about nine-tenths of her attention. May Matlin limped in and sat down, lumpishly.

Russell began earnestly, "Mr. Matlin, I don't know how this situation between you and the boys began. I can guess that the kids are much to blame. I imagine they enjoy it." He smiled. He wanted to be sympathetic towards this man.

"Of course they enjoy it." Matlin looked triumphant.

"They call me The Witch," the girl said. "Pretend they're scared of me. The devils. I'm scared of them."

Matlin flicked a nervous eye at the woman in the wheel chair.

"The truth is, Mr. Russell," he said in his high whine, "they're vicious."

"It's too bad," said his wife in a low voice. "I think it's dangerous."

"Mama, you mustn't worry," said the girl in an entirely new tone. "I won't let them hurt you. Nobody will hurt you."

"Be quiet, May," said Matlin. "You'll upset her. Of course nobody will hurt her."

"Yes, it is dangerous, Mrs. Matlin," said Russell quietly. "That's why I came over."

Matlin goggled. "What? What's this?"

"Could I possibly persuade you, sir, to spend the night away from this neighborhood . . . and depart noisily?"

"No," said Matlin, raring up, his ego bristling, "no you cannot! I will under no circumstances be driven away from my own home." His voice rose. "Furthermore, I certainly will not leave my wife and stepdaughter."

"We could manage, dear," said Mrs. Matlin anxiously.

Russell told them about the talk under the oak, the B.B. gun.

"Devils," said May Matlin, "absolutely . . ."

"Oh, Earl," trembled Mrs. Matlin, "maybe we had all better go away."

Matlin, red-necked, furious, said, "We own this property. We pay our taxes. We have our rights. Let them! Let them try something like that! Then, I think the law would have something to say. This is outrageous! I did not harm that animal. Therefore, I defy . . ." He looked solemn and silly, as the Judge had said, with his face crimson, his weak eyes rolling.

Russell rose. "I thought I ought to make the suggestion," he said mildly, "because it would be the safest thing to do. But don't worry, Mrs. Matlin, because I . . ."

"A B.B. gun can blind . . ." she said tensely.

"Or even worse," Mike agreed. "But I am thinking of the . . ."

"Just a minute," Matlin roared. "You can't come in here and terrify my wife! She is not strong. You have no right." He drew himself up with his feet at a right angle, his pudgy arm extended, his plump jowls quivering. "Get out," he cried. He looked ridiculous.

Whether the young man and the bewildered woman in the chair might have understood each other was not to be known. Russell, of course, got out. May Matlin hobbled to the door and as Russell went through it, she said, "Well, you warned us, anyhow." And her lips came together, sharply.

Russell plodded across the pavement again. Long enchanting shadows from the lowering sun struck aslant through the golden air and all the old houses were gilded and softened in their green setting. He moved toward the big oak. He hunkered down. The sun struck its golden shafts deep under the boughs. "How's it going?" he asked.

Freddy Titus looked frozen and still. "O.K.," said Phil Bourchard with elaborate ease. Light on his owlish glasses hid the eyes.

Mike opened his lips, hesitated. Supper time struck on the neighborhood clock. Calls, like chimes, were sounding.

". . . 's my Mom," said Ernie Allen. "See you after."

"See you after, Freddy."

"O.K."

"O.K."

Mrs. Somers' hoot had chimed with the rest and now Freddy got up, stiffly.

"O.K.?" said Mike Russell. The useful syllables that take any meaning at all in American mouths asked, "Are you feeling less bitter, boy? Are you any easier?"

"O.K.," said Freddy. The same syllables shut the man out.

Mike opened his lips. Closed them. Freddy went across the lawn to his kitchen door. There was a brown crockery bowl on the back stoop. His sneaker, rigid on the ankle, stepped over it. Mike Russell watched, and then, with a movement of his arms, almost as if he would wring his hands, he went up the Judge's steps.

"Well?" The Judge opened the door. "Did you talk to the boy?"

Russell didn't answer. He sat down.

The Judge stood over him. "The boy . . . The enormity of this whole idea *must* be explained to him."

"I can't explain," Mike said. "I open my mouth. Nothing comes out."

"Perhaps *I* had better . . ."

"What are you going to say, sir?"

"Why, give him the facts," the Judge cried.

"The facts are . . . the dog is dead."

"There are no facts that point to Matlin."

"There are no facts that point to a tramp, either. That's too sloppy, sir."

"What are you driving at?"

"Judge, the boy is more rightfully suspicious than we are."

"Nonsense," said the Judge. "The girl saw the dog's body before Matlin came . . ."

"There is no alibi for poison," Mike said sadly.

"Are you saying the man is a liar?"

"Liars," sighed Mike. "Truth and lies. How are those kids going to understand, sir? To that Mrs. Page, to the lot of them, Truth is only a subjective intention. 'I am no liar,' sez she, sez he. 'I *intend* to be truthful. So do not insult me.' Lord, when will we begin? It's what we were talking about at lunch, sir. What you and I believe. What the race has been told and told in such agony, in a million years of bitter lesson. *Error,* we were saying. Error is the enemy."

He flung out of the chair. "We know that to tell the truth is not merely a good intention. It's a damned difficult thing to do. It's a skill, to be practiced. It's a technique. It's an effort. It takes brains. It takes watching. It takes humility and self-examination. It's a science and an art . . .

"Why don't we tell the *kids* these things? Why is everyone locked up in anger, shouting liar at the other side? Why don't they automatically know how easy it is to be, not wicked, but mistaken? Why is there this notion of violence? Because Freddy doesn't think to himself, 'Wait a minute. I might be wrong.' The habit isn't there. Instead, there are the heroes—the big-muscled, noble-hearted, gun-toting heroes, blind in a righteousness totally arranged by the author. Excuse me, sir."

"All that may be," said the Judge grimly, "and I agree. But the police know the lesson. They . . ."

"They don't care."

"What?"

"Don't care enough, sir. None of us cares enough—about the dog."

"I see," said the Judge. "Yes, I see. We haven't the least idea what happened to the dog." He touched his pince-nez.

Mike rubbed his head wearily. "Don't know what to do except sit under his window the night through. Hardly seems good enough."

The Judge said, simply, "Why don't you find out what happened to the dog?"

The young man's face changed. "What we need, sir," said Mike slowly, "is to teach Freddy how to ask for it. Just to ask for it. Just to want it." The old man and the young man looked at each other. Past and future telescoped. *"Now,"* Mike said. "Before dark."

Supper time, for the kids, was only twenty minutes long. When the girl in the brown dress with the bare blonde head got out of the shabby coupé, the gang was gathered again in its hollow under the oak. She went to them and sank down on the ground. "Ah, Freddy, was it Bones? Your dear little dog you wrote about in the essay?"

"Yes, Miss Dana." Freddy's voice was shrill and hostile. *I won't be touched!* it cried to her. So she said no more, but sat there on the ground, and presently she began to cry. There was contagion. The simplest thing in the world. First, one of the smaller ones, whimpering. Finally, Freddy Titus, bending over. Her arm guided his head, and then he lay weeping in her lap.

Russell, up in the summer house, closed his eyes and praised the Lord. In a little while he swung his legs over the railing and slid down the bank. "How do? I'm Mike Russell."

"I'm Lillian Dana." She was quick and intelligent, and her tears were real.

"Fellows," said Mike briskly, "you know what's got to be done, don't you? We've got to solve this case."

They turned their woeful faces.

He said, deliberately, "It's just the same as a murder. It is a murder."

"Yeah," said Freddy and sat up, tears drying. "And it was ole Matlin."

"Then we have to prove it."

Miss Lillian Dana saw the boy's face lock. He didn't need to prove anything, the look proclaimed. He knew. She leaned over a little and said, "But we can't make an ugly mistake and put it on Bones's account. Bones was a fine dog. Oh, that would be a terrible monument." Freddy's eyes turned, startled.

"It's up to us," said Mike gratefully, "to go after the real facts, with real detective work. For Bones's sake."

"It's the least we can do for him," said Miss Dana, calmly and decisively.

Freddy's face lifted.

"Trouble is," Russell went on quickly, "people get things wrong. Sometimes they don't remember straight. They make mistakes."

"Ole Matlin tells lies," said Freddy.

"If he does," said Russell cheerfully, "then we've got to *prove* that he does. Now, I've figured out a plan, if Miss Dana will help us. You pick a couple of the fellows, Fred. Have to go to all the houses around and ask some questions. Better pick the smartest ones. To find out the truth is very hard," he challenged.

"And then?" said Miss Dana in a fluttery voice.

"Then they, and you, if you will . . ."

"Me?" She straightened. "I am a schoolteacher, Mr. Russell. Won't the police . . . ?"

"Not before dark."

"What are *you* going to be doing?"

"Dirtier work."

She bit her lip. "It's nosey. It's . . . not done."

"No," he agreed. "You may lose your job."

She wasn't a bad-looking young woman. Her eyes were fine. Her brow was serious, but there was the ghost of a dimple in her cheek. Her hands moved. "Oh, well, I can always take up beauty culture or something. What are the questions?" She had a pad of paper and a pencil half out of her purse, and looked alert and efficient.

Now, as the gang huddled, there was a warm sense of conspiracy growing. "Going to be the dickens of a job," Russell warned them. And he outlined some questions. "Now, don't let anybody fool you into taking a sloppy answer," he concluded. "Ask how they know. Get real evidence. But don't go to Matlin's—I'll go there."

"I'm not afraid of him." Freddy's nostrils flared.

"I think I stand a better chance of getting the answers," said Russell coolly. "Aren't we after the answers?"

Freddy swallowed. "And if it turns out . . . ?"

"It turns out the way it turns out," said Russell, rumpling the tow head. "Choose your henchmen. Tough, remember."

"Phil. Ernie." The kids who were left out wailed as the three small boys and their teacher, who wasn't a lot bigger, rose from the ground.

"It'll be tough, Mr. Russell," Miss Dana said grimly. "Whoever you are, thank you for getting me into this."

"I'm just a stranger," he said gently, looking down at the face. "But you are a friend and a teacher." Pain crossed her eyes. "You'll be teaching now, you know."

Her chin went up. "O.K., kids. I'll keep the paper and pencil. Freddy, wipe your face. Stick your shirt in, Phil. Now, let's organize . . ."

It was nearly nine o'clock when the boys and the teacher, looking rather exhausted, came back to the Judge's house. Russell, whose face was grave, reached for the papers in her hands.

"Just a minute," said Miss Dana. "Judge, we have some questions."

Ernie Allen bared all his heap of teeth and stepped forward. "Did you see Bones today?" he asked with the firm skill of repetition. The Judge nodded. "How many times and when?"

"Once. Er . . . shortly before noon. He crossed my yard, going east."

The boys bent over the pad. Then Freddy's lips opened hard. "How do you know the time, Judge Kittinger?"

"Well," said the Judge, "hm . . . let me think. I was looking out the window for my company and just then he arrived."

"Five minutes of one, sir," Mike said.

Freddy flashed around. "What makes you sure?"

"I looked at my watch," said Russell. "I was taught to be exactly five minutes early when I'm asked to a meal." There was a nodding among the boys, and Miss Dana wrote on the pad.

"Then I was mistaken," said the Judge, thoughtfully. "It was shortly before one. Of course."

Phil Bourchard took over. "Did you see anyone go into Matlin's driveway or back lot?"

"I did not."

"Were you out of doors or did you look up that way?"

"Yes, I . . . When we left the table. Mike?"

"At two-thirty, sir."

"How do you know that time for sure?" asked Freddy Titus.

"Because I wondered if I could politely stay a little longer." Russell's eyes congratulated Miss Lillian Dana. She had made them a team, and on it, Freddy was the How-do-you-know-for-sure Department.

"Can you swear," continued Phil to the Judge, "there was nobody at all around Matlin's back lot then?"

"As far as my view goes," answered the Judge cautiously.

Freddy said promptly, "He couldn't see much. Too many trees. We can't count that."

They looked at Miss Dana and she marked on the pad. "Thank you. Now, you have a cook, sir? We must question her."

"This way," said the Judge, rising and bowing.

Russell looked after them and his eyes were velvet again. He met the Judge's twinkle. Then he sat down and ran an eye quickly over some of the sheets of paper, passing each on to his host.

Startled, he looked up. Lillian Dana, standing in the door, was watching his face.

"Do you think, Mike . . . ?"

A paper drooped in the Judge's hand.

"We can't stop," she challenged.

Russell nodded and turned to the Judge. "May need some high brass, sir." The Judge rose. "And tell me, sir, where Matlin plays golf. And the telephone number of the Salvage League. No, Miss Dana, we can't stop. We'll take it where it turns."

"We must," she said.

It was nearly ten when the neighbors began to come in. The Judge greeted them soberly. The Chief of Police arrived. Mrs. Somers, looking grim and uprooted in a crêpe dress, came. Mr.

Matlin, Mrs. Page, Mr. and Mrs. Daugherty, a Mr. and Mrs. Baker, and Diane Bourchard who was sixteen. They looked curiously at the tight little group, the boys and their blonde teacher.

Last of all to arrive was young Mr. Russell, who slipped in from the dark veranda, accepted the Judge's nod, and called the meeting to order.

"We have been investigating the strange death of a dog," he began. "Chief Anderson, while we know your department would have done so in good time, we also know you are busy, and some of us," he glanced at the dark window pane, "couldn't wait. Will you help us now?"

The Chief said, genially, "That's why I'm here, I guess." It was the Judge and his stature that gave this meeting any standing. Naïve, young, a little absurd it might have seemed had not the old man sat so quietly attentive among them.

"Thank you, sir. Now, all we want to know is what happened to the dog." Russell looked about him. "First, let us demolish the tramp." Mrs. Page's feathers ruffled. Russell smiled at her. "Mrs. Page saw a man go down Matlin's drive this morning. The Salvage League sent a truck to pick up rags and papers which at ten forty-two was parked in front of the Daughertys'. The man, who seemed poorly dressed in his working clothes, went to the tool room behind Matlin's garage, as he had been instructed to. He picked up a bundle and returned to his truck. Mrs. Page," purred Mike to her scarlet face, "the man was there. It was only your opinion about him that proves to have been, not a lie, but an error."

He turned his head. "Now, we have tried to trace the dog's day and we have done remarkably well, too." As he traced it for them, some faces began to wear at least the ghost of a smile, seeing the little dog frisking through the neighborhood. "Just before one," Mike went on, "Bones ran across the Judge's yard to the Allens' where the kids were playing ball. Up to this time no one saw Bones *above* Greenwood Lane or *up* Hannibal Street. But Miss Diane Bourchard, recovering from a sore throat, was not in school today. After lunch, she sat on her porch directly across from Mr. Matlin's back lot. She was waiting for school to be out, when she expected her friends to come by.

"She saw, not Bones, but Corky, an animal belonging to Mr.

Daugherty, playing on Matlin's lot at about two o'clock. I want your opinion. If poisoned bait had been lying there at two would Corky have found it?''

"Seems so," said Daugherty. "Thank God Corky didn't." He bit his tongue. "Corky's a show dog," he blundered.

"But Bones," said Russell gently, "was more like a friend. That's why we care, of course."

"It's a damn shame!" Daugherty looked around angrily.

"It is," said Mrs. Baker. "He was a friend of mine, Bones was."

"Go on," growled Daugherty. "What else did you dig up?"

"Mr. Matlin left for his golf at eleven-thirty. Now, you see, it looks as if Matlin couldn't have left poison behind him."

"I most certainly did not," snapped Matlin. "I have said so. I will not stand for this sort of innuendo. I am not a liar. You said it was a conference . . ."

Mike held the man's eye. "We are simply trying to find out what happened to the dog," he said. Matlin fell silent.

"Surely you realize," purred Mike, "that, human frailty being what it is, there may have been other errors in what we were told this afternoon. There was at least one more.

"Mr. and Mrs. Baker," he continued, "worked in their garden this afternoon. Bones abandoned the ball game to visit the Bakers' dog, Smitty. At three o'clock, the Bakers, after discussing the time carefully, lest it be too late in the day, decided to bathe Smitty. When they caught him, for his ordeal, Bones was still there. . . . So, you see, Miss May Matlin, who says she saw Bones lying by the sidewalk *before three o'clock*, was mistaken."

Matlin twitched. Russell said sharply, "The testimony of the Bakers is extremely clear." The Bakers, who looked alike, both brown outdoor people, nodded vigorously.

"The time at which Mr. Matlin returned is quite well established. Diane saw him. Mrs. Daugherty, next door, decided to take a nap, at five after three. She had a roast to put in at four-thirty. Therefore, she is sure of the time. She went upstairs and from an upper window, she, too, saw Mr. Matlin come home. Both witnesses say he drove his car into the garage at three-ten, got out, and went around the building to the right of it—*on the weedy side*."

Mr. Matlin was sweating. His forehead was beaded. He did not speak.

Mike shifted papers. "Now, we know that the kids trooped up to Phil Bourchard's kitchen at about a quarter of three. Whereas Bones, realizing that Smitty was in for it, and shying away from soap and water like any sane dog, went up Hannibal Street at three o'clock sharp. He may have known in some doggy way where Freddy was. Can we see Bones loping up Hannibal Street, going *above* Greenwood Lane?"

"We can," said Daugherty. He was watching Matlin. "Besides, he was found above Greenwood Lane soon after."

"No one," said Mike slowly, "was seen in Matlin's back lot, except Matlin. Yet, almost immediately after Matlin was there, the little dog died."

"Didn't Diane . . . ?"

"Diane's friends came at three-twelve. Their evidence is not reliable." Diane blushed.

"This . . . this is intolerable!" croaked Matlin. "Why *my* back lot?"

Daugherty said, "There was no poison lying around my place, I'll tell you that."

"How do you know?" begged Matlin. And Freddy's eyes, with the smudges under them, followed to Russell's face. "Why not in the street? From some passing car?"

Mike said, "I'm afraid it's not likely. You see, Mr. Otis Carnavon was stalled at the corner of Hannibal and Lee. Trying to flag a push. Anything thrown from a car on that block, he ought to have seen."

"Was the poison quick?" demanded Daugherty. "What did he get?"

"It was quick. The dog could not go far after he got it. He got cyanide."

Matlin's shaking hand removed his glasses. They were wet.

"Some of you may be amateur photographers," Mike said. "Mr. Matlin, is there cyanide in your cellar darkroom?"

"Yes, but I keep it . . . most meticulously . . ." Matlin began to cough.

When the noise of his spasm died, Mike said, "The poison was embedded in ground meat which analyzed, roughly, half-beef and the rest pork and veal, half and half." Matlin encircled his throat with his fingers. "I've checked with four neighborhood butchers and the dickens of a time I had," said Mike. No one smiled. Only Freddy looked up at him with solemn sympathy. "Ground meat was delivered to at least five houses in the vicinity. Meat that *was* one-half beef, one-quarter pork, one-quarter veal, was delivered at ten this morning to Matlin's house."

A stir like an angry wind blew over the room. The Chief of Police made some shift of his weight so that his chair creaked.

"It begins to look . . ." growled Daugherty.

"Now," said Russell sharply, "we must be very careful. One more thing. The meat had been seasoned."

"Seasoned!"

"With salt. And with . . . thyme."

"Thyme," groaned Matlin.

Freddy looked up at Miss Dana with bewildered eyes. She put her arm around him.

"As far as motives are concerned," said Mike quietly, "I can't discuss them. It is inconceivable to me that any man would poison a dog." Nobody spoke. "However, where are we?" Mike's voice seemed to catch Matlin just in time to keep him from falling off the chair. "We don't know yet what happened to the dog." Mike's voice rang. "Mr. Matlin, will you help us to the answer?"

Matlin said thickly, "Better get those kids out of here."

Miss Dana moved, but Russell said, "No. They have worked hard for the truth. They have earned it. And if it is to be had, they shall have it."

"You know?" whimpered Matlin.

Mike said, "I called your golf club. I've looked into your trash incinerator. Yes, I know. But I want you to tell us."

Daugherty said, "Well? Well?" And Matlin covered his face.

Mike said, gently, "I think there was an error. Mr. Matlin, I'm afraid, did poison the dog. But he never meant to, and he didn't know he had done it."

Matlin said, "I'm sorry . . . It's . . . I can't . . . She means to do her best. But she's a terrible cook. Somebody gave her those . . . those herbs. Thyme . . . thyme in everything. She fixed me a lunch box. I . . . couldn't stomach it. I bought my lunch at the club.''

Mike nodded.

Matlin went on, his voice cracking. "I never . . . You see, I didn't even know it was meat the dog got. She said . . . she told me the dog was already dead.''

"And of course," said Mike, "in your righteous wrath, you never paused to say to yourself, 'Wait, what *did* happen to the dog?' ''

"Mr. Russell, I didn't lie. How could I know there was thyme in it? When I got home, I had to get rid of the hamburger she'd fixed for me—I didn't want to hurt her feelings. She tries . . . tries so hard . . .'' He sat up suddenly. *"But what she tried to do today,"* he said, with his eyes almost out of his head, *"was to poison me!"* His bulging eyes roved. They came to Freddy. He gasped. He said, "Your dog saved my life!''

"Yes," said Mike quickly, "Freddy's dog saved your life. You see, your stepdaughter would have kept trying.''

People drew in their breaths. "The buns are in your incinerator,'' Mike said. "She guessed what happened to the dog, went for the buns, and hid them. She was late, you remember, getting to the disturbance. And she did lie.''

Chief Anderson rose.

"Her mother . . .'' said Matlin frantically, "her mother . . .''

Mike Russell put his hand on the plump shoulder. "Her mother's been in torment, tortured by the rivalry between you. Don't you think her mother senses something wrong?''

Miss Lillian Dana wrapped Freddy in her arms. "Oh, what a wonderful dog Bones was!'' She covered the sound of the other voices. "Even when he died, he save a man's life. Oh, Freddy, he was a wonderful dog.''

And Freddy, not quite taking everything in yet, was released to simple sorrow and wept quietly against his friend . . .

When they went to fetch May Matlin, she was not in the house. They found her in the Tituses' back shed. She seemed to be looking for something.

Next day, when Mr. and Mrs. Titus came home, they found that although the little dog had died, their Freddy was all right. The Judge, Russell, and Miss Dana told them all about it.

Mrs. Titus wept. Mr. Titus swore. He wrung Russell's hand. ". . . for stealing the gun . . ." he babbled.

But the mother cried, ". . . for showing him, for teaching him. . . . Oh, Miss Dana, oh my dear!"

The Judge waved from his veranda as the dark head and the blonde drove away.

"I think Miss Dana likes him," said Ernie Allen.

"How do you know for sure?" said Freddy Titus.

William Bankier

William Bankier was born in Bellville, Ontario, Canada, and began writing when he was ten years old. His first published story, in *Liberty Magazine* (Toronto) won a Canadian Short Story of the Month Prize. With his family, he moved to London in 1974, leaving behind a job as creative director of a Montreal advertising agency. He writes full-time, when he is not involved with amateur theatrics, music or spectator sports. In 1980, along with Clark Howard, Ed Hoch and John Lutz, he was nominated for an Edgar for best mystery short story.

THE DOG WHO HATED JAZZ

BY WILLIAM BANKIER

I was walking through the lobby of the Coronet Hotel when Jack Danforth, the owner, called me over to the desk. "Have you got a minute, Norman?"

My grocery shopping was finished, I was only in for a beer. "Sure thing, Mr. Danforth." Even though I was now an English teacher at Baytown High School, I had never forgotten my first summer job as a bellboy at the Coronet. If the boss asked me to get the bags from room 311, I'd be up those stairs two at a time.

I followed him through the back lounge and into his private office, where I sat in a chair he indicated. I watched him close the window to exclude the noise from the parking lot. Danforth's shape was blocky, like a fullback gone to seed, and when he turned he showed me that belligerent face framed by close-cut black hair, the lower lip drawn down by the weight of a cigar stub. He looked stubborn, possibly dangerous.

It was the green eyes that gave him away, eyes narrowed with amusement and lit up with the pleasure of running a small hotel in a quiet town with the warm, dry summer at its height.

"You're pretty close to Joe Benson, aren't you?" he asked, swinging his shiny black boots onto a corner of the littered surface of his desk.

"I see Joe almost every day."

"I wonder if you'd mind putting an idea to him. I'd call him myself only he may need persuading and that will come better from you."

"Sounds mysterious."

"Not at all. I'm thinking of converting the back lounge into a piano bar. Joe Benson playing jazz could be an attraction."

"You're right about that." I could understand the reason for Mr. Danforth's hesitation. Joe Benson accompanied the hymn

45

singing at the United Church on Sunday mornings. He might consider it incongruous to be asked to spend Saturday nights in a smoky beer parlor playing the blues.

"Jazz is near and dear to Joe's heart," I confirmed. "I'm sure I can overcome any reluctance he may have."

The office door swung open. I recognized the lean and hungry shape of Lyndon Lee, a Torontonian who had met Jack Danforth's daughter Stella a few years ago and persuaded her to marry him. Lee was supposed to keep out of trouble by managing Jack's motel located ten miles down the highway. This was never easy for Lee—as I understood it, he managed to create several kinds of difficulty for himself most of the time. Antisocial is the nicest word we have for people like Lyndon Lee.

"Evening, Dad," he said, deliberately using that sadistic form of address. All he gave me was a nod.

Jack kicked shut the bottom drawer of his desk and kept his boot braced against it. The move was instinctive. I knew from my bellboy days that the boss liked to keep a metal box in there with a couple of hundred dollars in it. The flat-eyed Lee looked as if his tongue could snake into that drawer and snatch out tens like an armadillo sucking up ants from a hole in the ground. "What do you want, Lyndon?"

"Only to ask if you'd like a lift home. Stella's idea." It was a harmless suggestion, but as always when Lyndon Lee was in a room the air was electric with possibilities.

"I intend to stay here for a while," Danforth dismissed his son-in-law. "I'll call a cab when I'm ready to go home."

Lee went away and Jack said to me, "His latest enterprise was a poker game in one of the units at the motel."

"That's illegal, isn't it?"

"Especially the way my boy was doing it. Besides taking a percentage of every pot, he had something going with a marked deck of cards. One of the players threw a punch at him and came back later with the police."

"Nice for the motel."

"Fortunately, I'm on good terms with Chief Greb. But I had to be persuasive to cool that situation down."

I shook my head in sympathy. "When do you want to start the piano lounge?"

"Soon as possible. I see it as Fridays and Saturdays, eight till midnight. Half hour on, half hour off. If Joe is willing, he can ring me and we'll agree on money.''

"I'll go and see him tomorrow," I said, looking forward to the exciting mission.

Queenie greeted me when I arrived at Joe Benson's apartment after telephoning him the following morning. Joe ordered her into the living room and she went obediently. I followed him into the room, where I took my favorite armchair and watched as he lowered himself onto the piano bench. Queenie established herself at his feet.

"What's it all about, Norman? You sounded eager on the phone." Joe sat with his head tipped back, his eyes focused somewhere beyond the ceiling, as if he was receiving messages from above. Blind from birth, Joe Benson is not disfigured in any obvious way. The only sign of his handicap I can see is a slightly off-center condition of the eyes so that his face reminds me of a slot machine with the indicators jammed. Joe is in his mid-thirties, prematurely grey, with a neatly trimmed beard and moustache. He's tall and slim and he wears black trousers, black shoes, a white shirt, never a tie—a physicist on his day off.

"Jack Danforth at the Coronet Hotel has an idea," I said and went on to explain the concept of the piano lounge and Joe's place there as resident jazzman two nights a week. When I finished, Joe grinned at the ceiling. He turned to the piano, Queenie changing her position to let his legs pass, and allowed his hands to hang above the keyboard. They shifted this way and that, as if each finger was fitting into a familiar slot in the air.

"Here's something I'm doing for the Sunday School next week," he said. "It's one of their favorite hymns, but we haven't had it for a while. A real rouser." He struck a major chord, then began to sing, accompanying himself with percussive enthusiasm.

> "Though the angry surges roll
> On my tempest-driven soul . . .''

Joe completed a verse and one chorus, leaving no doubt that he possessed an Anchor safe and sure that would ever more endure. During the evangelical outburst, Queenie stretched out, lowered her fine alsatian head to her forearms, and closed her eyes. Her job was to guide Joe Benson along familiar streets, to prevent him walking in front of a car, and to keep him company here at home. If it was his habit to produce these sounds from time to time, that was his business. Queenie, in fact, seemed to find the gospel music pleasant.

"That should double the collection next Sunday," I said, "But what about the piano lounge?"

"You don't see any conflict in my banging out 'Flying Home' on Saturday night and 'Harvest Home' on Sunday morning?"

"If God had meant us to create music only in church," I said with utter sincerity, "he wouldn't have given us Art Tatum and Oscar Peterson."

"I can tell you somebody who isn't going to like it," Joe said, reminding me of a phenomenon that had slipped my mind. "But the idea appeals to me so she'll just have to put up with it."

The Benson fingers searched again for the familiar grooves. Joe struck a chord as different from the gospel introduction as beer is from beef tea. Queenie's ears came up and her chin rose an inch or so from its resting place. Joe shuffled through a progression of chords that changed the atmosphere in the room, changed the light, the temperature, moved us from where we were into a reality which was slightly better than the one I knew would be waiting for me when the music stopped. He began to play "I Can't Get Started" at a rather faster tempo than the Berrigan standard, left hand pumping a rhythm that was almost stride, right hand producing a tremolo at the end of each phrase. It was unique, a version never heard before, perhaps never to be heard again. And I was there.

Queenie moaned, the only time I have heard a dog utter such a sound. She dragged herself to her feet with the disgust of an elderly sunbather when the kids invade the beach with their frisbees and left the room with her head down. Through her master's exquisite music I heard her claws clicking down the corridor linoleum to the kitchen.

When Joe finished, I said, "That was prime."

"Thanks. But Queenie took off." He swept a hand below the bench to confirm his dog's absence.

"She reminds me of my old mother, rest her soul," I said. "A cultured lady, despite her nicotine addiction and a tendency to blow her top. I grew up surrounded by good music, knowing Tagliavini was a great tenor, understanding what a Gregorian chant sounded like. Our radio was quickly switched from speech; it broadcast music only, whether it was Schubert on a Sunday afternoon or the Foden Motor Works Brass Band playing 'Sons of the Brave' as I headed off to school in the morning."

"Musical Marchpast," Joe recalled the program.

"But when I became a teenager and I used my allowance to buy records, tolerance evaporated. I brought home Charlie Barnet's 'Scotch and Soda' and never got to play it above half volume. One time I said to her, 'Mom, listen, it's the Basie rhythm section—drums and bass and guitar playing like one man.' Do you know what her reaction was?"

"Same as Queenie's."

"She called it thump-thump-thump . . .."

That afternoon I wandered down to the Coronet, enjoying the sense of freedom I experienced when I passed the high school and saw the blind windows, noted the green scud of grass taking over the dirt playing field, and knew I wouldn't have to resume my slavery as slave-master at the head of Grade Eleven English for another six weeks.

As I walked into the hotel lobby, Stella Lee (the former Stella Danforth) was on her way out. I've always admired Stella's calm intelligent face, the thick sensible braid of her hair, the pool of quiet sanity that surrounds her wherever she goes. I like to brush up against that tranquil periphery, to slip inside and relax with her for a moment if I can. I think Stella's benign influence is, quite simply, what human evolution is all about. Give civilization another few thousand years and this will be the norm instead of the exception. Oh, to live in that paradise.

"Norman Craig, hello. I haven't seen you for a while. You look nice and relaxed."

"Hi, Stella. Summer vacation. I'm enjoying being a teacher." I mentioned the piano lounge and said I was going to see her father about Joe Benson's decision to take it on. "I'm glad he said yes. Dad's been talking about it for a year. I encouraged him to go ahead."

Just before we parted, I asked, "How's Lyndon?"

"Busy," she said, not in the way a nurse would have said that Doctor Schweitzer was busy. "I guess he can't help it."

"What do you mean?"

"I don't think it's the money—" she hesitated, then decided she trusted me enough to go on. "He never has enough. He takes things—and sells them. I've grown up with a copper coffee-mill my father's parents brought from Russia. It stood on the mantelpiece at home, and when I got married my father gave it to me."

"I can't believe this—"

"He did, Lyndon sold it to a dealer. When I missed it and asked him about it, he didn't even try to cover up." She shrugged philosophically. "Anyway, I made him hand over the money and I bought the coffee-mill back. Never mind."

Why Stella Danforth married Lyndon Lee is a tough question. The conclusion I have reached, the ony one I ever *will* reach, is that she, too, has her imperfection, the flaw in an otherwise perfect personality. She is so good, she must tie herself up with something bad. It can't be explained any more than science can explain magnetism. At one end you have positive, at the other, negative. Nature will not allow positive without negative. Go know.

I found Jack Danforth in the beverage room. He was enjoying himself, drawing glasses of beer. The bartender was reading a paper and Jack was running the tap, smiling to himself. The front door was open, warm fresh air drifting in from the street, and the place smelled beery and the drone of conversation around the room was like bees on a field of clover.

"Joe Benson likes the idea," I said.

Danforth pushed an overflowing glass my way. "On the house."

"Thanks. He'll call you to confirm it."

"Terrific. Perfect." My old boss looked as if he was proclaiming Christmas. "We'll start next Friday night."

I was there early that Friday to be sure of having a seat. The back lounge of the Coronet is not a large room, and preparations for the entertainment had made it smaller. A corner was cleared, an upright piano installed, and a space left open between it and the informal arrangement of upholstered chairs and small tables.

I sat near the door of Danforth's private office and ordered a beer. Shortly before eight, Jack emerged, locked the office door behind him, and joined me.

"Looks like a success already," he said, surveying the crowded room. A new cigar was plugged into his face—the hotel owner was about to enjoy himself. "Is somebody bringing Benson?"

"Queenie will look after it," I said. "They've been here before."

Lyndon Lee appeared from the beverage room. He was carrying a briefcase. "Can we go over the motel receipts?" he asked.

"Not now," Danforth said, looking straight ahead. "Joe Benson is going to play."

"I'll wait in the office."

"The office is locked."

Lee looked at Danforth. He looked at the office door. He looked at me. His eyes conveyed disbelief that grown men would waste time sitting in a smoky room listening to somebody playing the piano. As Shakespeare reminds us, let no such man be trusted.

Danforth's son-in-law went away just as Joe Benson arrived with Queenie leading him on a short leash. Joe's grin was in place, his eyes following closely the invisible map on the ceiling. In black slacks and turtleneck, he was elegant as a cat burglar. Queenie spotted the piano and led her master to it, sprawling on the floor as soon as he sat on the bench.

There was applause and a few words from Jack Danforth about his experimental entertainment policy, and then Benson warmed up with a couple of arpeggios. The room fell silent. Joe's fingers sought and found their starting position, hesitated, listening for the instruction from above. There was extreme tension in the air. Then Joe's left hand began to strike a repetitive boogie beat, deep and heavy and precise as if the notes were being produced by a clockwork mechanism. After four bars, the right hand introduced a rollicking figure that bounced off the base notes and tumbled and fell and rose again. It was something in the style of Pinetop Smith and the crowd responded instantly.

So did the dog. Queenie's head was up, her eyes fixed mournfully on her master. How could he do this to her? They were not safe at home, they were in a strange place. I watched the internal struggle expressed on those noble features and knew loyalty was going to lose out to the dog's musical snobbery. A moment later, Queenie got up and shuffled away, disgust and disapproval showing in every swing of her lowered head.

The crowd got the message and had to react. Joe's sensitive hearing picked it up and he knew what was happening. He stopped playing and said, "You can never please your own family."

Queenie came to me, her only friend in the room. Danforth got up and unlocked his office door, let the dog escape into the dark and quiet, then closed the door. "She's in my office, Joe," he reassured the piano player. "Carry on."

The evening was a terrific success. The local paper even managed to include a review in their weekend edition. Not that the hotel needed the plug. Joe Benson was a musical institution in Baytown and his presence would guarantee a sell-out every time.

I returned for a second transfusion the following night. As I entered the hotel, I passed Lyndon Lee lurking by the brass-plated doors. Shirt and tie, clean-shaven face, briefcase perpetually in hand—I reflected that Stella's husband presented an appearance that could give respectability a bad name.

"Nice night, Lyndon," I said.

"Mmmmmm." He had no use at the moment for a vacationing school teacher.

"Coming in to hear the music?"

"No, I have to go." He looked at his watch but made no move to depart.

As I passed through the lobby to the lounge, I glanced back and saw Lee poised in the doorway. Later I would recall his posture and the image would fall into place—Second World War assault troops looked like that in landing craft approaching a beach.

The crowd was even larger than on opening night. This time, Queenie was led away and stowed in the back office before Joe began to play. After the first set, she was let out to mingle with the customers during the interval, trudging solemnly from table to table for the pleasant ritual of the laying on of hands. Then, as Joe returned to the piano, Danforth put the dog back in the office, closed the door, and came to sit with me.

The entire second set turned out to be a tour-de-force built around the standard, "April In Paris." Joe began sweetly, almost in a classical vein. Then the earthy roots took hold and pushed up lush shoots that penetrated the melody and wove variations through it that threatened to bury the song—but never went quite that far. Chorus after chorus, the blind pianist came bursting through to emerge with the melody triumphantly at his fingertips.

The ending lasted, by itself, almost a quarter of an hour. Joe threw in the famous Basie coda, both hands in unison thundering out the swinging variation on the theme, and the people in the room cheered as he went on playing.

There was so much sound in the room—the fortissimo music, the crowd reaction—and our attention was so centered on the performance, I doubt if we would have heard a plane crash in the parking lot. Certainly nobody heard what must have been the intense, if brief, confrontation in Jack Danforth's back office. We knew nothing of that until the set ended and Jack went to retrieve Benson's dog.

I heard the sound my former boss made and saw him frozen in the doorway where he had switched on the light. I joined him inside and saw Queenie lying on the floor, bleeding from wounds in her neck and shoulder.

The window onto the parking lot had been forced open. I didn't see then but was told later by the police that there were signs of somebody trying to open the desk. The same implement used to do this and to jimmy the window had inflicted the wounds on the dog—probably a screwdriver.

Queenie had to be taken to the vet. Joe went with her and so did I. The damage was serious but not critical. She would be sedated, shaved, and stitched, and would spend the night at the surgery. Joe could have her back tomorrow.

I saw Joe home in a cab and promised to bring Queenie to him the next day.

After doing that in the late morning—she had numerous stitches around the neck, a Frankenstein dog—I went to the hotel and asked Jack Danforth if there was any news about the attempted robbery.

"Chief Greb came over himself," Jack said. "He found another blood specimen on the floor—not from the dog, he thinks. She must have got her teeth into whoever it was."

"Good," I said fervently.

We were still talking when the telephone rang. Jack answered and said, "Hello, Chief. Did you really?" He listened. "Well, that's a bit of luck. I'm not sure whether I'll press charges or not. I'll have to think about that."

As he put down the telephone, I asked, "A breakthrough?"

"They have the man. The dog did bite him and drew blood. He went home and had to tell his wife something, so he said it was a stray on the street. She's a knowledgable and sensible girl—the first thought she had was rabies, and she took him to the doctor for a shot. I wouldn't have given Greb credit for this much foresight, but apparently he asked all the doctors in town to report any dog bites. He didn't even have to do a blood sample—the guy admitted it."

"What guy?"

"Who else? Lyndon. He was after the cash in my bottom drawer. The room was dark, he mustn't have seen the dog till she went for him when he started jimmying the desk."

I can't say what punishment was meted out to Lyndon Lee. He still manages Jack's motel, and as far as I know the marriage to Stella is intact. Danforth's hands are tied—if he presses charges, his son-in-law will go to prison and his daughter could never live with that. But this story is not really about Lee, anyway. Queenie is the heroine and she holds the spotlight right to the end.

The following Friday Joe Benson reappeared at the Coronet lounge and received an ovation from a packed house, as did his heroic guide dog. When Joe sat at the piano, Jack took hold of Queenie's leash, led her into the back office, and closed the door. The room went silent as Joe prepared to play.

That was when we heard the plaintive whining behind the office door. Joe's hands settled onto his lap. "She's too smart to stay in there again, Jack," he said.

Danforth opened the door, ready to take the dog somewhere

else, but she was past him in a flash, between the tables and onto her spot beside the piano bench. There was applause and laughter. Joe stroked her head. "Lesser of two evils, love?" he said.

He began to play a slow, quiet blues with the measured pace of a man walking down a deserted street. Queenie's head went down for a moment, then it came up and her noble eyes rested on some point in space that only she could see.

Bless the dog, I said to myself as I sat back and lifted my glass of beer. She's going to try something my old mother refused to do—she's going to give jazz a chance.

Sir Arthur Conan Doyle

Creator of the most famous detective in literature, Sherlock Holmes, Sir Arthur Conan Doyle (1859-1930) was near apologetic in his autobiography, *Memories and Adventures*, (1924), about "Silver Blaze."

He writes: "Sometimes I have got upon dangerous ground where I have taken risks through my own want of knowledge of the correct atmosphere. I have, for example, never been a racing man, and yet I have ventured to write "Silver Blaze" in which the mystery depends upon the laws of training and racing. The story is all right, and Holmes may have been at the top of his form, but my ignorance cries aloud to heaven. I read an excellent and very damaging criticism of the story in some sporting paper, written clearly by a man who *did* know, in which he explained the exact penalties which would have come upon everyone concerned if they had acted as I described. Half would have been in jail, and the other half warned off the turf forever. However, I have never been nervous about details, and one must be masterful sometimes."

SILVER BLAZE

BY ARTHUR CONAN DOYLE

"I am afraid, Watson, that I shall have to go," said Holmes as we sat down together to our breakfast one morning.

"Go! Where to?"

"To Dartmoor; to King's Pyland."

I was not surprised. Indeed, my only wonder was that he had not already been mixed up in this extraordinary case, which was the one topic of conversation through the length and breadth of England. For a whole day my companion had rambled about the room with his chin upon his chest and his brows knitted, charging and recharging his pipe with the strongest black tobacco, and absolutely deaf to any of my questions or remarks. Fresh editions of every paper had been sent up by our news agent, only to be glanced over and tossed down into a corner. Yet, silent as he was, I knew perfectly well what it was over which he was brooding. There was but one problem before the public which could challenge his powers of analysis, and that was the singular disappearance of the favourite for the Wessex Cup, and the tragic murder of its trainer. When, therefore, he suddenly announced his intention of setting out for the scene of the drama, it was only what I had both expected and hoped for.

"I should be most happy to go down with you if I should not be in the way," said I.

"My dear Watson, you would confer a great favour upon me by coming. And I think that your time will not be misspent, for there are points about the case which promise to make it an absolutely unique one. We have, I think, just time to catch our train at Paddington, and I will go further into the matter upon our journey. You would oblige me by bringing with you your very excellent field-glass."

And so it happened that an hour or so later I found myself in the corner of a first-class carriage flying along enroute for

Exeter, while Sherlock Holmes, with his sharp, eager face framed in his ear-flapped travelling-cap, dipped rapidly into the bundle of fresh papers which he had procured at Paddington. We had left Reading far behind us before he thrust the last one of them under the seat and offered me his cigar-case.

"We are going well," said he, looking out of the window and glancing at his watch. "Our rate at present is fifty-three and a half miles an hour."

"I have not observed the quarter-mile posts," said I.

"Nor have I. But the telephone posts upon this line are sixty yards apart, and the calculation is a simple one. I presume that you have looked into this matter of the murder of John Straker and the disappearance of Silver Blaze?"

"I have seen what the *Telegraph* and the *Chronicle* have to say."

"It is one of those cases where the art of the reasoner should be used rather for the sifting of details than for the acquiring of fresh evidence. The tragedy has been so uncommon, so complete, and of such personal importance to so many people that we are suffering from a plethora of surmise, conjecture, and hypothesis. The difficulty is to detach the framework of fact—of absolute undeniable fact—from the embellishments of theorists and reporters. Then, having established ourselvess upon this sound basis, it is our duty to see what inferences may be drawn and what are the special points upon which the whole mystery turns. On Tuesday evening I received telegrams from both Colonel Ross, the owner of the horse, and from Inspector Gregory, who is looking after the case, inviting my coöperation."

"Tuesday evening!" I exclaimed. "And this is Thursday morning. Why didn't you go down yesterday?"

"Because I made a blunder, my dear Watson—which is, I am afraid, a more common occurrence than anyone would think who only knew me through your memoirs. The fact is that I could not believe it possible that the most remarkable horse in England could long remain concealed, especially in so sparsely inhabited a place as the north of Dartmoor. From hour to hour yesterday I expected to hear that he had been found, and that his abductor was the murderer of John Straker. When, however, another morning had come and I found that beyond the arrest of young Fitzroy Simpson nothing had been done, I felt that it was time for me to take action. Yet in some ways I feel that yesterday has not been wasted.''

"You have formed a theory, then?''

''At least I have got a grip of the essential facts of the case. I shall enumerate them to you, for nothing clears up a case so much as stating it to another person, and I can hardly expect your coöperation if I do not show you the position from which we start.''

I lay back against the cushions, puffing at my cigar, while Holmes, leaning forward, with his long, thin forefinger checking off the points upon the palm of his left hand, gave me a sketch of the events which had led to our journey.

''Silver Blaze,'' said he, ''is from the Somomy stock and holds as brilliant a record as his famous ancestor. He is now in his fifth year and has brought in turn each of the prizes of the turf to Colonel Ross, his fortunate owner. Up to the time of the catastrophe he was the first favourite for the Wessex Cup, the betting being three to one on him. He has always, however, been a prime favourite with the racing public and has never yet disappointed them, so that even at those odds enormous sums of money have been laid upon him. It is obvious, therefore, that there were many people who had the strongest interest in preventing Silver Blaze from being there at the fall of the flag next Tuesday.

''The fact was, of course, appreciated at King's Pyland, where the colonel's training stable is situated. Every precaution was taken to guard the favourite. The trainer, John Straker, is a retired jockey who rode in Colonel Ross's colours before he became too heavy for the weighing-chair. He has served the colonel for five years as jockey and for seven as trainer, and has always shown himself to be a zealous and honest servant. Under him were three lads, for the establishment was a small one, containing only four horses in all. One of these lads sat up each night in the stable, while the others slept in the loft. All three bore excellent characters. John Straker, who is a married man, lived in a small villa about two hundred yards from the stables. He has no children, keeps one maidservant, and is comfortably off. The country round is very lonely, but about half a mile to the north there is a small cluster of villas which have been built by a Tavistock contractor for the use of invalids and others who may wish to enjoy the pure Dartmoor air. Tavistock itself lies two miles to the west, while across the moor, also about two miles distant, is the larger training establishment of Mapleton, which belongs to Lord Backwater and is managed by Silas Brown. In every other direction the moor is a complete wilderness, inhabited only by a few roaming gypsies. Such was the general situation last Monday night when the catastrophe occurred.

"On that evening the horses had been exercised and watered as usual, and the stables were locked up at nine o'clock. Two of the lads walked up to the trainer's house, where they had supper in the kitchen, while the third, Ned Hunter, remained on guard. At a few minutes after nine the maid, Edith Baxter, carried down to the stables his supper, which consisted of a dish of curried mutton. She took no liquid, as there was a water-tap in the stables, and it was the rule that the lad on duty should drink nothing else. The maid carried a lantern with her, as it was very dark and the path ran across the open moor.

"Edith Baxter was within thirty yards of the stables when a man appeared out of the darkness and called to her to stop. As she stepped into the circle of yellow light thrown by the lantern she saw that he was a person of gentlemanly bearing, dressed in a gray suit of tweeds, with a cloth cap. He wore gaiters and carried a heavy stick with a knob to it. She was most impressed, however, by the extreme pallor of his face and by the nervousness of his manner. His age, she thought, would be rather over thirty than under it.

" 'Can you tell me where I am?' he asked. 'I had almost made up my mind to sleep on the moor when I saw the light of your lantern.'

" 'You are close to the King's Pyland training stables,' said she.

" 'Oh, indeed! What a stroke of luck!' he cried. 'I understand that a stable-boy sleeps there alone every night. Perhaps that is his supper which you are carrying to him. Now I am sure that you would not be too proud to earn the price of a new dress, would you?' He took a piece of white paper folded up out of his waistcoat pocket. 'See that the boy has this to-night, and you shall have the prettiest frock that money can buy.'

"She was frightened by the earnestness of his manner and ran past him to the window through which she was accustomed to hand the meals. It was already opened, and Hunter was seated at the small table inside. She had begun to tell him of what had happened when the stranger came up again.

" 'Good evening,' said he, looking through the window. 'I wanted to have a word with you.' The girl has sworn that as he spoke she noticed the corner of the little paper packet protruding from his closed hand.

" 'What business have you here?' asked the lad.

" 'It's business that may put something into your pocket,' said the other. 'You've two horses in for the Wessex Cup—Silver Blaze and Bayard. Let me have the straight tip and you won't be a loser. Is it a fact that at the weights Bayard could give the other a hundred yards in five furlongs, and that the stable have put their money on him?'

" 'So, you're one of those damned touts!' cried the lad. 'I'll show you how we serve them in King's Pyland.' He sprang up and rushed across the stable to unloose the dog. The girl fled away to the house, but as she ran she looked back and saw that the stranger was leaning through the window. A minute later, however, when Hunter rushed out with the hound he was gone, and though he ran all around the buildings he failed to find any trace of him."

"One moment," I asked. "Did the stable-boy, when he ran out with the dog, leave the door unlocked behind him?"

"Excellent, Watson, excellent!" murmured my companion. "The importance of the point struck me so forcibly that I sent a special wire to Dartmoor yesterday to clear the matter up. The boy locked the door before he left it. The window, I may add, was not large enough for a man to get through.

"Hunter waited until his fellow-grooms had returned, when he sent a message to the trainer and told him what had occurred. Straker was excited at hearing the account, although he does not seem to have quite realized its true significance. It left him, however, vaguely uneasy, and Mrs. Straker, waking at one in the morning, found that he was dressing. In reply to her inquiries, he said that he could not sleep on account of his anxiety about the horses, and that he intended to walk down to the stables to see that all was well. She begged him to remain at home, as she could hear the rain pattering against the window, but in spite of her entreaties he pulled on his large mackintosh and left the house.

"Mrs. Straker awoke at seven in the morning to find that her husband had not yet returned. She dressed herself hastily, called the maid, and set off for the stables. The door was open; inside, huddled together upon a chair, Hunter was sunk in a state of absolute stupor, the favourite's stall was empty, and there were no signs of his trainer.

"The two lads who slept in the chaff-cutting loft above the harness-room were quicky aroused. They had heard nothing during the night, for they are both sound sleepers. Hunter was obviously under the influence of some powerful drug, and as no sense could be got out of him, he was left to sleep it off while the two lads and the two women ran out in search of the absentees. They still had hopes that the trainer had for some reason taken out the horse for early exercise, but on ascending the knoll near the house, from which all the neighbouring moors were visible, they not only could see no signs of the missing favourite, but they perceived something which warned them that they were in the presence of a tragedy.

"About a quarter of a mile from the stables John Straker's overcoat was flapping from a furze-bush. Immediately beyond there was a bowl-shaped depression in the moor, and at the bottom of this was found the dead body of the unfortunate trainer. His head had been shattered by a savage blow from some heavy weapon, and he was wounded on the thigh, where there was a long, clean cut, inflicted evidently by some very sharp instrument. It was clear, however, that Straker had defended himself vigorously against his assailants, for in his right hand he held a small knife, which was clotted with blood up to the handle, while in his left he clasped a red-and-black silk cravat, which was recognized by the maid as having been worn on the preceding evening by the stranger who had visited the stables. Hunter, on recovering from his stupor, was also quite positive as to the ownership of the cravat. He was equally certain that the same stranger had, while standing at the window, drugged his curried mutton, and so deprived the stables of their watchman. As to the missing horse, there were abundant proofs in the mud which lay at the bottom of the fatal hollow that he had been there at the time of the struggle. But from that morning he has disappeared, and although a large reward has been offered, and all the gypsies of Dartmoor are on the alert, no news has come of him. Finally, an analysis has shown that the remains of his supper left by the stable-lad contained an appreciable quantity of powdered opium, while the people at the house partook of the same dish on the same night without any ill effect.

"Those are the main facts of the case, stripped of all surmise, and stated as baldly as possible. I shall now recapitulate what the police have done in the matter.

"Inspector Gregory, to whom the case has been committed, is an extremely competent officer. Were he but gifted with imagination he might rise to great heights in his profession. On his arrival he promptly found and arrested the man upon whom suspicion naturally rested. There was little difficulty in finding him, for he inhabited one of those villas which I have mentioned. His name, it appears, was Fitzroy Simpson. He was a man of excellent birth and education, who had squandered a fortune upon the turf, and who lived now by doing a little quiet and genteel book-making in the sporting clubs of London. An examination of his betting-book shows that bets to the amount of five thousand pounds had been registered by him against the favourite. On being arrested he volunteered the statement that he had come down to Dartmoor in the hope of getting some information about the King's Pyland horses, and also about Desborough, the second favourite, which was in charge of Silas Brown at the Mapleton stables. He did not attempt to deny that he had acted as described upon the evening before, but declared that he had no sinister designs and had simply wished to obtain first-hand information. When confronted with his cravat he turned very pale and was utterly unable to account for its presence in the hand of the murdered man. His wet clothing showed that he had been out in the storm of the night before, and his stick, which was a penang-lawyer weighted with lead, was just such a weapon as might, by repeated blows, have inflicted the terrible injuries to which the trainer had succumbed. On the other hand, there was no wound upon his person, while the state of Straker's knife would show that one at least of his assailants must bear his mark upon him. There you have it all in a nutshell, Watson, and if you can give me any light I shall be infinitely obliged to you.''

I had listened with the greatest interest to the statement which Holmes, with characteristic clearness, had laid before me. Though most of the facts were familiar to me, I had not sufficiently appreciated their relative importance, nor their connection to each other.

"Is it not possible," I suggested, "that the incised wound upon Straker may have been caused by his own knife in the convulsive struggles which follow any brain injury?"

"It is more than possible: it is probable," said Holmes. "In that case one of the main points in favour of the accused disappears."

"And yet," said I, "even now I fail to understand what the theory of the police can be."

"I am afraid that whatever theory we state has very grave objections to it," returned my companion. "The police imagine, I take it, that this Fitzroy Simpson, having drugged the lad, and having in some way obtained a duplicate key, opened the stable door and took out the horse, with the intention, apparently, of kidnapping him altogether. His bridle is missing, so that Simpson must have put this on. Then, having left the door open behind him, he was leading the horse away over the moor when he was either met or overtaken by the trainer. A row naturally ensued. Simpson beat out the trainer's brains with his heavy stick without receiving any injury from the small knife which Straker used in self-defence, and then the thief either led the horse on to some secret hiding-place, or else it may have bolted during the struggle, and be now wandering out on the moors. That is the case as it appears to the police, and improbable as it is, all other explanations are more improbable still. However, I shall very quickly test the matter when I am once upon the spot, and until then I cannot really see how we can get much further than our present position."

It was evening before we reached the little town of Tavistock, which lies, like the boss of a shield, in the middle of the huge circle of Dartmoor. Two gentlemen were awaiting us in the station—the one a tall, fair man with lion-like hair and beard and curiously penetrating light blue eyes; the other a small, alert person, very neat and dapper, in a frock-coat and gaiters, with trim little side-whiskers and an eyeglass. The latter was Colonel Ross, the well-known sportsman; the other, Inspector Gregory; a man who was rapidly making his name in the English detective service.

"I am delighted that you have come down, Mr. Holmes," said the colonel. "The inspector here has done all that could possibly be suggested, but I wish to leave no stone unturned in trying to avenge poor Straker and in recovering my horse."

"Have there been any fresh developments?" asked Holmes.

"I am sorry to say that we have made very little progress," said the inspector. "We have an open carriage outside, and as you would no doubt like to see the place before the light fails, we might talk it over as we drive."

A minute later we were all seated in a comfortable landau and were rattling through the quaint old Devonshire city. Inspector Gregory was full of his case and poured out a stream of remarks, while Holmes threw in an occasional question or interjection. Colonel Ross leaned back with his arms folded and his hat tilted over his eyes, while I listened with interest to the dialogue of the two detectives. Gregory was formulating his theory, which was almost exactly what Holmes had foretold in the train.

"The net is drawn pretty close round Fitzroy Simpson," he remarked, "and I believe myself that he is our man. At the same time I recognize that the evidence is purely circumstantial, and that some new development may upset it."

"How about Straker's knife?"

"We have quite come to the conclusion that he wounded himself in his fall."

"My friend Dr. Watson made that suggestion to me as we came down. If so, it would tell against this man Simpson."

"Undoubtedly. He has neither a knife nor any sign of a wound. The evidence against him is certainly very strong. He had a great interest in the disappearance of the favourite. He lies under suspicion of having poisoned the stable-boy; he was undoubtedly out in the storm; he was armed with a heavy stick, and his cravat was found in the dead man's hand. I really think we have enough to go before a jury."

Holmes shook his head. "A clever counsel would tear it all to rags," said he. "Why should he take the horse out of the stable? If he wished to injure it, why could he not do it there?

Has a duplicate key been found in his possession? What chemist sold him the powdered opium? Above all, where could he, a stranger to the district, hide a horse, and such a horse as this? What is his own explanation as to the paper which he wished the maid to give to the stable-boy?''

"He says that it was a ten-pound note. One was found in his purse. But your other difficulties are not so formidable as they seem. He is not a stranger to the district. He has twice lodged at Tavistock in the summer. The opium was probably brought from London. The key, having served its purpose, would be hurled away. The horse may be at the bottom of one of the pits or old mines upon the moor.''

"What does he say about the cravat?''

"He acknowledges that it is his and declares that he had lost it. But a new element has been introduced into the case which may account for his leading the horse from the stable.''

Holmes pricked up his ears.

"We have found traces which show that a party of gypsies encamped on Monday night within a mile of the spot where the murder took place. On Tuesday they were gone. Now, presuming that there was some understanding between Simpson and these gypsies, might he not have been leading the horse to them when he was overtaken, and may they not have him now?''

"It is certainly possible.''

"The moor is being scoured for these gypsies. I have also examined every stable and outhouse in Tavistock, and for a radius of ten miles.''

"There is another training-stable quite close, I understand?''

"Yes, and that is a factor which we must certainly not neglect. As Desborough, their horse, was second in the betting, they had an interest in the disappearance of the favourite. Silas Brown, the trainer, is known to have had large bets upon the event, and he was no friend to poor Straker. We have, however, examined the stables, and there is nothing to connect him with the affair.''

"And nothing to connect this man Simpson with the interests of the Mapleton stables?''

"Nothing at all.''

Holmes leaned back in the carriage, and the conversation ceased. A few minutes later our driver pulled up at a neat little red-brick villa with overhanging eaves which stood by the road. Some distance off, across a paddock, lay a long gray-tiled outbuilding. In every other direction the low curves of the moor, bronze-coloured from the fading ferns, stretched away to the sky-line, broken only by the steeples of Tavistock, and by a cluster of houses away to the westward which marked the Mapleton stables. We all sprang out with the exception of Holmes, who continued to lean back with his eyes fixed upon the sky in front of him, entirely absorbed in his own thoughts. It was only when I touched his arm that he roused himself with a violent start and stepped out of the carriage.

"Excuse me," said he, turning to Colonel Ross, who had looked at him in some surprise. "I was day-dreaming." There was a gleam in his eye and a suppressed excitement in his manner which convinced me, used as I was to his ways, that his hand was upon a clue, though I could not imagine where he had found it.

"Perhaps you would prefer at once to go on to the scene of the crime, Mr. Holmes?" said Gregory.

"I think that I should prefer to stay here a little and go into one or two questions of detail. Straker was brought back here, I presume?"

"Yes, he lies upstairs. The inquest is to-morrow."

"He has been in your service some years, Colonel Ross?"

"I have always found him an excellent servant."

"I presume that you made an inventory of what he had in his pockets at the time of his death, Inspector?"

"I have the things themselves in the sitting-room if you would care to see them."

"I should be very glad." We all filed into the front room and sat round the central table while the inspector unlocked a square tin box and laid a small heap of things before us. There was a box of vestas, two inches of tallow candle, an A D P brier-root pipe, a pouch of sealskin with half an ounce of long-cut Caven-dish, a silver watch with a gold chain, five sovereigns in gold, an aluminum pencil-case, a few papers, and an ivory-handled knife with a very delicate, inflexible blade marked Weiss & Co., London.

"This is a very singular knife," said Holmes, lifting it up and examining it minutely. "I presume, as I see blood-stains upon it, that it is the one which was found in the dead man's grasp. Watson, this knife is surely in your line?''

"It is what we call a cataract knife,'' said I.

"I thought so. A very delicate blade devised for very delicate work. A strange thing for a man to carry with him upon a rough expedition, especially as it would not shut in his pocket.''

"The tip was guarded by a disc of cork which we found beside his body,'' said the inspector. "His wife tells us that the knife had lain upon the dressing-table, and that he had picked it up as he left the room. It was a poor weapon, but perhaps the best that he could lay his hands on at the moment.''

"Very possibly. How about these papers?''

"Three of them are receipted hay-dealers' accounts. One of them is a letter of instructions from Colonel Ross. This other is a milliner's account for thirty-seven pounds fifteen made out by Madame Lesurier, of Bond Street, to William Derbyshire. Mrs. Straker tells us that Derbyshire was a friend of her husband's, and that occasionally his letters were addressed here.''

"Madame Derbyshire had somewhat expensive tastes,'' re-marked Holmes, glancing down the account. "Twenty-two guin-eas is rather heavy for a single costume. However, there appears to be nothing more to learn, and we may now go down to the scene of the crime.''

As we emerged from the sitting-room a woman, who had been waiting in the passage, took a step forward and laid her hand upon the inspector's sleeve. Her face was haggard and thin and eager, stamped with the print of a recent horror.

"Have you got them? Have you found them?'' she panted.

"No, Mrs. Straker. But Mr. Holmes here has come from London to help us, and we shall do all that is possible.''

"Surely I met you in Plymouth at a garden-party some little time ago, Mrs. Straker?'' said Holmes.

"No, sir; you are mistaken.''

"Dear me! Why, I could have sworn to it. You wore a costume of dove-coloured silk with ostrich-feather trimming.''

"I never had such a dress, sir,'' answered the lady.

"Ah, that quite settles it,'' said Holmes. And with an apol-ogy he followed the inspector outside. A short walk across the moor took us to the hollow in which the body had been found. At the brink of it was the furze-bush upon which the coat had been hung.

"There was no wind that night, I understand," said Holmes.

"None, but very heavy rain."

"In that case the overcoat was not blown against the furze-bushes, but placed there."

"Yes, it was laid across the bush."

"You fill me with interest. I perceive that the ground has been trampled up a good deal. No doubt many feet have been here since Monday night."

"A piece of matting has been laid here at the side, and we have all stood upon that."

"Excellent."

"In this bag I have one of the boots which Straker wore, one of Fitzroy Simpson's shoes, and a cast horseshoe of Silver Blaze."

"My dear Inspector, you surpass yourself!" Holmes took the bag, and, descending into the hollow, he pushed the matting into a more central position. Then stretching himself upon his face and leaning his chin upon his hands, he made a careful study of the trampled mud in front of him. "Hullo!" said he suddenly. "What's this?" It was a wax vesta, half burned, which was so coated with mud that it looked at first like a little chip of wood.

"I cannot think how I came to overlook it," said the inspector with an expression of annoyance.

"It was invisible, buried in the mud. I only saw it because I was looking for it."

"What! you expected to find it?"

"I thought it not unlikely."

He took the boots from the bag and compared the impressions of each of them with marks upon the ground. Then he clambered up to the rim of the hollow and crawled about among the ferns and bushes.

"I am afraid that there are no more tracks," said the inspector. "I have examined the ground very carefully for a hundred yards in each direction."

"Indeed!" said Holmes, rising. "I should not have the impertinence to do it again after what you say. But I should like to take a little walk over the moor before it grows dark that I may know my ground to-morrow, and I think that I shall put this horseshoe into my pocket for luck.''

Colonel Ross, who had shown some signs of impatience at my companion's quiet and systematic method of work, glanced at his watch. ''I wish you would come back with me, Inspector,'' said he. ''There are several points on which I should like your advice, and especially as to whether we do not owe it to the public to remove our horse's name from the entries for the cup.''

''Certainly not,'' cried Holmes with decision. ''I should let the name stand.''

The colonel bowed. ''I am very glad to have had your opinion, sir,'' said he. ''You will find us at poor Straker's house when you have finished your walk, and we can drive together into Tavistock.''

He turned back with the inspector, while Holmes and I walked slowly across the moor. The sun was beginning to sink behind the stable of Mapleton, and the long, sloping plain in front of us was tinged with gold, deepening into rich, ruddy browns where the faded ferns and brambles caught the evening light. But the glories of the landscape were all wasted upon my companion, who was sunk in the deepest thought.

''It's this way, Watson,'' said he at last. ''We may leave the question of who killed John Straker for the instant and confine ourselves to finding out what has become of the horse. Now, supposing that he broke away during or after the tragedy, where could he have gone to? The horse is a very gregarious creature. If left to himself his instincts would have been either to return to King's Pyland or go over to Mapleton. Why should he run wild upon the moor? He would surely have been seen by now. And why should gypsies kidnap him? These people always clear out when they hear of trouble, for they do not wish to be pestered by the police. They could not hope to sell such a horse. They would run a great risk and gain nothing by taking him. Surely that is clear.''

''Where is he, then?''

''I have already said that he must have gone to King's Pyland or to Mapleton. He is not at King's Pyland. Therefore he is at Mapleton. Let us take that as a working hypothesis and see what it leads us to. This part of the moor, as the inspector remarked, is very hard and dry. But it falls away towards Mapleton, and you can see from here that there is a long hollow over yonder, which must have been very wet on Monday night. If our supposition is correct, then the horse must have crossed that, and there is the point where we should look for his tracks.''

We had been walking briskly during this conversation, and a few more minutes brought us to the hollow in question. At Holmes's request I walked down the bank to the right, and he to the left, but I had not taken fifty paces before I heard him give a shout and saw him waving his hand to me. The track of a horse was plainly outlined in the soft earth in front of him, and the shoe which he took from his pocket exactly fitted the impression.

"See the value of imagination," said Holmes. "It is the one quality which Gregory lacks. We imagined what might have happened, acted upon the supposition, and find ourselves justified. Let us proceed."

We crossed the marshy bottom and passed over a quarter of a mile of dry, hard turf. Again the ground sloped, and again we came on the tracks. Then we lost them for half a mile, but only to pick them up once more quite close to Mapleton. It was Holmes who saw them first, and he stood pointing with a look of triumph upon his face. A man's track was visible beside the horse's.

"The horse was alone before," I cried.

"Quite so. It was alone before. Hullo, what is this?"

The double track turned sharp off and took the direction of King's Pyland. Holmes whistled, and we both followed along after it. His eyes were on the trail, but I happened to look a little to one side and saw to my surprise the same tracks coming back again in the opposite direction.

"One for you, Watson," said Holmes when I pointed it out. "You have saved us a long walk, which would have brought us back on our own traces. Let us follow the return track."

We had not to go far. It ended at the paving of asphalt which led up to the gates of the Mapleton stables. As we approached, a groom ran out from them.

"We don't want any loiterers about here," said he.

"I only wished to ask a question," said Holmes, with his finger and thumb in his waistcoat pocket. "Should I be too early to see your master, Mr. Silas Brown, if I were to call at five o'clock to-morrow morning?''

"Bless you, sir, if anyone is about he will be, for he is always the first stirring. But here he is, sir, to answer your questions for himself. No, sir, no, it is as much as my place is worth to let him see me touch your money. Afterwards, if you like.''

As Sherlock Holmes replaced the half-crown which he had drawn from his pocket, a fierce-looking elderly man strode out from the gate with a hunting-crop swinging in his hand.

"What's this, Dawson!'' he cried. "No gossiping! Go about your business! And you, what the devil do you want here?''

"Ten minutes' talk with you, my good sir,'' said Holmes in the sweetest of voices.

"I've no time to talk to every gadabout. We want no strangers here. Be off, or you may find a dog at your heels.''

Holmes leaned forward and whispered something in the trainer's ear. He started violently and flushed to the temples.

"It's a lie!'' he shouted. "An infernal lie!''

"Very good. Shall we argue about it here in public or talk it over in your parlour?''

"Oh, come in if you wish to.''

Holmes smiled. "I shall not keep you more than a few minutes, Watson,'' said he. "Now, Mr. Brown, I am quite at your disposal.''

It was twenty minutes, and the reds had all faded into grays before Holmes and the trainer reappeared. Never have I seen such a change as had been brought about in Silas Brown in that short time. His face was ashy pale, beads of perspiration shone upon his brow, and his hands shook until the hunting-crop wagged like a branch in the wind. His bullying, overbearing manner was all gone too, and he cringed along at my companion's side like a dog with its master.

"Your instructions will be done. It shall all be done,'' said he.

"There must be no mistake,'' said Holmes, looking round at him. The other winced as he read the menace in his eyes.

"Oh, no, there shall be no mistake. It shall be there. Should I change it first or not?''

Holmes thought a little and then burst out laughing. "No,

don't," said he, "I shall write to you about it. No tricks, now, or—"

"Oh, you can trust me, you can trust me!"

"Yes, I think I can. Well, you shall hear from me to-morrow." He turned upon his heel, disregarding the trembling hand which the other held out to him, and we set off for King's Pyland.

"A more perfect compound of the bully, coward, and sneak than Master Silas Brown I have seldom met with," remarked Holmes as we trudged along together.

"He has the horse, then?"

"He tried to bluster out of it, but I described to him so exactly what his actions had been upon that morning that he is convinced that I was watching him. Of course you observed the peculiarly square toes in the impressions, and that his own boots exactly corresponded to them. Again, of course no subordinate would have dared to do such a thing. I described to him how, when according to his custom he was the first down, he perceived a strange horse wandering over the moor. How he went out to it, and his astonishment at recognizing, from the white forehead which has given the favourite its name, that chance had put in his power the only horse which could beat the one upon which he had put his money. Then I described how his first impulse had been to lead him back to King's Pyland, and how the devil had shown him how he could hide the horse until the race was over, and how he had led it back and concealed it at Mapleton. When I told him every detail he gave it up and thought only of saving his own skin."

"But his stables had been searched?"

"Oh, an old horse-faker like him has many a dodge."

"But are you not afraid to leave the horse in his power now, since he has every interest in injuring it?"

"My dear fellow, he will guard it as the apple of his eye. He knows that his only hope of mercy is to produce it safe."

"Colonel Ross did not impress me as a man who would be likely to show much mercy in any case."

"The matter does not rest with Colonel Ross. I follow my own methods and tell as much or as little as I choose. That is the advantage of being unofficial. I don't know whether you observed it, Watson, but the colonel's manner has been just a trifle cavalier to me. I am inclined now to have a little amusement at his expense. Say nothing to him about the horse.''

''Certainly not without your permission.''

''And of course this is all quite a minor point compared to the question of who killed John Straker.''

''And you will devote yourself to that?''

''On the contrary, we both go back to London by the night train.''

I was thunderstruck by my friend's words. We had only been a few hours in Devonshire, and that he should give up an investigation which he had begun so brilliantly was quite incomprehensible to me. Not a word more could I draw from him until we were back at the trainer's house. The colonel and the inspector were awaiting us in the parlour.

''My friend and I return to town by the night-express,'' said Holmes. ''We have had a charming little breath of your beautiful Dartmoor air.''

The inspector opened his eyes, and the colonel's lip curled in a sneer.

''So you despair of arresting the murderer of poor Straker,'' said he.

Holmes shrugged his shoulders. ''There are certainly grave difficulties in the way,'' said he. ''I have every hope, however, that your horse will start upon Tuesday, and I beg that you will have your jockey in readiness. Might I ask for a photograph of Mr. John Straker?''

The inspector took one from an envelope and handed it to him.

''My dear Gregory, you anticipate all my wants. If I might ask you to wait here for an instant, I have a question which I should like to put to the maid.''

''I must say that I am rather disappointed in our London consultant,'' said Colonel Ross bluntly as my friend left the room. ''I do not see that we are any further than when he came.''

''At least you have his assurance that your horse will run,'' said I.

''Yes, I have his assurance,'' said the colonel with a shrug of his shoulders. ''I should prefer to have the horse.''

I was about to make some reply in defence of my friend when he entered the room again.

"Now, gentlemen," said he, "I am quite ready for Tavistock."

As we stepped into the carriage one of the stable-lads held the door open for us. A sudden idea seemed to occur to Holmes, for he leaned forward and touched the lad upon the sleeve.

"You have a few sheep in the paddock," he said. "Who attends to them?"

"I do, sir."

"Have you noticed anything amiss with them of late?"

"Well, sir, not of much account, but three of them have gone lame, sir."

I could see that Holmes was extremely pleased, for he chuckled and rubbed his hands together.

"A long shot, Watson, a very long shot," said he, pinching my arm. "Gregory, let me recommend to your attention this singular epidemic among the sheep. Drive on, coachman!"

Colonel Ross still wore an expression which showed the poor opinion which he had formed of my companion's ability, but I saw by the inspector's face that his attention had been keenly aroused.

"You consider that to be important?" he asked.

"Exceedingly so."

"Is there any point to which you would wish to draw my attention?"

"To the curious incident of the dog in the night-time."

"The dog did nothing in the night-time."

"That was the curious incident," remarked Sherlock Holmes.

Four days later Holmes and I were again in the train, bound for Winchester to see the race for the Wessex Cup. Colonel Ross met us by appointment outside the station, and we drove in his drag to the course beyond the town. His face was grave, and his manner was cold in the extreme.

"I have seen nothing of my horse," said he.

"I suppose that you would know him when you saw him?" asked Holmes.

The colonel was very angry. "I have been on the turf for twenty years and never was asked such a question as that before,'' said he. "A child would know Silver Blaze with his white forehead and his mottled off-foreleg.''

"How is the betting?''

"Well, that is the curious part of it. You could have got fifteen to one yesterday, but the price has become shorter and shorter, until you can hardly get three to one now.''

"Hum!'' said Holmes. "Somebody knows something, that is clear.''

As the drag drew up in the enclosure near the grandstand I glanced at the card to see the entries.

> Wessex Plate [it ran] 50 sovs. each h ft with 1000 sovs. added, for four and five year olds. Second, £300. Third, £200. New course (one mile and five furlongs).
> 1. Mr. Heath Newton's The Negro. Red cap, Cinnamon jacket.
> 2. Colonel Wardlaw's Pugilist. Pink cap, Blue and black jacket.
> 3. Lord Backwater's Desborough. Yellow cap and sleeves.
> 4. Colonel Ross's Silver Blaze. Black cap. Red jacket.
> 5. Duke of Balmoral's Iris. Yellow and black stripes.
> 6. Lord Singleford's Rasper. Purple cap. Black sleeves.

"We scratched our other one and put all hopes on your word,'' said the colonel. "Why, what is that? Silver Blaze favourite?''

"Five to four against Silver Blaze!'' roared the ring. "Five to four against Silver Blaze! Five to fifteen against Desborough! Five to four on the field!''

"There are the numbers up,'' I cried. "They are all six there.''

"All six there? Then my horse is running,'' cried the colonel in great agitation. "But I don't see him. My colours have not passed.''

"Only five have passed. This must be he.''

As I spoke a powerful bay horse swept out from the weighing enclosure and cantered past us, bearing on its back the well-known black and red of the colonel.

"That's not my horse,'' cried the owner. "That beast has not a white hair upon its body. What is this that you have done, Mr. Holmes?''

''Well, well, let us see how he gets on,'' said my friend imperturbably. For a few minutes he gazed through my field-glass. ''Capital! An excellent start!'' he cried suddenly. ''There they are, coming round the curve!''

From our drag we had a superb view as they came up the straight. The six horses were so close together that a carpet could have covered them, but halfway up the yellow of the Mapleton stable showed to the front. Before they reached us, however, Desborough's bolt was shot, and the colonel's horse, coming away with a rush, passed the post a good six lengths before its rival, the Duke of Balmoral's Iris making a bad third.

''It's my race, anyhow,'' gasped the colonel, passing his hand over his eyes. ''I confess that I can make neither head nor tail of it. Don't you think that you have kept up your mystery long enough, Mr. Holmes?''

''Certainly, Colonel, you shall know everything. Let us all go round and have a look at the horse together. Here he is,'' he continued as we made our way into the weighing enclosure, where only owners and their friends find admittance. ''You have only to wash his face and his legs in spirits of wine, and you will find that he is the same old Silver Blaze as ever.''

''You take my breath away!''

''I found him in the hands of a faker and took the liberty of running him just as he was sent over.''

''My dear sir, you have done wonders. The horse looks very fit and well. It never went better in its life. I owe you a thousand apologies for having doubted your ability. You have done me a great service by recovering my horse. You would do me a greater still if you could lay your hands on the murderer of John Straker.''

''I have done so,'' said Holmes quietly.

The colonel and I stared at him in amazement. ''You have got him! Where is he, then?''

''He is here.''

''Here! Where?''

''In my company at the present moment.''

The colonel flushed angrily. ''I quite recognize that I am under obligations to you, Mr. Holmes,'' said he, ''but I must regard what you have just said as either a very bad joke or an insult.''

Sherlock Holmes laughed. ''I assure you that I have not associated you with the crime, Colonel,'' said he. ''The real murderer is standing immediately behind you.'' He stepped past and laid his hand upon the glossy neck of the thoroughbred.

''The horse!'' cried both the colonel and myself.

''Yes, the horse. And it may lessen his guilt if I say that it was done in self-defence, and that John Straker was a man who was entirely unworthy of your confidence. But there goes the bell, and as I stand to win a little on this next race, I shall defer a lengthy explanation until a more fitting time.''

We had the corner of a Pullman car to ourselves that evening as we whirled back to London, and I fancy that the journey was a short one to Colonel Ross as well as to myself as we listened to our companion's narrative of the events which had occurred at the Dartmoor training-stables upon that Monday night, and the means by which he had unravelled them.

''I confess,'' said he, ''that any theories which I had formed from the newspaper reports were entirely erroneous. And yet there were indications there, had they not been overlaid by other details which concealed their true import. I went to Devonshire with the conviction that Fitzroy Simpson was the true culprit, although, of course, I saw that the evidence against him was by no means complete. It was while I was in the carriage, just as we reached the trainer's house, that the immense significance of the curried mutton occurred to me. You may remember that I was distrait and remained sitting after you had all alighted. I was marvelling in my own mind how I could possibly have overlooked so obvious a clue.''

''I confess,'' said the colonel, ''that even now I cannot see how it helps us.''

''It was the first link in my chain of reasoning. Powdered opium is by no means tasteless. The flavour is not disagreeable, but it is perceptible. Were it mixed with any ordinary dish the eater would undoubtedly detect it and would probably eat no more. A curry was exactly the medium which would disguise this taste. By no possible supposition could this stranger, Fitzroy Simpson, have caused curry to be served in the trainer's family that night, and it is surely too monstrous a coincidence to suppose that he happened to come along with powdered opium upon the very night when a dish happened to be served which would disguise the flavour. That is unthinkable. Therefore Simpson becomes eliminated from the case, and our attention centres upon Straker and his wife, the only two people who could have chosen curried mutton for supper that night. The opium was added after the dish was set aside for the stable-boy, for the others had the same for supper with no ill effects. Which of them, then, had access to that dish without the maid seeing them?

"Before deciding that question I had grasped the significance of the silence of the dog, for one true inference invariably suggests others. The Simpson incident had shown me that a dog was kept in the stables, and yet, though someone had been in and had fetched out a horse, he had not barked enough to arouse the two lads in the loft. Obviously the midnight visitor was someone whom the dog knew well.

"I was already convinced, or almost convinced, that John Straker went down to the stables in the dead of the night and took out Silver Blaze. For what purpose? For a dishonest one, obviously, or why should he drug his own stable-boy? And yet I was at a loss to know why. There have been cases before now where trainers have made sure of great sums of money by laying against their own horses through agents and then preventing them from winning by fraud. Sometimes it is a pulling jockey. Sometimes it is some surer and subtler means. What was it here? I hoped that the contents of his pockets might help me to form a conclusion.

"And they did so. You cannot have forgotten the singular knife which was found in the dead man's hand, a knife which certainly no sane man would choose for a weapon. It was, as Dr. Watson told us, a form of knife which is used for the most delicate operations known in surgery. And it was to be used for a delicate operation that night. You must know, with your wide experience of turf matters, Colonel Ross, that it is possible to make a slight nick upon the tendons of a horse's ham, and to do it subcutaneously, so as to leave absolutely no trace. A horse so treated would develop a slight lameness, which would be put down to a strain in exercise or a touch of rheumatism, but never to foul play.''

''Villain! Scoundrel!'' cried the colonel.

''We have here the explanation of why John Straker wished to take the horse out on to the moor. So spirited a creature would have certainly roused the soundest of sleepers when it felt the prick of the knife. It was absolutely necessary to do it in the open air.''

''I have been blind!'' cried the colonel. ''Of course that was why he needed the candle and struck the match.''

''Undoubtedly. But in examining his belongings I was fortunate enough to discover not only the method of the crime but even its motives. As a man of the world, Colonel, you know that men do not carry other people's bills about in their pockets. We have most of us quite enough to do to settle our own. I at once concluded that Straker was leading a double life and keeping a second establishment. The nature of the bill showed that there was a lady in the case, and one who had expensive tastes. Liberal as you are with your servants, one can hardly expect that they can buy twenty-guinea walking dresses for their ladies. I questioned Mrs. Straker as to the dress without her knowing it, and, having satisfied myself that it had never reached her, I made a note of the milliner's address and felt that by calling there with Straker's photograph I could easily dispose of the mythical Derbyshire.

''From that time on all was plain. Straker had led out the horse to a hollow where his light would be invisible. Simpson in his flight had dropped his cravat, and Straker had picked it up—with some idea, perhaps, that he might use it in securing the horse's leg. Once in the hollow, he had got behind the horse and had struck a light; but the creature, frightened at the sudden glare, and with the strange instinct of animals feeling that some mischief was intended, had lashed out, and the steel shoe had struck Straker full on the forehead. He had already, in spite of the rain, taken off his overcoat in order to do his delicate task, and so, as he fell, his knife gashed his thigh. Do I make it clear?''

''Wonderful!'' cried the colonel. ''Wonderful! You might have been there!''

''My final shot was, I confess, a very long one. It struck me that so astute a man as Straker would not undertake this delicate tendon-nicking without a little practice. What could he practise on? My eyes fell upon the sheep, and I asked a question which, rather to my surprise, showed that my surmise was correct.

"When I returned to London I called upon the milliner, who had recognized Straker as an excellent customer of the name of Derbyshire, who had a very dashing wife, with a strong partiality for expensive dresses. I have no doubt that this woman had plunged him over head and ears in debt, and so led him into this miserable plot."

"You have explained all but one thing," cried the colonel. "Where was the horse?"

"Ah, it bolted, and was cared for by one of your neighbours. We must have an amnesty in that direction, I think. This is Clapham Junction, if I am not mistaken, and we shall be in Victoria in less than ten minutes. If you care to smoke a cigar in our rooms, Colonel, I shall be happy to give you any other details which might interest you."

Paul W. Fairman

Prolific writer and editor, Paul W. Fairman wrote over two hundred novels using various names, and edited *Amazing, Fantastic,* and *Ellery Queen's Mystery Magazine.* His short stories, which began appearing in the 1930s in *The Saturday Evening Post, This Week, Cosmopolitan, Redbook* and other publications, were adapted for television shows and science fiction movies.

THE DARK ROAD HOME

BY PAUL W. FAIRMAN

The woman was in a terrible rage. The little girl, highly sensitive to human reactions—to fear and tension and anger—could feel the vibrations coming through the wall from the room beyond; coming into the place where she sat very still and waited.

The woman kept repeating a single word: "Stupid—stupid—stupid" and the man who was with her there in the other room growled his defense: "It wasn't my fault. How could I know? I just did like we planned. It wasn't my fault."

The little girl was not frightened in the accepted sense. She had known of too much oppression and injustice to panic even in a situation such as this.

"The important thing now, Helen," the man whined, "is what are we going to do?"

"What can we do? We've got to get rid of her. She's worthless. It's all danger now and no profit. We've got to get rid of her and give ourselves an even break."

"You mean—?"

"What else could I mean?"

The little girl didn't understand one word in ten but the woman's tone, the aura of poised violence, the fear in the man's last question, gave her the meaning. And she knew the Terror had returned; was here again; had to be reckoned with.

There had been a long, pleasant time beyond reach of the Terror; when they'd told her it would never come again. But she'd known that it would; that it was only waiting out there somewhere to sweep in and take her as it had taken her mother and her father and so many of the people she had known.

And what did you do when the Terror came? You did as you were told. You obeyed orders without question, knowing those who gave the orders loved you and wanted the best for you.

83

But it was different now. They were all gone. All except Uncle Hugo and maybe he was gone too. So it followed that you did the best you could; gave your own orders to yourself and then followed them.

And the order that came from deep in the little girl's highly sensitized mind was—*leave—get away from this place—make an effort to survive.*

Trust no one in this big black world and never, never, never give up.

This last was the most important lesson she'd learned in the whole eleven years of her life. The will to survive. This was a part of her as she got up from the chair they'd put her in and moved along the wall toward the window. She knew that haste was imperative but also that too much haste could be fatal, so she examined the window very carefully.

It was broken. Three jagged shards angled toward a smashed center and the little girl tested them carefully and found they were loose. Working carefully, she removed them one by one and then lifted herself even more carefully over the sill.

If she had an urge to leap out to freedom—to scream for help—to cry or act in any manner like a child—she stifled the demand because she had learned long ago to do none of these things. Trained for six of her eleven years in the wisdom of alert, deliberate movement, restraint had become a part of her nature even in the face of great peril.

So her seeming casualness, now, was logical as she stood outside in a soft, abandoned flower bed and marshaled all her knowledge of this particular situation.

She'd been brought in through the front door of this secluded house. It was set in a clearing, in a completely deserted section of a forest. There were trees on all sides but the safest direction to move was straight back because then the house itself might keep the man and the woman inside from seeing her.

There were other things she knew also; that the man had brought her some fifty kilometers north of where she had been; that the automobile in which they'd ridden had been an old one; that they had gone most of the distance on winding country roads with trees close in on both sides.

These things she'd learned even while bound and covered on the floor in the back of the car; learned and remembered.

It was some comfort too, to know that the direction in which she now moved—toward the forest behind the house—was bringing her closer to Uncle Hugo—if Uncle Hugo still lived. Not much closer, but south, in the right direction; only a few steps subtracted from fifty kilometers but even this was comfort for a child who had learned to live—as her parents had lived—from moment to moment. Because only hope supports such living; you learn to rely heavily on hope; so even knowledge of a right direction was a great comfort.

The little girl reached the trees safely; touched a young birch as though it were a loving friend; held its trunk in her arms while she allowed herself the luxury of a quick little-girl sob.

But only one and that but for a short moment because the Terror thrived on those who took time to feel sorry for themselves. It made short work of weak victims. That was why her mother and her father and the people she'd known had lasted so long in the face of the Terror; because they were filled with courage; because they stayed and lived on hope and didn't cry.

And so, after the stolen luxury of one small sob, the little girl circled the birch sapling and moved like a slim blond shadow into the forest . . .

The Doberman, a sleek, graceful unit of highly trained ferocity, whined to himself as he paced the eight-floor length of his kennel. He had been a witness and the incident at the child's playhouse in a secluded corner of the estate near his kennel had driven him momentarily mad; a weird silent madness during which he threw himself at the wire walls and the solid roof and had put bruises on his sleek hide.

The action had been over quickly but its image was sharp in the dog's memory; the tall, thin man; the blanket with its musty odor; the battered car the man had driven away.

The action finished, another man, a friend, was approaching the kennel and the Doberman paced restlessly, waiting to be let out so he could follow the car and set things right.

The friend was big, grizzled, slow of movement. He wore the clothing of a gardener, a caretaker, and his eyes were kindly. Exactly the opposite of the Doberman's because the dog had been meticulously trained to kill and death always lurked back behind his eyes; back in his memory.

The dog did not bark at Hugo Kroener because that had been

a part of his training also. Never any noise; run silent; run deadly; come out of nowhere to kill.

Kroener said, "Poor Prince." He smiled and put his hand on the wire as close to the dog's nose as possible. "You'd like to be out running like a dog should, wouldn't you? Out in the forest chasing rabbits."

The dog sat motionless now, waiting to be released. But Hugo Kroener had not seen the action at the playhouse. He took a piece of dog candy from his pocket and tossed it through the wire. The responsive move of the Doberman's head was automatic—the dog appearing to accept the favor as some sort of stupid but necessary preliminary to the important business at hand.

But Hugo Kroener was a great disappointment to the dog. He turned away and started back toward his work at the other side of the estate. After a few steps, he stopped and turned and again smiled. "You miss her, do you not, old fellow? You like to have her in your sight all the time. But that cannot be. She is probably in the great house playing with the other little girl."

The dog knew that the other little girl was afraid of him. He'd learned this while watching the two of them at play; while he'd watched with yearning from his heavy wire kennel. Now he watched Hugo Kroener; motionless; a statue; a rigid machine of man-made death. Tolerated because a little girl loved him.

Kroener moved out of sight and the dog began sniffing the ground along the fence that trapped him . . .

The little girl had been moving slowly and deliberately through the forest but now she was tired and felt herself entitled to a rest. Not a long one; just a few moments to ease the tension of eternal concentration.

She found a small pocket in the trunk of a big rotted-out tree and vanished from sight so completely that only a highly trained person could have located her.

Momentarily safe, she allowed her mind to slip its grasp on current reality; allowed it to rest and, automatically, memory took over. This was not a good thing, even while resting. In such circumstances as this she knew she should stay passively alert even while regaining her strength. But her longing was great and her thoughts went back . . .

. . . To the awful day when the Terror struck so savagely in

Budapest. There had been a very important meeting that morning in the cellar of the house where the little girl lived with her mother and father. Several men came quietly to talk over some important matters with her father.

Her father was a leader and the little girl had been very proud of him; proud of the respect and deference in the voices of the men who came. She had been proud of her mother also. Her mother never said a great deal but at times her opinion was asked on some matter of importance and she always had something very quiet and sensible to say and the men listened.

The little girl's mother and father talked together also, usually with the little girl in her mother's lap, feeling the gentle touch of her mother's hand and the warmth and comfort of her presence.

But on the awful day of the Terror, the little girl could tell by the tight feeling in the air, by the nervousness of her mother's hands, that things were very wrong.

Then had come the sounds of gunfire in the streets not far away and her father and the other men went there to see if they could help.

After a while the phone rang and the little girl sat very close to her mother while she answered and even though she didn't hear what was said over the phone there was her mother's choked sob and the little girl knew her father was dead.

But her mother did not cry, so the little girl did not cry. They sat alone in the quiet house for a long time, the mother holding the little girl close in her arms. There alone in the quiet house, waiting, while the Terror lashed back and forth in the streets around them.

Then the telephone rang again, a nerve-ripping jangle in the darkness, breaking in frighteningly upon the stillness.

More news came over the phone and the little girl knew it was bad because her mother's fingers closed over her arm, hurting her, but the little girl made no outcry because she knew her mother was not aware of the hurt.

Now her mother began using the telephone, desperately and after a while the little girl knew her mother was talking to Uncle Hugo.

Uncle Hugo tried to get the little girl's mother to run; to try to escape past the Terror through the streets but she refused. She said it was too dangerous—the two of them—out there in the bullet-riddled night. Besides, there was no time.

So she told Uncle Hugo what he was to do and then hung up the telephone and held the little girl tight in her arms for a little while. But even then she was not crying.

When there was no time left even for love, the little girl's mother said, "Now I want you to go to your hiding place under the porch. No matter what happens, you must not make a sound. Do you understand that, my darling? Not one single little sound. You must promise."

"I promise," the little girl said.

After her mother held her for a few scant seconds longer and gave her kisses she would always remember and she went as she had been ordered, to the snug little place under the front porch where—if you stayed quiet as a mouse—no one would ever know.

She'd hardly gotten there when heavy footsteps thumped across the porch over her head; the footsteps of the Terror shaking dust down into her hair.

The men went on into the house, smashing in the door with the butts of their rifles. Then there were deep gutteral sounds. There was the brutal laughter of men who took the Terror with them wherever they went.

They stayed in the house quite a while and the little girl's mother screamed twice before she was finally quiet.

But the little girl obeyed the orders of the one who loved her most and she was as quiet as the stones around her.

She did not cry out even when the men crossed the porch again, on their way out; even when she knew the body they dragged after them was the body of her mother.

Then it was very quiet in the house and on the streets around the house, with the gunfire dying down as though the Terror had spent itself and had to rest and gain new strength.

Still the little girl sat.

Then there was a soft sound close by. The little girl reached out and touched a cold, wet muzzle.

The dog had come . . .

But now, hiding again in the rotted tree, half a world away from Budapest and that awful night, the little girl felt a touch of alarm at allowing her mind to wander so far from this new time and this new place. A dangerous thing to do; dangerous because the Terror never rested. It was always alert; always ready to pounce down on the dreamer, the rememberer, the one who allowed mind and its senses to relax.

Besides, Uncle Hugo was fifty kilometers away and the little girl had to get back to him as soon as possible. Uncle Hugo couldn't possibly come for her this time because the little girl's mother hadn't been there to call him on the telephone and tell him where the little girl would be hiding. Therefore she would have to find Uncle Hugo all by herself. There was no one else to help her.

She pushed carefully out of her hiding place, scarcely stirring a leaf or a blade of grass as she tested for danger. There did not appear to be any at the moment so she came into view and continued on toward the south. Moving slowly and carefully through the forest because haste itself could be the greatest danger of all . . .

The man and the woman in the secluded house argued, berated, and cursed each other for half an hour before it was finally settled; before they agreed upon what needed to be done. Their mistake had to be obliterated; all evidence of it completely destroyed. And even though it would be a grim chore, it would not be difficult. After all—a child of eleven or twelve.

And there were any number of places to hide the body; places in the comparatively wild country where it might never be found; and would certainly remain hidden until time had worked in favor of the man and the woman.

"When?" the man asked sullenly.

"What's wrong with now?"

"I suppose so. How?"

"Do you know how to blow your nose?" Helen Mayhew asked contemptuously.

"Okay, okay."

The man prowled the room. He weighed the lethal comparatives of a milk bottle and a scarred rolling pin and selected the latter. He went to the door leading into the rear room and paused. "Maybe we ought to wait 'til dark."

"And lose the time? Who's around, you lamebrain? Have we got an audience or something?"

"Maybe we ought to take her where we're going to leave her first. Find the place."

"Get it over with, Mack—or haven't you got the guts? Do you want me to do it?"

"Quit riding me!"

Frank Macklin opened the door. He stood for a moment, looking into the back room, then lumbered forward. He found the closet empty, inspected the paneless window, and came back to Helen with a blindfold he'd just picked up from the floor.

"She's gone," he said.

Helen had been putting on lipstick with the aid of a piece of broken mirror on the table. She straightened with a look of fright.

"What do you mean—gone?"

"What I said. She took this off and blew."

Helen's rage flared again. She beat back her fear and made room for rage and if she'd had a weapon at that moment she would have killed Macklin. She glared at him and went back to the old word: "Stupid—stupid—stupid. I lay things out. I plan—"

Macklin took a menacing step forward. "But you didn't do none of the work. The dangerous stuff—"

"You fool—she saw *me*—not you. When I took the blindfold off and found you'd blundered."

"That's right," Macklin said virtuously. "She saw you—not me. I seized her from behind."

"I made the plans—you made the mistakes. Now you get out and find that kid because I swear if I'm dead you're dead too."

Macklin—for all his stupidity—was still blessed with a certain logic. He nodded stolidly. "Uh-huh. We're both in it. But there's no cause to worry. She couldn't go far in this kind of country."

"Then don't stand there! Move! Do something!"

Helen's rage was melting. The fear was seeping back. The man patted her arm clumsily. "Don't worry. I'll find her. Everything's going to be all right."

And obviously there was some sort of a distorted love between the two of them because Helen's face softened. "Be careful," she said.

Macklin laughed boisterously. "I got danger with a twelve-year-old kid?"

"Move, you fool! Find her."

"Sure, sure."

As he left the house to start searching Helen Mayhew's fear returned. She was crying when he closed the door.

Outside, Macklin went around to the paneless window and found the small shoe prints in the abandoned flowerbed. He scowled. Up to this time he had been very gentle with the little girl—careful, as with a thing of value. But now she was a potential danger and he hated her; hated her as a peril and also for having become valueless.

He followed the tracks over the soft earth to the wall of trees behind the house, muttering as he walked:

"I'll find her and kill her. She won't get us into no trouble. I'll find her. I'll kill her—real good . . ."

In the wooded, hilly country there were many summer homes owned by people who came north for the good months; many who felt a country summer to be incomplete without a pet to share it with—usually a dog because a dog will romp with its benefactors and show appreciation in many ways.

But later, many of these dogs become problems. What to do with them when summer is over? They would be annoyances in city apartments, needing attention and care. Everyone knows a dog is not happy in close quarters. They belong in the open where they can run and play.

So in many cases the problem is solved by driving away from it; by leaving these summer friends in the country where they gather in packs for mutual protection and are soon no longer pets.

Where they revert to the law of the wild and kill to live. They kill woodchucks and rabbits and pull down deer. Packs with a particularly savage leader will slaughter domestic animals for food. And some of these packs, reverting completely before they are hunted down, have been known to maim children.

Such a dog pack roamed the country through which the little girl moved. The leader, a big German Shepherd gone shaggy and vicious, caught her intriguing scent on the late autumn breeze and sat down on his haunches to consider the matter while his four followers awaited his decision.

The pack as yet had not gone totally vicious what with food still available and the weather still good. But they were farther along than they should have been because they'd been roughly handled. Chased off one farm with clubs, they'd approached the second with far too much trust and had been met by a load of buckshot.

The small Collie swung a loose foreleg as a result and the German Shepherd was in a sullen mood from a wounded jowl that hurt him whenever he opened his mouth to breath, which was most of the time.

The female Beagle, sensing his pain had tried to lick his wound and he'd slashed her shoulder by way of gratitude.

Still, the German Shepherd was not quite ready to take human life—to pass that point of no return in dogdom—but the scent made him quiver deep inside because while human it was not adult and a dog pack is attracted to helplessness.

The German Shepherd came off its haunches and circled restlessly, growled in its throat, and started off through the woods.

Moving with more decision as the scent grew stronger . . .

Neal Garrett looked up from the book he'd been reading and saw his caretaker approaching the patio across a hundred yards of lawn. There would have been time to read another page but Garrett put the book down because he enjoyed watching Kroener. Sight of the big European gave him a sense of satisfaction, Kroener being a reflection of Garrett's own generosity.

And Garrett had a right to this satisfaction. Wasn't he one of the comparative few who'd been thoughtful enough to extend a helping hand to those poor devils? Sharing good fortune with the unfortunate? God, what those damned Russians had put them through over in Hungary! Enough to make a man's blood boil. Of course, Kroener didn't talk much but it had come to Garrett from other sources. Facing death for the little girl. Getting across the border with Red bullets clipping at his heels. Who wouldn't want to help a guy like that?

Besides, there were rewards for Garrett's kind of virtue. Not that they'd been the first consideration of course. But good luck keeps an eye on generous men because Garrett had had to wait only three weeks after he'd first gotten the idea until they told him they had a crackerjack gardener for him.

And this specification hadn't been so unreasonable on his part. After all, didn't a top-notch grass and flower man rate a break as much as some slob who figured America owed the world a living and would just stand around and collect it? Hell yes!

Of course there weren't too many of that kind. European workmen hadn't been ruined by unions and prosperity and most of them appreciated a break. This Kroener for instance. He kept the whole damn ten acres looking like an exhibit and hadn't asked for a lick of help. One man doing the work of two and maybe even three.

Garrett was glad, now, that he'd gambled on the child. He'd almost turned them down on Kroener when they told him the little girl had to come too—figured maybe the guy would have her in tow all the time and let the place go to pot.

But it hadn't worked out that way at all. Just about the opposite in fact. The little girl had even been good for Cindy. Same age, same build. And two little blonde heads around the place were kind of cute.

So it had worked out fine. With both Kroener and the kid knowing their place and Kroener never letting her come into the house unless Grace invited her.

Garrett wondered. Maybe Grace had her up from the cottage a little too much. Not that he was a snob, mind you. Just for the kid's own good. Might be rough on her with so much here she couldn't have. In her condition it might be easy for a kid to turn morbid and get to be a problem.

But that was a minor point. Garrett forgot about it and wondered if he should ask Kroener to have a drink. Not that he wouldn't have done it automatically, but what the hell—how did they do it in Europe? That was how Americans got a bad name around the world; being too damn generous. Treating people as equals—peasants who weren't used to it and figured you for a peasant yourself just for fraternizing with them. They were queer ducks all right, some of them.

Hugo Kroener had arrived now. He took off his hat and spoke in careful, laborious English. "Mr. Garrett, sir. I have come to inquire of you if my little Tina is here. With your Cindy?"

Garrett got up and went out onto the lawn still carrying his scotch and soda. "Tina? Haven't seen her. I thought she was with Cindy—over in Cindy's playhouse."

"They were there. Now the playhouse is empty. There is no one there."

"Then they may be in the house. Upstairs in Cindy's room, maybe. Wait a minute."

Garrett went back into the screened patio and called, "Grace! Hey, Grace—is Tina in there anywhere?"

His voice was loud enough to reach all of the seventeen rooms and soon a tall, graceful woman appeared. She smiled and said, "Don't stand out there in the sun, Mr. Kroener. Come in where it's cool."

Hugo Kroener gravely obeyed and Neal Garrett said, "He's come for his little girl. I told you that. You could have brought her down and saved a trip."

Grace Garrett was surprised. "Why, I thought Tina was with you, Mr. Kroener. Cindy came back from the playhouse quite a while ago. She's upstairs in the bathtub."

Hugo Kroener was troubled. "Usually I watch them—to see that Tina is not left alone too long. But I got busy with the back shrubs."

"It was thoughtless of Cindy. Leaving her that way. I'll speak to her about it."

Garrett said, "She's probably roaming the grounds somewhere. Hope she's careful about not stepping on flowers and things."

"Tina is very careful," Hugo Kroener said.

Grace Garrett frowned slightly as she glanced at her husband. "I'm sure she couldn't have gone far."

Garrett sloshed his ice cubes around and said, "Sure. Let's face it—how far could a blind kid go?"

Grace Garrett was embarrassed—something in her husband's tone and manner. A crudeness. She said, "We'll help you look around, Mr. Kroener."

"Thank you, Mrs. Garrett, but I will find her. As Mr. Garrett said, she could not go very far."

A bell toned melodiously somewhere inside the house. "The front door," Neal Garrett said. "I'll get it, hon. Make yourself a drink and relax a while."

After her husband left, Grace Garrett asked, "Would you care for a drink, Mr. Kroener?"

"No thank you. I must go and look for Tina. I am sorry I have troubled you."

"It was no trouble. And Tina isn't, either. I think it's wonderful, she and Cindy having one another to play with."

"It is very good for Tina," Hugo Kroener said gravely. "She needs friends."

Hugo Kroener returned as he'd come, toward the wooded and shrubbed areas beyond the lawn. Tina had several hiding places around the estate and once in a while, when he was ahead in his work, she would select one and then Kroener would make an elaborate, noisy business out of finding her; calling her name in mock anger; bringing giggles from lips that seldom smiled.

But there was no time for a game now; a quicker way of finding her. The dog. He never made a game of it. He always went straight to where she was and licked her face in glee. The dog and the child loved each other and they belonged together but that was impossible. They could be together only when he was there to watch.

The Garretts were afraid of having the dog loose. And perhaps they were right although Hugo Kroener knew in his heart that Prince would die under torture before he would hurt a child. But there *were* other people around and you could never tell about a dog with his kind of background.

Hugo Kroener stopped and looked toward the kennel. Then he hurried forward. A hole had been dug underneath the wire.

The Doberman was gone . . .

The terror, Tina had learned, was not a single, clearly defined thing. It was a dark mixture of many evils. Basically, it was the nonlove, the hostility, of persons unknown, and this she had come to take for granted as a part of life, just as her mother had trained her to make the will to survive a part of her life.

You didn't waste mental energy wondering why the unknown persons wanted to destroy you. Instead, you used that energy to always fight back with whatever weapons were available, and Tina's weapons were incredibly keen ears, her every sense honed and sharpened to the uttermost in compensation for her blindness.

So her ability to walk a straight south line through a strange forest was not incredible; no more so than knowledge of the distance she had been driven, or her ability to read black intent from the tone of strange words and feel danger in the subtle vibrations around her.

A mixture of many evils, the Terror, with fatigue, hunger, and cold numbered among them because these weapons of the Terror were calculated to dull your senses, cripple your reactions, make you an easy target for the final attack.

Thus rest was not a luxury; it was a necessity, so in the sharpening chill of late autumn afternoon, Tina began looking for another sanctuary and found a snug hole under a cluster of boulders, probably the deserted nest of a fox or a woodchuck because it was heavy with old animal odors.

There she rested and as her mind again let go, it seemed she was back in the other cave under the porch in Budapest; just as she had been when Prince first came; his cold wet nose; his soft tongue . . .

In a sense, the Doberman too had been a victim of the Terror—trained to become a savage part of it—put to work in places where high walls and barb wire had sometimes failed. He had been skillfully brain-washed and taught to do his work well, his gentler instinct scientifically stifled.

Stifled but not quite destroyed as was proved that terrible night in Budapest when a cog in the machine of the Terror slipped and he was left to himself; no leash; no commands to sit, to stand, to heel—to kill.

A lean black shadow moving through the tense city; trying possibly, to escape the gunfire smells he had always hated; or perhaps keyed to destroy on his own whim if the need came.

He stopped in the vicinity of a darkened house—one that looked empty and deserted—giving it his attention because he knew this was not the case. Life still existed there and he crossed the street and found it in a small nestlike place under the front porch.

But he did not attack. There was something unusual about this helpless wisp of form and movement; something in the uncertainty of the hand that touched him. A confusing thing but oddly pleasant. He licked the small hand and allowed it to pat his nose.

The Doberman licked the little girl's face and she almost

laughed as she heard his tail thump but she caught herself in time and whispered, "Don't be afraid, doggie. I'll take care of you until Uncle Hugo comes."

The dog put his head into her lap and quivered as the little girl stroked him and they waited together.

Perhaps the strangest aspect of the phenomenon was the dog's complete trust in the little girl as was proven when Hugo Kroener crawled under the porch and knelt for a few tight seconds within inches of sudden death. But a whispered word from the little girl told the dog this was a friend and the dog understood.

But Hugo Kroener didn't. He tried to send the Doberman on its way but the dog stood firm, stubbornly demanding acceptance, until Kroener realized that henceforth the little girl's way was the dog's way also, and they moved in stealth through the strife-torn city—the man, the child, and the lean black shadow—avoiding destruction—escaping into Austria . . .

But now the Terror had come again and Tina was alone with only her hope and her instinct for survival. Reaching out from the near-edge of sleep, she whispered, "Prince—Prince—come and find me."

But this, she knew, was wishful thinking. Prince would not come. He was trapped in a kennel with wire over the top. No one would come, so she must rest and banish the weariness and then move on again . . .

Hugo Kroener returned to the big house at dusk. Neal and Grace Garrett were having coffee behind the screens of the patio. Kroener gripped his hat in his huge hands and said, "I have not found her. She is not anywhere on the grounds."

While Neal Garrett frowned out across the lawn, his wife said, "Then we must call the police. She has wandered off and must have gotten confused."

Neal Garrett did not appear to be convinced. "Are you sure you looked every place? This is a pretty good-sized layout. Maybe she got tired and dropped off to sleep under some bush."

"I looked everywhere," Kroener said. "I think the police should be called. It could be very dangerous."

"Dangerous? You've got your locations mixed. This isn't the

African jungle. Its urban United States—seventy miles north of New York City.''

"But the dog is with her. It might be dangerous for anyone who approached her to ask a question.''

"You mean she took that killer—?''

"No. He dug out under the wire of his kennel.''

"Then how do you know he's with her? He might have just taken off into the hills.''

"Wherever she went,'' Kroener said, "he is with her.''

"Okay—I guess we better call the State Troopers—have them check the neighborhood.'' There was an odd reluctance in his voice and Grace Garrett looked up quickly, wondering about it, feeling vaguely troubled . . .

They called the closest State Police barracks and were told that all cars in the area would be alerted. A search would be made. The Trooper on the phone said not to worry. They would find the child.

Hugo Kroener went back to his searching. After he left, the Garretts were silent for a time, with Grace Garrett watching her husband as he paced the floor.

Neal Garrett said, "I hope that beast doesn't take an arm off somebody. We'd be liable. I shouldn't have allowed them to bring the monster with them.''

"Neal—''

He didn't quite meet her eyes. "Yes—?''

"Has it occurred to you that Tina might have been kidnapped?''

He stared incredulously. "Kidnapped! Are you out of your mind? A nobody's kid. What would be the point?''

"Our Cindy isn't a nobody's child. You happen to be worth a great deal of money.''

"Nobody figures me in that class,'' he snapped.

"Someone might suspect.''

"Anyhow, you aren't making sense. We weren't talking about Cindy. She's safe upstairs in bed.''

"That's true, but she and Tina look very much alike.''

"What's that got to do with it?''

"You're being purposely dense. A mistake could have been made.''

"Why hell's bells! They're as different as night and day. The Hungarian kid is blind. Anyone could tell—''

"Of course, but very few people realize it at first glance. She lost her sight from scarlet fever when she was five years old but her eyes weren't damaged. And with the training she got from her mother—to hold her head up so proudly—she appears to be quite normal most of the time."

"You're crazy. Kidnappers are smart. They wouldn't make a mistake like that."

"I don't agree. I think the fact that they're kidnappers makes them stupid. And I think a situation might arise where a mistake like that could easily occur."

"I say you're off your rocker. Nobody could be sure I'd be able to pay. They wouldn't make the gamble. So that leaves some enemy or other and nobody's out to get even with me for anything. Not people like that, anyhow."

"Are you sure?"

"Of course I'm sure. What are you driving at?"

"Somehow I keep thinking of that Mayhew woman."

"Who's she?"

"The maid who worked for us a month or so last spring. She dropped a trayful of glasses, remember?"

"Oh—that one."

"You lost your temper and cursed her."

"She had it coming."

"Nobody deserves to be cursed for an accident. She cursed you back, you'll recall—said she'd get even with you."

"Hell—she probably forgot all about it the next day."

"Still, you've got to admit she became an enemy."

"You're way out in the left field. Kidnappers don't keep you in the dark. They leave a note or send one. They want money."

Grace Garrett studied her husband thoughtfully. "I suppose you're right." There was something distant and uncertain in her voice. She arose from her chair suddenly. "I'm going up to look in on Cindy," she said, and left the room.

Alone, Neal Garrett mixed himself a drink. He gulped it down. At intervals, he swore softly . . .

It had taken the Doberman less than five minutes to tunnel under the wire wall of his kennel—a felony he committed only after discovering that Kroener was not going to release him. He went straight to the spot where the hedge had been broken by the tall man's passage in and out; through which he'd carried the little girl wrapped tight in the blanket.

Just beyond the hedge was a point where a narrow country road wound in close to that corner of the grounds before it snaked off into the northern hills. That was where the car had stood; where the man had bound and blindfolded the little girl before finally covering her with the blanket on the floor in the back seat.

And the Doberman found something else; a heavy blood spoor. This came from the dead body of a robin that had been killed by hitting an overhead telephone wire in flight, the body later flattened by the rear wheel of the fast-traveling car.

So, as the dog loped north in pursuit, the blood spoor remained strong. The road also was a fortunate one for his purpose. In earlier years it had been a main thoroughfare but a six-lane parkway had been built a mile to the east and now the old road was used by the comparatively few people whose country homes bordered it.

Thus there was no heavy traffic to confuse the Doberman, a breed not noted for superior tracking abilities. In fact, if the kidnap car had turned off into any of the estate entrances, the dog would probably have been thrown into a fruitless circle.

But it stayed on the rutty blacktop mile after mile; until the country became more hilly and deserted and it finally dwindled into a dirt road, rough and tortuous; heavy with dust that held the blood spoor even better than the paved surface.

So the dog found no great problem until he came, after three hours of steady, mile-eating lope, into an area where the dirt road dwindled off and vanished into overgrown trails and footpaths. There, the scent wore out and the dog began circling; flushing out small game and ignoring it as he followed one false lead after another.

But he did not give up. That also was a characteristic of the breed and a marked trait of this particular dog. He would circle and follow, return and go forward, until he dropped in his tracks . . .

The frightened woman, left alone in the isolated house, made dozens of trips into the yard as the afternoon waned into evening. She kept watching the south forest line for a sign of the man's return and now her nerves were about as raw as she could stand. The surrounding woods with its whispering, menacing trees had begun to move in on her; to seem more and more like a big black trap.

She had admitted no guilt in front of the man but alone she conceded that she'd blundered also. That was what came from trying a thing you'd had no experience with. That way, you found out your mistakes after you made them.

First, she should not have moved in anger—she shouldn't have let that slob Garrett bug her so much. Of course, if he hadn't treated her like so much dirt, she wouldn't have gotten the idea in the first place. It had been strictly from revenge in the beginning, with Garrett's contempt and his curses and foul names eating at her until she decided to make him pay.

And it had looked so easy. Helen Mayhew had been sure Garrett would pay; that his wife wouldn't let him go to the cops. And afterwards, how could she and Mack be traced? Who could suspect? Neither of them had a record. When you hunted for a kidnapper, you went through the police files and looked for somebody with a criminal background. You didn't track down ordinary citizens who'd always minded their own business.

And with the kid back, the whole thing would have died down after a while. She and Mack would just have to be careful with the money—not flash it around.

But you should have checked one last time. It *had* been several months. She'd taken the chance from fear of being seen in the neighborhood; had gambled that things would be the same. But she'd told Mack that if things didn't look just right to just drive on by and come back.

So it wasn't her fault. She'd told him that and things hadn't been right. But he hadn't driven on by. He'd snatched the wrong kid. How could she have known he'd have a choice? Two kids. Both of them blonde and around eleven years old. Good God!

Thus the failure roiled around in Helen Mayhew's mind; accusation and alibi until the forest shrieked in her ears and she could stand it no longer.

Until she grabbed her purse and started the car and headed out. Out to anywhere. She didn't care. She only knew that she had to get away from this place and keep going. Keep going 'til she hit an ocean somewhere. And then keep going some more . . .

The wounded German Shepherd, viciousness flowing into it with its heightening hunger, circled the cluster of boulders under which the little girl waited. The dog could have gone on in and dragged her out but a thin edge of caution held him back; a caution requiring him to snarl and froth in his rising madness a while longer, working himself to a higher pitch of noncaution.

This caution was based on an instinctive fear of traps, the cave under the boulders having that aspect. The wild hunter, the pack leader to which the abused animal had reverted, prefers to work in the open; to circle and bring its quarry down with quick lunges at exposed flanks.

But with the agony of a torn jaw nourishing the dog's madness, the barrier of caution was fast vanishing. Soon he would be ready. He had already pushed to within inches of the crouching child, had ravened in her face and then pulled back at the last moment.

The pack milled restlessly, waiting for the leader to make his move; expecting him to make it, with the leader aware of this demand for leadership. He had to produce food and comfort or he would lose the pack.

The crippled Collie pressed a little too close and the German Shepherd whirled and ripped at the injured paw. The Collie shrieked in pain and limped away. The German Shepherd slavered a warning and moved back to the cave opening.

He was ready now. This time he would finish the chore. But at just that moment a furious black shadow came out of nowhere to bar the way, smashed against the German Shepherd and knocked him sprawling.

It was a pitifully unequal battle, the German Shepherd supported only by madness and instinct while the Doberman, silent as a well-oiled piston destroyed his enemy with a detached savagery born of cold, scientific training.

There was no time even for the pack to close in on its fallen leader and help with the kill; time only for surprise before the Doberman turned from the death he had dealt out and streaked for the Collie.

And thus the pack was informed of a difference here. This was not a new leader destroying the old one and taking over the pack. Here, the pack itself was in danger of annihilation and the dogs fled in all directions to look back in bewilderment from beyond the perimeter of danger and then go their separate ways.

The Doberman stood watch for a while, grinning at them as they left, and then entered the cave; wriggling along on his belly with strangely immature puppy whines of contentment.

The little girl's hand touched his bloody muzzle and did not draw back. She held the dog close and the dog quivered as from weakness when she whispered, "Prince—Prince. You *did* come and find me." Not in those words; in the soft guttural Hungarian the dog understood.

He put his head in her lap and banged his tail against the ground and after a while Tina—her courage and fortitude shredded by weariness—dropped off to sleep.

But the dog did not sleep. He lay unmoving with his head in the little girl's lap, a blood-spattered threat of sudden death to anyone who came too close . . .

The tall man had hunted through the forest all that day but had not found the little girl. After the tracks vanished into an unbroken carpet of dried leaves, he began moving in aimless circles, feeling that one direction was as good as another.

At one point he came upon the tracks again, or thought he did, but they proved to be a part of many others, converging upon a place where many children had come for a picnic— probably in early summer from the deserted look.

He went on with his wandering, hoping each moment to catch sight of a yellow cotton dress so he could finish the job he'd come to do.

But the little girl seemed to have been swallowed up and the man began cursing his evil luck.

How was it that not a damn thing ever worked out. How come even a sure thing went wrong? Garrett would have paid. And he'd have kept his mouth shut, too. He was that kind of a guy. Inside the law, but not wanting any cops snooping in his business.

That was how Helen Mayhew had it figured and she'd been around him long enough to know. Helen was smart. She knew what she was doing and just how things should have worked out.

Only one thing—they should have checked first and found

out about the second kid. Or would it have made any difference? Maybe not.

His weariness growing, Macklin turned back toward the deserted house. Deep in self-pity, he decided it wouldn't have made any difference. If it hadn't been two kids to trip him up there would have been something else. He'd never been able to ring up a score. Just a hard-luck guy from the beginning and he'd probably end that way.

He broke into the clearing and saw the house; no light; no sign of life. But Helen was probably playing it smart. Some local yokel might spot a light and start nosing around and more trouble would come down on them.

But no car either. What the hell had she done with the car? He called her name. There was no answer. Damn it all, she didn't have to play it that smart.

"Helen! Where the hell are you? It's Mack. You don't have to hide. I'm all alone." No answer. He plodded toward the house.

And even then it took him a good five minutes to realize the truth. She'd run out on him! She'd taken the car and headed out with him pounding the woods like a maniac trying to keep *her* out of trouble.

The lousy, cheap, conniving bitch! She'd taken off and left him to face the rap! He'd kill her by God! He'd find her and wring her goddam no-good neck!

But now he was hungry and he stopped reviling the woman long enough to wolf down some bread and cold meat she'd left in the house. Damned white of her not leaving him to starve to death.

His hunger dulled, fatigue took over, and an earlier resolution to get the hell out of there came up for reappraisal. Sure, he'd have to get away fast but not in a night so goddam black you could crack your skull on it. This was as safe a place to sleep as any. He'd rest up and hit out before dawn—straight south—through the woods; get down into civilization and keep going clear into the South maybe.

He bedded down in a corner of the room they'd first put the kid in and that made him remember her. Damn stupid little brat. Sneaking out and ruining everything. They weren't going to hurt her. But that was how things went for him. He was a hard luck guy . . .

He awoke, refreshed just before dawn as he had intended to, shook off the autumn chill, and ate the rest of the food. Then, as soon as it was light enough to keep from breaking your leg, he started south through the woods. Morning deepened and he moved faster . . .

Until, around ten o'clock, Macklin got his break. The kid. There she was; walking kind of slow and funny through the woods. Walking like she was afraid of falling over a cliff.

And damn if she didn't have a dog with her. Where had she picked up that mutt? A black Doberman. There'd been a dog like that back at Garrett's place; a dog that couldn't bark. It had gone crazy in its kennel when he took the kid.

This couldn't be the same one, though. Just a coincidence that they looked the same.

Mack picked up a section of fallen branch, a good strong club. Maybe he'd have to kill the dog first. Or maybe the mutt would run. A belt across the chops and it would get the message, anyhow.

The dog had turned and was eyeing Macklin; motionless and silent with no hint of what went on in its mind. The man and the dog stared at each other for long moments. Then the man raised the club and moved forward.

Macklin said, "One side, you black bastard or I'll—"

It was the evening of the second day and the State Police together with members of volunteer fire companies in the surrounding area were out beating the hills for some sign of the little blind girl. So far they'd seen nothing.

With lack of evidence to the contrary, it had been assumed that she'd wandered away into the hills and was perhaps hiding, weary and frightened, in some rock-pocket or thick undergrowth.

They had rimmed off the widest circle that a blind child could conceivably cross and were covering every inch of it.

But without result. Still, they kept on as others joined them and their wives leagued together and brought food and drink and began collecting flashlights and batteries in preparation for night search.

Hugo Kroener moved steadily, doggedly, silently over his apportioned segment refusing food or rest; like a man hunting for a time bomb with the minutes ticking away. Perhaps not even minutes now . . . Perhaps it was already too late.

Neal and Grace Garrett remained home on advice of the State Police; to be available in case the thing "took a new twist"— words with which the State trooper in charge framed his fear of kidnapping.

He was Sergeant Farrier, a pleasant young man with an air of efficiency about him. He made several visits to the Garrett home during the day and then, around six o'clock, he called from the Patrol barracks and talked to Grace Garrett.

"The little girl may have been found," he said. "We got word from Centerville, a little place about forty-five miles north of here. Something's been going on up there."

Grace Garrett's nerves were a trifle raw. "Just what do you mean by—*something's been going on?* Either they found her or they didn't. Is Tina—?"

Farrier forestalled the word *dead.* "We don't know yet. As I said, we got the report but in cases like this it's best to go up and find out first-hand. I'm leaving now. I'll be there in less than an hour."

"Shall I tell—?"

"Don't tell anyone. Let the hunt go right on until we find out what this is all about."

"Hurry—please hurry."

"I will." Farrier hesitated, then added, "I can tell you this much. The little girl they found is blind."

"Then it *is*—" . . .

"It would seem so. But there are other blind children and we want to be sure."

"Thank you. I'll be waiting right here."

Grace Garrett put the phone down and turned to her husband who stood waiting. "They think perhaps they have found Tina."

"Where for God's sake?"

"They aren't sure it's Tina yet. A call came in from a place forty-five miles north of here."

"That's silly. A blind child wandering that far."

"Sergeant Farrier is driving up to see. Until they know for sure we mustn't say anything about it."

"It—it just doesn't sound reasonable," Neal Garrett said.

"We can hope."

"I'm going to get a cup of coffee."

Grace Garrett followed her husband's exit with troubled eyes.

This affair had driven a wedge between them; mostly her fault, no doubt, because she hadn't inquired too deeply into the cause of his obvious upset. Concern was natural, of course, but Neal seemed to have a personal secret eating at him.

Perhaps, Grace Garrett thought, she should have kept probing until she'd brought it out. But she had a feeling that she knew what it was and had been hoping he would tell her of his own accord. Had she been right in thinking—? No. Of course not. How could she have gotten such an idea?

Her head ached dully and she took two aspirin before going upstairs to keep Cindy company. She had kept Cindy inside the whole day and it was difficult for the child . . .

Farrier returned around ten o'clock that night, bringing another Patrolman with him. They were met at the front door by the Garretts and Farrier said, "We had good luck. Things seem to be all right. The little girl is unharmed."

"Where is she?" Grace Garrett asked.

"There in the back seat. We fed her before we started back. She's sound asleep now."

Grace Garrett took a step forward but the second Trooper raised his hand. "She's perfectly comfortable. It might be better if we let her sleep until her uncle comes. He'll be better able to handle the dog."

"This is Trooper Kane," Farrier said. "He was in charge of things up at Centerville. He rode down with me to kind of wrap it up."

"The dog, you said?" Neal Garrett asked.

"A black Doberman. He's tied up but let me tell you—there's one rough customer."

"Thank God everything's all right," Neal Garrett said fervently. "I'll go out and find Kroener and tell him."

"That won't be necessary. We reported at the local barracks on the way over. The word was sent out to the uncle—and to call off the search. But there are a few things—"

"Come in, please," Grace Garrett said. "We shouldn't have kept you standing here."

"—a few things—" Farrier repeated over a cup of coffee in the study with Grace Garrett sitting on the edge of her chair and Neal Garrett with his back to the fireplace, tense and silent.

"Some pretty peculiar points, actually," Trooper Kane said.

He was an older man, stocky, with a bronzed, weatherbeaten face. "A man was killed."

Garrett winced. "You mean you killed someone rescuing her?"

"No, it wasn't quite like that," Trooper Kane frowned at the cup in his thick fingers. "Let's see if I can put it in some kind of sequence. First, a farmer outside of Centerville heard what sounded like a dog fight off in the woods late last evening.

"He went out this morning and found a dog dead there—a big German Shepherd. It looked as though it had been killed in the fight. That wouldn't have been too exceptional, though, because we're bothered up in that section by wild dogs. Summer people leave them when they go back to the city."

"You said a man was killed."

"I'm coming to that. A couple of hours later two fellows hunting rabbits came across this man about half a mile south of the dead dog. He was dead too. It was pretty bad. The man had obviously been killed by a savage animal. His throat had been—well anyhow, that was what we had; until we covered the section a little more thoroughly and came on the girl.

"We couldn't get to her, though, because she had a black Doberman with her—the one we've got in the car. He blocked us off from her—wouldn't let us get even close—so we brought out some nets and trapped him."

The Trooper shrugged and set his cup on the coffee table. "We didn't realize the little girl was blind for a few minutes; you'd certainly think she was all right to look at her. Then we found she couldn't speak much English; kept asking for her *Onkel* Hugo. There couldn't have been two like that roaming the woods so we were pretty sure we'd found your stray."

"But the dead man—" Grace Garrett said.

"We actually can't say the black dog killed him. It could have been the German Shepherd."

"Then there isn't any certain connection between the man and Tina."

"I wouldn't say that exactly. The man had some papers on him—a social security card. His name was Frank Macklin and we're checking him out."

Trooper Kane reached into his pocket and brought out a stamped, addressed envelope. He held it up. "The man was carrying this, too. All stamped and ready to put in a mail box. It's addressed to you, Mr. Garrett.''

Trooper Kane took out the single folded sheet of paper the envelope contained and flattened it out on the coffee table. ''A ransom demand,'' he said, forgetting to speak with his usual calmness.

The Garretts moved forward as one and read the scrawled words: *Drive north on Old Mill Road. Throw the satchel with the 25 Gs under the old bridge a mile south of King's Crossing. Then keep right on going. Do like we say and your little girl will be let go. Drop the stachel at 10 o'clock Friday night and keep right on going or it will be too bad.*

''Then Tina *was* kidnapped,'' Grace Garrett said.

''It looks that way,'' Sergeant Farrier answered.

''We'll find out exactly what happened—''

Trooper Kane broke off as Hugo Kroener entered from the patio side of the room without ceremony. ''I was told that you found Tina.''

Kroener was unshaven and haggard. He looked like a specter out of a bad dream. Grace Garrett went to him and laid a hand on his arm and said, ''Yes. She is asleep out in the car. We thought it best to wait for you. The dog is with her.''

He went past them, through the front door and when they reached the car behind him, he asked, ''What dog? What child? Is this a joke?''

The State Troopers peered into the car. ''They were there—in the back,'' Trooper Kane said.

''Then I think I know.''

''The dog was tied. The little girl was asleep.''

''The little girl was not asleep. And knots can be undone.''

He left them and walked off in the darkness, the others following. He crossed the estate to the Doberman's kennel and went in through the open gate to kneel in front of the dog house.

They were inside, the child and the dog; the dog motionless in the entrance; black head resting on tense paws; eyes as cold as an Arctic winter.

Hugo Kroener called, ''Tina,'' and the little girl answered. *''Uncle Hugo—I am so tired!''* she said in her native tongue. He lifted her out carefully. *''It is all right, my little one—it is all right now!"* And to the Doberman: "Come, old fellow. You may lie at the foot of her bed and watch over her . . ."

Later that night, after the Troopers had left, Grace Garrett faced her husband and put the question that had to be asked: "Why did you do it, Neal?"

He feigned surprise. "Do what for God's sake?"

"Cover it up—keep silent. You knew Tina had been kidnapped."

"I knew *what?"*

"Oh, don't pretend," she said wearily. "It will all come out. They aren't going to drop it here. They'll find the Mayhew woman and—"

"But you said I knew. The kidnap note was in Macklin's pocket—not mine."

She met his gaze unwaveringly.

"The second one—yes. The one he didn't mail. But the first one came when you and Hugo Kroener and I were on the patio. You went to the door."

"How did you know it was a kidnap note?"

"I saw the special delivery mailman driving away. And you didn't mention what he had brought. I know you so well, Neal. Your business mail never comes here—and you were careful not to mention it to me."

"All right—quit bugging me. It was a ransom note."

"But why did you conceal it—that's what I must know. Why did you keep saying Tina couldn't have been kidnapped."

"Twenty-five thousand dollars! That's why! I figured it might work out. And that's a lot of money to lay out for someone else's kid."

"I thought that was probably the reason."

"Well, why not? It's your money—and Cindy's—as well as mine."

"Tina took Cindy's place. She could have died for Cindy."

"All right. But would that have been my fault? Is that any reason for not being practical?"

"I suppose not, from your standards, Neal, but there's one more question I have to ask."

"Okay—get it over with. I'm tired."

"If there had been no mistake. If it *had* been Cindy. Would you have cringed at the thought of paying out."

"Grace! For God's sake! How can you ask a question like that? What do you think I am? Inhuman or something?"

"No—no Neal. I'm sorry. I don't think that at all."

"Then let's go to bed. Things worked out all right and that's the main thing."

"Yes, that's the main thing," Grace Garrett said. And it seemed to her that she had grown suddenly older as she got into bed beside her husband.

The next morning Hugo Kroener carefully explained to his niece that what had happened was a very exceptional thing, not an ordinary occurrence in America at all; that it could not possibly happen ever again and that it had nothing to do with the Terror.

Tina listened dutifully and nodded and agreed with her uncle because she loved him and knew he really thought he was right. But of course he wasn't. You couldn't hide from the Terror by simply crossing an ocean. It wasn't as easy as that. The Terror was many things and it would come back again. It always had.

The thing to do was to stay alert.

Stay alert and never, never give up.

Michael Gilbert

Michael Gilbert, English lawyer and detective-story writer, composes his short stories while commuting from his home in Kent to his London offices. Once Raymond Chandler's lawyer, he has written true crime novels, mystery dramas and hundreds of short stories, his preferred medium. His most famous characters are Inspector Hazelrigg, Detective Sergeant Patrick Petrella and counterintelligence agents Calder and Behrens. *Game Without Rules* (1967), a collection of short stories about Calder and Behrens was called by *Ellery Queen* the best volume of spy stories ever written, after W. Somerset Maugham's *Ashenden* (1928).

THE EMERGENCY EXIT AFFAIR

BY MICHAEL GILBERT

It was six o'clock, on as foul a morning as could be imagined.

In Warsaw it was raining, in the way it rained just before the rain turned to sleet and the sleet to the first snow of winter. The wind from the east lifted the rain and blew it, in a fine spray, down the Grodsky Boulevarde and into Katerina Square. In the far corner of the Square the electric sign of the Hotel Polanska was fighting a losing battle with the early morning light.

A man, dressed in an overcoat which hung nearly to his heels and armed with a long broom, was sweeping down the pavement which fronted the three cafés on the south side of the Square; he looked up from his task. Something was happening at the Hotel Polanska across the way.

The front door jerked open and two uniformed policemen came out. They were half carrying, half dragging a man who looked as if he had been pulled out of bed and had not been allowed to put on all his clothes. A police officer raised a gloved hand. A car slid up. The four of them bundled in. The car drove off.

A fresh gust of misty rain blew across the Square. It was as though a motion-picture director had said "Dissolve" and the scene had been wiped out. The Square was once more quiet and empty.

The sweeper rubbed a frayed cuff over his eyes, and bent to his work. He was paid by all three cafés, and if he swept for one better than the others there would be complaints.

When he had finished, he shouldered his broom and shambled off. His course took him past one of the kiosks which sold newspapers and cigarettes. He stopped to have a word with the bearded stall keeper who was taking down the shutters. The man listened, nodding occasionally. Later that morning he himself did some talking, into a telephone.

113

The news reached an office in Whitehall with the afternoon tea trays and was passed on to Mr. Fortescue, the Manager of the Westminster Branch of the London and Home Counties Bank, as he was getting ready to catch his train home that evening. The message said, "They've taken Rufus Oldroyd."

Mr. Fortescue considered the matter, standing in front of the fireplace, with its hideous chocolate-colored porcelain mantel. From the expression on his face you might have judged that the account of one of his most trusted customers had gone suddenly into the red.

Nine o'clock, on an autumn morning straight from paradise. The sun, clear of the mist, was full and golden, but not yet giving out much heat. In the drawing room of Craysfoot House a log fire was crackling in the grate, and the smell of percolating coffee was scenting the air.

"Damn the girl," said Admiral Lefroy, "how many times have I told her that I like my eggs boiled for four minutes!"

"I've told her a dozen times," said his wife.

"By the feel of this one it's been boiled for fourteen minutes."

"Give it to Sultan."

"I'll do nothing of the sort. The quickest way to ruin a dog's manners is to feed him at table. You'll have him begging next. Balancing lumps of sugar on his nose."

"When you were in command of a ship, I'm sure you were horrid to all the little midshipmen."

"It isn't a Captain's job to be horrid to midshipmen." The Admiral glared at the official letter he had just opened. "Damn!"

"What's up now?"

"Got to go to town. The First Sea Lord's called a conference. It's wonderful how busy they manage to keep us, considering we haven't got a navy."

"I'll go with you. We can come back together on Friday afternoon."

"Who have we got this weekend?"

"Your friend, Captain Rowlandson."

"Good."

"And Mrs. Orbiston."

"Oh, God!"

"You'll have to be nice to her. She's on the committee of the

Kennel Club. We can't have her blackballing Sultan when he comes up.''

Hearing his name, the dog got up from the rug in front of the fire and walked across to Lady Lefroy. He was nine months old, a puppy no longer, but a young dog with plenty of growth to come in his long springy body and barrel chest. A Persian deerhound of royal parentage, he wore the tuft of hair on the top of his head like a coronet. His eyes, which had been light yellow at birth, were deepening now into amber. His nose was blue-black, his skin the color of honey.

Lady Lefroy tickled the top of his head and said. "Sorry, no scraps for you.'' And to her husband, "I forgot. There's one more. Mr. Behrens.''

"Who's he?''

"You ought to know. You invited him.''

"Oh, the bee chap. Yes. I met him at my club. He's written a book about them. Knows a lot about medieval armor, too.''

"He can go for nice long walks with Mrs. Orbiston and talk to her about hives and helmets.''

Admiral Lefroy abandoned the egg in disgust, and started on the toast and marmalade. He said, "What are you planning to do up in town?''

"Shopping, and having my hair done.''

"By—what's the fellow's name—Michael?''

"Who else? And what are you snorting about?''

"You know damned well what I'm snorting about.''

"Now, Alaric . . . Michael is adorable. The things he says! Do you know what he told Lady Skeffington last week?''

"I'm not the least interested in what he told Lady Skeffington.''

The beauty salon was in two sections. The front had plush settees, low tables covered with glossy magazines, a thick carpet, and indirect lighting. At the back was a row of cubicles, with plain white wooden doors. On each door was the word *Michael's* in letters of brass script, and under each word the stylized painting of a different flower.

From behind the cubicles the snipping of scissors, the sudden gushing of water as a spray was turned on, the humming of a hair dryer. From in front, the hum of conversation. Mrs. Hetherington, county to the oblong ends of her brown shoes, was saying to Lady Lefroy, "So *she* said, when they have the next Cabinet reshuffle, Tom's been promised the Navy. Michael said—with a perfectly straight face—'What'll he do with it when he gets it? Play with it in his bath?' "

A Mrs. Toop, who was nobody in particular, and knew it, giggled sycophantically. Lady Lefroy, who had heard the story before, said, "Oh. What did she say?"

"Of course she pretended to be furious. I mean, Michael doesn't bother to be rude to you unless your husband's someone."

How Mrs. Toop wished that Michael would be rude to *her*!

"He goes too far sometimes," said Lady Lefroy. "Did you hear what he said to Lady Skeffington?"

"No. Tell, tell."

"Well, you know how she's always carrying on about her husband's polo. What the Duke said to him and what he said to the Duke—"

"Hold it," said Mrs. Hetherington regretfully.

The door with a chrysanthemum on it opened and Michael came out. He held the door open for Lady Skeffington, gave her a gentle pat on the back as she went past, and said, "There now, Lady S. You look a proper little tart. I 'ope your 'usband likes it."

"He'll hate it," said Lady Skeffington complacently.

"It'll keep his mind off things. You ought to see the cartoon in the *Mirror*."

"I never read the *Mirror*."

"You don't know what you're missing. They've got him to the life. Quintin as the lion, and 'im as the unicorn."

It was noticeable that Michael dealt with his aitches quite arbitrarily, sometimes dropping them, sometimes not. He helped Lady Skeffington into her coat, showed her out, and came back, casting an eye over the waiting victims.

"Come, on Lady L.," he said. "I'll wash your hair for you."

Mrs. Hetherington said, "What about me? I was next."

"Bert can take care of you," said Michael. "He'll be through in Delphinium in 'alf a mo'."

"It's sheer favoritism."

"You know what Mr. Asquith said. 'Favoritism's the secret of efficiency.' "

"It wasn't Asquith," said Mrs. Hetherington coldly. "It was Lord Fisher."

"Lady Marcia Lefroy," said Mr. Fortescue, "is not English at all, although to hear her speak you would never guess it. She's a French Lebanese girl, of good family." Mr. Fortescue paused, as though the next words he had to speak were precious, and needed to be weighed out very carefully. "She had been a trained Communist agent since she was sixteen."

The Under-Secretary of State stared at him in blank disbelief. He said, "Really, Fortescue. This sounds like something Security Executive has dreamed up. I've met Lady Lefroy a dozen times. She's an absolutely charming woman."

"She was trained to be charming. In fact, her earliest assignment was to charm Lefroy. He was only a Captain then, in command of our Eastern Meditterranean Cruiser Detachment. Her instructions were to seduce him. However, it served the purpose of her employers equally well when he carried her off and married her."

"This is quite fantastic. Who started this—this canard?"

"It was started by a disgruntled housemaid. She told us that once, when clearing away the coffee cups, she distinctly heard Admiral Lefroy telling his wife something—she was vague what it was but she was sure it was secret."

The Under-Secretary laughed. "And you believed that sort of evidence?"

"On the contrary, we put her down as a bad and spiteful witness. The information was pigeon holed. However, three months ago, when Heinrich Woolf defected to us—you remember—"

"Of course."

"One of the things he told us was that details of our agents in Eastern bloc countries were regularly reaching Moscow via Warsaw. They were known to be coming from the foreign-born wife of a senior Naval Officer with a post in Intelligence. The Lefroys filled the bill exactly. He's the naval representative on the Joint Staffs Intelligence Committee.

"We still didn't believe it, but we had Lady Lefroy watched. And noted that she had her hair—washed and set, I believe, is the right expression—by a fashionable hairdresser who calls himself Michael, speaks with a strong Cockney accent, was born in Lithuania, and has an occasional and inconspicuous rendezvous on Parliament Hill Fields with a Major Shollitov, who drives the Polish Ambassador's spare car.''

The Under-Secretary said, "Good God!" and then, "I hope you realize that this is a case where we can't afford—can't possibly afford—to make any mistake.''

"I can see that it would arouse considerable comment.''

"Comment! God in heaven, man, it's dynamite. And if it went off the wrong way it could—well it could blow quite a lot of people out of the office.''

Mr. Fortescue said in his gentlest voice, "I had not really considered the political angles. My objective is to stop it. You heard they picked up Rufus Oldroyd—''

"Was that—?''

"I imagine so. Admiral Lefroy knew all about Oldroyd. A single incautious word to his wife. The mention of a name even—''

"Yes. I can see that.''

"It must be stopped.'' Mr. Fortescue's eyes were as bleak and gray as the seas which washed his native Hebrides.

The Under-Secretary shifted uncomfortably in his padded chair. He was a Wykehamist. He disliked Intelligence work, its operations, its operators, and all its implications. It was only the accident of the particular seat he occupied at the Foreign Office which had forced him to have anything to do with it.

He said, "Alaric Lefroy's a public hero. Has been ever since he got his V.C. on the Russian convoy. He's a friend of Royalty. He could hardly be removed from the Committee without public explanation. And suppose we were forced—by questions in the House—to *give* an explanation. Could we prove it?''

"At the moment, almost certainly not.''

"Then couldn't we pull this fellow Michael in?''

"It would be ineffective. Marcia Lefroy is a professional. She'd lie low for a bit. Then she'd open up a new channel of communication—possibly one we didn't know about. Then we should be worse off.''

"I suppose you're right,'' said the Under-Secretary unhappily. "What are we going to do about it?''

"I had worked out a tentative plan—I could explain the details if you wished—"

The Under-Secretary said hastily that he had no desire to hear the details. He felt confident that the matter could be left entirely in Mr. Fortescue's hands.

Michael was uneasy. The causes of his uneasiness were trivial, but they were cumulative. There had been the trouble with the lock on the front door of his flat. The locksmith who had removed and replaced it had found the tip of a key broken off in the mechanism.

Michael had mentioned the matter to the hall porter, and in doing so had discovered that the regular porter, with whom he was on very good terms, had been replaced by a large and surly-looking individual who had treated him in a very offhand way. And the final straw—there had been the trouble with his car.

It had been his custom to make his trips to North London in an inconspicuous little Austin runabout. This had gone in for repairs a week ago, and had been promised to him for today. When he went to get the car it was not ready. Mysterious additional faults had developed. There was nothing he could do but use his second car, the extremely conspicuous, primrose-yellow Daimler with the personal license plate.

This he parked, as usual, in the backyard of the Spaniards, and made his way on foot down the complex of paths which led to the open spaces of Parliament Hill Fields. It was an ideal place for a rendezvous, with an almost panoramic view of London. Major Shollitov would come from the opposite direction, leaving his car in Swains Lane, and walking up to the meeting place.

And now, to add to, and cap, all the other doubts which had been nagging him, Major Shollitov was late. Michael, although a very minor player in the game, was sufficiently instructed to realize the significance of this. A rendezvous was always kept with scrupulous punctuality. If one party was late, it was a warning—a warning not to be disregarded. The other party took himself off, quickly and quietly.

Michael glanced at his watch. 2:59. From the seat on which he was sitting he could command all the paths leading up from the

Vale. It was one of its advantages. Thirty seconds to go. Major Shollitov was not coming.

When a hand touched him on the shoulder Michael jumped.

The man must have come up across the grass behind him. He was thick-set, middle-aged, and nondescript. He said, "Got a match?"

Michael's heart resumed a more normal rhythm. He said, "Sure."

"Mind if I sit down? Lovely view, isn't it?"

Michael said, "Yes." He wondered how soon he could move. To get straight up and walk off would look rude, and to be rude would attract attention.

The stranger said, "I wonder if you know why they call this spot Parliament Hill Fields?"

"No, I don't."

"You remember that crowd who were planning to blow up Parliament? Fifth of November, sixteen hundred and five. They'd got it all laid out, and were intending to scuttle off up north to start the revolt. And just about here was where they pulled up their horses, to have a view of the fireworks display. Dramatic, wasn't it?"

"Oh, very," said Michael. Give it one more minute.

"Only, as *we* know, the fireworks didn't go off. And they left poor old Guy Fawkes behind to carry the can. Interesting, don't you think?"

"Oh, very."

"I thought you'd be interested."

There was something about this last statement that Michael didn't like. He said sharply. "Why should it interest me, particularly?"

"Well," said the stranger, "after all it's much the sort of position you're in now, isn't it?"

The long silence that followed was broken by the distant voices of children playing, out of sight down the slope. At last Michael said, "What are you talking about?"

"Your old pal, Major Shollitov—the one you usually meet here. He's gone scuttling back to Warsaw, leaving you sitting here, like Guy Fawkes, waiting for the rack and thumbscrew."

"Who are you?"

"Never mind about me," said the stranger, with a sudden

brutal authority. "Let's talk about you. You're the one who's on the spot. You're a messenger boy for the Commies, aren't you? How did they rope you in? Through your old Mum and Dad in Lithuania? Not that it matters. They've finished with you now. You're blown."

"You're mad."

"If you think I'm mad I'd advise you to shout for help. Go on. There's a park attendant. Give him a yell. Tell him you're being annoyed by a lunatic."

Michael watched the park attendant approach them. He watched him walk away.

The stranger inhaled the last drop of smoke from his cigarette, dropped it, and stamped on it. He said, "You've had an easy run, so far. Listening to high-class tittle-tattle from Lady This, whose husband's in the Cabinet, and Mrs. That whose brother's on the Staff, and passing it on for a few pounds a time. They don't pay much for third class work like that. Well, that's all over now. It's you who's going to do the playing and—" The stranger leaned forward until his face was a few inches from Michael's. "—it's not going to be nice. They get rough, those Intelligence boys. They know what happens to *their* friends when they get caught, and they like a chance to pay a little of it back. The last one they brought in had both his legs broken. Jumping out of a car, *they* said—"

"He's yellow," said Mr. Calder to Mr. Fortescue. "Yellow as a daffodil. By the time I'd finished he was almost crying."

"I'm not surprised," said Mr. Fortescue. "Verbal bullies are often lacking in moral stamina. You were careful not to suggest any connection between him and Lady Lefroy?"

"Very careful. I kept it quite general. Listening to indiscreet gossip was how I put it."

"Excellent. We must hope that he'll act predictably."

It had not been an easy weekend, even for an experienced hostess like Marcia Lefroy. Captain Rowlandson and Mrs. Orbiston had not mixed well. The only real success had been Mr. Behrens, who had filled in awkward gaps in the conversation with stories about his bees.

The final straw for Lady Lefroy was when her husband

telephoned that he had to stay in London. The First Lord had called a conference for early the next day.

Lady Lefroy pondered these things as she lay in bed. Usually she fell asleep immediately after turning off the bedside lamp. Tonight she had not done so. Like all trained and experienced agents she possessed delicate antennas, on the alert for the unusual. It was most unusual for a conference to be called on a Saturday morning. If there had been a crisis of some sort, it would have have been understandable. But the international scene was flat as a pancake. Why then—?

The first handful of gravel against the window jerked her back to full wakefulness. As she got out of bed Sultan growled softly. "It's all right," she said. She struggled into her dressing gown without turning on the light.

She made her way downstairs into the drawing room and opened the long window giving onto the terrace. As a man slipped through she adjusted the curtains carefully and switched on a single wall light. When she saw who it was her anger exploded. "How *dare* you come here!"

"I wouldn't have come unless I had to," said Michael sulkily.

"Your instructions were clear. You were absolutely forbidden to write, telephone, or even speak to me, except in your shop."

"But I've got to get out. They're onto me."

"How do you know that?"

"They told me."

"An unusual proceeding," said Lady Lefroy coldly.

"This man, he met me, at the rendezvous. Shollitov's been sent home. He knew all about us."

"*Us?*"

"Well, about me."

"Did he mention my name?"

"Not your name particularly. He accused me of picking up gossip at the salon and passing it on. He made threats. They were going to—to do things to me."

"Have they done anything?"

"Not yet. But they will. I tried to get through—to the emergency number."

"Fool. Your line will be tapped."

"I couldn't, anyway. They said it had been disconnected."

"I see," said Lady Lefroy. It was a few moments before she spoke again.

"How did you come down?"

"By car. I'm sure I wasn't followed—I should have known at once. The roads were empty. I hid the car nearly a mile away and walked the rest of the way."

"You showed that much sense." There was no point in panicking him. He was frightened enough already. "What do you want?"

"Help. To get out."

"What makes you think I can help you?"

"You know the ropes. They told me that if I ever had to clear out I was to come to you."

"Then," said Lady Lefroy, "I must see what I can do." She walked across to her desk. As she did so, the door was pushed open. Her heart missed a beat, then steadied. It was Sultan.

"That's very naughty of you," she said. "I told you to stay put."

Sultan yawned. He wanted the man to go so that they could get back to bed.

Lady Lefroy unlocked the desk, and than a steel-lined drawer inside. From it she took a bulky packet which she weighed thoughtfully in her hand. She said, "You see this. It was left with me against such a contingency. But before I give it to you I must have your promise to use it exactly in the way I tell you."

"Of course. What is it?"

"It's called 'Emergency Exit.' Inside you'll find a passport. The photograph resembles you sufficiently. You'll have to make a few small changes. Arrange your air differently. That should be easy enough for a man of your talents." A smile twitched the corner of Lady Lefroy's mouth. "And wear glasses. You'll find them in the packet too. There's a wad of French and German money, and instructions as to what you're to do when you get to Cologne. From there you'll be flying to Berlin. There's a second passport to use in Berlin, and a second set of instructions. After you open the packet—which you're not to do until you're back in London—all instructions are to be learned by heart and then destroyed. And the first passport is to be destroyed when you reach Cologne. Is that clear?"

Michael let his breath out with a soft sigh. "All clear," he said. "And thank you."

"A final word. *These things aren't issued in duplicate*. So look after it carefully."

Michael made an unsuccessful attempt to stow the bulky oilskin-covered packet in his coat pocket. Lady Lefroy took it from him. She said, "Open the front of your shirt. That's right. Stow it down there. Now button it up again. Right. Don't open the curtains until I've turned the light off."

She stood for a few moments after Michael had gone. She was taut as a violin string. The young dog, crouched at her feet, sensed it and growled, low in his throat. The sound broke the tension.

"All right," said Lady Lefroy. "Back to bed. Nothing more to worry about."

Among other irritating habits Mrs. Orbiston was accustomed to turning on her portable radio for the seven o'clock news, and retailing the choicer items to the company at breakfast. Lady Lefroy had not appeared, so her audience consisted of Captain Rowlandson, who was never fully awake until he had finished his after-breakfast pipe, and Mr. Behrens whose mind appeared to be elsewhere.

"Burglars," she announced. "Stole jewelry worth fifteen thousand pounds. At Greystone House. That's not far from here, is it?"

"I've no idea," said Captain Rowlandson.

"Well, I'm sure it is nearby. Because the people were called Baynes, and I've heard Marcia talk about them."

"Serve them right. When you go away you ought to put your jewelry in the bank."

"That's just it. That's what made it so terrible. The men went *into* their bedroom, *while* they were there, and helped themselves to the jewel box *off* the dressing table. It makes your flesh creep. I was just saying, Marcia—"

"If it's the Bayneses you're talking about," said Lady Lefroy, who had come into the room at that moment, "I've just heard. Mary Baynes was on the telephone."

"One good thing," said Captain Rowlandson. "They wouldn't get away with it here. Sultan would see them off."

"He's a very light sleeper," agreed Lady Lefroy. "All the same, I can't help thinking that it might be better if he *didn't* give the alarm."

"Oh—why?"

"I gather these burglars are pretty desperate characters. And all my stuff is well insured."

"That's pure defeatism, Marcia. Don't you agree, Behrens?"

Mr. Behrens said, "Defeatism might be preferable to being shot."

Mrs. Orbiston, seeing the conversation drifting away from her, pulled it back sharply. She said, "And that wasn't the *only* exciting thing that happened in this part of the country. Roysters Cross is quite close to here, too, isn't it?"

"About four miles away," said Lady Lefroy. "Why?"

"There was a terrible accident there last night. A man blew himself up."

"Blew himself up?"

"That's what the news commentator said."

"Curious way of committing suicide," said Captain Rowlandson.

"The possibility of accident has not been ruled out."

"You can't very well blow yourself up by accident," said Mr. Behrens. "That is, unless you're carrying some sort of bomb."

"Perhaps it was a tire blowout," said Lady Lefroy. "Would you mind passing the marmalade?"

"It didn't sound like a tire blowout. They said the man *and* the car were blown to bits."

"Amatol or dextrol," said Mr. Calder. "Or just possibly good old-fashioned nitroglycerine, although that's got rather a detectable smell."

"What sort of fuse?" asked Mr. Fortescue.

"Something silent. Wire and acid?"

"Very likely," agreed Mr. Fortescue. "It's notoriously inaccurate. I've no doubt the thing was intended to go off a lot further away from Lady Lefroy's house. Or maybe he took longer to walk back to his car than she anticipated. How do you think she arranged it?"

"I imagine it was something she gave him to take back to London. A parcel of some sort."

"The whole thing," said Mr. Fortescue, "is most unfortunate. Michael was responding nicely to treatment. He would soon have been ready to cooperate."

"Evidently Marcia thought so, too."

"It demonstrates what we have always suspected—that she's a ruthless and unscrupulous woman."

"It demonstrates something else, too," said Mr. Calder. "If she tumbled to what we were doing—twisting Michael's tail so hard that he'd incriminate her—she must have suspected that we were onto her as well."

Mr. Fortescue said, "Hmm. Maybe."

"Not certain, I agree. But a workable assumption. And if it's true it must mean that she's decided to stay put and brazen it out. Because if she had decided to quit she'd have kept Michael on ice for a day or two, while she made all *her* preparations."

"It's a very unhappy conclusion. Now that she's been warned she'll sever all her contracts and lie low for a very long time. possibly forever."

"It would, I suppose, be a halfway solution," said Mr. Fortescue. He didn't sound very happy about it. "All the same, I don't think it's a chance we can take. Do you?"

"No," said Mr. Calder. "I don't." He added, "I read in the papers that there'd been another burglary down in the Petersfield area. It's some sort of gang. The police say that they're armed, and dangerous. They've put out a warning to all householders in the neighborhood."

Mr. Fortescue thought about this for a long time. Then he said, "Yes. I think that would be best. It'll mean keeping the Admiral up in London for another night. I'll get the Minister to reconvene the Conference."

"How's he going to get away with that one? He can't keep Senior Admirals and Generals in London on a Sunday. Not in peacetime."

"Then we'll have to declare war on someone," said Mr. Fortescue.

Marcia sat up in bed and said, "Stop it, Sultan. What's the matter with you?"

It had been a savage growl—no gentle rumbling warning, but a note of imminent danger.

The moon, cloud-wracked, was throwing a gray light into the room. As her sight adjusted itself, Marcia could dimly see the figure at which Sultan was snarling.

She twisted one hand into his collar, and with the other she switched on the bed-table lamp. A man was standing beside the dressing table, examining an opened jewel case. He put the case down and said, "If you don't keep that dog under control I shall have to shoot him. It wouldn't make a lot of noise, because this gun's silenced, but I'd hate to have to mess up a nice animal like that."

"If that jewel case interests you, you're welcome to it. It's got nothing but costume jewelry in it—stop it, Sultan—worth twenty-five pounds if you're lucky."

"And insured for five hundred, I don't doubt," said the intruder. "I'm not really interested in jewelry. That's just an excuse for meeting you. I wanted to get your version of what happened to Michael last night."

"Michael? Michael who?"

"The Michael who's been doing your hair for the last eighteen months. You can't have forgotten about him already. They've only just finished scraping bits of him off the signpost at Roysters Cross. That must have been a powerful bit of stuff you put in the packet you gave him."

"I've no idea what you're talking about," said Lady Lefroy. Her voice gave nothing away. Only her eyes were thoughtful, and the knuckles of the hand which held Sultan's collar showed white.

The door opened quietly. Calder's colleague, Mr. Behrens, looked in.

"You've come just at the right moment," said the first intruder. "Have you got the tape?"

"I have it," said Mr. Behrens, "and a recorder. I had to wire three rooms to be sure of getting it."

Lady Lefroy's look had hardened. She moved her head slowly, trying to sum up both men, to weigh this new development. It was the reaction of a professional, faced by a threat from a new quarter.

"You know each other, I see."

"Indeed, yes," said Mr. Behrens. "Calder and I have known each other for twenty years. Or is it twenty-five? Time goes so quickly when you're interested in your work."

"So you're in this together."

"We often work as a team."

"You do the snooping and sneaking, and he does the rough stuff."

"Exactly," said Mr. Behrens. "We find it an excellent arrangement." He was busy with the tape recorder. "Now perhaps we can convince you we're not bluffing. Where shall we start?"

There was a click, and they heard Lady Lefroy's voice say, "It's called 'Emergency Exit.' Inside you'll find a passport—" They listened in silence for a full minute. "Open the front of your shirt. That's right. Stow it down there—"

Mr. Behrens turned the machine off.

"A nice touch," he said. "It must have been resting on his stomach when it went off. No wonder there wasn't much of him left."

Lady Lefroy said, "That tape recording proves nothing. You say it's my voice. I say it's a clumsy fake. It doesn't even sound much like me."

"You mustn't forget that I saw Michael, both coming and going."

"Lies! Why do you bother me with such lies?" Again her eyes turned from one man to the other. She was trying to estimate which of them was the stronger character, which one she should attack, what weapons in her well-stocked armory she should use. It was confusing to have to deal with two at once.

In the end she said, with a well-contrived yawn. "Do I understand that this is all leading up to something? That you have some proposal to put to me? If so, please put it, so that I can get back to sleep."

"Our proposal," said Mr. Calder, "is this. If you will make a written statement, naming your employers, and your contacts, giving full details which can be verified in forty-eight hours, we'll give you the same length of time to get out of the country."

"We feel certain," said Mr. Behrens, "that you have all *your* arrangements made."

"More efficient, if less drastic, than the ones you made for Michael."

All expression had gone out of Lady Lefroy's face. It was a mask—a meticulously constructed mask behind which a quick brain weighed the advantages and disadvantages of the proposal. When she smiled, Mr. Behrens knew that they had lost.

"You're bluffing," she said. "I call your bluff. Go away."

"A pity," said Mr. Behrens.

"Very disappointing," said Mr. Calder. "We shall have to use plan Number Two."

"You do understand," said Mr. Behrens earnestly, "that you've brought this on yourself. We have no alternative."

Lady Lefroy said nothing. There was something here she found disturbing.

Mr. Calder said. "It's this gang of burglars, you see. Armed burglars. They've been breaking into houses round here. Tonight they turned their attention to this house. You woke up and caught one of them rifling your jewel case."

"And what happened then?"

"Then," said Mr. Calder, "he shot you."

Three things happened together: a scream from Marcia Lefroy, cut short; the resonant twang of the silenced automatic pistol; and a snarl of fury as the dog went for Mr. Calder's throat.

Mr. Behrens moved almost as quickly as the dog. He caught up the two corners of the blanket on which the dog had been lying and enveloped him in it, a growling writhing, murderous bundle. Mr. Calder dropped his gun, grabbed the other two corners of the blanket, knotted them together.

"It was unpardonable," said Mr. Fortescue.

"I know," said Mr. Calder. "But—"

"There are no 'buts' about it. It was an unnecessary complication, and a quite unjustifiable risk. Suppose he is recognized."

"All Persian deerhounds have a strong family resemblance. Once he's fully grown there'll be no risk at all. I'll rename him of course. I thought that Rasselas might be the appropriate name for an Eastern Prince—"

"I can't approve."

"He's beautifully bred. And he's got all the courage in the

world. You should have seen the way he came for me. Straight as an arrow. If Behrens hadn't got the blanket over him, he'd have had my throat for sure. What were we to do?''

''You should have immobilized him.''

''You can't immobilize a partly grown deerhound.''

''Then you should have shot him.''

''Shoot a dog like that,'' said Mr. Calder. ''You must be joking.''

Ron Goulart

The work of Ron Goulart has its roots in many genres. His science fiction has elements of mystery, his mysteries have elements of fantasy and almost everything is infused with wit. Under numerous pseudonyms he has written dozens of novels, short stories, novelizations and comic strips. In 1971, he won the Mystery Writers of America's Edgar Allen Poe Award.

HOW COME MY DOG DON'T BARK?

RON GOULART

They couldn't use those final pictures of him. The photos were too much even for *Worldwide Intruder*, which is why the last picture of Kerry Dent to run in that particular tabloid showed him looking tan, fit, and relatively unwrinkled.

It was the other photos in the *Intruder* which caused Dent to do what he did. If it hadn't been for those earlier pictures, and the unflattering little stories and captions accompanying them, he wouldn't have ended up out in San Fernando Valley in such terrible shape.

Well, his wife had something to do with it, of course. And that impossible dog, too.

Dent told me his suspicions concerning his wife when I visited him on the set of his television show late in the spring of last year. I'm sure you know he was married to Sue Bee Brannigan who does all the commercials for Galz beer. A striking girl, if not overly supportive. He was a shade over 29 years older than Sue Bee.

His suspicions and complaints about the dog I was already pretty familiar with. His feelings concerning Demon were why I was on the Wheelan Studios lot that bright, relatively clear morning. My avertising agency had bought his new show, "Demon & Co.," for our client, the Barx Smoke Alarm. That's the one that barks and howls like a dog to warn you that your house is on fire. Dent's show seemed perfect for Barx and within three weeks of its first airing, "Demon & Co." had shot up to the number three spot in the ratings. Not bad for a television show starring a German Shepherd and a 59-year-old daredevil actor.

The trouble was, Dent had developed the notion the dog was jealous of him. He took to calling me at the ad agency, and

132

eventually at my home in the best part of Santa Monica, to tell me how insanely jealous Demon was of him. Dent was convinced Demon was deliberately flubbing scenes, wasn't growling on cue, was mugging and letting his purplish tongue loll out during Dent's best dramatic moments and, on three occasions at least, nudging him off high places where only the actor's agility and long experience in action films saved him from serious injury. I'm not overly fond of animals, but I still found it difficult to accept most of what Dent told me.

As I approached the indoor set where Dent was supposed to be rescuing, aided by Demon, a country-and-western singer who was marooned in a flood I heard a great deal of snarling, barking, and shouting.

"Out, I want that gink out of here! Let me go, let me smack him in the beezer!"

That was Dent. You couldn't mistake his voice, which had never quite shaken his Bronx childhood.

"Easy, Kerry. Your pudgy face is getting all flushed. It's going to be coronary time if you don't watch it."

I reached the set in time to see Dent break free of the assistant director and key grip who'd been restraining him from charging at Ben Walden.

Walden was a tall, lean, and moderately handsome young man in his late twenties. He set his camera safely on a vacant canvas chair, pivoted, and stepped out of Dent's way.

"Gigolo!" accused Dent, spinning around. "I told you what I'd do with your camera if I ever caught you around me again!"

"Relax, Kerry," suggested Walden. "Your flabby body can't stand such stress."

"Flabby! I'll shove that—"

Dent, his narrowed eyes on the reporter, didn't notice the approach of Demon. He tripped over the dog and landed with a smack on the sound-stage floor.

Walden, snatching up his camera, clicked off six shots of the actor. "Beautiful, beautiful. All your chins are showing nicely." Then cradling the camera in his arms like a football, Walden jogged away.

He was out of the place by the time they got Dent on his feet again. "Didn't I give strict orders that nobody from the *Intruder* ever be allowed near me?"

The director patted Dent on the shoulder. "The guy slips in, Kerry, he's elusive."

"And you!" Dent kicked out at the dog, missed, and nearly lost his balance.

"Why don't we take five," the director urged. "Pull Dolly out of the tank, Skipper. We'll try the scene again in a few minutes."

"I can do it now," said Dent.

"Few minutes. Go sit down and have a drink."

"I don't drink. I haven't had a drink in three years, no matter what you read in the damn *Intruder*. 'Aging Hasbeen, Looking the Worse for Booze, Totters out of Gollywood Bistro on Arm of Long-Suffering Wife.' You better keep Walden off my set, off the lot. Otherwise there's going to be real trouble." He noticed me then and came hurrying over.

"You're looking well, Kerry," I made the mistake of saying.

"Why shouldn't I look well? I'm in damn fine shape. I do all my own stunts in this halfwit show," he told me, face still flushed. "Which is more than I can say for Demon, my illustrious co-star. He needs a double for all the difficult stuff. Come into my dressing room so we can talk."

I followed him through a doorway and down a corridor. "The client is a little worried about—"

"Did you see what he did just now? Tripped me so I couldn't wind Walden's clock for him."

"An accident, dogs aren't as bright as—"

"And look at this dressing room." He jerked the door open. "Cozy."

"Cozy my fanny! It's tiny. You know who had this dressing room before me? That clunk who starred in *Cybernetic Midget*. Yeah, this is a dwarf's old dressing room." He stalked to a small refrigerator, took out a bottle of Perrier water. "Demon has a kennel the size of Pickfair, while I—"

"The client was worried by the last story in the *Int*—"

"Listen, I'm a part of your life, right?" He gestured at one wall with his glass of sparkling water.

There were framed stills from some of his old movies mounted on the wall. A shot from *The Dancing Pirate*, two from *Captain Juggernaut*, one from *Fort Gordo*, and a whole series from *The Avenging Cavalier*, which was Dent's most popular movie.

"I saw most of your pictures," I admitted, "when I was a kid."

"Ha, ha. Very funny. You're as old as I am."

"I'm forty-four, you're fifty-nine."

"Forty-four isn't that far from fifty-nine. However, I don't have the problems you civilians do." He sipped at the water. "I take care of myself, good care." He patted his chin. "That's *one* chin you see, no matter what snide lies Walden writes in the *Intruder*."

"It's not so much the lies as the photographs. The client feels—"

"That bum hounds me! He sneaks around and snaps pictures of me when I'm at my worst. He waits for some unfortunate pose, then snaps and runs."

"The picture in this week's tab is particularly unfortunate. When you're hitting that blind beggar woman over the head with her own accordion."

"It only *looks* that way. Because of that wily jerk Walden," explained the actor. "I was helping the old bat adjust the damn thing and *snap* there's Walden and his camera."

"You were caught standing in front of the Naked Nikelodeon," I reminded. "With that poster behind you promising explicit romantic action inside."

"You don't understand what it is to be a celebrity," Dent said. "I can't take a walk or meet a friend without some nitwit reporter or photographer popping up and trying to make me look bad. The worst offender is that—"

"Maybe you should quit strolling in places like the Los Angeles tenderloin."

Finishing his Perrier, Dent turned to face me. "You recall the picture of me three weeks ago in the *Intruder*?"

"The one where you're doing a bellyflop in your pool. Flabby Kerry Does Flop. The client thought—"

"He climbed over the wall of my estate to snap that." The actor turned his back on me. "At least, I thought that was his only reason for being there. Now I—well, it's one of those little everyday troubles you have to live with."

I said, "I don't think the Barx Brothers can live with many more of your little everyday troubles, Kerry. What is it?"

He gestured at another wall of photos. "I've had four wives, everybody knows that. I swear the only one I ever cared for is Sue Bee.''

"She's a striking woman.''

"Of course she is. I only marry striking women. Sue Bee is also intelligent. How many people do you know who've read all the way through Proust's *Remembrance of Things Past*?''

"I read it in college, and my wife read it while she was in the hospital with—''

"Never mind,'' he cut in. "The trouble is, despite her intelligence—well, Sue Bee is being unfaithful.''

I nodded. "These days, Kerry, with society in a state of—''

"Unfaithful to *me*! And do you know who the guy is?''

"No, who?''

"Him! The jerk with the camera!''

"Ben Walden?''

"That bum with the camera, yes. Walden is cuckholding me.''

"You're absolutely sure?''

"Figures, doesn't it? Explains why he's trying to destroy me in the pages of that filthy rag. Over-the-hill Swashbuckler makes Feeble Attempt at Comeback. Feeble? He knows we knocked off the two top shows. The network ought to have a few more feeble swashbucklers like me.''

"Wait now,'' I said. "Do you know for certain your wife's having an affair with Walden, or do you just suppose she is?''

"I know *here*!'' He thumped his handsome chest. "Look, if you're an artist you *sense* things. I know. Old Man Dent Takes Snooze After Too Much Booze. He's trying to make me look ridiculous in the eyes of Sue Bee.''

"But a woman of her intelligence wouldn't—''

"Just because she's read Proust doesn't mean she wouldn't have an affair with Walden.''

I was silent for several seconds. "Going to be tough using any of this with the Barx Brothers,'' I finally told him. "If true, this is a logical explanation for why the *Intruder* seems to be picking on you. But the idea of your wife fooling around will upset them even more than—''

"You can tell the Barx boys to stick some of their smoke alarms—''

"Kerry, let me think about this. I'll see if I can—''

"Always the ad man. You can't react to anything with your *guts*. You have to write memos, take a couple dips in the think tank."

I cleared my throat. "This probably isn't the best time to ask you about the publicity stills."

"What stills?"

"Ones of you and Demon standing under a Barx alarm."

"Tell you what." Dent put a hand on my back. "We can use Demon's stand-in. That dog is an angel, a gem of a hound. Sweet, considerate, the absolute antithesis of Demon. I keep telling them to take Demon out and retire him or something and use the damn stand-in. They won't hear of it, especially Tessica Janes, the bimbo who claims to be Demon's trainer. She's got them all hoodwinked into thinking Demon is unique. He's unique all right, but—"

"Ready to shoot again, Mr. Dent," someone called outside the door.

Dent straightened, smiling. "Don't brood too much about anything that's happened today," he said to me. "I have an uncanny ability for bouncing back. And you're going to see one hell of a bounce any day now."

The agency sent me to Mentor, Ohio, a few days after that encounter with Kerry Dent and I didn't see him again for nearly a month. We'd been test-marketing a new bread in Mentor, a loaf which was 20 percent sawdust and called Lumberjack Bread, and some problems had arisen. Nearly everyone who ate so much as a slice of the experimental bread had come down with a disease closely resembling the flu. There was a definite danger of the media getting hold of the story. We couldn't afford to have the whole country hearing about a new blight known as the Lumberjack Bread Disease.

I was able, with a mixture of diplomacy and bribery, to keep the whole mess hushed up. Working very covertly we got all the test loaves out of the supermarkets and dumped into a handy river. That dumping gave us another problem, since it turned out that Lumberjack Bread was capable of killing fish even with its wrapper on.

As I say, I didn't get back to Los Angeles until a month or

more after my meeting with Kerry Dent on the "Demon and Co." set. Not that I hadn't been in communication with him, or rather he with me. Dent, possibly because he knew I'd been a fan of his swashbucklers in my youth, decided I was the one person he could confide in.

The phone in my slightly mildewed Mentor motel room rang at all hours. Dent's complaints were all variations on ones I'd heard before. Sue Bee continued to be unfaithful with Ben Walden of *Worldwide Intruder*, Demon loathed him and was making enormous efforts to sabotage his comeback, Walden was so audacious that when he sneaked into Dent's mansion to woo his wife he managed to snap unflattering photos of the dozing actor. Despite his claims of renewed vigor, Dent seemed to nap a good deal, as the frequent pictures showing up in the *Intruder* attested.

One particularly bleak morning in Ohio, just after my lovely secretary had rushed in to tell me 5000 dead fish had been sighted floating down the river with several loaves of Lumber-Jack Bread leading the pack, Dent phoned me collect. He claimed he had absolute proof that Demon not only hated him but was actually trying to kill him. In a scene for the eleventh episode of their show the dog was supposed to remove a smoking stick of dynamite from the vicinity of the bound-and-gagged Dent. He swore, and claimed to have witnesses, that Demon switched a real stick of dynamite for the prop one. If Dent hadn't sensed something was wrong and gone rolling over a low precipice he would have been blown up.

I pointed out that real dynamite could just as likely have blown up the dog when he snatched it up in his powerful jaws. Dent told me the dog had deliberately dawdled instead of rushing in to pick up the dynamite stick. Pacifying him as best I could, I went out to do something about all those dead fish.

My last, although I didn't know it at the time, encounter with Kerry Dent took place by accident. I was out in San Fernando Valley to call on a well-known sci-fi writer in Woodland Hills to see if we could persuade him to endorse a new pizza line the agency was involved with. The author, an extremely surly man, was not at all impressed by the Unidentified Flying Pizza and came close to punching me. Feeling very much like someone in an *Intruder* gossip item, I slunk away from his home and dropped into a valley restaurant for a cup of coffee to calm my nerves.

It was a noisy place, because of the prerecorded whip cracking and pistol shooting, and at first I wasn't aware of the hissing.

"Hsst, over here."

It was Dent, wearing a nylon jumpsuit and dark glasses and without his hairpiece. "Are you incognito?" I inquired, joining him in his booth.

"Used to know Whip in his heyday and I stop by here now and then."

Whip Wigransky's Burger Rancho was one of six such spots in the valley. It didn't seem to me that a nostalgia for the old B-Western actor was what had brought Dent here. "You have," I mentioned, "paw prints all over your front."

He glanced down, frowning, and brushed off some of the muddy spots. "Ho, ho," he said.

"You sound happy. I take it those prints aren't the leftovers from another attack by your co-star."

"That dumbunny isn't a co-star. I'm a star and he's only a bit player." Dent appeared considerably more relaxed than he'd been lately.

"I'm glad you're in a jovial mood. I thought maybe the picture in this week's *Intruder* would have—"

"Ho, ho, ho. That sort of guff rolls off my back. Fat Old Actor, Looking Terrible, Escorts Stunning Much Younger Wife to Premiere. Walden'll have to do a lot better than that to dampen Kerry Dent's spirits."

"I'll pass that news on to the Barx Brothers."

"Give them my love."

I watched his partially masked face. "What are you up to?"

"Having a Bar-B-Q Burger, Owlhoot Style," he said, smiling. "That's all."

"You're out here, disguised, looking smug. It's not like you."

"You didn't know me in my heyday," he replied. "I often went around looking smug. Recently I've found a way to return to the happier moods of yesteryear."

"Are you drinking again?"

"You can't drink and do your own stunts and keep a crazed hellhound from destroying you." He chuckled, relaxing even more. "I was stupid for a spell, now I'm getting all my old smarts back. There was a rock-and-roll tune I used to be fond of years ago. About a guy who suspected his wife was two-timing him. He asks the suspected lover, 'How come my dog don't bark when you come round to my door? Maybe it's because you been here before.' I was like that, stupid. Now I see things as they really are. I've devised a plan to bring me complete and total happiness."

"You haven't gone and joined some lunatic cult?"

"Cults join me." He locked his hands behind his head. "You and the Barx brood need have no fears. In a short time I shall have everything worked out to the satisfaction of one and all."

"Tessica Janes lives out here in the valley somewhere," I said, recalling the fact all at once. "You haven't been visiting her and making threats?"

"That bimbo and I have little to do with each other," Dent assured me. "She trains Demon, I am forced to act with him. That's our only link."

"She's a pretty large young woman. Doesn't look as though she could be intimidated."

"I don't blame Tess for what Demon does. He hates me and plots against me entirely on his own," he said. "Say, look who's coming in. It's old Whip Wigransky himself. Excuse me while I go wrestle with him. It's a long-standing custom."

"Sure, certainly." I sat there, not even turning to watch the good-natured horseplay which was amusing all the other customers. Deep inside I felt very uneasy. I had a premonition something was going to happen, something which would affect the show and annoy the Barx Brothers.

Immediately after this I had to leave town again. There'd been a disastrous fire in the Barx Brothers main factory in Trenton, New Jersey. The place had burned to the ground and not one of the 10,000 smoke alarms sitting in there had so much as yelped. The wire services had picked up the story and both *Newsmag* and *Tide* were sending people in. The Barx Brothers, with the exception of Carlos who refused to come back from Bermuda, met with me for two days while we worked out a rush campaign to counteract the effects of what had happened.

By the time I came up with a copy approach which satisfied us all, except for Jocko who went off to join Carlos in Bermuda, and wrote some commercials three weeks had passed. I was on the plane back to L.A. when the news came through. I learned about it because my stewardess was sobbing and I asked why.

"The poor darling old man," she managed to say between sobs. "He's been a part of my life since earliest girlhood. I simply adored his swashbuckuling films and his TV shows and—"

"Wait a minute. You can't be talking about—"

"Yes, isn't it awful? Kerry Dent is dead."

"Kerry Dent is dead?"

"I heard it on the news just before takeoff."

"How did it happen?"

"Oh, it's too terrible."

She was referring of course only to the official version of Dent's passing. Nobody ever released the true story, which was fortunate I suppose. It's possible that Ben Walden knows most of the truth, but he won't be writing it up in the *Intruder*. Not unless he can figure a way to make his own part of the events seem admirable. Which isn't likely.

As you probably know, I don't like to get too involved in affairs of this sort. Since I was curious, though, and since I felt I owed it to the agency to find out why the star of our top-rated show had been torn to pieces, I did some digging.

What follows is, I believe, a relatively accurate account of how Dent met his end. Some of it I've had to guess.

Dent had come up with a plan to remove the two prime sources of grief in his life—Ben Walden and Demon. He was certain Sue Bee would return to him completely when there was no more Ben Walden around. He also believed Demon could be very easily replaced on the show by the stand-in, a much more admirable dog. He figured it would be to the benefit of all concerned not even to let on there'd been a switch. One German Shepherd looked pretty much like another.

He arranged things so he could put his plan into action the night Tessica Janes, Demon's trainer, was not at home. The girl was scheduled to attend a screening of the punk rock remake of *Boys Town* on the night in question. Dent, with the help of Whip Wigransky, had already planted in Ben Walden's mind the idea that Dent was having an affair with Tessica. That fateful night Whip phoned Walden with a tip that the girl was going to skip the screening and spend the night with the aging actor. Dent assumed Walden wouldn't pass up a chance to get pictures of him in such a compromising situation.

Dent had been, very secretly, working out in San Fernando Valley at a seedy dog-training school. That was where he'd been the day I ran into him. The paw prints I'd noticed had come from the vicious German Shepherd that Dent was training. This dog was designed to be a watchdog, eager to kill anyone his master ordered him to kill. Dent was his master.

Actually it wasn't a bad plan. Lure Walden to Tessica's place and set this killer dog on him. The police would find the body of a snooping reporter who'd obviously been torn to pieces by a mad German Shepherd. There would be Demon in his cage looking sheepish.

Even if Tessica claimed the dog had been locked up all night, the evidence of a dead *Intruder* reporter would contradict her.

Dent arrived a half hour before the ten-o'clock assignation time that he'd had Whip pass on to Walden. It was an exceptionally clear night with more stars out than you usually see in Southern California.

Parking his rented van in a wooded area behind Tessica's spread, Dent led his killer dog out of the vehicle and down to the ranch. By diligent spying earlier he knew there was only one old servant to worry about. The man was in his late sixties and slept in a cottage near the main entrance of the ranch. There was a cyclone fence around the three acres, but it wasn't electrified. Dent had no trouble clipping a section out of it.

The police would naturally assume that Walden, hot after a hot story, had done the snipping.

Up to here Dent's plan went well. He crossed onto the ranch grounds with his dog.

There was an arbor to the left of the ranchouse. He took the German Shepherd there and crouched in the shadows to await Walden.

He debated whether or not he ought to let Demon loose after

the killing. He decided it would be safer not to. As he'd already figured out, no matter what Tessica and the old servant might claim, they'd never convince the police that it wasn't Demon who'd done the killing. There were only two collies and a spaniel in the kennels here. None of them could be blamed. The frame would fit only Demon.

Unfortunately there were three things Dent couldn't have anticipated. For one thing, he couldn't have known that Walden, who was spending some time with Sue Bee, would be late by about 20 minutes. Nor did Dent know that on the evenings when Tessica was away the old servant let Demon loose for a romp around the ranch.

The third thing he couldn't have expected was that his killer dog, while aggressive with people, was fearful of other German Shepherds.

So when the roaming Demon, sensing the presence of Dent and the dog in the arbor, came galloping in there, the killer dog yelped and ran away through the hole in the fence.

Demon then leaped straight at Dent.

I'd always thought Dent was exaggerating about the animosity Demon felt toward him. It turned out, though, Dent was absolutely right.

That dog really hated him.

Joyce Harrington

Author of two successful novels, *No One Knows My Name* (1980) and *Family Reunion* (1982), Joyce Harrington is best known for her New York City-set short stories. Her first mystery story, "The Purple Shroud" (1972), won an Edgar Award from the Mystery Writers of America. She has served on this organization's board of directors.

DISPATCHING BOOTSIE

BY JOYCE HARRINGTON

It was easy to *think* about killing Bootsie. But doing it, in real life, was a little more difficult. Let me tell you about Bootsie. She was Texas born and bred. Li'l ol' cow patty of a town in West Texas, as she liked to say. Her daddy was a wildcatter, and until she was seven years old, again according to her, they lived on pinto beans and the gusher that was going to come in tomorrow or the next day. All she would ever say about her mother was that she turned sorrowful and died before she had any fun out of life.

Well, gushers sometimes do come in, and Bootsie's daddy hit a whopper. What she remembered about that was first of all eating the first steak of her life and afterward getting sick, and second of all being sent off to boarding school. She learned a lot there. Not really how to read, although she could manage movie magazines if she tried real hard and there happened to be a picture of Burt Reynolds on the page; nothing whatever about math. As she liked to say, "I got so much money, I don't need to count it." No. What Bootsie learned at school was how to dress and what to do with her hair and how to spend all that money.

She also learned to smoke, both plain and funny cigarettes, drink whiskey, and generally behave like a Texas wild woman. Anything she wanted, she only had to ask Daddy.

I met Bootsie about a year after her Daddy had died. Killed in the crash of his private jet on the way to Acapulco. Five of the flower of Texas womanhood went with him. Daddy was evidently making up for all those years of pinto beans and sorrow. Bootsie, as she liked to tell it, cried a whole lot. But after the visit of the lawyers, she perked up. School, by that time, was boring and there was nothing else for her to learn. What she needed, she decided, was a change of scene.

She flipped a coin between New York and Los Angeles—she had learned enough geography to know that one was on the East Coast and the other on the West and both were large and expensive—and it came up in an easterly direction. She rented a suite in the Barclay and moved in with a little Tex-Mex woman named Josefa who washed and ironed her underwear, and a big old hound dog named Bruce. So Bootsie and Bruce and Josefa were set to see new York.

Josefa didn't speak a word of English, but she was quick and intelligent and got along with Bootsie by anticipating her every need. The few times she didn't, Bootsie would yell and scream and throw things at her until she got the drift. Example. "Dammit, Joe! Didn't I tell you yesterday to get rid of those flowers? The damn things remind me of funerals. Out! Out! Out!" And the vase would go sailing across the room, barely missing Josefa where she stood pretending to cower but with her dark eyes flashing malice. "Sí, sí, querida. Hija de puta. Las flores. Pronto. ¡Que tu murieras mil veces con tanto dolor! Gracias a Dios." That's the way it was between them. Screeching abuse on one side, and muttered maledictions of a thousand painful deaths on the other. Bruce terrorized the bellhops and all the other East Side dogs he met on his walks with Josefa. He adored Bootsie, and even when she kicked him was content to roll over at her feet and grovel abjectly.

I haven't told you what Bootsie looked like. She once showed me a snapshot of herself taken in pre-gusher days back in the cow-patty town. It was straight out of *The Grapes of Wrath*, not that she'd ever read the book or seen the movie, or even heard of the Dust Bowl. She stood, knobby-kneed, staring into the camera in a dress that was a couple of sizes too small and obviously had not been in the vicinity of soap and water for most of its career. Her feet were bare and her toes curled in the dust of the yard of a small shack that was out of focus in the background. Her hair hung lank about her face, chopped off in a homemade Dutch bob. But it was her eyes that dominated the picture. It was a black-and-white print, so you couldn't tell that the eyes were the color of Delft tiles, bright and pitiless blue. What stared at you out of the picture was a hunger so vast it seemed capable of devouring the earth for an appetizer and going on from there. That was then.

When I met her she was nothing short of gorgeous. The hair was a sleek shimmer of white-blonde silk falling straight to her shoulders, and the eyes had learned to sparkle and invite. She was tall, almost as tall as I am, and could have been bony and awkward. But the school had taught her to move gracefully, and nature had endowed her with just enough flesh in all the right places to make her entrances into Regine's the highlight of any evening. If you looked closely at her face, you might have seen the emptiness there, the total void, the hunger that still hadn't been assuaged. But few people ever got past the eyes, the cheekbones, the pale flawless skin, the wide mouth that laughed and chattered and told the grossest kind of jokes with an air of perverse innocence lent her by her West Texas drawl. And, of course, she absolutely reeked of money.

Did I think of playing Pygmalion to her Galatea? There might have been something of that in my attraction to her. I did take her to museums where she sniggered at Matisse and laughed out loud in front of Picasso's Guernica. "I never saw no horse that looked like that," she said. At concerts she fell asleep, and plays bored her into fidgets and twitches unless they were simple-minded musicals that she could leave with a song or two tinkling around inside her skull. What, then, did she like about New York? Because like it she did. "I purely love this town," she often said.

Well, for one thing, she could, and did, spend more money faster on everything from worthless junk to priceless antiques than she could do in the whole of Texas including Neiman-Marcus. She made a weekly pilgrimage to Cartier's the way ordinary mortals go to the A & P. Gucci's, Saks, Bergdorf's, and a host of snobby little boutiques in between grew to know and love her. She went slumming in Bloomingdale's. When I cautioned her about overspending and tried to lecture her on the wisdom of making sound investments, she quickly put me in my place.

"Don't you fret your li'l ol' head about that, honey. My lawyers take care of all that boring stuff."

And they did. Two of them flew up regularly from Texas, stiff men with bulging briefcases who out-Brooks-Brothered anything seen on Madison Avenue. They didn't like me, and I'm sure that behind closed doors they advised Bootsie to turf me out. By that time I was more or less permanently installed in the hotel suite, although I still kept my tiny one-room walkup in case this one went the way of my not-so-sound investments and the rather large sum of money left me by my dear deceased maternal relative.

And what, you might well ask, did fun-loving Bootsie see in me? I often asked myself whether, in her eyes, I fell into the category of worthless junk or priceless antique. I admit that she was the answer to an aging playboy's prayer. I bear a distinguished name, but the wealth that had made that name a household word had long since vanished. I am handsome, a claim I make with all due modesty, in a civilized kind of way quite different from the rawboned cowboys she must have known back home. No great thinker, but I did offer her a smattering of culture which awed her even as she resisted and mocked. Or was it simply that out of all the men who pursued her, I was the only one who was old enough to be her father?

Whatever the attraction, it was there and real enough for her one day to say to me, while we were sitting around the hotel suite trying to decide what to do for the evening, "Hey, why don't we get married?" Bootsie was like that. Spur of the moment, and if it seemed like a good idea, we did it. It seemed like a good idea to me.

"Why, indeed, not?" said I, with visions of sugar plums liberally coated with dollar signs dancing in my head.

The wedding took place just as soon as Bootsie had time to go shopping for a whole new wardrobe, and we gave a party that became as legendary as Truman Capote's Black and White Ball. Just three hundred of our closest friends. When the dust settled and we were about to gather up our luggage and Bruce and Josefa for an extended European honeymoon tour, I got the biggest shock of my life. I was looking forward to doing Europe in style. It had been a long time since I had stayed at the Ritz or basked on a Riveria beach. I had promised Bootsie all the great museums and cathedrals; I could almost taste the fabulous food and wine.

She mooched into the hotel suite, scowled at her matched set of Louis Vuitton luggage, kicked the nearest piece, and said, "Get on the phone, honey, and cancel the trip."

"But the reservations are all made," I protested. "The whole tour is planned."

"Who wants to go to boring old Europe?" she said. She pronounced it "Yerp."

She called Josefa out of the tiny room where she spent hours watching soap operas in Spanish and told her to start unpacking.

"What's wrong?" I asked. "If you're tired we can postpone the trip a few days."

"I ain't tired." She pronounced it "tard." The West Texas drawl was beginning to grate on my nerves. I was prepared to overlook certain things in exchange for certain other things, and she was reneging on her side of the bargain. She frowned as if puzzling over a vexing problem in higher math. "It just seems to me that we'd be spending an awful lot of my money to go round seein' a bunch of places that I don't want to see in the first place."

I can't tell you how ominous that sounded to me. And it was merely a foretaste of things to come. I got on the phone and called the travel agent.

The next day the lawyers appeared. I had thought that now, as Bootsie's husband, I would be privileged to sit in on their deliberations, but such was not the case. They invited me to take myself off while they conducted Bootsie's business. Their briefcases seemed exceedingly well stuffed this time. Bootsie merely shrugged and turned her blue eyes helplessly upward. Bootsie was about as helpless as a Sherman tank. I went to the movies.

When I got back, the lawyers had departed and Bootsie was looking thoughtful. That in itself should have warned me, but I was determined to be my usual carefree self.

"Well, my dear," I said, "where shall we dine tonight? Le Veau D'Or? Lutece? Or perhaps a simple meal from room service?"

"I sent Joe out for some Big Macs." She gazed at me, all bright blue enthusiasm. "You were so right, honey. I've been spending way too much. From here on in we're going to economize."

I managed to swallow that one without gagging, but felt entitled to a question or two. "We're . . . you're not broke, are you, my dear?"

She laughed. "Shoot, no! There's still plenty in the old kitty. But I'm a married lady now, and I got to think about the future. I want there to be something left over at the end of the trail."

A horrid suspicion crossed my mind. I was not temperamentally suited to fatherhood nor, although we had never discussed it, did I think that Bootsie was attuned to the patter of tiny feet. But the possibility existed and would account for her strange behavior. There was nothing to do but ask.

"Bootsie, are you, by any chance, pregnant?"

Again she laughed. "Naw. When I get ready to breed, I'll let you know right off. But I do have a little surprise for you. Them lawyers are pretty smart fellows, and they know people all over the place. They been worrying about you, and now that we're married, they feel like they have to look out for you. They found a job for you. Ain't that nice?"

"A job?" I repeated stupidly. "But, Bootsie, dearest, I've never worked at a job. I wouldn't have the foggiest idea what to do."

She came to me then, cuddling into my arms like a little girl and fixing me with her bright blue innocent stare. "That's all right. You'll figger it out. And you'll be making enough money so's I won't have to give you an allowance any more. Think what a saving that'll be. But you won't have to start until we move."

"Move!"

"Oh, yes. Do you realize what this hotel is costing me? I'm going to start looking for an apartment tomorrow. They say that rents are very cheap in Queens."

"Queens!" I was reduced to monosyllables. Marriage had turned my spendthrift Bootsie into a miser. Queens, indeed! I wondered if those smart lawyers could arrange an instant annulment of the marriage, but her next words started me thinking in another direction.

"There's one more thing. They didn't want me to tell you this but you're in it, so I told them you had a right to know. I made my will. It felt real creepy to think about dying, but they said I ought to do it. So I did."

I stroked her silky head and told her not to talk about it if it disturbed her. I told her that the lawyers were absolutely right in advising her to make the will, but that now she should just forget all about it and we'd live a long happy life together.

Tears of happiness rose in her blue eyes, and she kissed me while I pondered how and how soon I could arrange to benefit from her arrangements.

Josefa came in carrying a large white sack reeking of onions and greasy meat. Bruce bounded at her heels, as excited by the smell as I was repelled by it. I excused myself from the feast on the grounds of a slight headache and I went to lie down with my thoughts. As I closed the bedroom door, I heard Bootsie say, "I purely love Big Mac's, don't you, Joe?"

I managed to dissuade Bootsie from her plan of settling in Queens by appealing to her newfound parsimony. Every place we looked at involved a double fare, both bus and subway, for me to get to work. Oh, yes. I had decided to go along with the destiny her lawyers had mapped out for me. For the time being. We found a gloomy apartment on the Upper West Side, in what the corner newsstand proprietor assured me was a high-crime district. Josefa was delighted. At the hotel she could only communicate with the occasional Puerto Rican bellhop. Here, she chattered for hours with neighbors and shopkeepers, and even invited some of her new friends in for coffee. I didn't object, although I might have, on the grounds that some of them might have relatives adept in the arcane art of breaking and entering.

Bootsie loved the role she was playing. Happy little house-wife with a husband who went off every morning on the subway and returned every evening to a meal that she had prepared with her own hands. Her cooking was dreadful, but I pretended to enjoy it. I encouraged her to take Bruce for long walks in Central Park, both day and night. I told her she'd never be a true New Yorker until she learned to ignore traffic lights and dodge her way across streets in defiance of the speeding taxis and lumbering buses.

I pooh-poohed her concern that the building had no doorman and the elevator was a self-service one. And I told her that the roof was the ideal place for sunbathing. But while all around her, people were being mugged, knifed, shot, strangled in lonely elevators, run over by berserk drivers, pushed off roofs, and otherwise disposed of, Bootsie remained unscathed. I realized that if I expected to benefit from Bootsie's will, I would have to take a more active role. It was not enough to place her in jeopardy and then wait for the action to start.

In the meantime Bootsie's greatest happiness was the receipt of her monthly statement of account. She loved to watch her nest egg grow. She had sold off all her jewelry, returned as many of her expensive clothes as she could and peddled the rest to friends, got rid of the priceless antiques and the worthless junk at a handsome profit, and handed every cent over to the lawyers to reinvest. We lived off her income, but only a small portion of it, and she was constantly looking for new ways to cut corners.

She stopped going to the hairdresser and her dark roots began to show. Her face and body grew pudgy from the starchy meals she prepared. Pinto beans appeared three or four times a week. And the hunger in her blue, blue eyes grew ever more intense and frightening. If I'd had any sense at all, I would have left her then. But there was always the will, the will and the growing nest egg that was achieving the dimensions of something deposited by a dinosaur.

The job that Bootsie's lawyers had found for me was with a brokerage firm in Wall Street. Although I had frittered away some youthful years at Harvard achieving a gentleman's C and so could be considered one of the tribe, I was nothing more in the eyes of the firm than a glorified messenger boy. This suited me fine. While all around me serious younger men pondered portfolios and munched Mylanta tablets, I carred my Mark Cross attaché case (a gift from Bootsie before true parsimony set in) around the city and was reasonably happy in my work. My taxi fares went on the expense account and I had lots of free time.

Free time in which to brood. There had to be some way of dispatching Bootsie and coming into my inheritance. I could poison the pinto beans, but poison, I believed, was easily traced and I would surely be viewed as the most likely Borgia. It had to look like an accident or like one of the many wanton senseless murders that occurred with alarming regularity in our beloved town.

I thought about hiring a dispatcher—one of the small army of gun-toting desperados that the newspapers claimed infested our streets—but how to find one whom I could trust, one who would trust me and do the job on credit until Bootsie's will gave me the resources to pay for her demise? I even considered recruiting Josefa, whose maledictions those days had reached new heights and were conducted in a rapid screeching Spanglish, Josefa having taken the trouble of learning a few pungent items of New York street talk. The burden of Josefa's harangues seemed to be that Bootsie was stingy (agreed), that Bootsie was fat and lazy (becoming more true every day), and that she, Josefa, was homesick and wanted to return to West Texas if only Bootsie would give her the airfare.

Bootsie wouldn't. The terms of Josefa's employment, as far as I could gather, resembled indentured servitude. She received no salary. When times were good and Bootsie was spending freely, Josefa enjoyed the high life and only fulminated to keep in practise. But now that Bootsie was scrimping on everything, even Bruce's dog food, Josefa's curses achieved a kind of desperate poignancy. She might make a good ally.

As a kind of insurance I began smuggling in tidbits for Bruce. Bootsie had cut him off from meat entirely, doling out small portions of a substance that looked like wood chips and smelled like burnt rubber. Bruce grew thin and despondent, and developed a bad case of dandruff. The first time I brought him a snack, half a Sabrett's hot dog with onion sauce, he rewarded me with a limp thud of his tail and a grateful, if weak, bark. After that, I always had something in my attaché case for him when I got home from work, and soon he was my devoted friend. I doubted if I could convince him to rend Bootsie limb from limb, but at least he might not interfere if I had to do a little rending myself.

But still, the appropriate means eluded me and the frugal days stretched into penurious months. I thought often of Bootsie's beautiful money gathering mold and interest when it could be the comfort and solace of my declining years. Something would have to be done. When, on an October evening, I came home to find that she had replaced all the light bulbs with low-wattage numbers which she had no doubt stolen from the subway station, I knew the time had come.

Bruce bounded at me out of the gloom of the shabby flat and I slipped him a chunk of liverwurst that I'd bought at a deli on my way home. Josefa was in the kitchen, stirring the eternal pinto beans and singing dolefully of *amor desleal.*

"Where's Bootsie?" I asked her.

"Gong hout," she told me, adding, "I hope she fall en el río and drowng."

Stifling an urge to shout "Me, too," I reprimanded Josefa for her disloyal sentiments and opened the kitchen window to let out the thick aroma of the beans. The thick aroma of the garbage tossed into the airshaft by our neighbors came in, but I left the window open anyway. By craning outward and upward I could see the purple sky over Manhattan and the hazy reflection of the bright lights that should by rights be mine. I sat on the window sill and dreamed of all the gastronomic delights that were being served reverently by attentive waiters all over town, while a sullen Josefa clunked clumsy crockery onto the rickety table covered with a crumb-laden plastic cloth where we now took our meals. It was too much to be borne.

Bootsie came in while my mind's eye was combing the menu at Le Perigord. She carried a heavy sack which she thumped down onto the drainboard and then came over to me.

"Hi, honey," she cawed, "I just figgered out another way to cut down on our expenses." Beaming with pride, she flung a heavy arm across my shoulder. Her coat gave off the fusty fug of second-hand shops. "You know that vegetable market down the block? Well, they let me pick over all the stuff they were going to throw away. For free."

"Rotten apples?" I protested.

"Just a few spots. Josefa can make applesauce."

Behind her back Josefa made obscene gestures and mouthed indignities.

"And another thing," she rambled on "now that we're living so cheap, it's about time we started living on *your* salary. That way, we can save all *my* money so we'll be in really good shape at the end of the trail."

She bent to kiss me. All I did was flinch. There was something so repellent to me in her greedy blue eyes, her lips which had not seen lipstick these many months, her lank brown hair that smelled of cheap laundry soap, that I couldn't help myself. Where was the slender, sweetly perfumed, exquisitely made-up blonde girl whose money I had fallen in love with less than a year ago? As I say, I flinched, and in so doing overbalanced and felt myself slipping off the window sill on the wrong side of the window. I grabbed. It was only natural. And the nearest thing to grab for was Bootsie's arm. There was some thrashing about. I can't describe it; I was in the midst of it. But when it was over, I was sprawled on the kitchen floor and Bootsie was nowhere in sight.

Until I looked out the window.

"Ooong!" came Josefa's voice over my shoulder, "She gong! You killing her!"

Indeed. She seemed quite dead, lying there among the dented beer cans and defunct perambulators at the bottom of the airshaft. But I would have to make sure before I could allow my fledgling hopes to take flight. Bruce came to the window and whined. I turned to Josefa. "It was an accident. You are a witness to that."

"Sí, sí. Han haccident. La pobrecita. You fight her. She fall hout."

"No. I was falling and she tried to save me. You saw it happen."

She smiled, a dreadful knowing gap-toothed grin. "Oh, sí. I saw. You want to heat now?" She began spooning beans into two of the three bowls.

"God, no! I have to call the police."

She shrugged and sat down at the table. There was no telephone in the apartment—Bootsie had declined to bear the expense—so I had to go down to the corner bodega where the public telephone was strategically positioned adjacent to the crates of dried codfish. I dialed 911 and waited. Nothing. I tried again. Still nothing, not even a crackle on the line to show a sign of life.

"The phone is dead," I said to the shopkeeper, a thin young man standing importantly behind a counter crowded with candy bars, shoelaces, and gum.

"Yess," he said, "two, three months now they don't come to fix him. They say too much breaking the phone, taking the money, no more phone. What can I do? People around here don't have so much phones in the house. They come here to make phone call, buy a beer, buy a soda. buy some candy for the babies. Good for business, no? Now the phone don't work, they don't come. I'm only trying to make a living. Would I break the phone? I got a special on bananas today. Ten cents a pound. Take some home to your kids.''

I looked at the special bananas, Bootsie would have loved them, soft and brown-spotted, lying dispiritedly in a cardboard box.

"No, thanks. I need to call the police. My wife is dead."

"¡Ay, Dios!" The young man quickly turned his attention to important business at the back of the store. I could have walked off with all his shoelaces and overripe bananas.

"Where can I find a phone?" I called after him.

He reappeared from behind a stack of six-packs, making shooing motions with his hands. "Closing up now. Go away, please. No phone here."

Back on the street I wondered which way to turn to make my call. The idea of Bootsie dead was still so new to me I needed official confirmation to make it real. And I needed to make sure that the call came from me, establishing her death as an accident. Well, it *was* an accident. Even though I'd been thinking about ways to kill Bootsie, I hadn't thought about this way. It just happened. If it hadn't been Bootsie at the bottom of the airshaft, it would have been me. Not that there'd been any kind of struggle—me trying to push her out, or her trying to push me out—oh, no, officer, just a sad case of a loving wife trying to help a loving husband, and the whole thing ending in tragedy. I put on my tragic face and glanced back up the block.

A squad car was just pulling up in front of the building and Josefa came rushing out to meet it.

I ran. It would never do to let Josefa have the first word. Her command of English was imperfect and she might give the wrong impression.

She saw me coming and screeched, "¡Asesino!"

I peered into the police car. Two faces peered back at me, one black and one unmistakably Irish. With any luck their command of Spanish was imperfect and they wouldn't understand that Josefa had called me a murderer. I grabbed Josefa and clutched her head consolingly to my shoulder. "There, there," I murmured, "everything will be all right. Just shut your mouth and I'll cut you in on the will."

"The will? Ah, el testamento!" Her words were a breathy whisper flavored with pinto beans and onions. "She leave it all

to me, you go to jail, you no make trouble. Mi abogado me lo
ha dicho.''

"Well, your lawyer was wrong." Canny Josefa. Obviously
she had gained the impression that she benefited from Bootsie's
will, and she wanted to make sure that I would be in no position
to contest it. Some ally! I'd have to set her straight, and
quickly. "Bootsie made a will when we got married," I
whispered into her oiled black hair. "She left all her money to
me. She told me so. Behave yourself and I'll take care of you."

Black eyes squinted up at me. "¿Verdad?"

"I swear."

After a flood of Spanish invective Josefa nodded and said,
"Hokay." Then she turned on the waterworks.

The two policemen had by this time gotten out of the car and
come over to see what the trouble was.

"We got a call about a body at the bottom of an airshaft at this
address?"

I glanced at Josefa. She nodded. "I use the telephone of el
super." She cried some more.

"My wife," I told them. "It's terrible. She fell out the
window. Right before my eyes. There was nothing I could
do."

Josefa howled agreement.

We trooped through the building and out the back door. I saw
the round pale face of the super staring at us from the grimy
window of his basement apartment. From other windows surrounding the airshaft other faces stared down. The night was
very quiet and no one threw any garbage. After a while an
ambulance came and took Bootsie away.

When it was all over, after all the questions had been asked
and poor Bootsie's remains had been shipped back to West
Texas for burial next to those of her sorrowful mother and her
high-flying daddy, the lawyers came to town. Josefa and I were
summoned to their hotel suite for the reading of the will. The
suite reminded me poignantly of my early days with Bootsie,
days that I would be able to relive, alas, without her at my side.

The lawyers' first words were ominous.

"This is a very odd will," said one.

"Odd, but quite legal," said the other.

"Get on with it," I snapped. If they wanted to continue to

administer the estate, they had better get used to treating me as their employer and learn to show respect.

"Well," said Lawyer One, he of the round gold-rimmed spectacles and thinning hair, "she left everything to Bruce."

"Bruce!" My voice, I'm embarrassed to say, emerged in a squeak. "That's impossible! You can't leave money to a dog!"

"Well, you can," said Lawyer Two, long-faced and mournful. "You can and she did. But don't worry. You're both taken care of."

Josefa tugged at my sleeve. "¿Que dice?" she demanded, her dark eyes showing signs of an approaching storm.

"Relax," I told her, and settled back to hear the news.

Lawyer One bent his gold-rimmed spectacles to the blue-backed document and spouted about ten minutes of legalese. For another ten minutes Lawyer Two translated. What it boiled down to was this. Bootsie's fortune, and it was considerable, belonged to Bruce, for his lifetime. Josefa and I were appointed his guardians. We were charged with responsibility for his health and well-being. We were to buy him a ranch in West Texas and anything else his doggy heart desired.

We were to live on the ranch with him, keep him company, find him a suitable lady dog to share his bliss, and in general make his life a canine heaven on earth.

My agile mind instantly perceived that Bruce would require a Rolls-Royce for trips to the vet, a swimming pool to cool off in on hot West Texas afternoons, a tennis court on which to chase balls and a nine-hole golf course in which to bury bones, not to mention a bevy of nubile serving wenches to curry his coat and stuff him with dog biscuits.

If, by chance, Bruce predeceased his guardians, the money was to go to create the Bootsie and Bruce Foundation for Indigent Wildcatters. If either Josefa or I died before Bruce did, the surviving guardian was to have total control of the estate, subject to the advice of Goldrims and Longface. And if we both kicked off before the mutt, the legal beagles took charge.

I looked at Josefa. She looked back murderous questions.

"How old is Bruce?" I asked her.

She shrugged incomprehension.

"¿Cuantos años tiene Bruce?" Out of necessity, I'd picked

up a smattering of her lingo. She understood more than she let on and liked to pretend ignorance when it suited her.

"Dos, tres años. Yo no sé," she replied, followed by a muttered stream of abuse a la Zapata.

I nodded my agreement to the lawyers. A two- or three-year-old dog has another ten or twelve years in him. Contesting the will would take up precious time, during which I would be forced to work. Although Bruce was presently enfeebled by city life and poor diet, I would soon get him back in peak condition in the salubrious air of West Texas. And somehow, during his lifetime, I would figure out some way of gaining full control of Bootsie's money, or die trying. It was worth a period of exile.

The ranch is huge, acre upon acre of sagebrush and saguero, and the ranch house sprawls like an adobe version of Buckingham Palace. Josefa lives in her wing, surrounded by freeloading relatives. I live in mine, solaced by a rotating troop of imported beauties that make the Dallas Cowgirls look like bovine battleaxes. Ever since Josefa sent over her cousin Elizondo and his machete (I bear an interesting scar; Elizondo bears a chastened look at the imprint of my teeth on the remains of his left ear), my wing has been guarded by day and night Pinkertons. Josefa, unaccountably, believes I have attempted to poison her pinto beans and has posted platoons of grinning cousins in the kitchen and outside her quarters.

Bruce lives in oriental splendor in luxurious kennels out back. His every desire is satisfied. He is attended by emissaries of both camps, nymphs and cabelleros. Occasionally Josefa and I meet on neutral ground in Bruce's domain, when we both thoughtfully examine his muzzle for the first telltale sign of gray hairs, his joints for arthritis, and his fine brown eyes for the clouding over of cataracts. The years are going by.

It's a dog's life.

Edward D. Hoch

A full-time writer since 1968, Ed Hoch is certainly one of the two or three most prolific writers in the United States, with at least 600 stories in the mystery genre. He is best known for four series detectives: Rand, a British cipher expert; Nick Velvet; a most original thief, Simon Ark, a mystical detective and Captain Leopold, perhaps the best-known of his creations. Mr. Hoch is a winner of the Mystery Writers of America's highest award, The Edgar.

CAPTAIN LEOPOLD GOES TO THE DOGS

BY EDWARD D. HOCH

Eddie Sargasso was a gambler.

In his younger days he'd been known to bet on everything from the fall of a card to the virtue of a woman. Now that he'd passed 40 he was more likely to limit his wagers to recognized sporting events and games of chance, but he was still always on the lookout for an angle. He'd been in on the recent jai alai fixes until a grand-jury investigation broke the scandal wide open. Now it was greyhound racing which took his fancy.

Eddie Sargasso was fortunate to live in one of the few northeastern states where dog racing was legal. If he'd resided elsewhere it wouldn't have stopped him from betting, but it would have kept him from arranging to meet Aaron Flake—by convenient accident—in the Sportsman's Lounge one Sunday evening in July.

Flake was a little man with thin blond hair and glasses that were too big for his face. He was sitting alone at the bar, nursing a gin and tonic, when Eddie slipped onto the stool next to him. "Hey, aren't you Aaron Flake, the guy from the dog track?"

The man smiled thinly. "I'm a licensed hare controller, if that's what you mean. You may have seen me at the track."

"Damn right," Eddie said, building it up. "You were pointed out to me as knowing more about greyhound racing than anyone in the state."

"After working at something for sixteen years I suppose it's natural that you learn some facts about it."

Eddie Sargasso whistled. "Sixteen years! It hasn't even been legal that long, has it?"

"I worked the Florida tracks before I came north. New En-

161

gland was a whole new territory for me and I figured to get in on the ground floor.''

''You got a family here?''

Aaron Flake shook his head and took another sip of his drink. ''Wife and kids stayed in Florida. They liked the sun. I'm divorced now.''

''I do a little betting on the dogs,'' Eddie admitted.

''That's what we race 'em for.''

''I like them better than horses because they're harder to fix, you know? You bet on a greyhound and you know it's going to be a good honest race.''

''Well, there are ways of fixing them. Tampering with the dogs. I read a story once about dog racing in England and they had a dozen ways of making the dogs run faster, or slower, or whatever they wanted. We check 'em pretty careful over here, though.''

Eddie signaled the bartender for two more drinks, and Flake offered no objection. It was a Sunday, after all, and he didn't have to work again till Monday night. ''You control the mechanical rabbit, don't you?'' Eddie asked, pretending an ignorance of the sport's basics. ''How does that work?''

''I usually call it an artificial hare rather than a mechanical rabbit. There's nothing mechanical about it, really. It's a stuffed animal strapped to a device that moves around the track. It's powered by an electric motor and my job is to maintain just the correct speed for the hare. If it's too slow the lead dog might catch it, and if it's too fast and gets too far ahead of the dogs they lose interest. Judges have been known to declare a no-race if that happens.''

''How many dogs are there?''

''We race eight at a time in this state. Some places race nine.''

''You can keep them all in view during the race?''

''Sure, it's not hard. I'm in a little booth overlooking the track.''

''Which post position is best?''

''Number eight trap is on the outside of the oval, nearest the hare. That dog has to run a few more feet than the number one dog on the inside—but it's not enough to speak of. They usually bunch together after the start anyway. I wait till the hare's about twelve yards in front before I open the traps, and I try to maintain that distance. We have an electric-eye camera at the finish line to record the winner.''

"Sure sounds exciting. I've only been a couple of times, but I think I'll drive out again tomorrow night.''

Aaron Flake finished his drink. "You'll enjoy it,'' he said, sliding off the barstool. "See you around.''

Flake had left suddenly but that didn't bother Eddie Sargasso too much. At least he'd made contact, and with any luck he'd fare better than Marie did. Eddie and his wife lived in an expensive colonial house at the edge of the city, not far from the dog track, and driving home that evening he went over the possibilities in his mind. Somehow he needed an edge on the race fixing so he could get his cut of it and still avoid problems with the law. He had a lengthy arrest record over the years, and he knew there were some cops in the city just waiting for a misstep to nail him.

"How'd you make out?'' Marie asked as he entered the family room where she was watching television.

"Pretty good for the first meeting. If anyone knows when the fix is on it must be Flake. Watching the races that carefully every night he has to see something.''

"I hope you do better than me. I couldn't get to first base with him. He never even phoned me!''

He bent over and kissed her. "Don't let it bother you. I guess he doesn't go much for the ladies. I thought you could talk to him about Florida but it didn't work out.''

"Are we going to the track tomorrow night?''

"Sure. I told him I'd probably be there. We can use the old system till we latch onto something better.''

Monday was a warm night and that brought out a good crowd. Marie wore her white pants suit and Eddie had on his lucky brown jacket. He studied the dogs through binoculars, watching them break from their numbered traps to pursue the motorized rabbit.

After the third race he ran into Donald Wayne of the state betting commission. "Eddie! They haven't barred you from the track yet, I see.''

"Come on, Donald. I'm a solid citizen.''

"Sure, I know. Do you still make bets on things like whether the next girl into a bar will be wearing slacks or a skirt?"

"That was in my younger days, and I lost too much money. Now I try to bet only on sure things."

"I know. That's why we hate to see you at the dog tracks. We've had enough trouble with jai alai in this state."

"Would you be suspicious of a poker game at my place on Friday night?"

"That's more like it! Close up, I can keep my eyes on you."

Eddie chuckled and patted him on the shoulder. "Make it eight o'clock. I'll see who else I can round up."

It had been more than a year since the weekly poker games with Wayne and a few others. Eddie stopped asking him when Wayne was appointed to the state betting commission, fearing it might somehow compromise his friend's position. But if Wayne didn't mind coming, why should Eddie?

He made a bet on the fourth race, buying his ticket from one of the totalizator operators in their distinctive dark red jackets. Then he stood for a time watching the odds change right up to post time. It was much like horse racing in that respect. There was always big money bet in the closing minute, and late changes to lower odds often indicated inside information on a winner. Often when Eddie saw that happening he sent Marie out to stand in line at one group of windows while he went to a different selling location. When the odds changed on the totalizator screen they'd each buy a $100 ticket on the horse whose odds showed a sudden last-minute drop.

He went back to his seat in time to see the greyhound wearing the bright blue racing jacket numbered six cross the finish line first. "There was last-minute betting on him," Eddie told his wife. "The smart boys are at it again."

"You want me to get in line for the next race?"

"I think so. Until we get more friendly with Mr. Flake that's the only move we've got." He passed her a $100 bill. "Watch the odds and be close enough so you can make a last-minute bet just before the machines lock."

"You don't have to tell me. I've done it a thousand times."

He watched her head for the downstairs bank of selling windows and he went back to the windows nearest their seats. As he stood watching the totalizator board, another familiar figure passed into his line of vision. It was Sam Barth, one of the track stewards. "Sam!" Eddie called out.

"How's it going? Where's your lovely wife?"

"Downstairs, Sam. How about a poker game Friday night? Donald's coming over."

"Wayne? That's great! I think I can make it, but not till I get out of here at eleven. That okay?"

"Fine. Come when you can, Sam."

He watched the slender man walk away, wondering vaguely if a track steward could be in on any fixing. Stranger things had happened.

He got into the shorter of the two lines then, hoping he was timing it right. "Hi, Eddie. How they running?"

He turned at the sound of the woman's voice and saw Joyce Train, a woman he'd known quite well in his younger days. "Joyce! Good to see you! How's the family?"

"Who knows?" She smiled and winked. "I'm back to work."

"You are? Since when?"

"The spring. I couldn't take being a housewife."

Eddie chewed at his lower lip. "I'll keep it in mind. I might have something for you."

"I'm at the old place if you need to reach me."

"Fine." She still had a great figure and she knew how to show it off, wearing a dark brown jumpsuit with some frills at the neck and cuffs. A few years ago she'd quit the call-girl business to get married, but hardly anyone had thought it would last. Apparently it hadn't.

Thinking about her, Eddie wondered if he might try introducing her to Aaron Flake.

The totalizator screen was changing. He memorized the current odds and watched them shift. Minor changes, mostly, at one minute to post time.

Except—

Dog number four dropped from eight-to-one to seven-to-two. That meant a big last-minute bet. He hoped Marie had caught it at the other windows.

"One hundred on number four," he told the ticket seller when he reached the window a few seconds later. He was just walking away when he heard the snap of the machines locking as the starter signaled the release of the hare. Then there was a roar from the crowd as the eight greyhounds burst from their numbered traps.

He made it back to his seat in time to see them rounding the first curve of the oval track. The dogs were closing in on the electric rabbit, and the lead one looked to be almost within striking distance. He'd never seen them that close before. Maybe Flake—

The dogs were onto the rabbit, straining at their muzzles and sending up growls of frustration. Instantly the steward and judges were on the track, signaling it was a no-race. The message flashed on the tote board that all bets were off.

Eddie Sargasso couldn't figure it out. He met Marie by the steps and she was as baffled as he was. "What happened?" she asked.

"I don't know, but it'll probably cost Flake his job. We'll have to start all over with someone else."

They pushed their way through the crowd of disgruntled spectators, watching the trainers and track officials trying to bring some order from the confusion on the track. The dogs were growling and fighting among themselves, separating only reluctantly as the trainers pulled them apart.

The control booth for the hare was some distance away, near the starting gate, and by the time Eddie and Marie reached it he saw Donald Wayne coming out. His face was white as Eddie asked him, "What in hell happened?"

Wayne stared at him blankly, then seemed to recognize him and said, "Murder—that's what! Somebody stabbed Aaron Flake!"

Captain Leopold was not a gambler.

He'd been to the dog track once in his life, with Lieutenant Fletcher and his wife shortly after it opened. That night he'd managed to lose $12, enough to convince him he was no luckier with dogs than with horses. Now, as he pulled up to the main entrance with Fletcher at his side and the siren wailing, he wondered if he'd be any luckier this night.

"We should have gone home early," Fletcher decided, looking at the crowd of people. "Let the night shift handle it."

"Come on. Maybe it's an easy one—some drunk who's waiting to confess."

"Sure, Captain." Fletcher liked to use the title when he was being sarcastic. Most of the time they were good friends, and Leopold had been out to dinner at Fletcher's house twice so far during the summer. With Connie Trent away on vacation they'd been spending more hours together in the office too.

"This way, Captain," a voice called to him as they entered the stands. Leopold recognized Sam Barth, one of the track stewards whom he knew slightly. Barth stood at the top of a short flight of steps, wearing a dark red blazer like all the track personnel.

"What happened here?" Leopold asked. "The report said a homicide."

"That's it. Our hare operator, Aaron Flake, was stabbed in the back. It happened right during the race, and the dogs caught up with the hare!" That seemed to bother him more than the murder.

"All right, show us the way."

Leopold and Fletcher followed him to a little wooden booth overlooking the dog track. A husky man in a rumpled brown suit was there to greet them. "This is Donald Wayne of the state betting commission. He found the body," Barth said.

Leopold shook hands with Wayne and waited while the man opened the door of the control booth. Then he took a deep breath. The man they identified as Aaron Flake was slumped over in his chair, head down on the desk in front of him. Something—Leopold saw it was the evening's racing program—was pinned to his back with a bone-handled hunting knife.

"All right, Fletcher, get the photographer and the lab boys up here." Leopold glanced at the desk on which the body was slumped, and saw another racing program, an ashtray with one cigarette butt, some pencils, and a blank pad of paper. A pair of binoculars was mounted on a stand in front of the dead man's head.

He turned and looked at the door of the booth, observing a simple hook-and-eye latch. "Did he keep this door latched?"

Donald Wayne nodded. "It's something of an art, keeping that hare just the right distance ahead of the dogs. Flake didn't want anyone walking in during a race and ruining his concentration, so he kept the latch on. The door was unlocked when I found him, though."

"So he admitted his killer. It was someone he knew."

"Looks like it," Wayne agreed. "But that doesn't limit it very much. We have over fifty track employees, plus the owners and trainers of each dog. There are stewards, judges, a starter, a timekeeper, even a veterinary surgeon. Flake knew them all. Plus he might have admitted any one of the spectators that he knew."

"Make up a list of track employees for me," Leopold suggested. "And try to indicate where each one would have been during the race."

Sam Barth, the track steward, was standing outside the little booth. "I can probably do that better than Donald. I work with them. He was just a visitor tonight."

"How's that?" Leopold asked the stocky man.

"Well, I'm on the betting commission and I figure I should go around to the tracks once a week or so. We don't have thoroughbred racing in this state, but between the greyhounds and jai alai it keeps me busy."

"You were standing near this booth when it happened?"

"Not too far away," he told Leopold. "At first I couldn't believe my eyes! I've never seen the dogs catch the rabbit in all the years I've been coming here. It's something that just never happens! As soon as I realized something had gone wrong with Flake I hurried up here to the booth. But it was too late."

"Could you see the entrance from where you were standing?"

Barth shook his head. "You see the way these supporting girders stick out to hold the roof. There's a blind spot here so the door to the booth can't really be seen from the stands. Anyone could have entered without being seen."

While Fletcher made notes of the booth's measurements and other facts, and the medical examiner set about removing the knife from the wound, Leopold went down to the track with Sam Barth. "Never had anything like this happen, Captain. I still can't believe it!"

There was barking from a few frustrated dogs as Leopold walked along the edge of the track toward the kennels. One trainer was leading his muzzled greyhound for a trot around the exercise track. "Think we'll be able to finish the rest of the card, Sam?" he asked.

"Not a chance, Matt. They've scratched it all for tonight.

We'll try to get another hare controller up from Stamford for tomorrow's card.''

"No one seems to be mourning the dead man too much,'' Leopold observed.

"Aaron Flake was a loner. Stuck pretty much to himself. Behind his back they called him Flakey, of course. He probably had that all his life.''

"Was he married?''

"He told people he was divorced but it may not have been true. He came up from the Florida tracks when we started dog racing here. There was some sort of trouble at his last track, but the state investigated and decided he wasn't involved.''

"Trouble? Like fixed races?''

"No, something else. I don't know what.''

"Have there been any fixed races here?''

"I couldn't say, Captain.''

"All right,'' Leopold said. "I'll talk to you later.''

He'd ordered the gates closed shortly after his arrival, but of course the killer had had several minutes to make his escape before the Captain's arrival.

Leopold watched the progress of the lines without spotting any familiar faces, then went back to the booth where the medical examiner was just finishing. "What about the weapon?'' Leopold asked.

"Standard sort of hunting knife. You can buy them at any sporting goods or department store. Five-inch blade, about nine inches overall. Perfect for hiding in pocket or purse.''

"And the program skewered to the body?''

"Beats me! A message of some sort?'' He closed his bag and followed the stretcher out.

Fletcher came up the steps from the lower section. "I spotted an old friend of ours in the crowd.''

"Who's that?''

"Joyce Train. Used to be a call girl working out of the Harbor Motor Lodge. Remember?''

"How could I forget? She's back in the business, isn't she?''

"So I heard.''

"Let's go talk to her,'' Leopold decided.

They'd been given the use of Sam Barth's private office

under the grandstand for questioning, and Fletcher brought Joyce in there. "Hello, Joyce. Enjoying the races?"

"Leopold! So there's been a murder?"

He nodded. "Aaron Flake. Know him?"

"I know him by sight. He wasn't one of my customers, if that's what you mean."

"What can you tell us, Joyce?"

"Nothing. I was out here betting on the dogs like everyone else."

Fletcher perched himself on the edge of the desk. "In your line of work it's good to give the police tips once in a while."

"You're not the vice squad!"

"But they're right down the hall at headquarters. Come on, Joyce. Think hard and give us some information. Who had it in for Flake?"

"I don't know a thing, honest!"

Leopold tried a different approach. "You said he wasn't a customer and he didn't have a wife on the scene. Any chance he was homosexual?"

She shrugged. "Maybe. I saw him in bars with other men occasionally."

"How occasionally?"

"Last night."

"Who was the other man?"

She glanced away. "It was over at the Sportsman's Lounge. But it wasn't anything like that. This other guy's no queer."

"Suppose you let us decide that. Who was it?"

Joyce Train bit her lip and stalled for time. Leopold knew she would tell them the name, but she wanted to make it look like a difficult decision. "All right," she said finally. "It was Eddie Sargasso, the gambler."

"Sargasso!" Fletcher gave a low whistle. "Man, I'd like to hang something on him!"

"He's here tonight," Joyce added in a low voice.

"Here? At the track?"

She nodded. "You won't say it was me that told, will you?"

"Not unless we have to bring it out in court," Leopold promised. "He didn't see you at the Lounge last night?"

"No. I was in a booth with a—a friend."

"Thanks, Joyce. You've been a big help. We'll remember

it.'' He turned to Fletcher. "Let's go find Eddie Sargasso before he gets away.''

Eddie was standing in line with Marie, only three away from the officer taking down names and addresses of the personnel, when Leopold spotted him. He smiled and stuck out his hand. "Captain Leopold! This is a real pleasure!''

"Would you step into the office and have a word with us, Eddie? Your wife too?''

"And lose my place in line?'' he asked with a try at lightness.

"You won't have to wait in line,'' Leopold assured him.

Eddie and Marie followed Leopold into a little office under the grandstand. He knew it belonged to Sam Barth, and wondered where the steward was.

"Now what's on your mind, Captain?''

"The murder of Aaron Flake.''

"Terrible thing! Any idea who did it?''

"That's what we're working on. How well did you know him?''

The office door opened and Lieutenant Fletcher came in. That didn't surprise Eddie. He knew Leopold and Fletcher worked together. "Hardly at all,'' he answered. "I hardly knew him.''

"You were having a drink with him last night in the Sportsman's Lounge downtown.''

"Yeah? Hey, I guess that's right! Just happened to see him in there. That's the first time we ever talked, you know?''

"You're a gambler, Eddie, the sort who like to gamble on sure things. There've been some shady races run at this track lately. Not the sort of thing you'd want to gamble on unless you had inside information.''

"How do you fix a dog race?''

"That's what I'm asking you. Maybe you do it by bribing the hare operator.''

"Not a chance! You saw what happened if the hare isn't controlled just right. The dogs catch it, and there's no race. Those guys aren't licensed because they might be crooks. They're licensed because it takes a certain skill to run the hare at the proper distance from the dogs.''

"I don't need any instructions on dog racing,'' Leopold said. "Suppose you tell me what you and Flake talked about.''

"Nothing, I swear! Just barroom chat, that's all."

Leopold turned to Marie. "Were you with your husband at the time of the killing?"

She glanced sideways at Eddie and his heart skipped a beat. They were really out to hang this on him! If only Marie would say the right—

"Not the exact instant," Marie admitted, and his hopes died. "I came up from the lower ticket window just after the race was stopped."

"She was placing a last-minute bet for me," Eddie explained.

"And what were you doing?"

"I was placing a bet too." He knew it sounded foolish, so he explained. "Sometimes people with inside information wait till the last minute to place big bets, so it doesn't cause a run on a certain dog and lower the odds too much. I watch the tote board and if I see a drop in odds during the final minute before a race I usually put a hundred on the dog. The same thing holds with horses. It's just smart betting."

"It's smart betting if you suspect something crooked."

"Well, yeah."

"Why wasn't your wife with you?"

"Sometimes you figure the length of the line wrong and get shut out when the machines lock. I figured with Marie and me in separate lines, at least one of us would make it to the windows in time."

"Did anyone see you there?"

He remembered Joyce. "Girl I know—Joyce Train. I saw her in line just before the board changed."

"But she didn't see you after the race started?"

"Well, no. I was on my way back to our seats."

Fletcher picked that moment to lean across to Leopold and hand him something. It looked to Eddie like an address book. "This was in the dead man's pocket, Captain."

Leopold studied the entry Fletcher had indicated, then passed it along to Eddie. "What do you make of this?"

Marie S., it read, followed by a phone number. Eddie moistened his lips and said. "I don't know."

"Is that your number?"

"Yeah, I guess so."

He turned to Marie. "Mrs. Sargasso, do you have any explanation as to why the dead man had your name and phone number in his address book?''

''I—''

''Shut up, Marie!'' Eddie barked.

Leopold leaned forward. ''This is murder, Sargasso! And right now you're our prime suspect. You'd better let her talk.''

Marie looked at him. ''Eddie, we have to tell them what we know.''

''Yeah,'' he agreed reluctantly. ''I suppose so.''

''Eddie want me to meet Flake and strike up an acquaintance. He knew there was something crooked going on at the track and we figured he'd be a good one to know about it. We'd seen him drinking alone at the bars around town, and I gave it a try, but I didn't get anywhere. I told him my name was Marie Sullivan and he wrote it down, but he never called me.''

''How long ago was this?''

''Back in June, about a month ago.''

''So last night I tried it,'' Eddie said. ''I figured if he didn't like girls maybe I'd have better luck just chatting with him over a few drinks. But nothing came of it.''

''Something came of it,'' Leopold corrected him. ''Aaron Flake was murdered.''

''I don't know a thing about that.''

Suddenly Marie had a thought. ''Eddie, the tickets! We didn't cash them in yet. We've still got them!''

He saw at once what she was driving at. It just might be enough to save their skins. ''That's right! The lines were so long we decided to wait till tomorrow night to get our refunds for the canceled race. I've got my hundred-dollar ticket on number four, and you can check the totalizator records to see that the odds on number four took a big drop in the final minute before the race. That was our signal to buy. You got your ticket, Marie?''

She nodded and dug around in her purse, finally producing it. Leopold took the tickets and studied them. ''These were bought just before the race?''

''Less than a minute before. We didn't know which dog to bet on before that. And Flake was killed less than a minute into the race.''

''I'll agree with that,'' Leopold said. ''There's no way he

could have run that rabbit with the knife in his back. It killed him almost instantly.''

"Well there! I couldn't have gotten from the ticket window to that booth in anything like two minutes. It's impossible!''

Leopold frowned and said, "Time it, Fletcher.'' He glanced at Marie. "Where did you buy your tickets?''

"Downstairs.''

"Time it from where she was, too. And see if there's a ticket seller closer to Flake's booth.''

"Right, Captain.''

"Those are the only two grandstand banks of windows,'' Eddie said. "There's another in the clubhouse, but that's way down at the other end. Besides, this number on the ticket identifies the machine that sold it.''

Leopold nodded. "We'll see what Fletcher reports.''

Eddie used the few minutes for chatter about the track, and about gambling in general. "There was a time when I'd bet on anything, Captain.''

"Want to make a bet on whether I solve this case?''

"I might,'' Eddie answered carefully.

Fletcher came back shaking his head. "Looks like they're both in the clear, Captain. A fast walk from the upper windows to the booth took me two minutes and twenty-eight seconds. With the crowd here it would have been closer to three minutes. From downstairs where Marie bought her ticket it's even further— two minutes and forty-five seconds. They couldn't have bought these tickets and still gotten up to the booth in time to stab Flake.''

Leopold sighed. "All right, you can go now.''

Eddie got to his feet. "I'll lay two-to-one you don't crack this case, Captain.''

"I'm not a betting man.''

"That's too bad.''

After they'd gone Leopold and Fletcher went back to the kennel area, walking beneath the lights past row after row of barking dogs. "They're restless,'' he told Fletcher. "Unhappy, like me.''

"You still think Sargasso's guilty, don't you?''

"He's a two-bit gambler who never did an honest day's work

in his life. But we can't get a murder conviction on those grounds.''

Up ahead they saw the man from the betting commission and Leopold called to him. ''Mr. Wayne, do you have a minute?''

Donald Wayne turned and waited for them to catch up. ''Just talking to a few of the owners about what happened,'' he said.

''Do they have any information?''

''Nothing. No one can imagine Flake having an enemy. He was such a quiet guy.''

''How about friends? Did he have any of those?''

''Not many, according to Sam Barth. He knew Flake better than I did, certainly.''

''What's going on at this track?'' Leopold asked. ''They've been fixing races, haven't they?''

''What gives you that idea?''

''Eddie Sargasso told me a lot of money was being bet on certain dogs just before post time. And those dogs usually won.''

''I wish he'd make his accusations to me.''

''You a friend of Eddie's?''

Donald Wayne nodded. ''From the old days, before I was on the betting commission. We used to play poker together.''

''But not any more?''

''Matter of fact, he invited me over for a game on Friday night. Don't know if I'll be going now.''

''Who else was at these games?''

''Sam Barth, sometimes.''

''Mr. Wayne, if there was a fix in at this track, how could it be worked?''

''Oh, lots of ways. They run twelve races a night with eight dogs per race. That's nearly a hundred dogs each night. Of course most dogs race every evening, and travel a circuit through the three New England states that have dog tracks. The owners get to know one another. Sometimes they get to know each other so well that a group of them will get together and take turns winning. The other owners or trainers hold back their dogs by various methods and one man wins. Then it's someone else's turn.''

''Is that going on here?''

''To some extent.'' He spread his hands. ''To some extent it probably happens at race tracks—especially harness tracks—too. But that doesn't mean it led to Aaron Flake's death. He wouldn't have been a party to it.''

"Except that he's watching the race very carefully through binoculars, every foot of the way. He knows the way grey-hounds run, and he recognizes it when they're running different—either too fast or too slow. He could have been blackmailing somebody.''

"Yes, I suppose so. But who'd be foolish enough to kill him like that, in the middle of a race? A blackmail victim would more likely choose a dark street after the race, when there was less chance of discovery.''

"That's true," Leopold agreed. "It's almost as if the killer *had* to do it during the race.''

"And leave that program pinned to his back with the knife," Fletcher reminded them. "If you ask me it's some nut with a grudge against dog tracks.''

"Except that Flake unlatched the door for this person.''

"Couldn't the latch have been flipped from outside with a piece of plastic or a credit card?" Wayne suggested.

Fletcher shook his head. "I tried that. There's a strip of wood around the jamb that prevents it.''

Sam Barth came hurrying up from the direction of the grand-stand. "I've been looking for you, Captain. Here's that list of track personnel you requested. Any one of them could have gained admission to the booth.''

Leopold glanced at the typewritten sheets. "I think we can rule out the ticket sellers and gate personnel. And any security guards with fixed posts. Likewise the judges, the paddock steward, the starter, and the timekeeper. None of these people could have left their positions during the race. That still leaves stewards like yourself, plus most of the owners and trainers, the veterinarian, and others.''

"Plus Flake's friends.''

"Yes, if he had any." Leopold was staring up at the grand-stand, where the lights were beginning to go out.

"What are you thinking, Captain?" Fletcher asked.

"I'm thinking we should come back here tomorrow night.''

Leopold spent much of the following day on the phone to the

Florida police. When he'd finished, he thought he had the beginnings of an idea.

"Look here, Fletcher—Aaron Flake once worked at a dog track in Miami where an owner was knifed to death in his trailer."

"The same sort of weapon."

"Exactly. It's just possible that Flake was a blackmailer after all—but blackmailing a murderer instead of a race fixer."

"That still doesn't tell us who did it."

"Were there any fingerprints on the knife or the program?"

Fletcher shook his head. "Wiped clean."

"Blackmail or not, the killer still risked a great deal stabbing Flake during the race, when he knew people would rush to the booth to see what was wrong."

Fletcher brought in two cups of coffee from the temperamental machine in the hall. "Any chance the lever controlling the rabbit could have been turned on automatically, after the killer left the booth?"

"None at all. The starter signaled Flake to release the rabbit. He had to be alive then, even if the killer was standing right behind him in the booth."

Fletcher set the coffee cup on a square piece of cardboard that Leopold used as a coaster. Leopold stared at it in silence for a moment and then said, "You did that to protect the desk, in case the coffee spilled."

"What?"

"Just thinking out loud, Fletcher. I've got an idea who killed Aaron Flake, and I know how we can prove it at the track tonight."

News of the murder had obviously not hurt the dog track's business. By the time Leopold and Fletcher arrived, shortly after the gates opened, lines of people were pouring in.

"Curiosity seekers," Sam Barth said, standing in his red jacket just inside the entrance. "By next week they'll be onto something else."

"Have you seen Eddie Sargasso yet?" Leopold asked.

"Not yet, but he'll be here."

Leopold sent Fletcher to cover the lower-level ticket windows while he took the upstairs ones himself. Sargasso hadn't gone to the clubhouse the previous night, so he probably wouldn't go there tonight. It was just a matter of waiting.

"Looking for killers?" someone asked. It was Joyce Train, with a man the Captain didn't know.

"That's right," Leopold said. "I read somewhere they always return to the scene of the crime."

He chatted with her a moment and then glanced back at the lines. Eddie Sargasso was there, with his wife right behind him. Leopold hurried over, edging through the thickening crowd.

"Hello, Captain," Eddie said. "Break the case yet?"

"Just about."

Eddie reached the window and pushed a ticket through. "We're cashing in our tickets on the canceled race last night," he explained.

"I know," Leopold said.

Eddie took his $100 and stepped aside. Then, acting as fast as he could, Leopold's hand shot out to grip Marie Sargasso's wrist. "Not so fast, Marie. I want to see that."

Eddie made a move toward Leopold. "What in hell are you doing?"

"You may not know it, Eddie, but it was your wife who murdered Aaron Flake, and the proof of it is here in her hand."

"You're crazy!" Sargasso growled. "Marie, tell him he's crazy!"

But the life seemed to have gone out of her. "It's true, Eddie," she said simply. "I killed him."

Later, in Sam Barth's office under the grandstand, Leopold explained. "These tickets were the key to it," he said, fanning eight tickets on the previous night's race across the desk. "Marie's alibi, like her husband's, rested on the fact that she was in line, waiting for the odds to change so she could make a last-minute bet on a certain dog. And sure enough, she and Eddie each produced a ticket on the number four entry. Fletcher timed it and verified they couldn't have bought the tickets and still reached the booth in time to stab Flake."

"So how'd she do it?" Barth asked.

"Simply by purchasing one ticket on each of the eight dogs in the race, as soon as she went downstairs. This gave her time to reach the booth and kill Flake, and still hold a hundred-dollar ticket on whichever dog showed that last-minute odds change. Sure, it cost her eight hundred dollars, but she knew better than anyone else the race would never be completed. She knew she could get her money back on the tickets last night or today. I heard Eddie say they'd do it today because the lines were too long last night. Of course Eddie had no idea his wife was guilty. That was the main reason for her elaborate scheme. Most other people might have killed Flake in an alley, but Marie had to do it in such a way that she'd have a perfect alibi—not only for the police but for her husband!''

"But why did she kill him?" Sam Barth asked.

"We're digging into that. We think Marie killed a man at a Florida dog track years ago and got away with it. Eddie sent her to make Flake's acquaintance as part of their scheme to get inside dope on the fixed races. Flake recognized her from Florida and had some sort of knowledge connecting her with the prior killing. When he tried to blackmail her, she decided to kill him. She knew Eddie usually sent her to buy a last-minute ticket on the races, and she used that as her alibi. She went to the booth, pretending she had a blackmail payment for Flake, and he let her in. While his back was turned controlling the hare, she took the knife from her purse and stabbed him.''

"Through the program?" Fletcher asked.

"I saw that coaster under my coffee cup today and I got the idea, Fletcher. The knife blade was sticking through the program when she stabbed him, so it would act as a shield against possible bloodstains. That was the only likely explanation.

"So what did we know? The killer was someone Flake knew—either as a co-worker or an acquaintance. The killer found it necessary to murder Flake during the dog race, even with the risk involved. And the killer had to take great care to avoid even a speck of blood. Whom did that point to?''

"Couldn't it have been Sargasso as well as his wife?"

"Not likely. Eddie was wearing a dark brown jacket yesterday, remember? Likewise, Sam here and all the other track personnel wear dark red blazers. Even Donald Wayne had on a rumpled brown suit, and I think that girl Joyce wore brown too. Dark brown or dark red wouldn't likely show a bloodstain that obviously—not so the killer would find it necessary to use that program trick. But Marie Sargasso was wearing what?—a white pants suit! Even a speck of blood would have been fatal to her.''

There must have been a thousand other women at the track wearing white or light summer colors,'' Fletcher protested.

"But their names and phone numbers weren't in Flake's address book. And they weren't from Florida as Marie was.''

"Why'd she wear white if she was planning the murder?''

Leopold shrugged. "Maybe Eddie liked it on her, and she couldn't attract his suspicion by refusing to wear it. The important thing was that she avoided any blood splattering from the wound by using the program as a guard.''

Eddie Sargasso rode down to headquarters in the car with his wife and Leopold. She was silent and her head was bowed. Eddie held her hand all the way, and at one point he said, "You should have taken my bet, Leopold. You solved the case.''

"I told you I wasn't a gambler.''

"You gambled that she'd break down and confess. You had no real evidence against her.''

Leopold thought about it and said, "I suppose there are different sorts of gambling, Eddie. When you put it that way, maybe we're not so different after all.''

Warner Law

Warner Law's first story in *Playboy* magazine, "The Thousand Dollar Cup of Crazy German Coffee," won the prize for best fiction by a new writer in 1969. When asked why he specializes in crime fiction, he replied in 1971. "I have a criminal mind, but I'm too much of a coward to become a criminal myself." His best-known story to date may be "The Alarming Letters From Scottsdale Pennsylvania."

LINCOLN'S DOCTOR'S SON'S DOG

BY WARNER LAW

Among the local coterie of truly important writers, of which I am a leading member, it's legendary that Mark Twain once said that since books about Lincoln are proverbially best sellers, and since stories about doctors are always popular, and since Americans love to read about dogs, a story about Lincoln's doctor's dog must surely make a mint; and Twain said he was going to write it as soon as he could think of a story about the confounded dog.

After considerable research, I can't find that Mark Twain ever said this at all. But it's a widely printed anonymous witticism, and it sounds so much like Twain that if he didn't say it, he should have, so let's just accept it as a genuine Mark Twain quotation.

Since he never wrote the story, it's obvious that he had troubles with it. I can guess why. It wasn't the dog at all. There's a vital ingredient missing and, of all writers, Mark Twain should have spotted it. There is not a single freckle-faced American youngster with an engaging smile indicated in this story!

Once this sorry omission has been corrected, the story practically writes itself. And I have written it, in Mark Twain's honor. It's not that I want to make a mint—it's just that in this day of cynical literature, there's a crying need for old-fashioned stories that have true and heart-warming qualities and happy, upbeat endings, and here it is:

It was the fourth of March, in 1865. In Washington, Abraham Lincoln was being inaugurated for his second term.

Back in Springfield, Illinois, young Sam Haskins was alone in his parents' house on a quiet, tree-lined street.

Sam was the son of Dr. Amos Haskins, who was Abraham

182

Lincoln's kindly family doctor and who had delivered all four of the Lincoln boys. The Lincolns loved Dr. Haskins, and so the President had invited him and Mrs. Haskins to come to Washington and be his guests at the Inauguration.

Sam was twelve and an only child. He was disappointed at not being asked to Washington; but since he was a freckle-faced boy with an engaging smile, he was happy because at least his mother and father would be having a fine time. His Aunt Sally had come down from Chicago to look after Sam for the week his parents would be away.

Sam was a healthy, well-behaved boy, who seldom got into mischief. His only minor complaint was that his parents were strict vegetarians, so meat was never served in the Haskins family. But Sam was very fond of steaks and roasts and stews, and when he was nine, he'd stolen a meat pie from a neighbor woman's window ledge and his father had birched him for it. Sam knew he'd deserved the whipping and loved his parents just the same, for he was that kind of boy.

Next to his parents, Sam loved his dog, who was a lovable mongrel named Buddy. He was so lovable that everyone loved him—with the exception of Aunt Sally.

On this fourth of March, Aunt Sally had gone out to do some shopping and Sam was alone in the house. Suddenly, there was a banging on the front door. Sam went and opened it, to find Mr. Robbins standing there. He was their next-door neighbor and he was in an absolute fury.

"That damn dog of yours just chewed up my little baby boy!" he shouted at Sam. "He bit him in the calf!"

"Buddy!?" Sam exclaimed in disbelief. "No! Not Buddy! He loves your little boy! He'd never hurt him!"

"I found my little boy bleeding from bites in his leg! And Buddy was standing over him and there was blood around his mouth! He could have killed my little boy! He's a vicious dog and I'm going to see that he's destroyed!" Mr. Robbins stormed off.

A little later, Buddy slunk in the back door, looking guilty. Sam saw that there was, indeed, blood around his mouth. But he was sure it wasn't the blood of the Robbins boy, for Buddy was simply not that kind of dog.

Later on, Aunt Sally came home and Sam told her all about this, with tears in his eyes.

"I never *did* like that vicious mongrel!" Aunt Sally said. "Mr. Robbins is right! He *should* be destroyed!"

"But he's *not* a vicious mongrel!" Sam protested.

"There's always a first time!" Aunt Sally said.

Sam realized that he was not going to get too much support from Aunt Sally. He didn't know what to do. He couldn't get in touch with his parents, because he didn't know where in Washington they were staying.

Late that afternoon, Constable Ferguson came to Sam's house. He was a kindly man and Sam knew him well. Reluctantly, he told Sam that Mr. Robbins was bound and determined to have Buddy destroyed and that a court hearing was scheduled before kindly old Judge Lockwood the following afternoon and that Sam would have to appear and bring Buddy.

Now, Sam was desperate. He didn't know to whom to turn. Then he remembered Abraham Lincoln, who had always been so kind to him and who had sat Sam on his knee and told him amusing stories full of wisdom.

Sam ran down to the local telegraph office. The only person on duty was a young telegrapher who was about six years older than Sam. His name was Tom Edison and Sam knew that one day, Tom would amount to something. Young Tom was kindly and sympathized with Sam's problem and, between them, they composed a telegram:

PRESIDENT ABRAHAM LINCOLN. WASHINGTON. I AM SON OF DR. AMOS HASKINS. THEY ARE TRYING TO PUT MY DOG TO DEATH FOR SOMETHING HE DID NOT DO. PLEASE HELP ME. SAM HASKINS.

Young Tom rattled off the message on his key at lightning speed, but both boys wondered if Mr. Lincoln would ever actually see it himself. He would be a very busy man now, with the Inauguration and all.

That night, Sam held Buddy in his arms and cried himself to sleep.

Early the next morning, there was a banging on the Haskins

front door. Sam ran down and opened it, to find young Tom Edison with a telegram addressed to Sam. It read:

GO TO HERNDON'S OFFICE AND TELL THEM I WANT THEM TO HELP YOU. A. LINCOLN.

Sam knew that William Henry Herndon had been Lincoln's law partner for many years. As soon as he had dressed and gulped down some breakfast, Sam ran downtown to the law offices of Mr. Herndon. There, he found that Herndon and almost all the others in the fairly large firm had gone to Washington for the Inauguration. The only man in the office was a kindly gentleman named Mr. O'Reilly, who said he was a very fine attorney. Sam showed him the telegram from President Lincoln, and Mr. O'Reilly said he would be in court that afternoon and that he was a crackerjack orator and was sure he could talk the judge into sparing Buddy's life.

That afternoon, dressed in his Sunday best and accompanied by Aunt Sally, and with Buddy on a long rope, Sam set out for the Springfield courthouse. It was a long walk and Sam had somehow injured his right leg and it became sore, and Sam was limping.

Outside the courthouse, he took off his cap and saluted the American flag that flew over the building and then paid his respects to George Washington, whose statue stood in the courthouse square.

In the courtroom, Sam sat down at the defense table, next to Mr. O'Reilly. Buddy curled up at Sam's feet. Sam noticed that Mr. O'Reilly smelled of whiskey and seemed half asleep.

Then kindly old Judge Lockwood came in to preside over this informal hearing. Mr. Robbins told the judge what he'd seen with his own eyes and demanded that his vicious dog be destroyed before he bit any more innocent little children.

Mr. O'Reilly turned to Sam and whispered thickly: "I fear we don't have a chance, m'boy. This Robbins is the judge's brother-in-law."

"But that's not fair!" Sam cried.

"Quiet in the court!" the judge shouted, banging his gavel. Then he said, "Is there anyone here who has the effrontery to speak in defense of this miserable cur?"

At these words, Buddy got to his feet and growled and stared in the judge's direction, and his hair rose on his back.

Sam nudged Mr. O'Reilly. "Say something! Do something!" But Mr. O'Reilly's head had fallen forward onto his chest and he was snoring, in a drunken stupor.

"Well?" the judge demanded.

"*I* want to speak in defense of my dog, Buddy," Sam said bravely and rose to his feet. He addressed the judge, telling him how he had raised Buddy from a puppy and describing his gentle nature and assuring the judge that it was impossible for Buddy to have done this thing.

Judge Lockwood yawned and then said he was sorry but that the evidence indicated to him that the dog was guilty and should be destroyed. "Baliff," the judge ordered, "take this dog away and put him to death!"

At that moment, Buddy leaped in the direction of the judge's bench with an angry growl, pulling his rope out of Sam's hand. As the dog mounted the steps leading up from the courtroom floor, Judge Lockwood rose in fear, his gavel in hand to protect himself.

But Buddy darted past the judge's seat and began to wrestle with something on the floor. No one but the judge could see what it was.

"Good Lord!" the judge exclaimed. "It's a copperhead!"

What had happened was that Buddy had sensed that a deadly copperhead had slithered in from an adjoining room and was making for the judge, and Buddy had rushed to attack the snake to protect him. In a few moments, Buddy had killed the copperhead and the snake had been taken away.

Buddy returned at once to Sam, who petted him and said, "Good dog, good dog!"

Tears were forming in the judge's eyes. "Well, I'll be . . ." he said. "That dog saved my life! Here I'd sentenced him to death and he saved my life."

"That just *proves* what a good dog he is!" Sam said happily.

"It proves nothing of the kind, you young idiot!" the judge snapped. "All it proves is that this damn dog will bite anything that moves! If an innocent little baby boy had crawled up behind me, he would have tried to kill him, too!"

"That's not true!" Sam shouted.

"Oh, shut up and sit down!" the judge barked. "My order still stands! Baliff—take the dog!"

As the bailiff moved toward him, Sam rose. "Please your Honor—I believe in American justice, and if you say Buddy has to die, you must be right, because you're a judge. But wouldn't you let me take care of Buddy myself? Please?"

"How do you propose to destroy him?" the judge asked.

"Well, I'll take him out into the north woods near the old forked cottonwood on top of the hill," Sam answered. "And I'll dig a little grave, and then I'll shoot Buddy through the head with my father's Service pistol from the Mexican War—which was a just war, no matter what anyone says—and then I'll bury him."

"How do I know you'll actually do it?" the judge snarled.

"Because I give you my word of honor that I will, and I'm Abraham Lincoln's family doctor's son, and when I say I'll do a thing, I'll do it."

"*When* will you do it?" the judge demanded.

"This very afternoon, sir," Sam answered.

After a moment of glowering thought, the judge said, "Very well. But if you *don't* do it, I will hold you in contempt of this court and you could go to prison for thirty years."

And so it was that later that afternoon, Sam limped miserably into the woods north of Springfield and up the hill on which was the old forked cottonwood. Sam carried his father's loaded pistol in a sack and had a shovel over his shoulder. Buddy danced around him at the end of his rope, for Buddy loved to go for walks in the woods.

Sam tied Buddy to the tree and then dug a small grave. Watching, Buddy wagged his tail eagerly, for he was stupid enough to think that Sam was digging up a bone for him.

The grave finished, Sam got out the pistol and then called Buddy to him, and the dog came, waggling and wriggling with happiness. He licked Sam's hand—the same one that held the pistol.

Tears came once again to Sam's eyes and he felt he couldn't go through with it. But he had no intention of going to prison for thirty years, and so he cocked the trigger and took careful aim, directly between Buddy's soft and appealing eyes.

"Don't shoot that dog!" came a cry from the distance.

Sam turned to see Judge Lockwood running toward him, and just behind the judge was Dr. Morton, Sam's dentist. He was also Abraham Lincoln's family dentist.

"There might have been a miscarriage of justice!" the judge shouted.

"That dog might be innocent," said Dr. Morton, as he ran up. "Let me see his teeth!" He reached down and opened Buddy's mouth and looked into it. "I was right!" Dr. Morton announced.

"I don't understand!" Sam said.

Judge Lockwood explained: "Dr. Morton, here, happened to examine the Robbins boy's leg, and he didn't think that a dog of Buddy's size could have made those wounds at all."

"If it *was* a dog," Dr. Morton said carefully, "it would have to have been a very small one. Buddy's canines are too far apart."

"Well," Sam said, overjoyed. "I just knew for *certain* that Buddy hadn't done it."

The reason that Sam knew this for certain was that it had been Sam himself who had been chewing the Robbins boy in the calf when Buddy had come along and tried to protect the child by biting Sam in *his* calf. It had been Sam's blood in Buddy's mouth. This was why Sam had been limping.

As it happened, Dr. Morton knew the truth, for he was quite familiar with Sam's occlusion and had recognized the tooth marks as being Sam's.

However, Dr. Morton was a wise and kindly man, and he was also a student of the occult and he knew an incipient werewolf when he saw one. But, also, Dr. Morton knew the cure.

When Dr. Haskins returned from Washington, Dr. Morton went to him and said that it was vital that Sam have lots of red meat in his diet. "Otherwise," said the dentist, "all his teeth are going to fall out. Also, he may well go blind."

"Is that a true medical fact?" asked Dr. Haskins.

"I assure you that it is," Dr. Morton said. "In addition, his fingers and toes might fall off."

"Good heavens!" Dr. Haskins exclaimed. Not only was he a

badly educated doctor but he was also one of the most gullible men in Springfield. "Well, even though it's against my principles, Sam will have meat from now on."

From that day forward, Sam was given all the red meat he could eat—which was considerable. Dr. Morton was pleased to see that all of Sam's werewolf tendencies rapidly disappeared.

Buddy lived to a lovable old age.

As Sam grew up, his father pressed him to become a doctor or a lawyer, but Sam had other ideas. In later years, he was to become the most respected, successful, well-adjusted and sublimated retail butcher in all Springfield.

To me, this seems a perfectly straightforward and simple story, with touching human values and a happy, upbeat ending. In all modesty, I feel that the addition of young Tom Edison was a brilliant touch, verging on the profound.

I really don't know what kept Mark Twain from writing this story. But then, one of his great failings was that he wrote only what *he* wanted to write, rather than what people wanted to read.

This is, of course, why Mark Twain is not remembered as a writer today.

Francis M. Nevins, Jr.

Francis M. Nevins, Jr. is a leading authority in at least three fields: he is a nationally known expert on copyright law, a subject he teaches at Washington University Law School; a highly regarded authority on American popular culture, particularly film and television; and a prominent Edgar-Award-winning critic of mystery fiction, best known for his *Royal Bloodline: Ellery Queen, Author and Detective (1974)*. More recently, he is responsible for the long-overdue revival of the work of Cornell Woolrich. In addition, he has found time to write several mystery novels and a considerable number of short stories. Several, like the present selection, feature Milo Turner, a professional con-man and solver of crimes committed by others.

DOGSBODY

BY FRANCIS M. NEVINS, JR.

The Oakshade Inn had been touted to me as the most restful place to stay in Barhaven, and during the first three nights of my visit to that drowsy and affluent community I had no cause to dispute the assessment. Floorboards buffed to high gloss, homey maple furniture, bright chintz curtains, view of lush meadows from my second-floor window, fine classical music from the local university's radio station, breakfasts in the hotel dining room that were a trencherman's delight, and a scam that was progressing fantastically. No con man with a taste for the finer things could have asked for more.

Until that fourth night when the phone jolted me awake.

I sprang bolt upright and groped for the night table. The digital clock beside the phone proclaimed the time to be 1:14 A.M. I found the receiver and jammed one end to my ear. "Yes?" I spoke into the mouthpiece, fighting to make the word come out calm.

"Fritz!" replied an all-to-familiar voice, low and menacing like the growl of a German shepherd on guard duty. "Get your pants on and wait downstairs for a prowl car to pick you up. You've got four minutes."

For an awful moment I was convinced he'd tumbled to the scam and was arresting me over the phone. Then my brain came into gear and I exchanged a few sentences with my caller, hung up and dived for the clothes closet. Fully dressed and with my Vandyke brushed, I had all of ten seconds to wait in the dim empty lounge of the inn until the black-and-white braked in front of the picture window, the domelight whirling bloodily.

The scam had been going velvet-smooth till now. In fact, the only sour note in the orchestration was that Chief Knauf, for some private reason, kept calling me Fritz. My actual *nom de scam* this time was Horst—to be complete, professor Doktor

Horst Gerstad, formerly criminological consultant to the national police of the Federal Republic of Germany, currently president of Gerstad Security Systems, a corporation which analyzed and improved on existing security arrangements for businesses that were uptight about crime.

Professor Gerstad was one of my favorite identities and one of my most lucrative. The close-cropped military brush cut, the little Vandyke, the accent honed to a fine edge by hours of listening to tapes of Henry Kissinger's press conferences, all added up to the quintessence of a walking Teutonic efficiency machine.

I would present myself at a likely corporate headquarters, speak to its top management, learn its security arrangements, punch a few simple holes in them, and offer to lease the corporation my own comprehensive security system, which of course had as much real existence as a hippo-griff. If the corporation didn't agree, I could always recoup my losses by selling the information I'd picked up to a potential thief.

I had come to Barhaven to make my pitch at the university, and it was in the office of its president, Herbert J. Stockford, A.B., M.A., D.Ed., that I had chanced to meet Stockford's brother-in-law, the chief of the Barhaven police.

E. W. Knaup preferred to be called Duke—I gathered because the E. stood for Elmer or Ethelbert, or something equally unmacho. He was a short, tubby, gravel-voiced, genially pushy specimen, and he had a blind spot wide enough to drive a semi through. He was a gun nut. No man or woman who encountered him, however casually, could escape one of his monologues on weaponry. One might glance at the sky and remark that it looked like rain, and Knaup would say, "If you want to see a rain of lead, buddy, try the VC-70 heckler and Koch automatic pistol. Nineteen shots, double action, comes with a stock you can use for a holster *and* which you can attach to the pistol and turn it into a submachine gun. Brip brip brip, brip brip brip! Love those three-shot bursts."

The chief's personal police cruiser sported a rear-window sticker attesting to his life membership in the National Rifle Association, three separate anti-gun control stickers, a God Bless America tag, a Support Your Local Police tag, and a flag decal. No ambiguity about ol' Duke's sympathies.

After that first meeting in Stockford's office I hadn't expected to see Knaup again, but the very next day, a little before noon, while I was in a conference room on the third floor of the university administration building, poring learnedly over security plans with the chief and deputy chief of the school force, he came striding into the room in full uniform, the polished butt of his Colt Python protruding from his buttoned-down leather holster.

"Fritz!" he barked, like an actor trying out for the voice of the Lord in a De Mille Movie.

I looked curiously around the room to see if any of the security guards happened to be named Fritz. Nobody even looked up.

"No, *you*, dummy," he growled at me. That was the way he spoke to people he liked. "We're lunching."

"May I point out that my name is not Fritz?" I said in my most unruffled Kissinger tone.

"We in the law enforcement community eat Mex food for lunch. I hope you like tacos, Fritz," he said, and led me out by the elbow.

Over the guacamole salad at Panchito's he explained his sudden interest in me. "Now here's what it is, Fritz." He wolfed down great gobs of guacamole on taco chips between sentences. "As head honcho of the college, my brother-in-law Herbie Stockford is the one who has to decide about this security package of yours." Chomp crunch. "Only he doesn't know enough about security to hit the dirt when a Remington High Standard Model 10 goes off at him, so he's asked me to sort of help him make a decision." Crunch chomp. "Those retired village constables he uses for campus security aren't much better than Herbie, so he's relying on the only pro in town." Crunch crunch. "Me." Burp.

So I repeated my well-rehearsed pitch to the Duke, being careful to throw in as many gun references as I dared. And before we had demolished our *quesodillas* he had unsubtly switched the subject to weaponry. "What kind of contacts you got in Charter Arms, or Ruger, or Dan Wesson? I've got a little proposition for you."

When I modestly lied that my connections with several of the firms he'd mentioned were at moderately high levels of management, his eyes brightened. "We in the law enforcement community appreciate the work of the arms manufacturers,'' he said. ''And now that we're getting a lot of federal money from LEAA, we'd like to show our appreciation by placing some big orders. Like maybe a gross of M-16 or Armalite 180 rifles, a few dozen folding stock shotguns, all the Glaser Safety Slugs we can lay our mitts on. Say, if I get some of the chiefs in the neighboring towns to come in with me on a shopping list, you think you can get us, say, a thirty percent discount on a two-hundred-thousand-dollar order?''

He wasn't so crude as to make it explicit that his recommendation to his brother-in-law depended on my help in fixing him up with an arsenal, but I got the message loud and clear and assured him of my fullest cooperation. And that was how things stood between me and the gun-loving chief when, thirty-six hours later, the black-and-white whisked me through the sleeping streets of Barhaven to I knew not what destination.

* * *

We skirted the edge of the university grounds and swung north into the low foothills which sheltered the hundred-thousand-dollar homes. The black-and-white made a sharp turn into a private lane and then into the driveway of a fieldstone and redwood showplace halfway up the slope. Half of the house's windows were lit, and floodlights blazed across the broad lawn.

Duke Knaup strode tubbily into the path of the black-and-white and thrust out his palm like a crossing guard. The cop behind the wheel slammed the brakes, and I emerged from the rear with what dignity I could muster. Behind the chief shuffled a slim balding man in silk dressing gown and slippers whom I recognized as none other than President Stockford of Barhaven University. His face looked ghastly, as if his best friends had turned into a cheese Danish before his eyes. Without a word they led me across fifty yards of grass still wet from the early-evening storm to the foot of a stately old elm. The body of a large reddish-yellow dog lay beside the trunk.

''Someone poisoned the poor mutt,'' Knaup muttered. ''Can't tell what was used—lab will give me a report in the morning. About an hour ago Herbie heard the dog whining and came out to investigate and found him lying here. Looks like he'd crawled under the tree to die.''

A short dumpy woman in a blue wrapper trotted out of the house to join us. ''My sister, Mrs. Stockford. This is Dr. Fritz Gerstad, a visiting criminologist,'' Knaup introduced us.

''Oh, are you going to help my brother find the—the animal who did this to Thor?'' she demanded as we shook hands.

''It is possible I can be of assistance?'' I murmured, wondering what the hell I was doing here and how best to stay in character.

''Tell Fritz what you told me about the dog's routine after dark,'' Knaup directed his brother-in-law.

''He was a trained guard dog,'' Stockford replied dully. ''We let him out every night at sundown and he'd roam the grounds. We haven't had a burglary here since we got him three years ago.''

''And have you had a burglary tonight?'' I asked.

''No, nothing,'' Mrs. Stockford said. ''I've just finished checking to see if anything is missing.''

''Someone probably threw a poisoned meat patty onto the lawn to get rid of Thor,'' her husband added, ''but he hasn't come back yet to break in.''

''He'd probably wait till the wee hours before he came back,'' Knaup pointed out. ''But with all the lights on and cops around the house, he won't show now. I'll assign a car to stand by the rest of the night just in case.''

''Do I assume correctly, sir, that neither you nor Mrs. Stockford observed any strange automobiles on the private road this evening?''

''The storm was quite heavy up here for a while,'' the shaken president replied. ''We couldn't see as far as the road during that period. That was probably when he came by and threw out the poisoned meant.''

Chief Knaup clawed at my arm. ''Come over here with me, Fritz.'' He led me across the squishy grass to a rose arbor behind the house. ''Want to explain why I sent for you,'' he whispered. ''You see, I don't believe Thor was killed by somebody who was out to burglarize the house. I think whoever did it wanted to kill the dog and that was all.''

''A crazed dog poisoner in Barhaven?'' I clucked mildly,

trying to suggest his theory was ridiculous without actually insulting the man.

"It makes sense if you know the background," Knaup went on. "Thor was trained as a killer, the kind of dog they use for night security in big empty stores. When the college was going through the anti-war riots six years ago, Herbie hired an outfit that trains these dogs to let some of them run loose at night in the administration building and the ROTC building and some other vulnerable spots. A few long-haired kids broke into the ROTC building one night with a can of paint to put peace symbols on the walls. Couple of them got chewed up pretty bad by the dogs. Caused a big stink, the school went on strike for two days, and Herbie had to cancel the contract for the dogs. When the outfit went bust three years ago he bought one of those same dogs for his personal protection."

"Thor was one of the dogs involved in the incident in the ROTC building?"

"That's right. Half Irish wolfhound and half Pyrenean bearhound. Weight about one ten, a shade bigger than a full-grown German shepherd, and a hell of a lot meaner."

"I'm sure he was an excellent guard dog," I murmured, "but I fail to see why you wish to involve me in the matter." And, like a tyro swimmer who suddenly realizes he's drifted two miles out from the beach, I was becoming distinctly queasy.

"Herbie loved that dog like a son," Knaup explained, "and I owe him a lot of favors, like my job, for instance. He wants me to pull out all the stops to nail whoever poisoned Thor. Trouble is, if I give the case any more than routine attention, the papers will stomp all over me about misusing police resources. I can do without that grief."

I knew exactly what he meant, having taken the trouble to read the back issues of the Barhaven newspapers before I had made my appearance. Last year Knaup had come close to being removed from office over a little matter of assigning three patrolmen, while on duty, to paint his house and oil his gun collection. "That's why you're here, Fritz. You're going to be my dogicide squad for a while. Let's see how good a criminologist you really are."

I do not shy away from new experiences, but this one made me fight hard to repress a shudder. Very few con men have found themselves drafted into the police force while on a scam. I was far from enthusiastic but saw no way to extricate myself short of blowing town. I made an instant decision and held out my hand to Knaup gravely. "So be it," I pronounced as we shook. "Although I wish it explicitly understood that my success will guarantee a favorable recommendation by you of my security system."

Duke Knaup stuck thoughtful fingers under his chin. "I don't know if you have a saying for it in sauerkrautland, Fritz, but here in America, you scratch my back and I'll scratch yours."

* * *

It occurred to me, as the black-and-white sped me back to the Oakshade Inn, that there were two dogsbodies in this case. I was the second. The old English word *dogsbody*, meaning an insignificant underling, a lackey, fitted my present situation like pantyhose. Even worse, I had become a detective in spite of myself. But I had had enough experience putting myself in the shoes of the authorities to make me believe I could pull the thing off—with a large dose of luck.

It was too late to start on the case tonight, so I decided that tomorrow morning I would visit the college administration building, get the names of the students whom Thor had maimed six years ago, and then try to learn if they or anyone close to them still lived in Barhaven. And if someone in that category happened also to have access to the college chem lab, we might have our poisoner before the next nightfall.

The mellow sunlight of Friday morning was drenching my room when the phone exploded again. The digital clock read 7:12, and I was not yet in any mood to face the day. I made a kind of glunking noise into the mouthpiece.

"Fritz!" Even half awake it did not take me three guesses to identify my caller. "Get your rear end down to the station, *mach schnell*. All hell's broke loose!"

Thirty minutes later I stumbled out of a cab into the city hall and down a marble staircase to the basement, which was the police headquarters. I informed the fat asthmatic desk sergeant that Chief Knaup was expecting me, but before the sergeant could pick up the interoffice phone, a door flew open behind me and there he stood, posing with his hand on his holster for all the world like a short pudgy version of Randolph Scott playing marshal of Tombstone.

"Get in here!" he roared, and stalked ahead of me through the detective squad room and into his own office.

"Read this, and that, and this one." He tossed a stack of police reports across his desk at me. "We've been getting calls all night. Some nut's been driving around the county making war on the dog population of the area!"

On a first reading of the reports I almost agreed with the sputtering chief. Our devotee of the spiked hamburger had cut himself a wide swath last night.

Winston, age five, Boston bull terrier, property of Mr. and Mrs. Horace Burgess of Newcomb Heights, found dead in the service pantry of the Burgess home at 6:00 A.M.

El Toro, French poodle, age two, owned by Miss Lucretia Runcible of Barhaven, found dead in its basket in the kitchen when Miss Runcible woke up hungry at 3:25 A.M. and went to the refrigerator for some yogurt.

Cincinnatus, mutt, age seven, belonging to Professor Featherstone of the classics department at the college, found dead behind the professor's front door at 1:30 A.M. when the professor returned home from the annual banquet of the Lucullus club.

Including Thor, a total of seven canines had been transported overnight to that Big Kennel in the Sky, four within the Barhaven city limits and three in outlying communities.

"Has it been confirmed that the cause of death in each case was poison?"

"Only in the first three so far," Knaup told me. "County lab's been working all night on it. The others will prove out the same. This is a pattern, Fritz."

"Perhaps not the pattern you thought," I murmured, and shuffled through the police reports again. "Observe the addresses of the late dogs' master and mistresses. Five seem to be private homes, but Miss Runcible is 243 Westview, apartment 18-D, and Mr. Henry Wampler is 4576 North Wood Avenue, Apartment 907. Does this suggest anything to you?"

Before the chief could figure out what to say, his phone buzzed and he made a grab for it. "Knaup," he barked. "Yeah,

Sergeant I . . . *What?* . . . No, no, I'll go out on this one myself.'' He slammed down the phone and groped for his visored cap. "Let's go, Fritz.''

"Dogsbody Number Eight?'' I inquired.

"Catsbody Number One,'' he snarled. "Our nutcake's started zapping the cat population too!''

* * *

Knaup drove us in his own cruiser, the one with all the gun stickers on the bumper. Ten minutes out of town we turned in between a pair of stone pillars and onto another one of those private drives. The cruiser splashed through a mud puddle in a depression of the road, then sped along clean smooth macadam until the drive ended in a parking circle at the side of a huge Victorian stone monstrosity of a mansion.

"Who is the owner of this establishment?'' I asked as Knaup rang the symphonic chime beside the front door.

"Used to be Franklin Bagnell, the big steel manufacturer. He died five or six years ago.''

"Ah, yes, I remember seeing him on television—when he visited the Federal Republic of Germany, of course.'' I had almost blown my scam with that careless remark. I did remember seeing old Bagnell several times on TV newscasts, a cadaverous old reactionary who was forever ranting about Communist-inspired legal restraints on the American businessman. When he was upset a muscle in his cheek would twitch—a Bagnell family trait, I remembered having read in the news magazine.

"Ever since the old man died,'' Knaup continued, "the lawyers have been fighting in court over who owns the house and the money. For all practical purposes the dog owns it, I guess.''

Before I could ask him to clarify that last enigmatic remark, the door was inched open and a trim, tired-looking young lady in a pink pantsuit, inspected us, made a lightning deduction from the chief's uniform that he was fuzz, and threw the door wide. "Hey! Mama!'' she bellowed into the depths of the house. "Cops here!''

A gray, fiftyish woman descended the oak staircase to meet us in the foyer, where she stood under a huge oil portrait of skeletal old Bagnell and threw out her hands to the Duke. "Oh, Chief Knaup, it's so good of you to come. It's not many high officials who would come in person when a cat is murdered."

"We in the law enforcement community love cats deeply," Knaup orated. "Oh, this is Dr. Gerstad, the famous criminologist. Fritz, may I present Madge Slocum, the caretaker here, and her daughter Lila. What happened to the cat, honey?"

Her mother answered for her, sniffing back the hint of a tear. "I just don't know what happened, Chief Knaup. I put Kikimora's supper out for her at 5:45 yesterday evening the way I always do, and then I whistled for Barnaby to come in from the yard for *his* supper, and around then it started raining, and Lila and I ate at 6:30. We watched TV together and went to bed early and I found poor Kiki when I came down this morning to get her and Barnaby breakfast. She was lying in her little cat box so stiff and still I knew something was wrong with her, so I picked her up and listened for her little heartbeat, and she was dead."

"Is Barnaby your husband, madam?" I asked the sorrowing caretaker.

"He gets better care than a lot of husbands I know," Lila answered pertly. "He's the dog that more or less owns the place."

I took a casual stroll the length of the hallway to a parquet-floored conservatory at the back of the house. A riot of potted plants, hanging ferns, and crawling greenery almost suffocated me. I looked out the rear window on broad landscaped terraces stretching for a few hundred yards, dotted with bright flower beds. A large gray dog of indeterminate breed was romping in the middle distance, chasing a rabbit or something. Barnaby seemed a hell of a lot more carefree than most rich people of my acquaintance.

"It's the cat we're interested in, remember?" Knaup snaked an arm through the plant life and plucked me out of the conversatory, leading me through a side corridor and a butler's pantry into a barnlike kitchen and over to a wicker basket heaped with fluffy little pillows, where the eighth victim lay. Kikimora was a broad-headed white Maltese with a black notch down the middle of her forehead.

"The cat was merely a personal pet of Mrs. Slocum, I take

it?'' I asked Knaup. ''And the care of the dog is her job, like the care of the house?''

''You got it. Old Bagnell picked up Barnaby about five years before he died. Just a mutt, but the old man grew to love him a lot more than he loved the couple of relatives he had left. So he put most of his money in a fund to care for the dog as long as the dog lived. Honorary trust, it's called. Dog's got the run of the house and grounds, eats better than a lot of people, vet comes out to look it over twice a week. The Slocum women's pay, the taxes on the property, everything gets paid out of the trust as long as Barnaby's alive.''

''And when he dies?'' I murmured.

''The property and money get divided among seven or eight charities and those two relatives. Second or third cousins, I think. Morton Godfrey, a lawyer in California, and a young kid named George Bagnell. They're the ones who started the lawsuit to knock out the will on the idea the old man was bananas. It's been in the courts for years.''

I paced back and forth across the spotless kitchen floor. The extent to which I'd become my own fictitious creation was beginning to frighten me, but with a wild sense of excitement I realized that I might be on the brink of actually solving this case. ''But why should the cat have died?'' I mumbled half to myself. ''Everything else I can account for, but not the cat.''

''Fritz, what the hell are you muttering about?''

''Last night you believed that Thor was the intended victim of someone who drove near the Stockford house and threw a poisoned meat patty for him to eat. The rash of dog deaths during the night established that animosity against Thor was not the motive. But you still believe that the killer was a person who spent yesterday evening driving through the area dropping poisoned meat on lawns. This cannot be so. I remind you that at least two of the dogs lived in high-rise apartments. Where do they roam? How does our killer deposit the meat in front of them? You have misconceived the technique of the crimes.''

''Now wait a minute, Fritz,'' Knaup objected, banging on the door of the walk-in meat keeper for emphasis. ''Why couldn't the cat over there have picked up something with the poison in it yesterday? It could have been out in the grass playing with Barnaby all evening for all you know.''

"We drove through a mud puddle," I reminded the chief, "just inside the private drive leading here. The macadam between that puddle and this house was clean and unmarked until your own car traversed it. You will recall that it rained heavily last evening. No automobile crossed the puddle between its formation and this morning. This is at least circumstantial evidence that there is no madman driving around your community with poisoned meat. Kikimora was poisoned here in the house. And the seven dead dogs were poisoned in their respective homes also."

Something like understanding was beginning to dawn over the chief's dumpy face. "I submit that it was the food their masters served them that was poisoned," I went on. "It is the only hypothesis that explains everything. Well, almost everything—everything but the cat. You must call your brother-in-law at the university and ask him where he purchases dog food. Then you must call each of the other owners and ask the same question. I predict you will receive the same answer. Go." I pointed to the phone extension hanging on the kitchen wall next to a memo board. To give orders to a police chief in his own bailiwick tickled my soul.

Knaup pressed touch-tone buttons, got the university switchboard, and asked for President Stockford's office. "Yeah, Herbie, he wants me to ask you. Where did you buy Thor's chow? . . . Fourfooted Gourmet, huh? Okay, Herbie, buzz you later."

He hung up and turned to me. "Herbie fed the dog a special-quality ground chuck he bought at The Fourfooted Gourmet. That's a specialty shop we have in town—finest cuts of meat and other goodies specially prepared for pets. It's where all the pet pamperers go."

"Than that is the place where the poison was mixed with the dog food," I insisted. "Call your office, have your sergeant phone each of the others, and ask them the same question you put to Mr. Stockford, then report back to you. Meanwhile I must deal with the problem of the cat."

Knaup whirled back to the phone while I went through the swinging doors in and out of the butler's pantry and down the long hallway into the drawing room, where the Slocum women waited. They sat on matching armchairs upholstered in rich blue velvet, talking together in hushed tones.

"Excuse me, ladies." I stepped in front of them and executed a slight bow. "Where do you purchase Barnaby's meals?"

Madge Slocum stared up at me with a look of puzzlement behind her shell-rimmed glasses. "Why, what a strange question! Well, you know, Barnaby is not what you'd call an aristocrat among dogs. He was just a stray that Mr. Bagnell found as a puppy and grew extremely attached to. After Mr. Bagnell's death I tried to get Barnaby to eat the finest foods available but he would always turn up his nose, so ever since I've just served him canned dog food I get at the supermarket."

"And where do you obtain the food for your cat?" I continued.

This time Lila Slocum did the honors. "That's a funny story too. Like Mama said, she tried to get Barnaby to eat fancy food. There's a special grade of ground chuck she bought for him but he wouldn't eat the stuff. But Kiki went crazy over it, so ever since then we bought the ground chuck for her."

"Every Thursday afternoon I did my weekly shopping for Kiki," her mother added helpfully.

"Did you follow this procedure yesterday as well?" I inquired. Both women indicated that they had.

I didn't need to ask the next question, but I asked it anyway. "And the name of the establishment where you procured these culinary delights?"

"It's called The Fourfooted Gourmet," Lila said.

"Thank you." I practically clicked my heels at them Prussian-style, and wheeled back out to the kitchen, where Knaup was just hanging up the phone. "Sarge made four of those calls so far. You were right, by damn! They all bought that special ground chuck at The Fourfooted Gourmet."

"As did Mrs. Slocum for her cat," I reported. "The pattern is now clear. Someone poisoned the food at its source. And the rest of a week's supply is sitting in that meat keeper at this moment, and no doubt in the refrigerators of every other bereaved pet owner in this case. Call headquarters and send men out to collect the meat at once. Then let us pay a visit to these canine caterers."

We rocketed back through the mud puddle and roared onto the state highway back to town. Knaup drove with one hand on the wheel and the other on the butt of the Colt Python in its holster. We turned into the main business district in the center of Barhaven and pulled up short in the middle of a tiny parking lot next to a low tan-brick building. "That's the place," Knaup said.

"Is it permitted to part this way?" I asked. Every slot along the sides of the lot seemed to be taken, and he was blocking at least a dozen cars the way he was positioned.

"Man, I'm the law in this town, anything I do is permitted. Let's go."

And as casually as two dog owners about to pick up their pets' dinners, we stepped into the premises of The Fourfooted Gourmet. A bell over the door tinkled as we walked in. The establishment looked more like a real-estate office than a food store. Pickled-pine paneling, Muzak box bracketed to the wall near the ceiling, imitation-brick tile on the floor, an occasional poster of a dog or cat carefully posed to look irresistibly cuddly.

Behind a gold-flecked Formica counter at the far end of the shop there was a long line of refrigerator cabinets. A pale and very thin young man in a white apron, with hair the color of cooked noodles, was weighing meat in a scale for a customer. "What's your pleasure, gentlemen?" he began as he looked at us.

And then he registered Knaup's uniform, and a muscle in his cheek began to twitch. I studied his cadaverous face more closely, compared it with a painted face I had seen this morning, and made one of the rashest statements of my career.

"This is Mr. George Bagnell," I announced, turning to Knaup, "the animal poisoner."

And instantly the place was a madhouse. George flung the package of meat at us, scored a direct hit on Knaup's face, and sprang through a doorway to the rear. Dripping with meat juice, Knaup vaulted the counter and clawed for his gun, shouting, "Police, halt!" as he and I ran through the rear storage area and out a side door into the parking lot.

George was gunning a blue Pinto out of the lot and smashed head-on into Knaup's cruiser. He flew out the door of the Pinto and started sprinting toward the street. Knaup snapped a shot at him, aiming low for his leg. He missed George but hit the right front tire of his own cruiser.

George was almost out of the long narrow lot when suddenly

a two-tone convertible sped into the area with a fat blond woman in the front seat and a huge German shepherd in the rear. The kid had to swerve out of the car's way in a split second. He slammed against the wall as Knaup fired again, and the dog leaped out of the car and dived for George as if the kid were a cat.

The fat woman floored her brakes and screeched, "Oh, my God! Down, Schnitzel, down!" and waddled out of the convertible just as Knaup was ramming his Python into the small of George's back and motioning him to assume the frisking position against the wall.

Knaup had to radio for another car to come and haul the prisoner away. While we were waiting for the nearest service station to send someone over to change the flat on Knaup's cruiser, I explained the rest of my conclusions to him.

"As long as Barnaby lived, Bagnell's cousins profited nothing. George Bagnell came to Barhaven for the express purpose of killing the dog. He probably shadowed Mrs. Slocum on her shopping trips, observed her weekly visits to The Fourfooted Gourmet for ground chuck, and reasonably but wrongly assumed that the food was for the dog.

"He proceeded to obtain a job at the shop and some poison elsewhere and waited his chance to impregnate a supply of the special ground chuck with the poison just prior to one of Mrs. Slocum's Thursday visits. Altogether a foolish and wasteful plan, and one that betrayed its perpetrator's inexperience. Any other dog owner who picked Thursday to shop would find his animal dead too, but I suppose George was not displeased by that. The more dead dogs, the less it would appear that one particular dog was the target.

"And remember that you must arrange for announcements in the newspapers and radio and television that all patrons of The Fourfooted Gourmet must bring their meat in at once for analysis. We want no more dead animals."

"I know it was the twitch that told you the kid was a Bagnell," the chief asked, "but why couldn't he have been Morton Godfrey, the other cousin?"

Actually, of course, he could have been, and I had taken a fifty-fifty chance, but it wouldn't do to let Knaup know that.

"Being an attorney," I rationalized sagely, "Morton Godfrey

would depend on his suit contesting the will, simply because if he should win, the entire Bagnell estate would pass by the law of intestacy, with the charities taking nothing and the two cousins everything. Would he have been so foolish as to try to kill the dog for a small share of the estate when by lawful means he stood to gain so much more? No, it was clearly not a legal mind that conceived these crimes.''

"Sharp thinking, Fritz.'' Knaup clapped me on the shoulder. "And you can bet on it I'll make sure old Herbie signs that contract with your company for security services. Uhh—provided you put through that little side deal we talked about?''

I looked at the hapless chief, with his uniform dripping meat juice and his tire flattened by his own well-placed slug, and struggled to keep from laughing aloud as I shook his hand again. "We in the criminological community,'' I assured him, "support a well-armed police force.''

Q. Patrick

Q. Patrick, also known as Patrick Quentin, is a catch-all pseudonym of four authors who combined efforts from time to time. Richard Wilson Webb originated the pseudonym and wrote, in turn, with Mary (Patsy) Mott Kelly, Mary Louise Aswell and Hugh Wheeler. He and Wheeler were the most prolific and also wrote together under the pseudonym of Jonathan Stagge. From the early 1950s until 1965, when he began to write plays, Wheeler carried on alone. He won the New York Drama Critics Circle Award and a Tony for both *A Little Night Music* (1972) and *Candide* (1974).

PUZZLE FOR POPPY

BY Q. PATRICK

"Yes, Miss Crump," snapped Iris into the phone. "No, Miss Crump. Oh, nuts, Miss Crump."

My wife flung down the receiver.

"Well?" I asked.

"She won't let us use the patio. It's that dog, that great fat St. Bernard. It mustn't be disturbed."

"Why?"

"It has to be alone with its beautiful thoughts. It's going to become a mother. Peter, it's revolting. There must be something in the lease."

"There isn't," I said.

When I'd rented our half of this La Jolla hacienda for my shore leave, the lease specified that all rights to the enclosed patio belonged to our eccentric co-tenant. It oughtn't to have mattered, but it did because Iris had recently skyrocketed to fame as a movie star and it was impossible for us to appear on the streets without being mobbed. For the last couple of days we had been virtually beleaguered in our apartment. We were crazy about being beleaguered together, but even Héloise and Abelard needed a little fresh air once in a while.

That's why the patio was so important.

Iris was staring through the locked French windows at the forbidden delights of the patio. Suddenly she turned.

"Peter, I'll die if I don't get things into my lungs—ozone and things. We'll just have to go to the beach."

"And be torn limb from limb by your public again?"

"I'm sorry, darling. I'm terribly sorry." Iris unzipped herself from her housecoat and scrambled into slacks and a shirt-waist. She tossed me my naval hat. "Come, Lieutenant—to the slaughter."

When we emerged on the street, we collided head on with a

208

man carrying groceries into the house. As we disentangled ourselves from celery stalks, there was a click and a squeal of delight followed by a powerful whistle. I turned to see a small girl who had been lying in wait with a camera. She was an unsightly little girl with sandy pigtails and a brace on her teeth.

"Geeth," she announced. "I can get two buckth for thith thnap from Barney Thtone. He'th thappy about you, Mith Duluth."

Other children, materializing in response to her whistle, were galloping toward us. The grocery man came out of the house. Passers-by stopped, stared and closed in—a woman in scarlet slacks, two sailors, a flurry of bobby-soxers, a policeman.

"This," said Iris grimly, "is the end."

She escaped from her fans and marched back to the two front doors of our hacienda. She rang the buzzer on the door that wasn't ours. She rang persistently. At length there was the clatter of a chain sliding into place and the door opened wide enough to reveal the face of Miss Crump. It was a small, faded face with a most uncordial expression.

"Yes?" asked Miss Crump.

"We're the Duluths," said Iris. "I just called you. I know about your dog, but . . ."

"Not *my* dog," corrected Miss Crump. "Mrs. Wilberframe's dog. The late Mrs. Wilberframe of Glendale who has a nephew and a niece-in-law of whom I know a great deal in Ogden Bluffs, Utah. At least, they *ought* to be in Ogden Bluffs."

This unnecessary information was flung at us like a challenge. Then Miss Crump's face flushed into sudden, dimpled pleasure.

"Duluth! You're *the* Iris Duluth of the movies?"

"Yes," said Iris.

"Oh, why didn't you tell me over the phone? My favorite actress! How exciting! Poor thing—mobbed by your fans. Of course you may use the patio. I will give you the key to open your French windows. Any time."

Miraculously the chain was off the door. It opened halfway and then stopped. Miss Crump was staring at me with a return of suspicion.

"You *are* Miss Duluth's husband?"

"Mrs. Duluth's husband," I corrected her. "Lieutenant Duluth."

She still peered. "I mean, you have proof?"

I was beyond being surprised by Miss Crump. I fumbled from my wallet a dog-eared snapshot of Iris and me in full wedding regailia outside the church. Miss Crump studied it carefully and then returned it.

"You must please excuse me. What a sweet bride! It's just that I can't be too careful—for Poppy."

"Poppy?" queried Iris. "The St. Bernard?"

Miss Crump nodded. "It is Poppy's house, you see. Poppy pays the rent."

"The dog," said Iris faintly, "pays the rent?"

"Yes, my dear. Poppy is very well-to-do. She is hardly more than a puppy, but she is one of the richest dogs, I suppose, in the whole world."

Although we entertained grave doubts as to Miss Crump's sanity, we were soon in swimming suits and stepping through our open French windows into the sunshine of the patio. Miss Crump introduced us to Poppy.

In spite of our former prejudices, Poppy disarmed us immediately. She was just a big, bouncing, natural girl unspoiled by wealth. She greeted us with great thumps of her tail. She leaped up at Iris, dabbing at her cheek with a long, pink tongue. Later, when we had settled on striped mattresses under orange trees, she curled into a big clumsy ball at my side and laid her vast muzzle on my stomach.

"Look, she likes you." Miss Crump was glowing. "Oh, I knew she would!"

Iris, luxuriating in the sunshine, asked the polite question. "Tell us about Poppy. How did she make her money?"

"Oh, she did not make it. She inherited it." Miss Crump sat down on a white iron chair. "Mrs. Wilberframe was a very wealthy woman. She was devoted to Poppy."

"And left her all her money?" I asked.

"Not quite all. There was a little nest egg for me. I was her companion, you see, for many years. But I am to look after Poppy. That is why I received the nest egg. Poppy pays me a generous salary too." She fingered nondescript beads at her throat. "Mrs. Wilberframe was anxious for Poppy to have only the best and I am sure I try to do the right thing. Poppy has the master bedroom, of course. I take the little one in front. And then, if Poppy has steak for dinner, I have hamburger.'' She stared intensely. ''I would not have an easy moment if I felt that Poppy did not get the best.''

Poppy, her head on my stomach, coughed. She banged her tail against the flagstones apologetically.

Iris reached across me to pat her. ''Has she been rich for long?''

''Oh, no. Mrs. Wilberframe passed on only a few weeks ago.'' Miss Crump paused. ''And it has been a great responsibility for me.'' She paused again and then blurted: ''You're my friends, aren't you? Oh, I am sure you are. Please, please, won't you help me? I am all alone and I am so frightened.''

''Frightened?'' I looked up and, sure enough, her little bird face was peaked with fear.

''For Poppy.'' Miss Crump leaned forward. ''Oh Lieutenant, it is like a nightmare. Because I know. I just know they are trying to murder her!''

''They?'' Iris sat up straight.

''Mrs. Wilberframe's nephew and his wife. From Ogden Bluffs, Utah.''

''You mentioned them when you opened the door.''

''I mention them to everyone who comes to the house. You see, I do not know what they look like and I do not want them to think I am not on my guard.''

I watched her. She might have looked like a silly spinster with a bee in her bonnet. She didn't. She looked nice and quite sane, only scared.

''Oh, they are not good people. Not at all. There is nothing they would not stoop to. Back in Glendale, I found pieces of meat in the front yard. Poisoned meat, I know. And on a lonely road, they shot at Poppy. Oh, the police laughed at me. A car backfiring, they said. But I know differently. I know they won't stop till Poppy is dead.'' She threw her little hands up to her face. ''I ran away from them in Glendale. That is why I came to La Jolla. But they have caught up with us. I know. Oh, dear, poor Poppy who is so sweet without a nasty thought in her head.''

Poppy, hearing her name mentioned, smiled and panted.

"But this nephew and his wife from Ogden Bluffs, why should they want to murder her?" My wife's eyes were gleaming with a detective enthusiasm I knew of old. "Are they after her money?"

"Of course," said Miss Crump passionately. "It's the will. The nephew is Mrs. Wilberframe's only living relative, but she deliberately cut him off and I am sure I do not blame her. All the money goes to Poppy and—er—Poppy's little ones."

"Isn't the nephew contesting a screwy will like that?" I asked.

"Not yet. To contest a will takes a great deal of money— lawyers' fees and things. It would be much, much cheaper for him to kill Poppy. You see, one thing is not covered by the will. If Poppy were to die before she became a mother, the nephew would inherit the whole estate. Oh, I have done everything in my power. The moment the—er—suitable season arrived, I found a husband for Poppy. In a few weeks now, the—the little ones are expected. But these next few weeks . . ."

Miss Crump dabbed at her eyes with a small handkerchief. "Oh, the Glendale police were most unsympathetic. They even mentioned the fact that the sentence for shooting or killing a dog in this state is shockingly light—a small fine at most. I called the police here and asked for protection. They said they'd send a man around some time but they were hardly civil. So you see, there is no protection from the law and no redress. There is no one to help me."

"You've got us," said Iris in a burst of sympathy.

"Oh . . . oh . . ." The handkerchief fluttered from Miss Crump's face. "I knew you were my friends. You dear, dear things. Oh, Poppy, they are going to help us."

Poppy, busy licking my stomach, did not reply. Somewhat appalled by Iris' hasty promise but ready to stand by her, I said:

"Sure we'll help, Miss Crump. First, what's the nephew's name?"

"Henry. Henry Blodgett. But he won't use that name. Oh, no, he will be too clever for that."

"And you don't know what he looks like?"

"Mrs. Wilberframe destroyed his photograph many years ago when he bit her as a small boy. With yellow curls, I understand. That is when the trouble between them started."

"At least you know what age he is?"

"He should be about thirty."

"And the wife?" asked Iris.

"I know nothing about her," said Miss Crump coldly, "except that she is supposed to be a red-headed person, a former actress."

"And what makes you so sure one or both of them have come to La Jolla?"

Miss Crump folded her arms in her lap. "Last night. A telephone call."

"A telephone call?"

"A voice asking if I was Miss Crump, and then—silence." Miss Crump leaned toward me. "Oh, now they know I am here. They know I never let Poppy out. They know every morning I search the patio for meat, traps. They must realize that the only possible way to reach her is to enter the house."

"Break in?"

Miss Crump shook her tight curls. "It is possible. But I believe they will rely on guile rather than violence. It is against that we must be on our guard. You are the only people who have come to the door since that telephone call. Now anyone else that comes to your apartment or mine, whatever their excuse . . ." She lowered her voice. "Anyone may be Henry Blodgett or his wife and we will have to outwit them."

A fly settled on one of Poppy's valuable ears. She did not seem to notice it. Miss Crump watched us earnestly and then gave a self-scolding cluck.

"Dear me, here I have been burdening you with Poppy's problems and you must be hungry. How about a little salad for luncheon? I always feel guilty about eating in the middle of the day when Poppy has her one meal at night. But with guests— yes, and allies—I am sure Mrs. Wilberframe would not have grudged the expense."

With a smile that was half-shy, half-conspiratorial, she fluttered away.

I looked at Iris. "Well," I said, "is she a nut or do we believe her?"

"I rather think," said my wife, "that we believe her."

"Why?"

"Just because." Iris' face wore the entranced expression

which had won her so many fans in her last picture. "Oh, Peter, don't you see what fun it will be? A beautiful St. Bernard in peril. A wicked villain with golden curls who bit his aunt."

"He won't have golden curls any more," I said. "He's a big boy now."

Iris, her body warm from the sun, leaned over me and put both arms around Poppy's massive neck.

"Poor Poppy," she said. "Really, this shouldn't happen to a dog!"

The first thing happened some hours after Miss Crump's little salad luncheon while Iris and I were still sunning ourselves. Miss Crump, who had been preparing Poppy's dinner and her own in her apartment, came running to announce:

"There is a man at the door! He claims he is from the electric light company to read the meter. Oh, dear, if he is legitimate and we do not let him in, there will be trouble with the electric light company and if . . ." She wrung her hands. "Oh, what shall we do?"

I reached for a bathrobe. "You and Iris stay here. And for Mrs. Wilberframe's sake, hang on to Poppy."

I found the man outside the locked front door. He was about thirty with thinning hair and wore an army discharge button. He showed me his credentials. They seemed in perfect order. There was nothing for it but to let him in. I took him into the kitchen where Poppy's luscious steak and Miss Crump's modest hamburger were lying where Miss Crump had left them on the table. I hovered over the man while he located the meter. I never let him out of my sight until he had departed. In answer to Miss Crump's anxious questioning, I could only say that if the man had been Henry Blodgett he knew how much electricity she'd used in the past month—but that was all.

The next caller showed up a few minutes later. Leaving Iris, indignant at being out of things, to stand by Poppy, Miss Crump and I handled the visitor. This time it was a slim brash girl with bright auburn hair and a navy-blue slack suit. She was, she said, the sister of the woman who owned the hacienda. She wanted a photograph for the newspapers—a photograph of her Uncle William who had just been promoted to Rear Admiral in the Pacific. The photograph was in a trunk in the attic.

Miss Crump, reacting to the unlikeliness of the request, refused entry. The redhead wasn't the type that wilted. When she started talking darkly of eviction, I overrode Miss Crump and offered to conduct her to the attic. The girl gave me one quick, experienced look and flounced past me into the hall.

The attic was reached by the back stairs through the kitchen. I conducted the redhead directly to her claimed destination. There were trunks. She searched through them. At length she produced a photograph of a limp young man in a raccoon coat.

"My Uncle William," she snapped, "as a youth."

"Pretty," I said.

I took her back to the front door. On the threshold she gave me another of her bold, appraising stares.

"You know something?" she said. "I was hoping you'd make a pass at me in the attic."

"Why?" I asked.

"So's I could tear your ears off."

She left. If she had been Mrs. Blodgett, she knew how to take care of herself, she knew how many trunks there were in the attic—and that was all.

Iris and I had dressed and were drinking Daiquiris under a green and white striped umbrella when Miss Crump appeared followed by a young policeman. She was very pleased about the policeman. He had come, she said, in answer to her complaint. She showed him Poppy; she babbled out her story of the Blodgetts. He obviously thought she was a harmless lunatic, but she didn't seem to realize it. After she had let him out, she settled beamingly down with us.

"I suppose," said Iris, "you asked him for his credentials?"

"I . . ." Miss Crump's face clouded. "My dear, you don't think that perhaps he wasn't a real police . . . ?"

"To me," said Iris, "everyone's a Blodgett until proved to the contrary."

"Oh, dear," said Miss Crump.

Nothing else happened. By evening Iris and I were back in our part of the house. Poppy had hated to see us go. We had hated to leave her. A mutual crush had developed between us in those few hours.

But now we were alone again, the sinister Blodgetts did not seem very substantial. Iris made a creditable *Boeuf Stroganov* from yesterday's leftovers and changed into a lime green négligée which would have inflamed the whole Pacific Fleet. I was busy being a sailor on leave with his girl when the phone rang. I reached over Iris for the receiver, said "Hello," and then sat rigid listening.

It was Miss Crump's voice. But something was horribly wrong with it. It came across hoarse and gasping.

"Come," it said. "Oh, come. The French windows. Oh, please . . ."

The voice faded. I heard the clatter of a dropped receiver.

"It must be Poppy," I said to Iris. "Quick."

We ran out into the dark patio. Across it, I could see the lighted French windows to Miss Crump's apartment. They were half open, and as I looked Poppy squirmed through to the patio. She bounded toward us, whining.

"Poppy's all right," said Iris. "Quick!"

We ran to Miss Crump's windows. Poppy barged past us into the living room. We followed. All the lights were on. Poppy had galloped around a high-backed davenport. We went to it and looked over it.

Poppy was crouching on the carpet, her huge muzzle dropped on her paws. She was howling and staring straight at Miss Crump.

Poppy's paid companion was on the floor too. She lay motionless on her back, her legs twisted under her, her small, gray face distorted, her lips stretched in a dreadful smile.

I knelt down by Poppy. I picked up Miss Crump's thin wrist and felt for the pulse. Poppy was still howling. Iris stood, straight and white.

"Peter, tell me. Is she dead?"

"Not quite. But only just not quite. Poison. It looks like strychnine. . . ."

We called a doctor. We called the police. The doctor came, muttered a shocked diagnosis of strychnine poisoning and rushed Miss Crump to the hospital. I asked if she had a chance. He didn't answer. I knew what that meant. Soon the police came and there was so much to say and do and think that I hadn't time to brood about poor Miss Crump.

We told Inspector Green the Blodgett story. It was obvious to us that somehow Miss Crump had been poisoned by them in mistake for Poppy. Since no one had entered the house that day except the three callers, one of them, we said, must have been a Blodgett. All the Inspector had to do, we said, was to locate those three people and find out which was a Blodgett.

Inspector Green watched us poker-faced and made no comment. After he'd left, we took the companionless Poppy back to our part of the house. She climbed on the bed and stretched out between us, her tail thumping, her head flopped on the pillows. We didn't have the heart to evict her. It was not one of our better nights.

Early next morning, a policeman took us to Miss Crump's apartment. Inspector Green was waiting in the living room. I didn't like his stare.

"We've analyzed the hamburger she was eating last night," he said. "There was enough strychnine in it to kill an elephant."

"Hamburger!" exclaimed Iris. "Then that proves she was poisoned by the Blodgetts!"

"Why?" asked Inspector Green.

"They didn't know how conscientious Miss Crump was. They didn't know she always bought steak for Poppy and hamburger for herself. They saw the steak and the hamburger and they naturally assumed the hamburger was for Poppy, so they poisoned that."

"That's right," I cut in. "The steak and the hamburger were lying right on the kitchen table when all three of those people came in yesterday."

"I see," said the Inspector.

He nodded to a policeman who left the room and returned with three people—the balding young man from the electric light company, the redheaded vixen, and the young policeman. None of them looked happy.

"You're willing to swear," the Inspector asked us, "that these were the only three people who entered this house yesterday?"

"Yes," said Iris.

"And you think one of them is either Henry Blodgett or his wife?"

"They've got to be."

Inspector Green smiled faintly. "Mr. Burns here has been with the electric light company for five years except for a year when he was in the Army. The electric light company is willing to vouch for that. Miss Curtis has been identified as the sister of the lady who owns this house and the niece of Rear Admiral Moss. She has no connections with any Blodgetts and has never been in Utah." He paused. "As for Officer Patterson, he has been a member of the police force here for eight years. I personally sent him around yesterday to follow up Miss Crump's complaint."

The Inspector produced an envelope from his pocket and tossed it to me. "I've had these photographs of Mr. and Mrs. Henry Blodgett flown from the files of the Ogden Bluffs *Tribune*."

I pulled the photographs out of the envelope. We stared at them. Neither Mr. or Mrs. Blodgett looked at all the sort of person you would like to know. But neither of them bore the slightest resemblance to any of the three suspects in front of us.

"It might also interest you," said the Inspector quietly, "that I've checked with the Ogden Bluffs police. Mr. Blodgett has been sick in bed for over a week and his wife has been nursing him. There is a doctor's certificate to that effect."

Inspector Green gazed down at his hands. They were competent hands. "It looks to me that the whole Blodgett story was built up in Miss Crump's mind—or yours." His gray eyes stared right through us. "If we have to eliminate the Blodgetts and these three people from suspicion, that leaves only two others who had the slightest chance of poisoning the hamburger."

Iris blinked. "Us?"

"You," said Inspector Green almost sadly.

They didn't arrest us, of course. We had no conceivable motive. But Inspector Green questioned us minutely and when he left there was a policeman lounging outside our door.

We spent a harried afternoon racking our brains and getting nowhere. Iris was the one who had the inspiration. Suddenly, just after she had fed Poppy the remains of the *Stroganov*, she exclaimed:

"Good heavens above, of course!"

"Of course, what?"

She spun to me, her eyes shining. "Barney Thtone," she lisped. "Why didn't we realize? Come on!"

She ran out of the house into the street. She grabbed the lounging policeman by the arm.

"You live here," she said. "Who's Barney Stone?"

"Barney Stone?" The policeman stared. "He's the son of the druggist on the corner."

Iris raced me to the drugstore. She was attracting quite a crowd. The policeman followed, too.

In the drugstore, a thin young man with spectacles stood behind the prescription counter.

"Mr. Stone?" asked Iris.

His mouth dropped open. "Gee, Miss Duluth. I never dreamed . . . Gee, Miss Duluth, what can I do for you? Cigarettes? An alarm clock?"

"A little girl," said Iris. "A little girl with sandy pigtails and a brace on her teeth. What's her name? Where does she live?"

Barney Stone said promptly: "You mean Daisy Kornfeld. Kind of homely. Just down the block. Seven-twelve. Miss Duluth, I certainly . . ."

"Thanks," cut in Iris and we were off again with our ever growing escort.

Daisy was sitting in the Kornfeld parlor, glumly thumping the piano. Ushered in by an excited, cooing Mrs. Kornfeld, Iris interrupted Daisy's rendition of *The Jolly Farmer*.

"Daisy, that picture you took of me yesterday to sell to Mr. Stone, is it developed yet?"

"Geeth no, Mith Duluth. I ain't got the developing money yet. Theventy-five thenth. Ma don't give me but a nickel an hour for practithing thith gothdarn piano."

"Here." Iris thrust a ten-dollar bill into her hand. "I'll buy the whole roll. Run get the camera. We'll have it developed right away."

"Geeth." The mercenary Daisy stared with blank incredulity at the ten-dollar bill.

I stared just as blankly myself. I wasn't being bright at all.

I wasn't much brighter an hour later. We were back in our apartment, waiting for Inspector Green. Poppy, all for love, was trying to climb into my lap. Iris, who had charmed Barney Stone into developing Daisy's films, clutched the yellow envelope of snaps in her hand. She had sent our policeman away on a secret mission, but an infuriating passion for the dramatic had kept her from telling or showing me anything. I had to wait for Inspector Green.

Eventually Iris' policeman returned and whispered with her in the hall. Then Inspector Green came. He looked cold and hostile. Poppy didn't like him. She growled. Sometimes Poppy was smart.

Inspector Green said: "You've been running all over town. I told you to stay here."

"I know." Iris' voice was meek. "It's just that I wanted to solve poor Miss Crump's poisoning."

"Solve it?" Inspector Green's query was skeptical.

"Yes. It's awfully simple really. I can't imagine why we didn't think of it from the start."

"You mean you know who poisoned her?"

"Of course." Iris smiled, a maddening smile. "Henry Blodgett."

"But . . ."

"Check with the airlines. I think you'll find that Blodgett flew in from Ogden Bluffs a few days ago and flew back today. As for his being sick in bed under his wife's care, I guess that'll make Mrs. Blodgett an accessory before the fact, won't it?"

Inspector Green was pop-eyed.

"Oh, it's my fault really," continued Iris. "I said no one came to the house yesterday except those three people. There was someone else, but he was so ordinary, so run-of-the-mill, that I forgot him completely."

I was beginning to see then. Inspector Green snapped: "And this run-of-the-mill character?"

"The man," said Iris sweetly, "who had the best chance of all to poison the hamburger, *the man who delivered it*—the man from the supermarket. We don't have to guess. We have proof." Iris fumbled in the yellow envelope. "Yesterday morning as we were going out, we bumped into the man delivering Miss Crump's groceries. Just at that moment, a sweet little girl took a snap of us. This snap."

She selected a print and handed it to Inspector Green. I moved to look at it over his shoulder.

"I'm afraid Daisy in an impressionistic photographer," murmured Iris. "That hip on the right is me. The buttocks are my husband. But the figure in the middle—quite a masterly likeness of Henry Blodgett, isn't it? Of course, there's the grocery apron, the unshaven chin . . .''

She was right. Daisy had only winged Iris and me but with the grocery man she had scored a direct hit. And the grocery man was unquestionably Henry Blodgett.

Iris nodded to her policeman. "Sergeant Blair took a copy of the snap around the neighborhood groceries. They recognized Blodgett at the supermarket. They hired him day before yesterday. He made a few deliveries this morning, including Miss Crump's, and took a powder without his pay.''

"Well . . .'' stammered Inspector Green. "Well . . .''

"Just how many charges can you get him on?'' asked my wife hopefully. "Attempted homicide, conspiracy to defraud, illegal possession of poisonous drugs. . . . The rat, I hope you give him the works when you get him.''

"We'll get him all right,'' said Inspector Green.

Iris leaned over and patted Poppy's head affectionately.

"Don't worry, darling. I'm sure Miss Crump will get well and we'll throw a lovely christening party for your little strangers. . . .''

Iris was right about the Blodgetts. Henry got the works. And his wife was held as an accessory. Iris was right about Miss Crump too. She is still in the hospital but improving steadily and will almost certainly be well enough to attend the christening party.

Meanwhile, at her request, Poppy is staying with us, awaiting maternity with rollicking unconcern.

It's nice having a dog who pays the rent.

Hugh Pentecost

One of the great veterans of crime fiction, Hugh Pentecost (Judson P. Philips) was awarded the prestigious Grand Master Award of the Mystery Writers of America in 1973 for a lifetime of contributions to the field, including more than one hundred novels and hundreds of short stories. However, the award, while certainly deserved, was premature in the sense that he is still going strong and has produced more than a dozen books since that date. His work under his famous pen name and under his real name features strong plotting and solid character development, especially those stories that portray young people under stress. Hugh Pentecost is truly a professional's professional.

CHAMBRUN GETS THE MESSAGE

BY HUGH PENTECOST

There is an old story about two wealthy gentlemen having dinner together in one of their homes. After dinner they retire to the library where the butler serves brandy and coffee and passes the cigars. The host stands with his back to the fireplace where, over the mantel, is a stuffed moose head. "Did I ever tell you about my moose hunt?" the host asks. "No, but don't," says his friend. "Because I know how it came out."

This story would be a kind of a "moose head" to anyone who is a regular patron of the Beaumont, New York's top luxury hotel. It you were to go into the Trapeze Bar for a cocktail any evening after work, you would see Victoria Haven at her usual corner table, accompanied by her Japanese friend, and holding court as usual. There is no way to create suspense over whether or not she survived the attempt to murder her because there she is, "alive and well and living in Paris" as the song goes. This cannot be called a "whodunit" because it wasn't "dun," but the story of how Victoria Haven kept herself from being murdered in cold blood is, I think, worth the telling.

In a time when everyone calls everyone else by his or her first name, Victoria Haven calls me Haskell, never once using my first name, Mark. It reminds me of when I was a kid in prep school and I was Haskell, M. when they called the roll in study hall. I have a crush on the lady, which may produce a snicker here and there. Mrs. Victoria Haven admits, without a blush to having been born in 1900. I am thirty-five, the Public Relations Director of the Hotel Beaumont. Mrs. Haven lives in a penthouse on the roof and I see her almost every day of my life and look forward to it. She is something!

The Beaumont is famous for a number of things, primarily for its legendary manager, Pierre Chambrun. He is the king, the mayor, the boss of a small city within a city. He presides over

223

his own police force, a shopping center, restaurants and bars, a
bank, a health club, hospital facilities, and the living quarters
for a thousand guests. Some of us who work for Chambrun
think he has a magical radar system located behind his bright
black eyes. He seems able to sense a malfunction in the Swiss-
watch operations of the world he rules even before it happens.

Unfortunately Chambrun can't change human nature. He can't
eliminate greed, or jealousy, or a passion for revenge, or the
impulse toward treachery and betrayal in the individual man or
woman. And so, as in every other place on earth, these ugly
psychoses erupt in Chambrun's world too, and hamper man's
efforts to lead peaceful and orderly lives.

It was one of these dark and twisted impulses that threatened
the life of Victoria Haven in the spring of this year.

Not long ago a film company was considering one of the
stories I've written about Chambrun. They asked me if I could
suggest any actor who might play the role of the Great Man.
Unfortunately the perfect choice is no longer available, the late
Claude Rains. Chambrun is short, stocky, but elegant in his
movements. His dark eyes are buried in deep pouches, and they
can twinkle with humor, grow warm with compassion, or turn
as cold as a hanging judge's. His clothes are custom tailored,
his shirts, ties, and shoes made to order. He is something of a
Beau Brummell, but he handles it naturally, without affectation.

He, too, has a very special place in his heart for Victoria
Haven. It is whispered backstage that long ago there was a
young man-older-woman relationship between the two of them.
She obviously has some kind of special drag with Chambrun
because she is allowed to break so many house rules.

Chambrun became the managing genius of the Beaumont in
the early '50s, and, at the same time, Victoria Haven bought
one of the three penthouses on the roof, a cooperative arrangement at that time. She was obviously a woman of means,
because even in those days it was an expensive piece of real
estate. There are two other penthouses flanking the lady's residence. Chambrun lives in one of them and the other is held in
reserve for visiting foreign diplomats, in New York on United
Nations business.

Only one elevator goes to that top level, and the man who
operates it won't take you there without word from the front

desk that Chambrun, or Mrs. Haven, or the guest in Penthouse Number 3 has approved, in effect has given the green light. You are as safe up there from unwanted intrusion as if you were detached from the rest of the world. Or so it seemed.

I have mentioned Mrs. Haven's Japanese friend who sits with her in the Trapeze Bar at the cocktail hour. He is one of the house rules that Mrs. Haven is allowed to break. He is a small snubnosed Japanese Spaniel, snarling, unfriendly, contemptuous. He sits on his own chair, on his own red satin cushion, and indicates clearly that he is bored with the sophisticated social world of the Beaumont. His name to Toto.

Actually in my time at the hotel, there have been two Totos, and I understand that there was still another before that. Pets are not allowed in the hotel, but Toto is the exception. Mrs. Haven and "my Japanese gentleman friend" are, you might say, landmarks. If for some reason they miss the cocktail hour in the Trapeze, or are late appearing, Mr. Del Greco, the maitre d', is swamped with anxious inquiries from the regulars who fear something may have happened to the lady and her companion.

She is not inconspicuous.

At eighty-one Victoria Haven is tall, ramrod-straight. She walks briskly, like a woman of thirty. Her hair, quantities of it, is piled on top of her head, a henna-red that God never dreamed of. She wears plain, black silk dresses, sedate and proper, but she has on enough dazzling rings, bracelets, pendants, and earrings to send the manager of Tiffany's racing back to his store to check on the inventory.

"I have been a kept woman all my life, Haskell," she told me one day, "but not one of these baubles came to me for any other reason than love—good, sensuous, passionate love."

She had started out toward the end of World War One as a dancer in a cabaret, Chambrun told me. "She had legs that put the Betty Grables of her time to shame."

At eighty-one she is an outrageous and altogether charming flirt. I've never seen her with a woman friend, but men of all ages flock to her table in the Trapeze, ignoring Toto's growling hostility. She is still all woman, and fifty years ago she must have been the living end.

She was dangerously close to another kind of end that spring day. Afterward she told me she had wondered. "I felt a little like William Saroyan,'' she said, ''who said to the press just before the end that he'd been told that all of us have to face death, but he'd supposed an exception would be made in his case. I've always thought that, Haskell, but yesterday I wasn't so sure. Not sure at all.''

The complex problems of maintenance in an establishment like the Beaumont are beyond imagination. I'm not talking about maid service, cleaning crews, waiters and maitre d's, chefs, kitchen staffs, bellboys, telephone switchboard operators—services supplied by people. I was thinking of the maintenance of machinery. I'm talking about a forty-story building that has to be heated in winter, air-conditioned in summer, about two banks of elevators that have to be kept in service around the clock, about ice machines, refrigerator rooms, hundreds of different electrical gadgets that supply special luxuries to the guests—portable broiler-ovens, toasters, drink mixers, and on and on. There are three chief engineers, each working an eight-hour shift plus a crew of men who know exactly how everything works and where everything is located.

That staff of experts was prepared to deal with any sort of emergency that might develop in the hotel's equipment, and to maintain regular maintenance checks. Occasionally, however, outside specialists become involved. Twice a year the two banks of elevators are checked out by experts from the manufacturer. If any parts or cables or controls need replacing, these outsiders deal with the problem. It is a part of some kind of warranty.

Their presence is never particularly noticed, because they put only one car at a time out of commission. In the case of the roof and its three penthouses, however, this makes for a brief dislocation for the top-level residents—Chambrun, Mrs. Haven, and whoever may be in Penthouse Number 3. Only one elevator goes to the roof and when that is being checked out, it means the boss, Mrs. Haven, and the guest in Number 3 will have to use the fire stairs from the fortieth floor to the thirty-ninth, to come and go for perhaps two or three hours.

Chambrun, of course, knows when it is going to happen and arranges accordingly. Mrs. Haven and the guest in Number 3 are notified a couple of days in advance, reminded, and re-

reminded. The period of non-service is always from ten in the morning till about two in the afternoon.

One of the extraordinary things about Chambrun is his knowledge of the personal lives of all the hundreds of people who work for him, from Betsy Ruysdale, his fabulous secretary, down to the lowliest dishwasher in the main kitchen. He knows family histories, how many children there are, the schools they go to, medical problems, and so on. People will give an arm for him because he is aware of their problems before he is told. He does not have this kind of special knowledge, however, of the people who come in from the outside, like the elevator experts. That lack of knowledge came close to costing Victoria Haven her life.

The hotel's security force in command of Jerry Dodd, a wiry, bright-eyed, very tough former F.B.I. agent, is a marvel of efficiency. You go into the hotel and wander down some corridor where you are not supposed to go, or open the door of some anteroom, and someone is almost instantly at your elbow, asking you what cooks. But when special service people come in no one checks on them. They have free run of the place to do their jobs, whatever they may be. So what happened to Victoria Haven could not be blamed on Chambrun or Jerry Dodd. Neither one of them is psychic, although I sometimes wonder about Chambrun.

One more note before the curtain rises on a beautiful spring day with Death threatening to play the leading role. When I first came to know Mrs. Haven she had a routine that has since been abandoned. Three times a day and once in the latish evening she charged through the lobby with Toto under her arm. The little spaniel had to "do his duty." On a summer day, when a topcoat wasn't necessary, she was quite a sight, her jewelry glittering and flashing. I remember remarking to Chambrun that she was asking for trouble with all the junkies and muggers populating the streets. Every day we heard of someone snatching a gold chain or some other piece of jewelry off a lady's neck, or wrist, or hand. Victoria Haven was too inviting a target, I thought.

Chambrun gave me a wry smile and said nothing. But I learned, doing my own snooping, that every time she went out one of Jerry Dodd's men strolled after her. If anyone had even so much as taken a step toward the lady he would have been instantly confronted by an armed and tough security man. No one, I learned, had ever told the lady she was being protected, but I think she was too clever, too observant, not to have noticed it. I tell this only to show how closely Chambrun watched over her. When the city passed a law that pet owners had to follow their dogs equipped with scoopers, Mrs. Haven abandoned her outdoor forays.

"I would not be caught dead following Toto around with a shovel," she announced to the world at large.

A special place in her roof garden was set aside for Toto's problem, which explains why, on the day the elevator to the roof was out of service, Mrs. Haven had no reason to leave her penthouse.

On that day, a few minutes after noon, Victoria Haven came face to face with Death. He didn't look like Death or anyone dangerous. He was a small, dark young man sitting just outside her garden hedge, eating his lunch from a brown paper bag. Mrs. Haven was made aware of his presence by Toto, who, spotting a stranger, made bloodcurdling noises of protest through his upturned nose. Looking over her garden hedge, Mrs. Haven saw the man, and that he was wearing grease-stained coveralls.

"Toto!" she called. "My dog isn't partial to strangers. You are working on the elevator?"

The man—almost a boy, she thought—gave her a bright smile. "Lunch break," he said.

"What is your name?" she asked.

"Carl," he said.

"I'm not partial to first names," Mrs. Haven told him. "What is your last name?"

"Stratton," he said. "I am Carl Stratton. And you, ma'am?"

"I am Mrs. Victoria Haven," she said.

His smile became even brighter. "Victoria is a nice name—Victoria."

There was a kind of impertinent flirtatiousness about him that pleased the lady. "It's pretty hot out here in the sun," she said.

"After working in the dark shaft all morning it is pleasant," Stratton said. "But if I'm in the way—"

"Would you like some iced tea to go with your sandwich?" she asked. "I have some already made in the refrigerator."

"That would be most pleasant," he said. He was not looking her in the eyes any longer. His attention seemed to be directed toward her conspicuous display of rings, bracelets, and pendants.

"Come on inside and I'll pour you some," Mrs. Haven said.

Toto expressed his outrage with a snarl and disappeared into the garden. Mrs. Haven preceded the expectant Stratton through the front door into her penthouse.

I imagine Stratton was as astonished by what confronted him inside this obviously rich lady's living quarters as I was the first time I saw it. You expected elegance and grandeur but that isn't what you saw. The first impression one had was of total disorder, a crowded storage space for junk. There was twice as much old Victorian furniture as the place could comfortably contain. Heavy red velvet drapes shut out the world, day and night. Bookcases overflowed into stacks of books on the floor and stacks of newspapers from God-knows-how-far-back.

When you first recover from this apartment's incredible collection of rubble, you make a discovery. There isn't a speck of dust anywhere. The entire apartment is spotless. What appears to be total disorder is obviously perfect order to Mrs. Haven. "Ask for an article from the op-ed page of *The New York Times* from ten years back," Chambrun once told me, "and she will reach out, probably not moving from her chair, and produce it for you. She knows exactly where anything she cherishes is located."

Mrs. Haven left Stratton in this antique-dealer's paradise and went to the kitchen to get him the promised iced tea. He looked around him, intently curious, not daring to move anything from a chair in order to sit down. Mrs. Haven reappeared with iced tea in a frosted glass.

"Just throw that stuff off that chair, there, Stratton, and sit," the lady said.

He picked up some papers from a Windsor chair as if he might find a Black Widow spider hiding beneath them. He accepted the tea, his eyes focused on the diamond-studded pin that decorated the front of her dress.

"You have jewels for a queen," he said.

She smiled at him. "I had more fun acquiring them than most queens do," she said.

"The way things are today you must have a good safe to keep them in," Stratton remarked.

"Jewels are no fun if you keep them locked away," she said. "Will the elevator be running when they promised—at two o'clock?"

"Before that if all goes well," he said.

"Splendid. I have an appointment at five—as usual."

"You're not afraid of thieves?" he asked.

"I am as well guarded in this hotel as if it were Fort Knox," she said.

Casual talk and the time came for Carl Stratton to get back on the job. He thanked the lady politely, carried his empty glass back into the kitchen, thanked the lady again, and departed.

A nothing moment, if you had asked Mrs. Haven just then. She had done a kindness for a maintenance man who was, indirectly, making certain a service she counted on was in working order. She would have given a cold drink to almost anyone on a hot day. An unmemorable moment in an unmemorable day—so far.

At five o'clock that afternoon Mrs. Haven and Toto went down for their customary cocktail hour in the Trapeze Bar. It was an early evening when many friends stopped by her table to chat. A British diplomat whom she'd met years ago in Cairo was delighted to encounter her again and invited her to dine with him.

"Lord Ormsby," she told us later. "Willie Belton when I met him just after World War One. Damned near as old as I am. Horrible shape, though. Walks with a stick."

They dined in the Blue Lagoon, our night club. Toto is not allowed in the main dining room. The two old people apparently had a lovely time reliving half a century or more. It was nearly eleven when Mrs. Haven and Toto returned to her penthouse.

"Willie offered to escort me up to the roof," Mrs. Haven told us later, "but I told him chivalry didn't have to go that far. Good thing he accepted the idea. The dear old boy might have got himself killed!"

So it was that she returned to the roof alone, except, of course, for Toto. The little dog was left in the garden. He had a special "dog door" in and out of the kitchen which he could manage by himself. Mrs. Haven let herself in at the front door, switched on the lights, and found herself facing Carl Stratton standing in the doorway to the kitchen.

"How did you get in here?" Mrs. Haven asked sharply.

"Fixed the lock on the kitchen door when I was here earlier," Stratton said. "Where do you keep them?"

"Keep what?"

"Your jewels, Victoria. Where do you keep them? I've turned the place upside down—no safe, no strongbox. Where are they?"

Maybe she made some kind of instinctive gesture, because he stepped forward and snatched away her suitcase-like handbag, and backed away, opening it.

"My God!" he said.

"Safest place to keep them is with me," Mrs. Haven said.

"My God!" Stratton said again. "In here—and on you—there must be a million bucks' worth!"

"I should have estimated it a little higher than that," Mrs. Haven said. She dropped down in the big armchair which Chambrun called her throne. "So you've got them, Stratton. Would you mind very much leaving me the privacy to go to bed?"

He moistened his lips. "How old are you, Victoria?" he asked.

"Eighty-one—if it matters," she said.

"It matters," Stratton said, his eyes very bright. "Eighty-one years is quite a lot of living. It makes what I have to do a little less difficult."

"What you have to do?"

"Well, I can't go off with your million dollars and leave you to tell the police who was responsible." He shifted her bag under one arm, and from inside his coat he produced a switchblade knife. "I'm going to have to silence you rather permanently, Victoria. I'll try to make it as painless as possible."

He took a step toward her and out of the kitchen came Toto, snarling fiercely.

"I'll cut your stinking little head off, buster, if you don't stay away from me!" Stratton shouted.

"Toto!" The old woman's voice was clear and controlled. "Go somewhere and tend to your own business!"

The little dog gave Stratton a parting snarl, and headed back for the kitchen. Mrs. Haven leaned back in her chair.

"I suppose you have no choice, Stratton," she said. "Perhaps you would let me have one cigarette before you cut my throat."

Without waiting for Stratton to answer, she began fumbling in the stack of newspapers next to her chair. When she turned to face him again she was holding a giant handgun, a small cannon, aimed straight at his heart.

"Now, my young idiot," she said, "you will bring me that telephone and we'll put an end to this. It has a nice long cord on it."

He stared at her, like a bird fascinated by a cobra. "The phone won't work, Victoria. I cut the wires when I first let myself in."

"Then we'll just have to wait, won't we?" Mrs. Haven said.

"Wait for what?"

"Why, for someone to come."

"When will that be?"

"Who knows? I rather doubt there will be anyone before the maid who comes about nine in the morning."

The heavy gun was steady as a rock in Mrs. Haven's hand, her elbow resting on the arm of her chair. Stratton must have been thinking the old woman couldn't keep it steady for too long. He moistened his lips, and there were little beads of sweat on his forehead. The light glittered on the blade of his knife.

"Do you really know how to use that thing, Victoria?" he asked.

"Oh, my, do I know how!" Mrs. Haven said, smiling at him. "One of the first men in my life was a very rich oil man from Texas. He saw me at a nightclub where I was dancing."

"You were a dancer?" The young man was playing for time, trying to judge the distance between himself and the "throne."

"A very good one," Mrs. Haven said. "But my Texas friend was traveling around the world in those days. He wanted me with him and I wanted to be with him. He was afraid someone might try to get at him through me, so he taught me how to handle a gun. Would you believe I can still hit a fifty-cent piece at fifty paces?"

"Not really," Stratton said.

"You had better believe." Mrs. Haven smiled grimly. "My Texas friend gave me this diamond clasp I'm wearing." She touched the pin on the front of her dress with her free hand. "That was over fifty years ago. I suggest you sit down, young man. It will be a long time until the maid comes."

He sat down, facing her, wondering how long it would be before the gun hand wavered. It couldn't be too long now.

"My friend from Texas taught me to shoot with both hands," Mrs. Haven said, almost casually. "I am as good left-handed as I am right-handed." With which she shifted the gun from one hand to the other. That way, Stratton realized, she could hold out for a long, long time.

Could she really handle the gun, he wondered? If he made a quick lunge at her would she react in time? Something in her cold blue eyes warned him to wait. In time fatigue would overtake this aged crone.

"If you'd care for a little music while we wait," Mrs. Haven said, "you can turn on the hi-fi set over there in the corner."

"You're as crazy as a bedbug, Victoria," Stratton said. "I can last longer than you can last."

"I know what you're hoping for, Stratton," she said. "Don't count on it."

An hour went by, with two people staring at each other, with Death waiting for one of them in the wings. Then Toto reappeared, snarling and whimpering.

"Toto! I told you to go somewhere and tend to your own business!" Mrs. Haven said, a sharp edge to her voice.

The little dog gave her a sullen look and padded back into the kitchen.

A little after midnight I went up to Chambrun's penthouse with him. There was some kind of convention being held in the Beaumont the next day and Chambrun had a list of names he wanted me to have which he hadn't brought down to his second-floor office. We sat there, having a drink and going over the next day's details, when I heard an unusual sound.

"You got rats in the woodwork?" I asked Chambrun.

"I think not," he said. He walked over to the garden door and opened it. There, looking up at us sullenly, was Toto, Mrs. Haven's Japanese friend.

"I didn't know you and Toto were friends," I said.

"We're not," Chambrun said. "He hates my guts." Even as he spoke he was picking up the phone. "Get me Jerry Dodd," he said. A moment later he had our head security man on the line. "There's something wrong in Mrs. Haven's penthouse," Chambrun told him. "Get the passkeys and get up here on the double."

I couldn't believe it. "She's sick, you think? Let's get over there, boss."

"We'll wait for Jerry," he said.

It seemed like forever—I suppose it was less than ten minutes—before Jerry Dodd arrived. We could tell there were lights on in Mrs. Haven's penthouse, but we couldn't see in.

"Damned drapes are always drawn," Chambrun said. "Give me the front-door passkey, Jerry. You take the back." He glanced at his watch. "Twelve seventeen. We'll all go in at precisely twenty past."

And we did.

Mrs. Haven sat there, holding her gun on Stratton. When he saw Chambrun he decided to make a run for it. As he passed the kitchen door, Jerry Dodd knocked him cold with the butt of his gun.

Mrs. Haven's pale blue eyelids lowered for a moment as she put her cannon down on the stack of newspapers beside her chair. Then she gave us a report on what had happened.

"Would you have shot him, Victoria?" Chambrun asked.

"I haven't fired a gun for more than fifty-five years," Mrs. Haven said. "And anyway, I took the bullets out of this thing years ago. I was afraid someone would stumble on it and hurt themselves."

"An empty gun!" I heard Jerry Dodd mutter. He was hand-cuffing the unconscious Stratton behind his back.

"I always said, Dodd, that I could have been a very good actress," Mrs. Haven said. "That misguided young man seems to have bought my performance. I had to be good, you know. He was going to kill me."

Toto was sniffling on the floor beside her chair.

"Extraordinary that he had the instinct to go for help," I said.

Chambrun gave Mrs. Haven a wry smile. "We'd better show

Mark how it works, Victoria,'' he said, ''or we'll have a whole new folklore about animals.''

Mrs. Haven stood up and looked down at the little dog.

"Go somewhere, Toto, and tend to your own business," she said.

Toto gave her a bored look and went out to the kitchen. I could hear his little dog door open and close. Mrs. Haven went to one of the windows and opened the drape. She beckoned to me and I could see Toto trotting across the roof to Chambrun's penthouse. We watched him reach the garden door and scratch on it.

"I have trained him to follow that command—'go tend to your own business,'" Mrs. Haven said. "Pierre has always been concerned about my having so much of value here. If Toto ever scratched on his door he'd know I had more trouble than a stomachache. Tonight I had to send him twice before you came upstairs, Pierre."

So that was how Chambrun got the message.

Barry Perowne

Barry Perowne (aka Philip Atkey), born in Wiltshire, England, began his literary career editing two magazines publishing romantic and humorous fiction, and writing stories and paperback originals about Dick Turpin the highwayman and Red Jim the first air detective. He acquired rights to E.W. Hornung's character, the cracksman Raffles, and updated him. Fourteen of these stories, oginally published in *Ellery Queen's Mystery Magazine*, were anthologized in *Raffles Revisited* (1974).

RAFFLES ON THE TRAIL OF THE HOUND

BY BARRY PEROWNE

"I wonder if by any chance, Mr. Raffles, you're one of those discriminating people who may be described, perhaps, as Sherlockians?"

The question was tossed suddenly at A. J. Raffles by Mr. Greenhough Smith, distinguished editor of England's leading monthly periodical, *The Strand Magazine.*

It was a morning in dubious springtime, and a fitful sun shone in through the windows of Mr. Smith's editorial sanctum in Southampton Street, just off London's busy Strand.

Mr. Smith had invited Raffles, England's best-known cricketer, to contribute an article on the game, and dropping in on Mr. Smith to discuss the matter, Raffles had brought me along with him.

Knowing what I knew about the least suspected side of Raffles' life, the criminal side, I felt uncomfortable when Mr. Smith, agreement having been reached with Raffles for the cricket article, asked his unexpected question.

"Why, yes, Mr. Smith," Raffles replied, at ease in a saddle-bag chair, his suit immaculate, a pearl in his cravat, his dark hair crisp, his keen face tanned. "I think Bunny Manders and I can claim to be—shall we say—amateur Sherlockians. Eh, Bunny?"

"Certainly, Raffles," I murmured uneasily, taking my cue from him and accepting a Sullivan from his proffered cigarette-case.

"You may be interested, then," said Mr. Greenhough Smith, "to note this big basketful of letters on my desk. They're just a small part of the mail that's been flooding in from readers of Dr. Conan Doyle's latest tale, *The Hound of the Baskervilles.* It's the twenty-sixth published adventure of Sherlock Holmes.

237

Its first installment appeared last year, in *The Strand Magazine* for August 1901. It's eighth and final installment is in the current issue—practically vanished already from the bookstalls. You may have been reading the tale?''

''Bunny Manders and I consider it,'' said Raffles, ''the most enthralling Holmes adventure that's so far appeared.''

''An opinion, to judge from these letters,'' said Mr. Smith, ''concurred in by most readers—with one curious exception.''

The jingle of passing hansoms was faintly audible from South-ampton Street as Mr. Smith, polishing his scholarly glasses, frowned at a letter that lay open before him on his blotting-pad.

''You know, Mr. Raffles,'' he went on, ''Dr. Doyle was asked recently if he'd based the character of Sherlock Holmes on any real-life original. He replied that he had had in mind a preceptor of his undergraduate days at Edinburgh University, a certain Dr. Joseph Bell. On being told of this, Dr. Bell smiled. He said that Dr. Doyle's kind remembrance of his old teacher had made much of very little and that the real-life Sherlock Holmes is, in fact, Dr. Conan Doyle himself.''

My palms moistened with embarrassment, for Raffles and I knew from personal experience that Dr. Joseph Bell's remark was only too true. Back at a time when Dr. Conan Doyle had been an obscure medical practitioner in the naval town of Portsmouth and had published, to no great acclaim, only the first of his Sherlock Holmes tales, *A Study in Scarlet*, Raffles and I had had an encounter with Dr. Doyle and had nearly gone to prison as a result.

Now here in Mr. Greenhough Smith's editorial sanctum twenty-five Sherlock Holmes tales later, with the great detective and his creator known the world over, the conversation had taken a turn I found distinctly disquieting.

But Raffles merely tapped ash casually from his cigarette and said, ''To amateur Sherlockians, Dr. Joseph Bell's remark provides food for thought, Mr. Smith.''

''Of late,'' Mr. Smith said, ''Dr. Doyle's own great investigative ability has been concentrated on a challenge of the times we live in. As you may know, on the success of the Holmes tales, he abandoned medicine for literature. However, when the recent regrettable war with the Boers broke out, he abandoned literature for medicine—in order to serve in South Africa with the Langman Field Hospital. That photograph of him was taken at the time.''

Among the framed drawings and signed photographs on the walls of Mr. Smith's Sanctum was the original, I saw now, of an illustration for *The Hound of the Baskervilles*, depicting Sherlock Holmes, in deerstalker cap and Inverness cape, firing his revolver at the apparition of a gigantic hound charging with lambent eyes and slavering jaws out of the fog of a Dartmoor night.

Beside this illustration of the fictional Holmes hung a photograph of his creator, the real-life Sherlock Holmes. Big, burly, bushy-moustached, wearing khaki fatigues and a sun-helmet and smoking a Boer curved pipe, he was shown standing, a stalwart, uncompromising figure, against a background of Red Cross bell-tents on the parched South African *veld*.

"You may have met Dr. Doyle out there?" Mr. Smith asked.

"As Yeomanry subalterns for the duration, Bunny Manders and I served in a different sector," said Raffles, naturally making no mention of our Portsmouth encounter with Dr. Doyle, which had occurred years before the Boer War.

"Now that peace has been restored," said Mr. Smith, "Dr. Doyle has felt it his duty to investigate foreign allegations, not made by the Boers themselves, that the British used dum-dum bullets and committed other transgressions. As a doctor who had a good many Boer prisoners, wounded and sick, pass through his hands, he saw no evidence to support the allegations. He considers them to emanate from tainted sources with a vested interest in maintaining discord among nations."

"The traffickers in armaments," said Raffles.

"Exactly! And our government," said Mr. Smith, "apparently considering it beneath its dignity to heed such allegations, Dr. Doyle has undertaken the task of investigation himself, at great personal expense of time and money. He has, nowadays, a world-wide audience. He feels a duty to it and to the cause of Peace, for he knows that when he speaks it's with a voice known to the world—the voice of Sherlock Holmes."

"Quite so," said Raffles.

"Dr. Doyle has gathered his documented evidence in rebuttal," said Mr. Smith, "in a book he calls *The South African War: Its Cause and Conduct*, written without fee and printed far below cost by a sympathetic publisher. With the object of financing the translation of the book into many languages and its printing and world-wide distribution, gratis, a Fund has been opened for the receipt of contributions—''

''A Fund?'' said Raffles, his grey eyes alert.

''A 'War Book Fund,' '' said Mr. Smith, ''administered by Dr. Doyle's own bank—and also, you may recall, as Sherlockians, Holmes's bank—the Capital and Counties, Oxford Street branch. Of course, this great task which Dr. Doyle has taken upon his broad shoulders leaves him no time for fiction. In fact, he tells me he intends *The Hound of the Baskervilles* to be his last Holmes tale—which is bad news, of course, for the writers of all these letters. Strange as it may seem, I dare not bother him with them in his present mood—which is a pity, because there's one here in particular that—''

He broke off and called, ''Come in!''

The door opened to admit a tall young man, meticulously frock-coated, with a high collar and clean-cut, intellectual features.

''My Assistant Editor,'' said Mr. Smith, introducing us and handing the newcomer a sheaf of page proofs. ''You want these for Mr. W. W. Jacobs? Very well, they can go off to him now. We mustn't keep humorists waiting. By the way, I was thinking of getting Mr. Raffles' impression of that letter from Dartmoor.''

''It's a hoax, Mr. Smith,'' said the Assistant Editor firmly. ''It's another humorist at work—an unlicensed one. It'd be a mistake to bother Dr. Doyle with it, especially at this time. An impudent hoax would not only annoy Dr. Doyle, it'd just about put the lid on his determination to write no more Holmes tales. Gentlemen, if you'll excuse me—''

With a brisk nod to Raffles and myself, the Assistant Editor, obviously busy, left us.

''He's probably right about this letter,'' said Mr. Smith, as the door closed. ''It came in this morning, in an envelope postmarked Bovey Tracey. That's a small town—the 'Coombe Tracey' of *The Hound of the Baskervilles*—on the edge of Dartmoor. No harm in getting a fresh eye cast on this letter. As a man of the world, Mr. Raffles, what d'you make of this?''

I read the letter, amateurishly typewritten on a machine with a faded blue ribbon, over Raffles' shoulder:

Dartmoor,
Devonshire.
27th March 1902

The Editor,
The Strand Magazine,
London.

Sir,

As a resident in the Dartmoor area, scene of *The Hound of the Baskervilles*, now concluded in the current issue of your magazine, I have read the narrative with particular interest.

Your author, A. Conan Doyle, has based his tale on the case, well known in this area since 1677, of Sir Richard Cabell, Lord of the Manor of Brooke in the parish of Buckfastleigh. This evil-living baronet, in the act of raping a virgin, had his throat torn out by an avenging hound, which then, according to legend, took on phantom form, to range evermore upon Dartmoor.

Your author has adapted the legend to his own purpose, making the Phantom Hound "the curse of the Baskervilles" and skillfully using the topography and certain phenomena of Dartmoor to lend his tale verisimilitude. Among such phenomena mentioned by him are strange nocturnal howlings sometimes heard, as indeed of some huge hound baying the moon. Sceptics attribute these sounds to natural causes—the wind in the rocks of the moorland tors, or the slow upwelling and escape of vegetable gas from the depths of the treacherous Dartmoor mires, such as the Fox Tor morass which your author chooses to call "the great Grimpen Mire."

These sounds, and other phenomena mentioned in his tale, have never in fact been satisfactorily explained. I had hoped that your author might advance some theory to account for them. I now find, however, that he is content to end his tale with Mr. Sherlock Holmes destroying the "phantom hound" with five shots from a revolver, proving the beast to be mortal and doctored with phosphorescent paste in order for an evildoer to secure an inheritance by chicanery.

Sir, I must confess to a slight sense of disappointment, and I feel constrained to describe to you a recent experience of my own.

As something of a folklorist, I have cultivated the acquaintance, for the sake of his unique knowledge of the moor, of a certain local deer-poacher, sheep-stealer, all-around ne'er-do-well. I am, frankly, ashamed of my furtive association with the man. However, he came stealing one night to my back door not long ago. His poacher's sawed-off shotgun had been confiscated.

He begged the loan of my twelve-bore and a handful of cartridges. For some time, I gathered, a lurcher-like bitch he owned, a rangy, grizzly-grey beast he called Skaur, had been wild on the moor. Trouble was now brewing over sheep wantonly hamstrung and other depredations. The police were on the look-out for the culprit—Skaur, my acquaintance was certain, though he had long ago given it out that the bitch was dead and buried. If the police now got her and proved his ownership, it would mean gaol for him, as he could not pay the fines and damages.

He was in such a panic to down Skaur before the police did so that I lent him my gun. About a week later, he appeared again one night at my door, a deeply shaken man. He had sighted Skaur, shot her, and crippled her. Following her blood trail, he found her laired among the rocks. She lay panting, bloodstained, with three grizzly-grey whelps so savagely at her dogs that she was like to be eaten while yet alive.

As he crouched, peering into the lair in the failing daylight and howling wind, some instinct made him look round. He swears that, stealing towards him, was a creature, big as a pony, shadowy—some species of enormous hound. He shot at it, wildly—and the apparition was gone.

The fellow was in such a state when he came to me that it was all I could do to get him, the following day, to take me on the long, rough trudge across some of the worst parts of Dartmoor to the alleged lair.

It exists. Skaur lay there dead, ripped and torn by her

own whelps. Sir, I have never seen on canine pelts such curious markings as those on these savage creatures. I have penned them into the lair and, at considerable inconvenience, kept them alive. Curious as to their sire, I have maintained long vigils at the lair by day and night, but have caught no glimpse of the creature described by my ne'er-do-well acquaintance, though I have heard, on two occasions, a distant, grievous, hound-like howling—but no conclusion, of course, can be drawn from that nocturnal phenomenon.

I can devote no further time to this matter. I intend to shoot the whelps. I have no desire, as you will appreciate, for my association with my unsavoury acquaintance to become known. I must guard my local good repute—and hence maintain my anonymity in this matter. However, I will make this much concession: If your author should wish to view the strange whelps, he should insert forthwith, in the Personal column of the daily *Devon & Cornwall Gazette*, an announcement to this effect: 'Sirius—instructions awaited.'

There will then be mailed to your office a map of Dartmoor with, clearly marked upon it, the precise location of the lair of the strange whelps. What your author may then choose to do about them, should he look into the matter, will be his responsibility, not mine.

In the event of no announcement appearing, as specified above, by 7th April, I shall carry out the intention I have expressed in this notification.

Meantime, I have the honour to be, Sir, yours truly,

SIRIUS

"Well, Mr. Raffles?" said Mr. Greenhough Smith, as Raffles returned the letter to him.

"A hoax, obviously," Raffles said. "Eh, Bunny?"

"Undoubtedly, Raffles," I said.

"How well, Mr. Smith," Raffles asked, glancing at the illustration of the fictional Sherlock Holmes and the photograph of the real-life Sherlock Holmes, on the wall, "is Dr. Doyle actually acquainted with Dartmoor?"

"He spent a few days there, researching for *The Hound of the*

Baskervilles," said Mr. Smith, "at just about this time last year. He was with his friend, Mr. Fletcher Robinson, of Ipplepen, Devonshire, who knows Dartmoor well and told Dr. Doyle of the legend of the Phantom Hound which inspired his *Baskerville* tale. You know, I'm sorry—in a way—that you consider this letter a hoax. I had just a faint hope that, if I let Dr. Doyle see it, it might kindle a spark in his creative mind—and result perhaps in a sequel to *The Hound of the Baskervilles*."

"I'm afraid," Raffles said, with a smile, "it would be more likely to annoy him, as your Assistant Editor remarked."

"Common sense tells me you're right, of course. Ah, well!" Mr. Smith put the letter, rather reluctantly, into a drawer of his desk and became business-like. "Now, Mr. Raffles, about a delivery date for your cricket article—"

A date readily agreed upon by Raffles, we took our leave.

"I suppose that, as usual when you get an invitation to write about cricket, Raffles," I said, as we sauntered down Southampton Street, "you expect me, as a one-time journalist, to ghost-write this article for you?"

"Why else, except for you to hear Mr. Smith's briefing for it, would I have brought you with me this morning, Bunny? Innocent appearances in print are useful cover for—shall we say—less innocent activities. But literary toil's more your cup of tea than mine, though it would have been impolitic to mention your spectral function to Mr. Smith."

"I appreciate that," I said. "I'm not complaining. I just feel, seeing that the throes of composition fall upon me, that you might have held out for a later delivery date."

"You'll manage, Bunny," said Raffles absently. "Dartmoor air will stimulate your muse."

"Dartmoor air?" I stopped dead. "Why should we go to Dartmoor?"

Raffles gave me a strange look.

"To see a man about a dog, Bunny—if we can find him!"

In the first-class smoking compartment we had to ourselves in the train going down to Devonshire next day, Raffles explained his reasoning to me.

"Dr. Doyle's probably long ago forgotten our Portsmouth encounter with him, Bunny, but I never have. I made a humiliating mistake on that occasion. He detected it. I respect that man. The figure I cut in his eyes on that Portsmouth occasion is something I can't forget till I've levelled the score with him. If I could do him a service, even though he may never know of it, I'd feel—in my own mind—that I'd settled an account long outstanding to my own self-respect. And I could turn the page and forget.''

A heavy shower lashed the train windows.

''Raffles,'' I said uneasily, ''we'd be well advised to let sleeping dogs lie.''

''Every instinct tells me, Bunny, that the dog in that 'Sirius' letter is very wide-awake. I think that letter's an attempt to set a trap. I think 'Sirius' is a man with a mission. I think he's a running dog of those 'tainted sources' who'd like to stop the translation and free world-wide distribution of Dr. Doyle's book disproving their mischief-making allegations. He carries that whole project on his own shoulders. Remove Dr. Doyle, in some way that would appear mere accident, and the world-wide project would die on the vine, and, incidentally, the career of the fictional Sherlock Holmes would end with the career of the real-life one.''

''Who,'' I argued, ''being what we know him to be, would be as quick as you are to suspect a trap in that letter!''

''Of course he would, Bunny. And, being the man he is, he might decide—if he saw that letter—to track down 'Sirius' himself. That's why I told Mr. Greenhough Smith I thought the letter a hoax. 'Sirius' thought, of course, that the letter would be passed on immediately to Dr. Doyle. 'Sirius' couldn't know what we know, which is that Mr. Smith was in two minds about it—an editorial predicament. *We* don't want Dr. Doyle to see that letter, Bunny, because *we* want to be the ones to kennel 'Sirius'!''

''How?''

''He has a weak spot, Bunny. His whole letter proclaims it. He's a Sherlockian!''

I stared. The train rat-tatted along, vibrating, through the wind-blown rain. Raffles offered me a Sullivan from his case.

''Consider what's probably happened, Bunny. Assume 'Sirius' to be a man briefed to queer Dr. Doyle's pitch. Seeking ways and means to get at him, 'Sirius' reads *The Hound of the*

Baskervilles—with its vivid descriptions of the natural hazards of Dartmoor. Where most likely, thinks 'Sirius,' for Dr. Doyle to meet with a fatal accident than among the scenes of his own tale—if somehow he could be lured there?''

My heart began to thump.

''If I'm right,'' said Raffles, ''the idea of a trap probably began to shape in the mind of 'Sirius' as he finished his reading of *The Hound of the Baskervilles*—the end of which, he says, 'disappointed' him. It's highly unlikely that the man is, in fact, a Dartmoor resident. So what would he do?''

''Reconnoitre the area himself,'' I said, ''to decide just where and how he could best contrive a trap.''

''Furthermore, Bunny, he'd want to find out just how familiar Dr. Doyle really is with the area. 'Sirius' would probably ask a question here and there, to find out if Dr. Doyle had personally explored Dartmoor and, if so, how extensively. So—what are you and I to look for?''

''An inquisitive stranger!''

''Asking questions, Bunny, within—probably—the past couple of weeks, because the current issue of *The Strand Magazine*, containing the end of the *Baskerville* tale, only became available about then. No, Bunny, 'Sirius' shouldn't be hard to find. He's like you and me—a deviant Sherlockian.''

''Deviant?''

''Avowed Sherlockians, Bunny, are interested in the *fictional* Sherlock Holmes. You and I are interested in tracing the footsteps of the real-life Sherlock Holmes, Dr. Doyle. So, I suspect, is 'Sirius.' Now, as Mr. Greenhough Smith told us, Dr. Doyle *did* visit Dartmoor almost exactly a year ago. If we can find out who's been sniffing, just recently, to pick up a scent of Doyle on Dartmoor, we'll have discovered the prowling hound, the deviant Sherlockian—'Sirius.' And here, by the look of it,'' Raffles added, ''is our first glimpse of the moor coming up.''

The daylight was fading. Bleak hills swept by wind and rain loomed in the distance—the outlying bastions of Dartmoor with its sombre tors and quaking morasses, its neolithic hut circles and notorious prison. As I peered through the train window at those brooding sentinel hills, my own reading of *The Hound of the Baskervilles* gave me a haunting sense of having been here before—in the company of Sherlock Holmes, Dr. Watson, and the menaced Sir Henry Baskerville.

After changing to a local train, Raffles and I arrived that night at Lydford Station and put up at an inn under Black Down on the moor's edge.

"Dr. Conan Doyle?" said the landlady, in reply to Raffles' inquiry. "In these parts this time last year? No, sir, I don't recolleck any Dr. Doyle."

"Have you had any visitor during the last couple of weeks?" Raffles asked.

"No, sir, you're the first for many a month. Dartmoor gets visitors in the summer, more. Mostly they like to see the Sepulchre—which is the tomb of Sir Richard Cabell, 'im as was Lord o' the Manor, wenching and carrying on in 'is prime, over Buckfastleigh way. Ended up with 'is throat tore out by the 'Ound that turned phantom, as is well known in these parts."

Raffles and I exchanged a glance.

"There's a key'ole in the door of Sir Richard's tomb," said the landlady, "an' to this day, if you pokes yer finger through, 'is skeleton'll up an' gnaw at it."

"There are mysteries on Dartmoor, Missus," agreed Raffles, "and you'll join us in a nightcap to steady us. What'll you take?"

"Just a small port-and-peppermint," said Missus graciously.

All next day Raffles was out on the moor on a hired hunter, seeking word of Dr. Doyle's visit to these parts a year ago. The weather was vile, and I was not sorry that my duty as Raffles' "ghost" kept me indoors by the snuggery fire, working on his cricket article while the wind wuthered in the thatched and dripping eaves.

As the wan daylight faded and Missus brought the lamp in, lighted, and drew closed the snuggery curtains against the howling dark, there still was no sign of Raffles. It was a night when one could believe in the Phantom Hound, a night for it to be abroad on the desolate moor. I began to grow anxious. But, at last, Raffles returned, soaked to the skin. And when he had changed, and Missus set before us on the snuggery table a great round of beef and a foaming jug of nut-brown ale drawn from the wood, I was left alone with him, and I asked how he had got on.

"Not badly, Bunny," he said. "I made a start at Bovey Tracey, on the far side of the moor. That's the 'Coombe Tracey' of *The Hound of the Baskervilles*, and I struck what we're seeking—the trail behind the tale." He began, obviously famished, to carve the juicy sirloin, perfectly roast. "Dr. Conan Doyle's remembered at Bovey Tracey, both he and his friend Mr. Fletcher Robinson. Two big, genial, moustached gentlemen, Bunny, making a holiday of their explorations on Dartmoor for Dr. Doyle's tale of the Hound."

"What about 'Sirius'?"

"Not a sniff, as yet, of that inquisitive Sherlockian. I'll get his scent tomorrow, with luck. After you with the horseradish, Bunny."

But it was not until our fourth night at the Black Down inn that Raffles returned from his own explorations with a glint in his eyes that I knew well.

"Got him, Bunny! I picked up his scent at Widecombe-in-the-Moor. I had the luck to fall into conversation with the Vicar there—elderly man, a devoted Sherlockian himself. He told me about a man who'd called at the Vicarage about ten days ago—a tall, lean, mean-eyed individual, a stranger to the Vicar, who said there was something about the look of the chap that made him think of some lines the poet Shelley once wrote. The old Vicar quoted them to me:

> "I met Murder on the way.
> He had a mask like Castlereagh.
> Very grey he looked and grim.
> Seven bloodhounds followed him."

"My God, Raffles!" I breathed.

"Apparently," Raffles said, "he told the Vicar he was a bookdealer visiting country houses and would give a good price for any first editions they might care to part with—such as first editions of Dr. Conan Doyle's books. A good gambit, Bunny, to start asking if Dr. Doyle was known to have visited the area."

"It's 'Sirius,' for a certainty!"

"You can lay to that. But there are only *two* bloodhounds following him—you and me, Bunny. And the scent's now hot and rank, because the old Vicar told me he recognised the horse the fellow was riding—a hack hired from an inn called Rowe's Duchy Hotel at Princetown.''

"That's where that damnable prison is, Raffles."

"The highest point on Dartmoor, Bunny—Princetown. And we'll shift our base to there in the morning."

In the night, the wind dropped. The weather changed. We hired a dogcart from Missus. Raffles took the reins. Under a leaden sky, we clattered along the potholed road to Princetown. A strange stillness brooded over the moor, its desolation relieved here and there by great, smooth patches of green among the rocks and heather—the deceptive, inviting green of the deadly quagmires. The distant tors loomed up, strange and jagged in the distance, out of a growing hint of mist.

Suddenly, on that lonely road, we came upon a grisly procession—a shuffling file of convicts in knickerbockers and tunics stamped with broad arrows. Under a strong escort of blue-uniformed Civil Guards armed with carbines and fixed bayonets, Britain's born losers trudged along with picks and shovels over their shoulders, their sullen, shaved heads sunk on their chests.

"There, Bunny," Raffles muttered, "but for the grace of God—"

I knocked on wood as our dogcart clattered on past. And, about lunchtime, there loomed up ahead of us the house of a thousand hatreds, the most notorious of penitentiaries, its great, gaunt complex of buildings towering starkly over the squat little cluster of dwellings, Princetown, isolated under the gunmetal sky.

"Caution's our watchword, Bunny," Raffles said, as he reined in our horse before the long, low, stone-built inn that faced the prison across a deep dip in the moor. "We'll feel out the ground."

We found the landlord behind his counter in the Bar Parlour. A stout man in his shirtsleeves, with an oiled cowlick of hair, he was polishing the shove-ha'p'ny board. He gave us good-day and Raffles ordered a Scotch-and-soda for each of us.

"See any lags on the road?" a voice asked.

We turned from the bar. There was one other customer

present, sitting on a settle by the window. Lean, tall, powerfully built, gaunt of face, with a mean, tight mouth under a small, wax-pointed, sergeant-major type moustache, he wore a buttoned-up frockcoat and a bowler.

"Yes," Raffles said, "we saw a group."

"Being marched in from the stone quarries, huh? At this hour? That means there's fog coming up."

The man drained his tankard, mopped his moustache with a red bandanna handkerchief, stood up and, with a curt nod to the landlord, went out.

"Have a drink yourself, landlord," said Raffles.

"Thank 'ee, sir—just a small nip o' gin, then, to give me an appetite. You gents on holiday?"

"Snatching a few days from the treadmill," said Raffles. "Like that gentleman, perhaps, who just went out?"

"Well, no, sir, that's—but I better not mention his name, he likes to keep it quiet." The landlord glanced around, lowered his voice. "Between ourselves, gents, he's the Man with the Cat."

I stared. We had come to Dartmoor to see a man about a dog.

"The Man with the Cat?" said Raffles.

The landlord nodded. "It's not like the bad old days, sir, when it was done 'ap'azard. We're in a new century now. When a lag's ordered strokes nowadays, it has to be done civilized. So the Man with the Cat comes down from the Prison Commissioners in London to do it. He brings the Cat-o-Nine-Tails in proper hygienic wrappings. He has to do the job within a prescribed time of the lag bein' sentenced, to avoid mental anguish, and lay the Cat on for the best effect—scientific.

"He lodges with me for a night or two when he comes down on 'is business. If 'e lodges in the prison, the lags seem to smell 'e's arrived. They catcalls all night, yowling *miaouw miaouw* like a thousand randy toms on the roof, to keep him from sleepin'. They kick up a hell of a shindy, to sap 'is strength. The man's a bit too much in love with 'is work, for my taste. I gets a lodgin' allowance for him from the Commission, but I can't say I like the man."

"I'm sure," said Raffles. "Landlord, I think we'll have another drink. Is that gentleman your only guest just now?"

"No, sir, we've one other in the house. Book-dealer gent. Rides round to country 'ouses, tryin' to buy up old books, not that he seems to have much luck. Asked me, he did, when he arrived a week or so ago, if I'd 'appened to read the tale about our Phantom 'Ound in a magazine. Well, I don't get the time for reading, but we had the writer of it lodgin' here about a year ago, a Dr. Doyle, 'oo 'ad a Mr. Robinson an' Mr. Baskerville with him."

"Mr. *Baskerville*?" Raffles exclaimed.

The landlord chuckled. "I showed the book-dealer gent our Guest Book to prove it." He produced a leather-covered volume from under his counter, consulted the pages, then turned the book to Raffles and me. "See for yourselves, sir."

Under the date 2nd April 1901 were two signatures, one firm and clear, the other boldly scrawled:

A. Conan Doyle, M.D., Norwood, London.

Fletcher Robinson, Ipplepen, Devon (and coachman, Harry M. Baskerville)

"Mr. Robinson brought 'is own dogcart and coachman, see," said the landlord. "Mr. Baskerville'd drive the two gents 'ere an' there on the moor, then wait with the dogcart when the gents trudged off to points they could only get to afoot. Mr. Baskerville took 'is meals in the kitchen with me an' my family an' staff. 'E was tickled pink because Dr. Doyle'd asked him if he'd mind bein' knighted and put in a tale as Sir 'Enry Baskerville. Talk about laugh."

"Well, well!" said Raffles. "There's more behind some of these magazine stories than meets the eye. Is your book-dealer guest still staying here?"

"Yes, sir. He's out just now. He's out all day, most days, on a horse I hires him. If he ain't back well before dark, by the look of it, he'll get fogged in an' have to put up in some shepherd's bothy. Dartmoor's dangerous in fog."

"Then perhaps we'd be wise to spend the night here ourselves," said Raffles. "Got a couple of vacant rooms?"

"Certainly, sir."

As soon as we had been shown to our rooms, I joined Raffles in his.

"The so-called book-dealer's our man, Bunny. He's 'Sirius,' all right. I want to find his room and take a look at his things

while he's out.'' Raffles opened a door, listened at the crack,
then turned. ''Mealtime sounds from downstairs, Bunny. The
inn folk are in the kitchen, eating. Now's my chance. Watch
from that window. If a grey-faced man on a horse arrives, open
this door and start whistling *Drink, Puppy, Drink*.''

He was gone. I watched from the window. I thought of the
'Sirius' letter that implied the existence of ''Baskerville whelps,''
and Whyte-Melville's old hunting ditty ran eerily through my
mind:

> ''Drink, puppy, drink, and let every puppy drink.
> That's old enough to lap and swallow,
> For he'll grow into a hound, so let's pass the bottle round,
> And merrily we'll whoop and hollo!''

Outside, a stealing mist was beginning faintly to obscure the
gaunt building of the prison across the plunging dip in the
moorland. In front of the inn our dogcart still stood, the horse
munching in its nosebag. No man came riding enigmatic out of
the mist. And suddenly, silently, Raffles was back in the room.

''Got him, Bunny—knew his room because it's the only one
with a few books in it. There was a locked portmanteau. I
opened it with the little gadget I carry. There's a small Blick
typewriter with a faded ribbon in the portmanteau.''

''That settles it,'' I said.

''Not quite, Bunny. There's also an envelope containing five
sheaves of currency notes, each sheaf £100. I dared not take it,
of course. There's an Ordinance Survey map of Dartmoor in the
portmanteau. I took a look at the map. I could faintly make out
the pressure marks left by a pencil when a tracing had been
made over the map, and a small *x* marked on it.''

''The alleged 'lair of the whelps,' Raffles!''

''Not only that, Bunny. There's also in the portmanteau a
copy of the daily *Devon & Cornwall Gazette*, with a small
announcement in the Personal column ringed round in pencil:
'Sirius—instructions awaited.' ''

My heart stopped.

''The one thing we didn't want, Bunny,'' Raffles said, his
grey eyes hard, ''must have happened. Mr. Greenhough Smith
has shown the 'Sirius' letter to Dr. Doyle, and that real-life
Sherlock Holmes has smelled the trap in it—damn it, he'd be

bound to, knowing what *we* know of him! If he inserted that announcement, it's because he's decided to catch 'Sirius' himself, knowing the 'tainted sources' he's probably working for. But, Bunny, that copy of the *Devon & Cornwall Gazette* is four days old! I checked the date on it.''

Raffles was searching, as he spoke, through the things in his own valise.

''You see what it means, Bunny? If the map tracing showing the alleged lair of the whelps was posted to *The Strand Magazine* the day the announcement appeared in the *Gazette*, the tracing could have reached Dr. Doyle the day before yesterday, assuming normal mail. He may be on the moor now—the real-life Holmes! He may already have caught 'Sirius' in a counter-trap.''

''Or''—I hardly dared say it—'' 'Sirius' caught him?''

''My money—remembering Portsmouth—is on the real-life Holmes,'' Raffles said grimly. He was studying his own Ordinance Map, dug out from his valise. He made a small x on the map with a pencil. ''There we are, Bunny. There it is—out on the moor—the alleged 'lair of the whelps,' at the neolithic Stone Rows near Higher White Tor. There's where 'Sirius' has set his trap and where he's been keeping vigil over it every day for Doyle to walk blindly into it, 'Sirius' *hopes*!''

''For all we know,'' I said, ''he may be out there at this moment!''

''Bunny,'' Raffles said grimly, ''they may *both* be out there at this moment, stalking each other in this fog that's closing in. There may be *just* a chance that we can take a hand and square a long-outstanding account. The dogcart's outside. The map shows Higher White Tor and the Stone Rows to lie almost due north from Princetown here. Come on!''

Raffles at the reins, the horse jingled along, now at a trot, now at a canter, along a rough track through the heather, the wheels of the dogcart jolting and grinding. Mist, slowly deepening over the moor, was beginning to take on the grey tinge that presaged the menace of a Dartmoor peasouper.

Presently, the track became impossible for the dogcart. We left it and trudged on afoot. Heather, sparse and tough, grew among scattered, loose flints, which became more plentiful as we went on.

"Prehistoric flint-chippings, Bunny," Raffles said, "workings of our skin-clad ancestors, the beetle-browed Dawn Men. We must be getting near their settlement, the Stone Rows."

Suddenly a cry came, thin and inhuman, from somewhere ahead. We checked, listening. Again came the cry, soaring to a neighing, despairing screech, and abruptly ceased.

"There's a Dartmoor pony gone," said Raffles, "mired in some morass, and not far off."

I felt the insidious vapour, dankly chill like grave sweat on my face, as we trudged on—blindly, for my part—up a slope that now was virtually a glacis of flint-chippings, debris of the Dawn Men.

"Down!" breathed Raffles. "Listen!"

Flat on my belly beside him, I discerned a thickening in the mist ahead. A little above our level, the thickening was probably one of the Stone Age hut circles, up there on a small plateau. I heard a slight crunching sound. Somebody was walking around among the ruins.

Raffles inched higher, keeping flat. I followed. The rock-edge of the plateau loomed now just above us. I made out the shadowy form of a man up there. From our low-angle viewpoint, he looked like a very thin, tall funeral mute in a high hat and cemetery black.

"The 'book-dealer,' " Raffles breathed in my ear. " 'Sirius.' "

The man's elongated legs moved like scissors as he paced slowly to and fro between the plateau-edge and a ruined hut-wall dimly perceptible in the mist. A strange figure, this gaunt assassin who had been riding about Dartmoor on a hired horse, sniffing at the year-old trail of the author of *The Hound of the Baskervilles*.

The man passed from view around the angle of the hut wall. We seized our chance to clamber higher, then froze as he reappeared. He resumed his pacing. We kept low. I could feel the thumping of my heart against the ground. Hours seemed to pass. A man of deadly patience, this "Sirius," who must thus for two, perhaps three days now have been keeping vigil here over his trap, baited with whelps that never were.

Even as the thought crossed my mind, as I crouched there beside Raffles on the steep slope in this mist-muffled, silent solitude, the man checked his pacing and stood as though intently listening. Then he did a thing that raised the hair on my head.

He howled like a mournful hound.

The wailing cry died away in the mist. All was still, the man a long shadow, listening. I heard faintly, as from the further slope of this tumulus or plateau, the clink of a shod horse's hooves, then walking. The sounds stopped.

A yelp sounded, a sudden ky-yi-ing as of pain, a sharp bark, snarls and growling. Had the human source of these canine sounds not been dimly visible there above on the ledge, I would have sworn they emanated from a litter of whelps contending in a lair among the ruins.

"Bait," Raffles breathed. "He's got a revolver in his hand now. He's holding it clubbed. He's drawing his man on to look for the lair. As he comes around the hut wall, he'll be clubbed senseless and dragged down for disposal in the mire where we heard that pony scream as it was sucked under."

"Who comes?" I whispered. "Dr. Doyle?"

I had no answer from Raffles, for just then, out of the mist-dim ruins of the Dawn Age dwellings, a voice rang, calling: "Is there anybody here?"

Silence. Then sudden, sharp barks, on a note of challenge and interrogation, as from the hidden lair of the "Baskerville Whelps." And, before I sensed his intention, Raffles lunged upwards to the ledge, seized the barking man by the ankles, and jerked his feet out from under him.

He toppled backwards against the hut wall, tore his ankles free, aimed a kick at Raffles' head, then with flying coat-tails made a huge bound clean over the both of us. He landed on the glacis, went slithering down it in a cascade of loose flints, and vanished into the mist.

"Who's there?"—again the voice, peremptory above us.

We looked up. From our angle, the man who stood now on the ledge above us loomed tall in the mist—not a burly figure like Dr. Conan Doyle, but a lean man, a man in a deerstalker cap and an Inverness cape, a figure known the world over, a figure out of *The Hound of the Baskervilles*.

I seemed to hear the cracking of the thin ice of human reason.

Neither Raffles nor I moved, staring up.

"Who are you?" the man on the ledge demanded, firmly authoritative, conspicuous on his eminence. "I require an answer. You recognise with whom you have to deal!"

I heard Raffles, beside me, draw in his breath, slowly, deeply, as though released from a thrall. Clambering up to the ledge, he stood erect there.

"Yes, we have met," he told the newcomer courteously. "You're the Assistant Editor of *The Strand Magazine*. How d'you do?"

My own bespelled trance dissolved. My reason restored to me, with reservations regarding the newcomer's garments, I clambered up on to the ledge.

Glibly, Raffles explained that, as amateur Sherlockians, he and I had been prompted by our reading of *The Hound of the Baskervilles* to spend a few days on Dartmoor while he worked on his cricket article. Visiting this prehistoric site, the Stone Rows, we had noticed a man here who was behaving oddly. As we watched the man, he suddenly had begun to foam at the mouth and emit canine sounds. Believing him to be seized of a fit of some kind, we had tried to succour him, but he had eluded our helpful attentions and bolted.

"I thought I heard a horse galloping away," said Raffles. "He must have had one tethered down there in the mist somewhere."

"But good God!" exclaimed the Assistant Editor. "Don't you realize, Mr. Raffles? That must've been the man himself—'Sirius'—the *Baskerville* hoaxer!"

"Indeed?" said Raffles, astonished. "Bunny, what a pity we lost him!"

The Assistant Editor, seeming rather nettled by our ineptitude, explained that he had been convinced from the first that the "Sirius" letter was a hoax. To prove it to Mr. Greenhough Smith, who still had been half inclined to let Dr. Doyle see the letter, the Assistant Editor had persuaded Mr. Smith to let him insert the reply—"Instructions awaited"—in *The Devon & Cornwall Gazette*.

On receipt by mail of a map tracing marked with the lair of

the alleged whelps, he had come down from London by train, spent the night at Coryton, then hired a horse and set out across the moor to find the marked spot, the Stone Rows.

"Lucky to find the spot, with this mist coming on," he said, not knowing how lucky he was not to have had his skull fractured, in mistake for Dr. Doyle's, and to have ended up in the mire that had swallowed the pony. "I borrowed this deer-stalker and cape," he said, "from the studio of our artist, Sidney Paget, who illustrates the Holmes stories. My idea was, if the hoaxer should show himself, to give the fellow the shock of his life by suddenly appearing before him as—Sherlock Holmes!"

"You gave *us* a shock," said Raffles ruefully. "Eh, Bunny?"

"Absolutely, Raffles," I said.

"Listen!" exclaimed the Assistant Editor. "What's that sound?"

From somewhere distant in the mist came, faintly, a prolonged, eerie howling. The Assistant Editor blenched, listening, a wild surmise in his eyes.

"It's all right," said Raffles. "That, I think, comes from Dartmoor Prison. The convicts must have learned they have a certain visitor in the vicinity."

From time to time, that night, we heard yowling and catcalling from the nearby prison.

Raffles mentioned it when we set off, very early next morning, in the dogcart, to return it to Missus and catch our train at Lydford. The Assistant Editor, who had also put up at Rowe's Duchy Hotel and who was to go up to London in the same train with us, was astride his hired horse, trotting a hundred yards ahead of us in the grey, foggy morning.

"The yowling from the prison didn't keep the Man with the Cat awake, Bunny," Raffles said. "He was snoring when I paid his room a visit in the night. Have a look in my valise."

Mystified, I unstrapped his valise and took out, in its hygienic wrappings bearing the seal of the Prison Commissioners, the Cat-o'-Nine-Tails.

"If sentence must be carried out within a prescribed time of its order," Raffles said, "there's a chance we may have saved some poor devil a flayed back today. There's a nice little quagmire just ahead on the left.''

He reined in the horse, looked each way along the road, took the Cat from me and, standing up in the cart, hurled the Cat from him, overarm. It arched high through the air, fell in the green scum, remained for a moment upright like some sordid Excalibur, then was dragged under by its heavy stock.

"The other visit I paid in the night, Bunny," said Raffles, as the horse jingled us on again, "was to the room of 'Sirius.' We gave him a shock at the Stone Rows. He hadn't returned to the inn. He wasn't in his room. I think he must have left Dartmoor. So I now have in my pocket the £500 from his portmanteau."

Raffles was mistaken, however. "Sirius" had not left Dartmoor, as I learned two days later, when I completed the cricket article to be signed "by A. J. Raffles" and took it round to his rooms in The Albany, just off Piccadilly.

He showed me a brief newspaper item. It stated that the finding of a riderless horse had led to the discovery on Dartmoor of a man, a guest at Rowe's Duchy Hotel, whose identity had not been satisfactorily established. The horse evidently had had a fall. The man's neck was broken.

"That's what comes," said Raffles, "of galloping a horse in a Dartmoor fog. Not really a clever man, Bunny—certainly not clever enough to catch the real-life Sherlock Holmes in a trap, even if Dr. Doyle had been shown the 'Sirius' letter. Now, about this money. Tainted as its source is, we'll retain £100 to cover our expenses. For the rest, we have an account to settle. It's been outstanding since twenty-five Sherlock Holmes stories ago, so it's high time we squared the account, for the sake of our self-esteem."

We jingled round in a hansom, in the springtime sunshine, to the bank mentioned to us by Mr. Greenhough Smith—Dr. Conan Doyle's own bank, the Oxford Street branch of the Capital & Counties, which he had named in his tales as the bank also of his fictional alter ego, Mr. Sherlock Holmes.

"There is here," Raffles said to the cashier at the counter, "the sum of £400—a contribution to the Fund for the translation into many languages and free world-wide distribution of Dr. Conan Doyle's book exposing the evil of slander between nations."

"Very good, sir," said the cashier, counting the currency notes with deft finger. "To whom do you wish this handsome contribution to be attributed?"

"As amateur Sherlockians, keenly looking forward to the appearance, some day, of a sequel to *The Hound of the Baskervilles*, my friend here and I would like to honour the gentleman who inspired Dr. Doyle's tale of the Phantom Hound. So attribute this contribution, please, to Sir Richard Cabell, and post the formal acknowledgment," said A. J. Raffles, "to his country seat—The Sepulchre, Parish of Buckfastleigh, Dartmoor, Devon."

Bill Pronzini and Jeffrey Wallmann

The multitalented Bill Pronzini has been entertaining mystery and suspense readers since the mid-1960s. His novels featuring "the nameless detective" are particularly popular and are to some extent autobiographical, since "Nameless," like his creator, is Italian, likes beer and owns a large collection of pulp magazines. Pronzini's large number of excellent short stories are only now beginning to be collected. He has also written extensively on the mystery field, and his *Gun In Cheek,* a masterful study of the genre through its *worst* works, is certain to become a landmark work. Jeffrey Wallmann has collaborated on several stories with him, including the one we offer here.

COYOTE AND QUARTER MOON

BY BILL PRONZINI AND
JEFFREY WALLMANN

With the Laurel County Deputy Sheriff beside her, Jill Quarter-Moon waited for the locksmith to finish unlatching the garage door. Inside, the dog—a good-sized Doberman; she had identified it through the window—continued its frantic barking.

The house to which the garage belonged was only a few years old, a big ranch-style set at the end of a cul-de-sac and somewhat removed from its neighbors in the expensive Oregon Estates development. Since it was a fair Friday morning in June, several of the neighbors were out and mingling in a wide crescent around the property; some of them Jill recognized from her previous visit here. Two little boys were chasing each other around her Animal Regulation Agency truck, stirring up a pair of other barking dogs nearby. It only added to the din being raised by the Doberman.

At length the locksmith finished and stepped back. "It's all yours," he said.

"You'd better let me go in with you," the deputy said to Jill.

There was a taint of chauvinism in his offer, but she didn't let it upset her. She was a mature twenty-six, and a full-blooded Umatilla Indian, and she was comfortable with both her womanhood and her role in society. She was also strikingly attractive, in the light-skinned way of Pacific Northwest Indians, with hip-length brown hair and a long willowy body. Some men, the deputy being one of them, seemed to feel protective, if not downright chivalric, toward her. Nothing made her like a man less than being considered a pretty-and-helpless female.

She shook her head at him and said, "No thanks. I've got my tranquilizer dart gun."

"Suit yourself, then." The deputy gave her a disapproving frown and stepped back out of her way. "It's your throat."

261

*   *   *

Jill drew a heavy padded glove over her left hand, gripped the dart gun with her right. Then she caught hold of the door latch and depressed it. The Doberman stopped barking; all she could hear from inside were low growls. The dog sensed that someone was coming in, and when she opened the door it would do one of two things: back off and watch her, or attack. She had no way of telling beforehand which it would be.

The Doberman had been locked up inside the garage for at least thirty-six hours. That was how long ago it had first started howling and barking and upsetting the neighbors enough so that one of them had complained to the Agency. The owner of the house, Jill had learned in her capacity as field agent, was named Edward Benham; none of the neighbors knew him—he'd kept to himself during the six months he had lived here—and none of them knew anything at all about his dog. Benham hadn't answered his door, nor had she been able to reach him by telephone or track down any local relatives. Finally she had requested, through the Agency offices, a court order to enter the premises. A judge had granted it, and along with the deputy and the locksmith, here she was to release the animal.

She hesitated a moment longer with her hand on the door latch. If the Doberman backed off, she stood a good chance of gentling it enough to lead it out to the truck; she had a way with animals, dogs in particular—something else she could attribute to her Indian heritage. But if it attacked she would have no choice except to shoot it with the tranquilizer gun. An attack-trained, or even an untrained but high-strung, Doberman could tear your throat out in a matter of seconds.

Taking a breath, she opened the door and stepped just inside the entrance. She was careful to act natural, confident; too much caution could be as provoking to a nervous animal as movements too bold or too sudden. Black and short-haired, the Doberman was over near one of the walls—yellowish eyes staring at her, fangs bared and gleaming in the light from the open doorway and the single dusty window. But it stood its ground, forelegs spread, rear end flattened into a crouch.

"Easy," Jill said soothingly. "I'm not going to hurt you."

She started forward, extending her hand, murmuring the words of a lullabye in Shahaptian dialect. The dog cocked its head, ears perked, still growling, still tensed—but it continued to stay where it was and its snub of a tail began to quiver. That was a good sign, Jill knew. No dog wagged its tail before it attacked.

As her eyes became more accustomed to the half light, she could see that there were three small plastic bowls near the Doberman; each of them had been gnawed and deeply scratched. The condition of the bowls told her that the dog had not been fed or watered during the past thirty-six hours. She could also see that in one corner was a wicker sleeping basket about a foot and a half in diameter, and that on a nearby shelf lay a curry comb. These things told her something else, but just what it meant she had no way of knowing yet.

"Easy, boy . . . calm," she said in English. She was within a few paces of the dog now and it still showed no inclination to jump at her. Carefully she removed the thick glove, stretched her hand out so that the Doberman could better take her scent. "That's it, just stay easy, stay easy . . ."

The dog stopped growling. The tail stub began to quiver faster, the massive head came forward and she felt the dryness of its nose as it investigated her hand. The yellow eyes looked up at her with what she sensed was a wary acceptance.

Slowly she put away the tranquilizer gun and knelt beside the animal, murmuring the lullabye again, stroking her hand around its neck and ears. When she felt it was ready to trust her she straightened and patted the dog, took a step toward the entrance. The Doberman followed. And kept on following as she retraced her path toward the door.

They were halfway there when the deputy appeared in the doorway. "You all right in there, lady?" he called.

The Doberman bristled, snarled again low in its throat. Jill stopped and stood still. "Get away, will you?" she said to the deputy, using her normal voice, masking her annoyance so the dog wouldn't sense it. "Get out of sight. And find a hose or a faucet, get some water puddled close by. This animal is dehydrated."

The deputy retreated. Jill reached down to stroke the Doberman another time, then led it slowly out into the sunlight. When they emerged she saw that the deputy had turned on a faucet built into the garage wall; he was backed off to one side now, one hand on the weapon holstered at his side, like an actor in a B movie. The dog paid no attention to him or to anyone else. It went straight for the water and began to lap at it greedily. Jill went with it, again bent down to soothe it with her hands and voice.

While she was doing that she also checked the license and rabies tags attached to its collar, making a mental note of the numbers stamped into the thin aluminum. Now that the tenseness of the situation had eased, anger was building within her again at the way the dog had been abused. Edward Benham, whoever he was, would pay for that, she thought. She'd make certain of it.

The moment the Doberman finished drinking, Jill stood and faced the bystanders. "All of you move away from the truck," she told them. "And keep those other dogs quiet."

"You want me to get the back open for you?" the deputy asked.

"No. He goes up front with me."

"Up front? Are you crazy, lady?"

"This dog has been cooped up for a long time," Jill said. "If I put him back, in the cage, he's liable to have a fit. And he might never trust me again. Up front I can open the window, talk to him, keep him calmed down.

The deputy pursed his lips reprovingly. But as he had earlier, he said, "It's your throat," and backed off with the others.

When the other dogs were still Jill caught hold of the Doberman's collar and led it down the driveway to the truck. She opened the passenger door, patted the seat. The Doberman didn't want to go in at first, but she talked to it, coaxing, and finally it obeyed. She shut the door and went around and slid in under the wheel.

"Good boy," she told the dog, smiling. "We showed them, eh?"

Jill put the truck in gear, turned it around, and waved at the scowling deputy as she passed him by.

At the agency—a massive old brick building not far from the university—she turned the Doberman over to Sam Wyatt, the resident veterinarian, for examination and treatment. Then she went to her desk in the office area reserved for field agents and sat down with the Benham case file.

The initial report form had been filled out by the dispatcher who had logged the complaint from one of Benham's neighbors. That report listed the breed of Benham's dog as an Alaskan husky, female—not a Doberman, male. Jill had been mildly surprised when she went out to the house and discovered that the trapped dog was a Doberman. But then, the Agency was a bureaucratic organization, and like all bureaucratic organizations it made mistakes in paperwork more often than it ought to. It was likely that the dispatcher, in checking the registry files for the Benham name, had either pulled the wrong card or miscopied the information from the right one.

But Jill kept thinking about the sleeping basket and the curry comb inside the garage. The basket had been too small for the Doberman but about the right size for a female husky. And curry combs were made for long-haired, not short-haired dogs.

The situation puzzled as well as angered her. And made her more than a little curious. One of the primary character traits of the Umatilla was inquisitiveness, and Jill had inherited it along with her self-reliance and her way with animals. She had her grandmother to thank for honing her curiosity, though, for teaching her never to accept any half-truth or partial answer. She could also thank her grandmother who had been born in the days when the tribe lived not on the reservation in northeastern Oregon but along the Umatilla River—the name itself meant "many rocks" or "water rippling over sand"—for nurturing her love for animals and leading her into her present job with the Agency. As far back as Jill could remember, the old woman had told and retold the ancient legends about "the people"—the giant creatures, Salmon and Eagle and Fox and the greatest of all, Coyote, the battler of monsters, who ruled the earth before the human beings were created, before all animals shrank to their present size.

But she was not just curious about Benham for her own satisfaction: she had to have the proper data for her report. If the Agency pressed charges for animal abuse, which was what she wanted to see happen, and a heavy fine was to be levied against Benham, all pertinent information had to be correct.

*   *   *

She went to the registry files and pulled the card on Edward Benham. The dispatcher, it turned out, *hadn't* made a mistake after all: the breed of dog listed as being owned by Benham was an Alaskan husky, female. Also, the license and rabies tag numbers on the card were different from those she had copied down from the Doberman's collar.

One good thing about bureaucratic organizations, she thought, was that they had their filing systems cross-referenced. So she went to the files arranged according to tag numbers and looked up the listed owner of the Doberman.

The card said: *Fox Hollow Kennels, 1423 Canyon Road, Laurel County, Oregon.*

Jill had heard of Fox Hollow Kennels; it was a fairly large place some distance outside the city, operated by a man named Largo or Fargo, which specialized in raising a variety of pure-bred dogs. She had been there once on a field investigation that had only peripherally concerned the kennel. She was going to make her second visit, she decided, within the next hour.

The only problem with that decision was that her supervisor, Lloyd Mortisse, vetoed it when she went in to tell him where she was going. Mortisse was a lean, mournful-looking man in his late forties, with wild gray hair that reminded Jill of the beads her grandmother had strung into ornamental baskets. He was also a confirmed bureaucrat, which meant that he loved paperwork, hated anything that upset the routine, and was suspicious of the agents' motives every time they went out into the field.

"Call up Fox Hollow," he told her. "You don't need to go out there; the matter doesn't warrant it."

"I think it does."

"You have other work to do, Ms. Quarter-Moon."

"Not as important as this, Mr. Mortisse."

She and Mortisse were constantly at odds. There was a mutual animosity, albeit low-key, based on his part by a certain condescension—either because she was a woman or an Indian, or maybe both—and on her part by a lack of respect. It made for less than ideal working conditions.

He said, "And I say it's not important enough for you to neglect your other duties."

"Ask that poor Doberman how important it is."

"I repeat, you're not to pursue the matter beyond a routine telephone call," Mortisse told her sententiously. "Now is that understood?"

"Yes. It's understood."

Jill pivoted, stalked out of the office, and kept right on stalking through the rear entrance and out to her truck. Twenty minutes later she was turning onto the long gravel drive, bordered by pine and Douglas fir, that led to the Fox Hollow Kennels.

She was still so annoyed at Mortisse, and preoccupied with Edward Benham, that she almost didn't see the large truck that came barreling toward her along the drive until it was too late. As it was, she managed to swerve off onto the soft shoulder just in time, and to answer the truck's horn blast with one of her own. It was an old Ford stakebed, she saw as it passed her and braked for the turn onto Canyon Road, with the words *Fox Hollow Kennels* on the driver's door. Three slat-and-wire crates were tied together on the bed, each of which contained what appeared to be a mongrel dog. The dogs had begun barking at the sound of the horns and she could see two of them pawing at the wire mesh.

Again she felt both her curiosity and her anger aroused. Transporting dogs in bunches via truck wasn't exactly inhuman treatment, but it was still a damned poor way to handle animals. And what was an American Kennel Club-registered outfit which specialized in purebreds doing with mongrels?

Jill drove up the access drive and emerged into a wide gravel parking area. The long whitewashed building that housed Fox Hollow's office was on her right, with a horseshoe arrangement of some thirty kennels and an exercise yard behind it. Pine woods surrounded the complex, giving it a rustic atmosphere.

When she parked and got out, the sound of more barking came to her from the vicinity of the exercise yard. She glanced inside the office, saw that it was empty, and went through a swing-gate that led to the back. There, beside a low fence, a man stood tossing dog biscuits into the concrete run on the other side, where half a dozen dogs—all of these purebred setters—crowded and barked together. He was in his late thirties, average-sized, with bald head and nondescript features, wearing Levi's and a University of Oregon sweatshirt. Jill recognized him as the owner, Largo or Fargo.

"Mr. Largo?" she said.

He turned, saying, "The name is Fargo." Then he set the food sack down and wiped his hands on his Levi's. His eyes were speculative as he studied both her and her tan Agency uniform. "Something I can do for you, miss?"

Jill identified herself. "I'm here about a dog," she said, "a male Doberman, about three years old. It was abandoned inside a house in Oregon Estates at least two days ago; we went in and released it this morning. The house belongs to a man named Benham, Edward Benham, but the Doberman is registered to Fox Hollow."

Fargo's brows pulled down. "Benham, did you say?"

"That's right. Edward Benham. Do you know him?"

"Well, I don't recognize the name."

"Is it possible you sold him the Doberman?"

"I suppose it is," Fargo said. "'Some people don't bother to change the registration. Makes a lot of trouble for all of us when they don't."

"Yes, it does. Would you mind checking your records?"

"Not at all."

He led her around and inside the kennel office. It was a cluttered room that smelled peculiarly of dog, dust, and cheap men's cologne. An open door on the far side led to an attached workroom; Jill could see a bench littered with tools, stacks of lumber, and several slat-and-wire crates of the type she had noticed on the truck, some finished and some under construction.

Along one wall was a filing cabinet and Fargo crossed to it, began to rummage inside. After a time he came out with a folder, opened it, consulted the papers it held, and put it away again. He turned to face Jill.

"Yep," he said, "Edward Benham. He bought the Doberman about three weeks ago. I didn't handle the sale myself, one of my assistants took care of it. That's why I didn't recognize the name."

"Is your assistant here now?"

"No, I gave him a three-day weekend to go fishing."

"Is the Doberman the only animal Benham has bought from you?"

"As far as the records show, it is."

"Benham is the registered owner of a female Alaskan husky," Jill said. "Do you know anyone who specializes in that breed?"

"Not offhand. Check with the American Kennel Club; they might be able to help you."

"I'll do that." Jill paused. "I passed your truck on the way in, Mr. Fargo. Do you do a lot of shipping of dogs?"

"Some, yes. Why?"

"Just curious. Where are those three today bound?"

"Portland." Fargo made a deliberate point of looking at his watch. "If you'll excuse me, I've got work to do . . ."

"Just one more thing. I'd like to see your American Kennel Club registration on the Doberman you sold Benham."

"Can't help you there, I'm afraid," Fargo said. "There wasn't any AKC registration on that Doberman."

"No? Why not? He's certainly a purebred."

"Maybe so, but the animal wasn't bred here. We bought it from a private party who didn't even know the AKC existed."

"What was this private party's name?"

"Adams. Charles Adams. From out of state—California. That's why Fox Hollow was the first to register the dog with you people."

Jill decided not to press the matter, at least not with Fargo personally. She had other ways of finding out information about him, about Fox Hollow, and about Edward Benham. She thanked Fargo for his time, left the office, and headed her truck back to the Agency.

When she got there she went first to see Sam Wyatt, to check on the Doberman's health. There was nothing wrong with the animal, Wyatt told her, except for minor malnutrition and dehydration. It had been fed, exercised, and put into one of the larger cages.

She looked in on it. The dog seemed glad to see her; the stub of a tail began to wag when she approached the cage. She played her fingers through the mesh grille, let the Doberman nuzzle them.

While she was doing that the kennel attendant, a young redhead named Lena Stark, came out of the dispensary. "Hi, Jill," she said. "The patient looks pretty good, doesn't he?"

"He'll look a lot better when we find him a decent owner."

"That's for sure."

"Funny thing—he's registered to the Fox Hollow Kennels, but they say he was sold to one Edward Benham. It was Benham's garage he was locked up in."

"Why is that funny?"

"Well, purebred Dobermans don't come cheap. Why would anybody who'd pay for one suddenly go off and desert him?"

"I guess that is kind of odd," Lena admitted. "Unless Benham was called out of town on an urgent matter or something. That would explain it."

"Maybe," Jill said.

"Some people should never own pets, you know? Benham should have left the dog at Fox Hollow; at least they care about the welfare of animals."

"Why do you say that?"

"Because every now and then one of their guys comes in and takes most of our strays."

"Oh? For what reason?"

"They train them and then find homes for them in other parts of the state. A pretty nice gesture, don't you think?"

"Yes," Jill said thoughtfully. "A pretty nice gesture."

She went inside and straight to the filing room, where she pulled the Fox Hollow folder. At her desk she spread out the kennel's animal licensing applications and studied them. It stood to reason that there would be a large number and there were; but as she sifted through them Jill was struck by a peculiarity. Not counting the strays Fox Hollow had "adopted" from the Agency, which by law had to be vaccinated and licensed before being released, there were less than a dozen dogs brought in and registered over the past twelve months. For a kennel which claimed to specialize in purebreds, this was suspiciously odd. Yet no one else had noticed it in the normal bureaucratic shuffle, just as no one had paid much attention to Fox Hollow's gathering of Agency strays.

And why *was* Fox Hollow in the market for so many stray dogs? Having met Fargo, she doubted that he was the humanitarian type motivated by a desire to save mongrels from euthanasia, a dog's fate if kept unclaimed at the Agency for more than four days. No, it sounded as if he were in some sort of strange wholesale pet business—as if the rest of the state, not to mention the rest of the country, didn't have their own animal overpopulation problems.

But where did Edward Benham, and the Doberman, fit in? Jill reviewed the Benham file again, but it had nothing new to tell her. She wished she knew where he'd gone, or of some way to get in touch with him. The obvious way, of course, was through his place of employment; unfortunately, however, pet license applications did not list employment of owners, only home address and telephone number. Nor had any of his neighbors known where he worked.

Briefly she considered trying to bluff information out of one of the credit-reporting companies in the city. Benham had bought rather then rented or leased his house, which meant that he probably carried a mortgage, which meant credit, which meant an application listing his employment. The problem was that legitimate members of such credit companies used special secret numbers to identify themselves when requesting information, so any ruse she might attempt would no doubt fail, and might even backfire and land her in trouble with Mortisse.

Then she thought of Pete Olafson, the office manager for Mid-Valley Adjustment Bureau, a local bad-debt collection service. Mid-Valley could certainly belong to a credit-reporting company. And she knew Pete pretty well, had dated him a few times in recent months. There wasn't any torrid romance brewing between her and the sandy-haired bachelor, but she knew he liked her a good deal—maybe enough to bend the rules a little and check Benham's credit as a favor.

She looked up Mid-Valley's number, dialed it, and was talking to Pete fifteen seconds later. "You must be a mind-reader, Jill," he said after she identified herself. "I was going to call you later. The University Theater is putting on 'Our Town' tomorrow night and I've wangled a couple of free passes. Would you like to go?"

"Sure. If you'll do me a favor in return."

Pete sighed dramatically. "Nothing is free these days, it seems. Okay, what is it?"

"I want to know where a man named Edward Benham is

employed. Could you track down his credit applications and find out from them?''

"I can if he's got credit somewhere.''

"Well, he owns his own home, out in Oregon Estates. The name is Benham, B-e-n-h-a-m, Edward. How fast can you find out for me?''

"It shouldn't take long. Sit tight; I'll get back to you.''

Jill replaced the handset and sat with her chin propped in one palm brooding. If the lead to Edward Benham through Pete didn't pan out, then what? Talk to his neighbors again? Through them she could find out the name of the real estate agent who had sold Benham his home . . . but it was unlikely that they would divulge personal information about him, since she had no official capacity. Talk to Fargo again? That probably wouldn't do her any good either. . . .

The door to Lloyd Mortisse's private office opened; Jill saw him thrust his wild-maned head out and look in her direction. It was not a look of pleasure. "Ms. Quarter-Moon," he said. "Come into my office, please.''

Jill complied. Mortisse shut the door behind her, sat down at his desk, and glared at her. "I thought," he said stiffly, "that I told you not to go out to Fox Hollow Kennels.''

Surprised, Jill asked, "How did you know about that?''

"Mr. Fargo called me. He wanted to know why you were out there asking all sorts of questions. He wasn't particularly pleased by your visit; neither am I. Why did you disobey me?''

"I felt the trip was necessary.''

"Oh, you felt it was necessary. I see. That makes it all right, I suppose.''

"Look, Mr. Mortisse—''

"I do not like disobedience," Mortisse said. "I won't stand for it again, is that clear? Nor will I stand for you harassing private facilities like Fox Hollow. This Agency's sole concern in the Benham matter is to house the Doberman for ninety-six hours or until it is claimed. And I'll be the one, not you, to decide if any misdemeanor animal-abuse charges are to be filed against Mr. Benham.''

Jill thought that it was too bad these weren't the old days, when one of the Umatilla customs in tribal disputes was to hold a potlatch—a fierce social competition at which rival chiefs gave away or destroyed large numbers of blankets, coppers, and slaves in an effort to outdo and therefore vanquish each other. She would have liked nothing better than to challenge Mortisse in this sort of duel, using bureaucratic attitudes and red tape as the throwaway material. She also decided there was no point in trying to explain her suspicions to him; he would only have said in his supercilious way that none of it was Agency business. If she was going to get to the bottom of what was going on at Fox Hollow, she would have to do it on her own.

"Do you understand?" Mortisse was saying. "You're to drop this matter and attend to your assigned duties. And you're not to disobey a direct order again, under any circumstances."

"I understand," Jill said thinly. "Is that all?"

"That's all."

She stood and left the office, resisting an impulse to slam the door. The wall clock said that it was 4:10—less than an hour until quitting time for the weekend. All right, she thought as she crossed to her desk. I'll drop the matter while I'm on Agency time. But what I do and where I go on my own time is *my* business, Mortisse or no Mortisse.

It was another ten minutes, during which time she typed up a pair of two-day-old reports, before Pete Olafson called her back. "Got what you asked for, Jill," he said. "Edward Benham has a pretty fair credit rating, considering he's modestly employed."

"What does he do?"

"He's a deliveryman, it says here. For a kennel."

Jill sat up straight. "Kennel?"

"That's right," Pete said. "Place called Fox Hollow outside the city. Is that what you're after?"

"It's a lot more than I expected," Jill told him. Quickly she arranged tomorrow night's date with him, then replaced the receiver and sat mulling over this latest bit of news.

If she had needed anything more to convince her that something was amiss at Fox Hollow, this was it. Fargo had claimed he didn't know Edward Benham; now it turned out that Benham worked for Fargo. Why had he lied? What was he trying to cover up? And where was Benham? And where did the Doberman fit in?

She spent another half hour at her desk, keeping one eye on the clock and pretending to work while she sorted through questions, facts, and options in her mind. At ten minutes of five, when she couldn't take any more of the inactivity, she went out into the kennel area to see Lena Stark.

"Release the Doberman to me, will you, Lena?" she asked. "I'll bring him back later tonight and check him in with the night attendant."

"Why do you want him?"

"I like his looks and I want to get better acquainted. If it turns out neither Fox Hollow nor Benham decides to claim him, I may just adopt him myself."

"I don't know, Jill . . ."

"He's all right, isn't he? Sam Wyatt said he was."

"Sure, he's fine. But the rules—"

"Oh, hang the rules. Nobody has to know except you and me and the night attendant. I'll take full responsibility."

"Well . . . okay, I guess you know what you're doing."

Lena opened the cage and the Doberman came out, stubby tail quivering, and nuzzled Jill's hand. She led it out through the rear door, into the parking lot to where her compact was parked. Obediently, as if delighted to be free and in her company, the dog jumped onto the front seat and sat down with an expectant look.

Jill stroked its ears as she drove out of the lot. "I don't want to keep calling you 'boy'," she said. "I think I'll give you a name, even if it's only temporary. How about Tyee?" In the old Chinook jargon, the mixed trade language of Indians and whites in frontier days, *tyee* was the word for chief. "You like that? Tyee?"

The dog cocked its head and made a rumbly sound in its throat.

"Good," Jill said. "Tyee it is."

She drove across the city and into Oregon Estates. Edward Benham's house, she saw when she braked at the end of the cul-de-sac, looked as deserted as it had this morning. This was confirmed when she went up and rang the doorbell several times without getting a response.

She took Tyee with her and let him sniff around both front and back. The Doberman showed none of the easy familiarity of a dog on its own turf; rather, she sensed a wary tenseness in the way he moved and keened the air. And when she led him near the garage he bristled, Jill thought. But then why had he been locked in Benham's garage?

She would have liked to go inside for a better look around, but the locksmith had relocked the doors, as dictated by law, before leaving the premises that morning. The house was securely locked too, as were each of the windows. And drawn drapes and blinds made it impossible to see into any of the rooms from outside.

Jill took Tyee back to her compact. She sat for a time, considering. Then she started the engine and pointed the car in an easterly direction.

It was just seven o'clock when she came up the access drive to Fox Hollow Kennels and coasted to a stop on the gravel parking area near the main building. There were no other vehicles around, a *Closed* sign was propped in one dusty pane of the front door, and the complex had a deserted aura; even the dogs in the near kennels were quiet.

She got out, motioning for Tyee to stay where he was on the front seat. The setting sun hung above the tops of the pines straight ahead, bathing everything in a dark-orange radiance. Jill judged that there was about an hour of daylight left, which meant that an hour was all she would have to look around. Prowling in daylight was risky enough, though if she were seen she might be able to bluff her way out of trouble by claiming she had brought Tyee back to his registered owner. If she were caught here after dark, no kind of bluff would be worth much.

The office door was locked, but when she shook it, it rattled loosely in its frame. Jill bent for a closer look at the latch. It was a spring-type lock, rather than a deadbolt. She straightened again, gnawing at her lower lip. Detectives in movies and on TV were forever opening spring locks with credit cards or pieces of celluloid; there was no reason why she couldn't do the same thing. No reason, that was, except that it was illegal and would cost her her job, if not a prison term, were she to be caught. She could imagine Lloyd Mortisse smiling like a Cheshire Cat at news of her arrest.

But she was already here, and the need to sate her curiosity was overpowering. The debate with her better judgment lasted all of ten seconds. Then she thought: Well, fools rush in— and she went back to the car to get a credit card from her purse.

Less than a minute of maneuvering with the card rewarded her with a sharp click as the lock snapped free. The door opened under her hand. Enough of the waning orange sunlight penetrated through the windows, she saw when she stepped inside, so that she didn't need any other kind of light. She went straight to the filing cabinets, began to shuffle through the folders inside.

The kennel records were in something of a shambles; Jill realized quickly that it would take hours, maybe even days, to sort through all the receipts, partial entries, and scraps of paper. But one file was complete enough to hold her attention and to prove interesting. It consisted of truck expenses—repair bills, oil company credit card receipts, and the like—and what intrigued her was that, taken together, they showed that the Fox Hollow delivery truck consistently traveled to certain towns in Oregon, northern California, and southern Washington. Forest Grove, Corvallis, Portland, McMinnville, Ashland, La Grande, Arcata, Kirkland. . . . These, and a few others, comprised a regular route.

Which might explain why Edward Benham was nowhere to be found at the moment; some of the towns were at least an overnight's drive away, and it was Benham's signature that was on most of the receipts. But the evident truck route also raised more questions. Why such long hauls for a small kennel? Why to some points out of state? And why to these particular towns, when there were numerous others of similar size along the way?

"Curiouser and curiouser," Jill murmured to herself.

She shut the file drawers and turned to the desk. Two of the drawers were locked; she decided it would be best not to try forcing them. None of the other drawers, nor any of the clutter spread across the top, told her anything incriminating or enlightening.

The door to the adjacent workroom was closed, but when she tried the knob it opened right up. That room was dimmer but there was still enough daylight filtering in to let her see the tools, workbench, stacks of lumber, finished and unfinished crates. She picked through the farrago of items on the bench; caught up slats and corner posts of an unassembled cage, started to put them down again. Then, frowning, she studied one of the wooden posts more carefully.

The post was hollow. So were the others; the inner lengths of all four had been bored out by a large drill bit. When fitted into the frame of a fully constructed cage the posts would appear solid, their holes concealed by the top and bottom sections. Only when the cage was apart, like now, would the secret compartments be exposed, to be filled or emptied.

Of what?

Jill renewed her search. In a back corner were three rolls of cage wire—and caught on a snag of mesh on one roll was a small cellophane bag. The bag was out of easy sight and difficult to reach, but she managed to retrieve it. It looked new, unopened, and it was maybe 3x5 inches in size. The kind of bag—

And then she knew. All at once, with a kind of wrenching insight, she understood what the bag was for, why the corner posts were hollowed out, what Fox Hollow was involved in. And it was ugly enough and frightening enough to make her feel a chill of apprehension, make her want to get away from there in a hurry. It was more than she had bargained for—considerably more.

She ran out of the workroom, still clutching the cellophane bag in her left hand. At the office door she peered through the glass before letting herself out, to make sure the parking area remained deserted. Then she set the button-lock on the knob, stepped outside, pulled the door shut, and started across to her compact.

Tyee was gone.

She stopped, staring in at the empty front seat. She had left the driver's window all the way down and he must have jumped out. Turning, she peered through gathering shadows toward the kennels. But the dogs were still quiet back there, and they wouldn't be if the Doberman had gone prowling in that direction. Where, then? Back down the drive? The pine woods somewhere?

Jill hesitated. The sense of urgency and apprehension demanded that she climb into the car, Tyee or no Tyee, and drive away pronto. But she couldn't just leave him here while she went to tell her suspicions to the country sheriff. The law would not come out here tonight no matter what she told them; they'd wait until tomorrow, when the kennel was open for business and when they could obtain a search warrant. And once she left here herself she had no intention of coming back again after dark.

She moved away from the car, toward the dark line of evergreens beyond. It was quiet here, with dust settling, and sounds carried some distance; the scratching noises reached her ears when she was still twenty paces from the woods. She'd heard enough dogs digging into soft earth to recognize the sound and she quickened her pace. Off to one side was a beaten-down area, not quite a path, and she went into the trees at that point. The digging sounds grew louder. Then she saw Tyee, over behind a decayed moss-festooned log, making earth and dry needles fly out behind him with his forepaws.

"What are you doing?" she called to him. "Come here, Tyee."

The Doberman kept on digging, paying no attention to her. She hurried over to him, around the bulky shape of the log. And then she stopped abruptly, made a startled gasping sound.

A man's arm and clenched hand lay partially uncovered in the soft ground.

Tyee was still digging, still scattering dirt and pine needles. Jill stood frozen, watching part of a broad back encased in a khaki shirt appear.

Now she knew what had happened to Edward Benham.

She made herself move, step forward and catch hold of the Doberman's collar. He resisted at first when she tried to tug him away from the shallow grave and what was in it; but she got a firmer grip and pulled harder, and finally he quit struggling. She dragged him around the log, back out of the trees.

Most of the daylight was gone now; the sky was grayish, streaked with red, like bloody fingermarks on faded cloth. A light wind had come up and she felt herself shiver as she took the Doberman toward her compact. She was anything but a shrinking violet, but what she had found at Fox Hollow tonight was enough to frighten Old Chief Joseph or any of the other venerable Shahaptian warriors. The sooner she was sitting in the safety of the Laurel County Sheriff's office, the better she—

And the sudden figure of a man came out from behind her car.

She was ten feet from the driver's door, her right hand on Tyee's collar, and the man just rose up into view like Nashlah, the legendary monster of the Columbia River. Jill made an involuntary cry, stiffened into a standstill. The Doberman seemed to go as tense as she did; a low rumble sounded in his throat as the man came toward them.

Fargo. With a gun in his hand.

"You just keep on holding that dog," he said. He stopped fifteen feet away, holding the gun out at arm's length. "You're both dead if you let go his collar."

She was incapable of speech for five or six seconds. Then she made herself say, "There's no need for that gun, Mr. Fargo. I'm only here to return the Doberman. . . ."

"Sure you are. Let's not play games. You're here because you're a damned snoop. And I'm here because you tripped a silent alarm connected to my house when you broke into the office."

It was not in Jill's nature to panic in a crisis; she got a grip on her fear and held it down, smothered it. "The office door was unlocked," she said. "Maybe you think you locked it when you left but you didn't. I just glanced inside."

"I don't buy that either," Fargo said. "I saw you come out of the office; I left my car down the road and walked up here through the trees. I saw you go into the woods over there, too."

"I went to find the dog, that's all."

"But that's not what you found, right? He's got dirt all over his forepaws—he's been doing some digging. You found Benham. And now you know too much about everything.''

"I don't know what you're talking about."

"I say you do. So does that cellophane bag you're carrying."

Jill looked down at her left hand; she had forgotten all about the bag. And she had never even considered the possibility of a silent alarm system. She had a lot to learn about being a detective—if she survived to profit by her mistakes.

"All right," she said. "It's drugs, isn't it? That's the filthy business you're in."

"You got it."

"Selling drugs to college kids all over the Pacific Northwest," she said. That was the significance of the towns on the Fox Hollow shipping route: they were all college or university towns. Humboldt State in Arcata, Lewis & Clark in Portland, Linfield College in McMinnville, Eastern Oregon College in La Grande. And the state university right here in this city. That was also why Fox Hollow had taken so many stray dogs from the Agency; they needed a constant supply to cover their shipment of drugs—cocaine and heroin, probably, the kind usually packaged and shipped in small cellophane bags—to the various suppliers along their network. "Where does it come from? Canada?"

"Mexico," Fargo said. "They bring it up by ship, we cut and package and distribute it."

"To kennels in those other cities, I suppose."

"That's right. They make a nice cover."

"What happens to the dogs you ship?"

"What do you think happens to them? Dogs don't matter when you're running a multi-million-dollar operation. Neither do snoops like you. Nobody fouls up this kind of operation and gets away with it."

Tyee growled again, shifted his weight; Jill tightened her grip on his collar. "Did Benham foul it up? Is that why he's dead?"

"He tried to. His percentage wasn't enough for him and he got greedy; he decided to hijack a shipment for himself—substitute milk sugar and then make off with the real stuff. When he left here on Wednesday for Corvallis he detoured over to his house and made the switch. Only one of the crates had the drugs in it, like always; he had to let the dog out of that one to get at the shipment and it turned on him, tried to bite him."

"This dog, the Doberman."

"Yeah. He managed to lock it up inside his garage, but that left him with an empty crate and he couldn't deliver an empty, not without making the Corvallis contact suspicious. So he loaded his own dog, the Husky, inside the crate and delivered it instead. But our man checked the dope anyway, discovered the switch, and called me. I was waiting for Benham when he got back here."

"And you killed him."

Fargo shrugged. "I had no choice."

"Like you've got no choice with me?"

He shrugged again. "I forgot all about the Doberman, that was my mistake. If I hadn't, I wouldn't have you on my hands. But it just didn't occur to me the dog would raise a ruckus and a nosy Agency worker would decide to investigate."

"Why did you lie to me before about knowing Benham?"

"I didn't want you doing any more snooping. I figured if I gave you that story about selling him the Doberman, you'd come up against a dead-end and drop the whole thing. Same reason I called your supervisor: I thought he'd make you drop it. Besides, you had no official capacity. It was your word against mine."

"Lying to me was your second mistake," Jill said. "If you kill me, it'll be your third."

"How do you figure that?"

"I told somebody I came out here tonight. He'll go to the county sheriff if I disappear, and they'll come straight to you."

"That's a bluff," Fargo said. "And I don't bluff. You didn't tell anybody about coming here; nobody knows but you and me. And pretty soon it'll just be me." He made a gesture with the gun. "Look at it this way. You're only one person, but I got a lot of people depending on me: others in the operation, all those kids we supply."

All those kids, Jill thought, and there was a good hot rage inside her now. College kids, some of them still in their teens. White kids, black kids—Indian kids. She had seen too many Indian youths with drug habits; she had talked to the parents of a sixteen-year-old boy who had died from an overdose of heroin on the Umatilla reservation, of a seventeen-year-old girl, an honor student, killed in a drug raid at Trout Lake near the Warm Springs development. Any minority, especially its restless and sometimes disenchanted youth, was susceptible to drug exploitation; and Indians were a minority long oppressed in their own country. That was why she hated drugs, and hated these new oppressors, the drug dealers like Fargo, even more.

Fargo said, "Okay, we've done enough talking—no use in prolonging things. Turn around, walk into the woods."

"So you can bury me next to Benham?"

"Never mind that. Just move."

"No," she said, and she let her body go limp, sank onto her knees. She dropped the cellophane bag as she did so and then put that hand flat on the gravel beside her, keeping her other hand on Tyee's collar. The Doberman, sensing the increase of tension between her and Fargo, had his fangs bared now, growling steadily.

"What the hell?" Fargo said. "Get up."

Jill lowered her chin to her chest and began to chant in a soft voice—a Shahaptian prayer.

"I said get up!"

She kept on chanting.

Fargo took two steps toward her, a third, a fourth. That put less than five feet of ground between them. "I'll shoot you right where you are, I mean it—"

She swept up a handful of gravel, hurled it at his face, let go of Tyee's collar, and flung herself to one side.

The gun sent off and she heard the bullet strike the ground near her head, felt the sting of a pebble kicked up against her cheek. Then Fargo screamed, and when Jill rolled over she saw that Tyee had done what she'd prayed he would—attacked Fargo the instant he was released. He had driven the man backward and knocked him down and was shaking his captured wrist as if it were a stick; the gun had popped loose and sailed off to one side. Fargo cried out again, tried to club the Doberman with his free hand. Blood from where Tyee's teeth had bitten into his wrist flowed down along his right arm.

Jill scrambled to her feet, ran to where the gun lay and scooped it up. But before she could level it at Fargo, he jacknifed his body backwards, trying to escape from the Doberman, and cracked his head against the front bumper of her compact; she heard the thunking sound it made in the stillness, saw him go limp. Tyee still straddled the inert form, growling, shaking the bloody wrist.

She went over there, caught the dog's collar again, talked to him until he let go of Fargo and backed off with her. But he stood close, alert, alternately looking at the unconscious man and up at her. She knelt and hugged him, and there were tears in her eyes. She disliked women who cried, particularly self-sufficient Indian women, but sometimes . . . sometimes it was a necessary release.

"You know who you are?" she said to him. "You're not Tyee, you're Coyote. You do battle with monsters and evil beings and you save Indians from harm."

The Doberman licked her hand.

"The Great One isn't supposed to return until the year 2000, when the world changes again and all darkness is gone; but you're here already and I won't let you go away. You're mine and I'm yours from now on—Coyote and Quarter-Moon."

Then she stood, shaking but smiling, and went to re-pick the lock on the office door so she could call the Laurel County sheriff.

John Rudin

"Sellin' Some Wood" was John Rudin's first story, published in 1973. At the time he was 45, married, with four children.

SELLIN' SOME WOOD

BY JOHN RUDIN

"Mornin', Edward."

"Hello, Mr. Bill."

"Selling some wood this mornin'?"

"Sellin' some wood, Mr. Bill."

"Hello, Edward."

"Hello, Mr. Tucker, sellin' some wood this mornin'."

The two men watched as the homemade cart rattled by, piled high with fireplace logs and pulled by the big boy. The foolish grin and empty stare didn't change as Edward's head turned back from the two men to the direction in which he was heading. A mongrel dog, with just a trace of a limp, trotted at his side.

"Shame," said one of the men as he turned and entered the store.

"Yeah," said the other, following.

Down the street, along the two-block business section of the town, similar greetings passed between the townspeople and the big slow-witted boy. He proudly explained to each that he was "sellin' some wood this mornin' " They usually smiled and acknowledged that was good and they were glad for him. But after he had passed, their smiles usually changed to looks of pity before they went about their business.

Edward never saw the pity. He wouldn't have understood if he had seen it. He could understand some things though—like pride. He was proud of his pull-cart, which he had made all by himself. Well, almost by himself. Mr. Sam at the gas station helped him some with the hard things like figuring out where the axles go and how to fasten them on. But Edward had done a lot—like hammering in the nails where Mr. Sam showed him, and bending the cotter pin in the hole at the end of the axle to hold the wheels on.

285

It was all pretty hard, and he had painted the whole thing without any help at all except just a little bit. Everybody told him it was a nice cart and that made him feel good. He knew it was a nice cart, but it was extra good if other people noticed, too. He thought about things like that while he was delivering and stacking the wood.

Edward felt very fortunate. He loved the feel of the ax and the saw in his hands. He was careful, too. Every piece of wood was cut to exactly the same length. He had a special stick that he used to measure every piece before he cut it.

One time he lost his measuring stick and had to make a new one. He went to a house where he had delivered wood before and made the new measuring stick just as long as the wood there. He was glad he had figured out to do that. If the logs were too thick to burn well he split them into thinner pieces, which also made it easier to stack when he delivered the wood.

That was one of the things he did best of all—stacking the wood. He took special care that everything was just right. No piece could stick out any farther than the others. And the stacks had to be perfectly straight. He always walked around and looked at the stack from all sides to make sure it was perfect before he knocked on the door for his money.

This morning, after he checked the stack, he knocked for Mrs. Sinclair. She came out, examined the stack as she knew she was expected to do, paid him, and said, "That's fine, Edward, and this morning I have a bone for your dog."

"Yes'm," said Edward, "he likes 'em." He accepted the package from her, grinned, and backed away to his cart.

As he reached for the pull-rope he stopped and inspected one wheel partly submerged in a puddle. He frowned. "Mud," he said, and for the first time that day he looked unhappy.

"We have to go to Mr. Sam's," he explained to the mongrel, and promptly forgot the wrapped bone in his hand. Edward headed down the driveway, pulling his cart, and turned up the street with purpose. The dog, bone-scent fresh in his nostrils and tail a-twitter, kept pace.

At the service station Sam heard the rattle of the cart and turned, recognition already on his face. "Hello, Edward, sell some wood this mornin'?"

Edward ignored the question and pointed to the left front wheel of his cart.

"Jammed with mud," he said.

Sam looked closer. "Edward, I don't think there's any mud in the bearing. Just on the wheel."

"Won't work if it's jammed with mud. Can I clean it, Mr. Sam?"

"But I don't think—" Sam stopped, eyeing the boy closely. "Sure, Edward, go ahead."

Sam watched Edward pull the cart over to the side of the station. He remembered all the trouble he'd had helping the boy build the cart, the difficulty he'd had trying to explain to him how to take care of it. Edward had not had the cart long when he had come by the station one day, trying to pull the cart against an impossible cake of dried mud on each wheel. Sam had stopped him and patiently explained that the wheel bearings could not be allowed to get fouled.

He had then carefully showed Edward how to remove the hubs, pull the cotter pins, and wash out and relubricate the bearings. It was a long and difficult job, but Edward eventually learned, and since then he stopped often, much more often than necessary, to remove and clean the wheels.

"Won't work if it's jammed with mud," Edward invariably said, and he had said it again today.

He started to turn the cart on its side when it dawned on him that he was being encumbered by the wrapped bone still in his hand. His mouth split in a sheepish grin. He tore off the wrapper and handed the bone to the dog. The mongrel took it and padded off to worry the bone on the grass at the edge of the driveway. Edward settled to his task.

The last wheel was cleaned and oiled and Edward was struggling with the final cotter pin when a mud-spattered pickup truck wheeled sharply in under the canopy. The front fender narrowly missed Edward's upturned cart and the groaning of the brakes testified to the driver's irritation. Ed Barr leaped out of the truck.

"Damn it, Sam," Barr growled, "why do you let that moron clutter up this place?"

"Hell, he's not hurtin' anything, Ed."

"Well, the damn fool oughta be locked up."

"He's all right, I tell you. He don't mean any harm." Sam started gassing the truck and Barr strode toward Edward. He stopped six feet away as if to avoid anything resembling social contact.

"Hey, boy, why don't you keep that damn wagon outta the way?"

Edward simply stood and stared, slack-jawed, uncomprehending. He wondered why Mr. Barr always called him "boy" instead of Edward and why the man always acted this way toward him. He didn't even realize they had the same first name, and would never have understood what effect that unhappy coincidence could have on a man like Ed Barr.

"I'm fixin' the wheels, Mr. Barr. Won't work if they're jammed with mud."

"You and your damn wheels. You deliver my wood this mornin', boy?"

"Yes, sir, Mr. Barr. Early this mornin', Mr. Barr."

"You put it in the shed this time, like I said, boy?"

"Yes, sir, Mr. Barr. Like you said, right in the shed by the back door."

"Well, it better be."

Edward just nodded his head vigorously, up and down. He had remembered all right. He'd done it, but he hadn't liked it. Not only had there been a muddy spot by the shed door, but when he was carrying in the wood he'd seen the shotgun. Right up there on the wall. Mr. Barr's shotgun.

When Edward had first seen it he stopped and gawked, recognizing it as the thing that had hurt his dog. It was all he could do to tear his eyes away each time he walked in with another armful of wood. He'd tried to keep his back to it while he was stacking the wood, so he wouldn't have to look at it. He was glad when he was done and could leave.

Barr swore, spit on the pavement, and turned toward the rest rooms. He didn't see Edward's dog lying in the grass by the drive or he wouldn't have walked up on him so fast. The dog was startled as Barr's foot slapped the concrete next to him and instinctively turned and snapped at the offending foot, at the same time giving a warning bark.

The movement and noise would have given anyone a start, but Barr let out a frightened shout and jumped back, cracking his elbow against the brick of the station wall. He realized immediately what had happened and stepped forward, lashing out viciously with his foot at the dog. The dog's reflexes were excellent and he avoided the kick, but Barr's momentum carried him onto the grass.

He fell, sprawling on the spot the dog had just left. The man was livid. He cursed and swore and, as he got up, hurled obscenities at Edward, the dog, Sam, the station—everything in sight.

Sam suppressed an urge to laugh. As he approached Barr, he pretended real concern.

"You okay, Ed?"

Barr was brushing himself off and cradling his bruised elbow. "Yes, no thanks to that imbecile and his damned mutt."

"Just an accident. Could have happened to anybody," said Sam, and they went into the station together.

Edward didn't really understand what had happened except that Mr. Barr had fallen. He hadn't seen the whole thing because he had been busy trying to right his cart. He was glad Mr. Barr wasn't hurt even if he did act awful mad, and he had long since stopped wondering why Mr. Barr didn't like his dog. He didn't and that was that.

His job finished, Edward called to the dog and started off down the street, pulling the car behind him. He was pleased with the way it rolled on its freshly oiled bearings. The immediate past incident was already forgotten. When Barr's truck pulled up beside him, it was as if nothing had happened so far as Edward was concerned.

"Hello, Mr. Barr."

"Come here, boy."

The truck had stopped and Edward dropped his pull-rope. He walked over to the open window on the passenger's side.

"Yes, sir, Mr. Barr."

"I want you to bring me some wood, boy."

"I brought it this mornin', Mr. Barr, early. I stacked it in the shed just like you told me. And I was very careful to—"

"Yeah, yeah, I know, but I want some more."

"Some more, Mr. Barr?"

"Oh, for God's sake, boy, I want you to bring some more wood!"

"Yes, sir, Mr. Barr." He finally understood. "I'll bring some more wood in the mornin'. I'll cut it this afternoon, Mr. Barr, and I'll bring it in the mornin'."

Barr was frowning. "I want it this afternoon."

Edward was puzzled again. "I got to cut it this afternoon, Mr. Barr."

"Can't you bring it when you're through cutting?"

Edward thought a few moments. "At sundown? You want me to bring it at sundown, Mr. Barr?"

"Yes, boy, at sundown. Bring it at sundown and be sure you don't forget."

The pickup lurched ahead and sped off down the street. Edward stood a while and watched until it disappeared around the curve, heading out of town toward Barr's place. He still wasn't sure why, but he knew Mr. Barr wanted more wood and he was going to be sure he got it there by sundown. Anyone besides Edward who had seen the hatred and anger on Barr's face as he drove away would have advised Edward to stay away from Barr, especially that day.

The little patch of woods that was Edward's source of supply was on the edge of town and not far from where Barr lived. Edward worked hard that afternoon, as he always did, and by the time the sun was very low, the cart was loaded, and they were on their way.

They were little more than specks when Barr saw them on the road heading his way. As he watched, his anticipation grew and he shifted uneasily on the rock he was sitting on in the tall grass. He had been leaning back against the fence post, but now he shifted forward, sitting up a little straighter to see better through the grass and bushes in which he was hidden. The shotgun was heavy across his knees.

As Barr watched, the dog would run ahead of the boy and the cart, searching the grass on either side of the road looking for whatever dogs hope to find. Barr wasn't sure, but once or twice he thought he heard a childish laugh as the dog returned now and again to his master, and each time Barr gripped the gun tighter and swore to himself.

They were closer now and Barr tingled as they veered off the road onto the long curving path that led up along the small front pasture to the house. Barr had warned the boy once before to keep his mutt out of the fenced area. But dogs pay little attention to barbed wire, and he had fired at him with the shotgun. It was at long range and he had only nicked one of the mutt's legs.

This time would be different, and it would help make up for the rankling embarrassment this idiot and his dog had caused him this morning. Barr thought about the incident in the gas station and even more bitterness churned inside him.

Now he could hear the rattle of the cart and through the grass he saw the dog's shadow prancing into the field. It was time, and Barr rose with the sweetness of revenge replacing the bitterness in his throat.

As he stood, the shotgun came to his shoulder and he shouted, "I warned you about that mutt, boy."

"Can't shoot my dog, Mr. Barr," yelled Edward.

Barr's finger tightened on the trigger.

"CAN'T SHOOT HIM!"

In absolute glee Barr pulled the trigger. With a grinding, shattering roar the world came apart in his face.

The searing flash was the last thing Barr saw. The last thing he smelled was a mixture of burnt powder and burnt flesh. And as he toppled backward, the last thing he heard was, ". . . jammed it full of mud, Mr. Barr."

Rex Stout

America's best-known fictional detective is most likely Rex Stout's corpulent creation, Nero Wolfe. His New York brownstone, it's inhabitants, his lifestyle and idiosyncracies are nearly as familiar to the reader as are Holmes's digs at 221B Baker Street.

Stout was in love with the English language and a stickler (as is Nero Wolfe) for its correct usage. He used it gracefully, ingeniously and with good humor.

A DOG IN THE DAYTIME

BY REX STOUT

I do sometimes treat myself to a walk in the rain, though I prefer sunshine as a general rule. That rainy Wednesday, however, there was a special inducement: I wanted his raincoat to be good and wet when I delivered it. So with it on my back and my old brown felt on my head, I left Nero Wolfe's brownstone house on West 35th Street, Borough of Manhattan, and set out for Arbor Street, which is down in Greenwich Village.

Halfway there the rain stopped and my blood had pumped me warm, so I took the coat off, folded it wet side in, hung it on my arm, and proceeded. Arbor Street, narrow and only three blocks long, had on either side an assortment of old brick houses, mostly of four stories, which were neither spick nor span. Number 29 would be about the middle of the first block.

I reached it, but I didn't enter it. There was a party going on in the middle of the block. A police car was double-parked in front of one of the houses, and a uniformed cop was on the sidewalk in an attitude of authority toward a small gathering of citizens confronting him. As I approached I heard him demanding, "Whose dog is this?"

He was referring, evidently, to an animal with a wet black coat standing behind him. I heard no one claim the dog, but I wouldn't have, anyway, because my attention was diverted. Another police car rolled up and stopped behind the first one, and a man got out, nodded to the cop without halting, and went in the entrance of Number 29.

The trouble was, I knew the man, which is an understatement. I do not begin to tremble at the sight of Sergeant Purley Stebbins of Manhattan Homicide West, but his presence and manner made it a cinch that there was a corpse in that house, and if I demanded entry on the ground that I wanted to swap raincoats with a guy who had walked off with mine, there was no question what would happen. My prompt appearance at the scene of a homicide would arouse all Purley's worst instincts, and I might not get home in time for dinner, which was going to be featured by grilled squab with a brown sauce which Fritz calls *lenitienne* and is one of his best.

Purley had disappeared inside without spotting me. The cop was a complete stranger. As I slowed down to detour past him on the narrow sidewalk, he gave me an eye and demanded, "That your dog?"

The dog was nuzzling my knee, and I stooped to give him a pat on his wet black head. Then, telling the cop he wasn't mine, I went on by. At the next corner I turned right, heading back uptown. A wind had started in from the west, but everything was still damp from the rain.

I was well on my way before I saw the dog. Stopping for a light on Ninth Avenue in the Twenties, I felt something at my knee, and there he was. My hand started for his head in reflex, but I pulled it back. I was in a fix. Apparently he had picked me for a pal, and if I just went on he would follow, and you can't chase a dog on Ninth Avenue by throwing rocks. I could have ditched him by taking a taxi the rest of the way, but that would have been pretty rude after the appreciation he had shown of my charm. He had a collar on with a tag and could be identified, and the station house was only a few blocks away, so the simplest way was to convoy him there. I moved to the curb to reconnoiter, and as I did so a cyclone sailed around the corner and took my hat with it into the middle of the avenue.

I didn't dash out into the traffic, but you should have seen that dog. He sprang across the bow of a big truck, wiping its left front fender with his tail, braked landing to let a car by, sprang again and was under another car—or I thought he was—and then I saw him on the opposite sidewalk. He snatched the hat from under the feet of a pedestrian, turned on a dime, and started back. This time his crossing wasn't so spectacular, but he didn't dally. He came to me and stood, lifting his head and wagging his tail. I took the hat. It had skimmed a puddle of water on its trip, but I thought he would be disappointed if I didn't put it on, so I did. Naturally, that settled it. I flagged a cab, took the dog in with me, and gave the driver the address of Wolfe's house.

My idea was to take my hat hound upstairs to my room, give him some refreshment, and phone the ASPCA to send for him. But there was no sense in passing up such an opportunity for a little buzz at Wolfe, so, after leaving my hat and the raincoat on the rack in the hall, I proceeded to the office and entered.

"Where the deuce have you been?" Wolfe asked grumpily. "We were going over some lists at six o'clock, and it's a quarter to seven." He was in his oversized chair behind his desk with a book, and his eyes hadn't left the page to spare me a glance.

I answered him. "Returning that fool raincoat. Only, I didn't deliver it, because—"

"What's that?" he snapped. He was glaring at my companion.

"A dog."

"I see it is. I'm in no temper for buffoonery. Get it out of here."

"Yes, sir, right away. I can keep him in my room most of the time, but of course he'll have to come downstairs and through the hall when I take him out. He's a hat hound. There is a sort of problem. His name is Nero, which as you know means 'black,' and of course I'll have to change it. Ebony would do, or Jet, or Inky, or—"

"Bah. Flummery!"

"No, sir. I get pretty darned lonesome around here, especially during the four hours a day you're up in the plant rooms. You have your orchids, and Fritz has his turtle, and Theodore has his parakeets up in the potting room, so why shouldn't I have a dog? I admit I'll have to change his name, through he is registered as Champion Nero Charcoal of Bantyscoot."

It was a fizzle. I had expected to induce a major outburst, even possibly something as frantic as Wolfe leaving his chair to evict the beast himself, and there he was gazing at Nero with an expression I had never seen him aim at any human, including me.

"It's not a hound," he said. "It's a Labrador retriever."

That didn't faze me, from a bird who reads as many books as Wolfe does. "Yes, sir," I agreed. "I only said hound because it would be natural for a private detective to have a hound."

"Labradors," he said, "have a wider skull than any other dog, for brain room. A dog I had when I was a boy, in

Montenegro, a small brown mongrel, had a rather narrow skull, but I did not regard it as a defect. I do not remember that I considered that dog to have a defect. Today I suppose I would be more critical. . . . When you smuggled that creature in here did you take into account the disruption it would cause in this household?''

It had backfired on me. I had learned something new about the big, fat genius: he would enjoy having a dog around, provided he could blame it on me and so be free to beef when he felt like it. As for me, when I retire to the country I'll have a dog, and maybe two, but not in town.

I snapped into reverse. "I guess I didn't," I confessed. "Okay, I'll get rid of him. After all, it's your house."

"I do not want to feel responsible," he said stiffly, "for your privation. I would almost rather put up with the dog than with your reproaches."

"Forget it." I waved a hand.

"Another thing," he persisted. "I refuse to interfere with any commitment you have made."

"I have made no commitment."

"Then where did you get it?"

"Well, I'll tell you."

I went and sat at my desk and did so. Nero—the four-legged one—came and lay at my feet with his nose just not touching the toe of my shoe. I reported the whole event, with as much detail as if I had been reporting a major case, and when I had finished Wolfe was, of course, quite aware that my presentation of Nero had been a gag. Ordinarily, he would have made his opinion of my performance clear, but this time he skipped it, and it was easy to see why. The idea of having a dog that he could blame on me had got in and stuck. When I came to the end there was a moment's silence; then he said:

"Jet would be an acceptable name for that dog."

"Yeah." I swiveled and reached for the phone. "I'll call the ASPCA to come for him."

"No." He was emphatic.

"Why not?"

"Because there is a better alternative. Call someone you know in the Police Department, anyone, give him the number on the dog's tag, and ask him to find out who the owner is. Then you can inform the owner directly.''

He was playing for time. It could happen that the owner was dead or in jail or didn't want the dog back, and, if so, Wolfe could take the position that I had committed myself by bringing the dog home in a taxi and that it would be dishonorable to renege. However, I didn't want to argue, so I phoned a precinct sergeant I knew. He took Nero's number and said he would call me back. Then Fritz entered to announce dinner.

The squabs with the sauce were absolutely edible, as they always are, but other phenomena in the next couple of hours were not so pleasing. The table talk in the dining room was mostly one-sided and mostly about dogs. Wolfe kept it on a high level, no maudlin sentiment. He maintained that the Basenji was the oldest breed on earth, having originated in Central Africa around 5,000 B.C., whereas there was no trace of the Afghan hound earlier than around 4,000 B.C. To me, all it proved was that he had read a book.

Nero ate in the kitchen with Fritz and made a hit. Wolfe had told Fritz to call him Jet. When Fritz brought in the salad he announced that Jet had wonderful manners and was very smart.

''Nevertheless,'' Wolfe asked, ''wouldn't you think him an insufferable nuisance as a member of the household?''

On the contrary, Fritz declared, Jet would be most welcome.

After dinner, feeling that the newly formed Canine Canonizing League needed slowing down, I first took Nero out for a brief tour and then escorted him up the two flights to my room and left him there. I had to admit he was well-behaved. If I had wanted to take on a dog in town it could have been this one. In my room I told him to lie down, and he did, and when I went to the door to leave, his eyes, which were the color of caramel, made it plain that he would love to come along, but he didn't get up.

Down in the office Wolfe and I got at the lists. They were special offerings from orchid growers and collectors from all over the world, and it was quite a job to check the thousands of items and pick the few that Wolfe might want to give a try. I sat at his desk, across from him, with trays of cards from our files, and we were in the middle of it, around ten thirty, when the doorbell rang. I went to the hall and flipped a light switch and saw out on the stoop, through the one-way glass panel in the door, a familiar figure—Inspector Cramer of Homicide.

I went to the door, opened it six inches, and asked politely, "Now what?"

"I want to see Wolfe."

"It's pretty late. What about?"

"About a dog."

It is understood that no visitor, and especially no officer of the law, is to be conducted to the office until Wolfe has been consulted, but this seemed to rate an exception. I considered the matter for about two seconds, and then swung the door open and invited cordially:

"Step right in."

"Properly speaking," Cramer declared as one who wanted above all to be perfectly fair and square, "it's Goodwin I want information from."

He was in the red-leather chair at the end of Wolfe's desk, just about filling it. His big, round face was no redder than usual, his gray eyes no colder, his voice no gruffer. Merely normal.

Wolfe came at me: "Then why did you bring him in here without even asking?"

Cramer interfered for me: "I asked for you. Of course, you're in it. I want to know where the dog fits in. Where is it, Goodwin?"

I inquired innocently, "Dog?"

His lips tightened. "All right; I'll spell it. You phoned the precinct and gave them a tag number and wanted to know who owns the dog. When the sergeant learned that the owner was a man named Philip Kampf, who was murdered this afternoon in a house at Twenty-nine Arbor Street, he notified Homicide. The officer who had been on post in front of that house had told us that the dog went off with a man who had said it wasn't his dog. After we learned of your inquiry about the owner, the officer was shown a picture of you, and said it was you who enticed the dog. He's outside in my car. Do you want to bring him in?"

"No, thanks. I didn't entice."

"The dog followed you."

I gestured modestly. "Girls follow me, dogs follow me, sometimes even your own dicks follow me. I can't help—"

"Skip the comedy. The dog belonged to a murder victim, and you removed it from the scene of the murder. Where is the dog?"

Wolfe butted in. "You persist," he objected, "in imputing an action to Mr. Goodwin without warrant. He did not 'remove' the dog. I advise you to shift your ground if you expect us to listen."

His tone was firm but not hostile. I cocked an eye at him. He was probably being indulgent because he had learned that Jet's owner was dead.

"I've got another ground," Cramer asserted. "A man who lives in that house, named Richard Meegan, and who was in it at the time Kampf was murdered, has stated that he came here to see you this morning and asked you to do a job for him. He says you refused the job. That's what he says."

Cramer jutted his chin. "Now. A man at the scene of a murder admits he consulted you this morning. Goodwin shows up at the scene half an hour after the murder was committed, and he entices—okay, the dog goes away with him. The dog that belonged to the victim and had gone to that house with him. How does that look?" He pulled his chin in. "You know the last thing I want in a homicide is to find you or Goodwin anywhere within ten miles of it, because I know from experience what to expect. But when you're there, there you are, and I want to know how and why, and what, and I intend to. Where's the dog?"

Wolfe sighed and shook his head. "In this instance," he said, almost genially, "you're wasting your time. As for Mr. Meegan, he phoned this morning to make an appointment and came at eleven. Our conversation was brief. He wanted a man shadowed, but divulged no name or any other specific detail, because in his first breath he mentioned his wife—he was overwrought—and I gathered that his difficulty was marital. As you know, I don't touch that kind of work, and I stopped him. My bluntness enraged him and he dashed out. On his way he took his hat from the rack in the hall, and he took Mr. Goodwin's raincoat instead of his own. Now, Archie, proceed."

Cramer's eyes swiveled to me, and I obeyed: "I didn't find

out about the switch in coats until the middle of the afternoon. His was the same color as mine, but mine's newer. When he phoned for an appointment this morning he gave me his name and address. I wanted to phone him to tell him to bring my coat back, but he wasn't listed, and Information said she didn't have him, so I decided to go get it. I walked, wearing Meegan's coat. There was a cop and a crowd and a PD car in front of Twenty-nine Arbor Street, and as I approached another PD car came, and Purley Stebbins got out and went in, so I decided to skip it, not wanting to go through the torture. There was a dog present, and it nuzzled me, and I patted it. Then I headed for home.''

"Did you call the dog or signal it?"

"No. I was at Twenty-eighth Street and Ninth Avenue before I knew it was tailing me. I did not entice or remove. If I did—if there's some kind of a dodge about the dog—please tell me why I phoned the precinct to get the name of his owner."

"I don't know. With Wolfe and you I never know. Where is it?"

I blurted it out before Wolfe could stop me: "Upstairs in my room."

"Bring it down here."

I was up and going, but Wolfe called me sharply: "Archie!" I turned. "Yes, sir."

"There's no frantic urgency." He said to Cramer. "The animal seems intelligent, but I doubt if it's up to answering questions. I don't want it capering around my office."

"Neither do I."

"Then why bring it down?"

"I'm taking it downtown. We want to try something with it."

Wolfe pursed his lips. "I doubt if that's feasible. Mr. Goodwin has assumed an obligation and will have to honor it. The creature has no master, and so presumably no home. It will have to be tolerated here until Mr. Goodwin gets satisfactory assurance of its future welfare. Archie?"

If we had been alone I would have made my position clear, but with Cramer there I was stuck. "Absolutely," I agreed, sitting down again.

"You see," Wolfe told Cramer, "I'm afraid we can't permit the dog's removal."

"Nuts. I'm taking it."

"Indeed? What writ have you? Replevin? Warrant for arrest as a material witness?"

Cramer opened his mouth, and shut it again. He put his elbows on the chair arms, interlaced his fingers, and leaned forward. "Look. You and Meegan check, either because you're telling it straight, or because you've framed it. But I'm taking the dog. Kampf, the man who was killed, lived on Perry Street, a few blocks away from Arbor Street. He arrived at Twenty-nine Arbor Street, with the dog on a leash, about five twenty this afternoon.

"The janitor of the house, named Olsen, lives in the basement, and he was sitting at his front window when he saw Kampf arrive with the dog and turn in at the entrance. About ten minutes later he saw the dog come out, with no leash, and right after the dog a man came out. The man was Victor Talento, a lawyer, the tenant of the ground-floor apartment. Talento's story is that he left his apartment to go to an appointment, saw the dog in the hall, thought it was a stray, and chased it out. Olsen say Talento walked off and the dog stayed there on the sidewalk."

Cramer unlaced his fingers and sat back. "About twenty minutes later, around ten minutes to six, Olsen heard someone yelling his name, and went to the rear and up one flight to the ground-floor hall. Two men were there—a live one and a dead one. The live one was Ross Chaffee, a painter, the tenant of the top-floor studio—that's the fourth floor. The dead one was the man that had arrived with the dog. He had been strangled with the dog's leash, and the body was at the bottom of the stairs. Chaffee says he found it when he came down to go to an appointment, and that's all he knows. He stayed there while Olsen went downstairs to phone. A squad car arrived at five fifty-eight. Sergeant Stebbins arrived at six ten. Goodwin arrived at six ten. Excellent timing."

Wolfe merely grunted.

Cramer continued: "You can have it all. The dog's leash was in the pocket of Kampf's raincoat, which was on him. The laboratory says it was used to strangle him. The routine is still in process. I'll answer questions within reason. The four tenants of the house were all there when Kampf arrived: Victor Talento, the lawyer, on the ground floor; Richard Meegan, whose job you say you wouldn't take, second floor; Jerome Aland, a nightclub comedian, third floor; and Ross Chaffee, the painter, with the top-floor studio. Aland says he was sound asleep until we banged on his door just before taking him down to look at the corpse. Meegan says he heard nothing and knows nothing.''

Cramer sat forward again. ''Okay, what happened? Kampf went there to see one of those four men, and had his dog with him. It's possible he took the leash off in the lower hall and left the dog there, but I doubt it. At least, it's just as possible that he took the dog along to the door of one of the apartments, and the dog was wet and the tenant wouldn't let it enter, so Kampf left it outside. Another possibility is that the dog was actually present when Kampf was killed, but we'll know more about that after we see and handle the dog. What we're going to do is take the dog in that house and see which door it goes to. We're going to do that now. There's a man out in my car who knows dogs.'' Cramer stood up.

Wolfe shook his head. ''You must be hard put. You say Mr. Kampf lived on Perry street. With a family?''

''No. Bachelor. Some kind of a writer. He didn't have to make a living; he had means.''

''Then the beast is orphaned. He's in your room, Archie?''

''Yes, sir.'' I got up and started for the door.

Wolfe halted me. ''One moment. Go in your room, lock the door, and stay there till I notify you. Go!''

I went. It was either that or quit my job on the spot, and I resign only when we haven't got company. Also assuming that there was a valid reason for refusing to surrender the dog to the cops, Wolfe was justified. Cramer, needing no warrant to enter the house because he was already in, wouldn't hesitate to mount to my room to do his own fetching, and stopping him physically would have raised some delicate points. Whereas breaking through a locked door would be another matter.

I didn't lock it, because it hadn't been locked for ten years and I didn't remember where the key was, as I left it open and stood on the sill to listen. If I heard Cramer coming I would shut the door and brace it with my foot. Nero, or Jet, depending on where you stand, came over to me, but I ordered him back, and he went without a murmur. From below came voices, not cordial, but not raised enough for me to get words. Before long there was the sound of Cramer's heavy steps tramping along the hall, then the slam of the front door.

I called down: "All clear?"

"No!" It was a bellow. "Wait till I bolt it!" And after a moment: "All right!"

I shut my door and descended the stairs. Wolfe was back in his chair behind his desk, sitting straight. As I entered he snapped at me: "A pretty mess. You sneak a dog in here to badger me, and what now?"

I crossed to my desk, sat, and spoke calmly: "We're 'way beyond that. You will never admit you bollixed it up yourself, so forget it. When you ask me what now, that's easy. I could say I'll take the dog down and deliver him at Homicide, but we're beyond that too. Not only have you learned that he is orphaned, as you put it, and therefore adopting him will probably be simple, but also you have taken a stand with Cramer, and of course you won't back up. If we sit tight, with the door bolted, I suppose I can take the dog out back for his outings, but what if the law shows up tomorrow with a writ?"

He leaned back and shut his eyes. I looked up at the wall clock: two minutes past eleven. I looked at my wrist watch: also two minutes past eleven. They both said six minutes past when Wolfe opened his eyes.

"From Mr. Cramer's information," he said, "I doubt if the case holds any formidable difficulties."

I had no comment.

"If it were speedily solved," he went on, "your commitment to the dog could be honored, at leisure. Clearly, the simplest way to settle this matter is to find out who killed Mr. Kampf. It may not be much of a job; if it proves otherwise, we can reconsider. An immediate exploration is the thing, and luckily we have a pretext for it. You can go to Arbor Street to get your raincoat, taking Mr. Meegan's with you, and proceed as the occasion offers. The best course would be to bring him here; but, as you know, I rely wholly on your discretion and enterprise in such a juncture."

"Thank you very much," I said bitterly. "You mean now?"

"Yes."

"They may still have Meegan downtown."

"I doubt if they'll keep him overnight. In the morning they'll probably have him again."

"I'll be hanged." I arose. "No client, no fee—no nothing except a dog with a wide skull for brain room." I went to the hall rack for my hat and Meegan's coat, and beat it.

The rain had ended and the wind was down. Dismissing the taxi at the end of Arbor Street, I walked to Number 29, with the raincoat hung over my arm. There was light behind the curtains of the windows on the ground floor, but none anywhere above, and none in the basement. Entering the vestibule, I inspected the labels in the slots between the mailboxes and the buttons. From the bottom up they read: Talento, Meegan, Aland, and Chaffee. I pushed Meegan's button, put my hand on the doorknob, and waited. No click. I twisted the knob and it wouldn't turn. Another long push on the button, and a long wait. Nothing doing.

I considered pushing the button of Victor Talento, the lawyer who lived on the ground floor, where light was showing; instead, I voted to wait a while for Meegan, with whom I had an in. I moved to the sidewalk, propped myself against a fire hydrant, and waited.

I hadn't been there long enough to shift position more than a couple of times when the light disappeared on the ground floor of Number 29. A little later the vestibule door opened and a man came out. He turned toward me, gave me a glance as he passed, and kept going.

Thinking it unlikely that any occupant of that house was being extended the freedom of the city that night, I cast my eyes around, and, sure enough when the subject had gone some thirty paces a figure emerged from an area way across the street and started strolling after him. I shook my head in disapproval. I would have waited until the guy was ten paces farther. Saul Panzer would have made it ten more than that, but Saul is the best trailer alive.

As I stood deploring that faulty performance, an idea hit me. They might keep Meegan downtown another two hours, or all night, or he might even be up in his bed asleep. This was at least a chance to take a stab at something. I shoved off, in the direction taken by the subject, who was now a block away.

Stepping along, I gained on him. A little beyond the corner I came abreast of the city employee, who was keeping to the other side of the street, but I wasn't interested in him. It seemed to me that the subject was upping the stroke a little, so I did, too, and as he reached the next intersection I was beside him.

I said: "Victor Talento?"

"No comment," he said, and kept going. So did I.

"Thanks for the compliment," I said, "but I'm not a reporter. My name's Archie Goodwin, and I work for Nero Wolfe. If you'll stop a second I'll show you my credentials."

"I'm not interested in your credentials."

"Okay. If you just came out for a breath of air you won't be interested in this, either. Otherwise, you may be. Please don't scream or look around, but you've got a homicide dick on your tail. He's across the street, ninety feet back."

"Yes," he conceded, without changing pace, "that's interesting. Is this your good deed for the day?"

"No. I'm out dowsing for Mr. Wolfe. He's investigating a murder just for practice, and I'm looking for a seam. I thought if I gave you a break you might feel like reciprocating. If you're just out for a walk, forget it, and sorry I interrupted. If you're headed for something you'd like to keep private, maybe you could use some expert advice. In this part of town at this time of night there are only two approved methods for shaking a tail, and I'd be glad to oblige."

He looked it over for half a block, with me keeping step, and then spoke: "You mentioned credentials."

"Right. We might as well stop under that light. The dick will, of course, keep his distance."

We stopped. I got out my wallet and let him have a look at my licenses, detective and driver's. He didn't skimp it, being a lawyer.

"Of course," he said. "I was aware that I might be followed."

"Sure."

"I intended to take precautions. But I suppose it's not always as simple as it seems. I have had no experience at this kind of maneuver. Who hired Wolfe to investigate?"

"I don't know. He says he needs practice."

He stood sizing me up by the street light. He was an inch shorter than I am, and some older, with his weight starting to collect around the middle. He was dark-skinned, with eyes to match.

"I have an appointment," he said.

I waited.

He went on: "A woman phoned me and I arranged to meet her. My wire could have been tapped."

"I doubt it. They're not that fast."

"I suppose not. The woman had nothing to do with the murder, and neither had I, but of course anything I do and anyone I see is suspect. I have no right to expose her to possible embarrassment. I can't be sure of shaking that man off."

I grinned at him. "And me, too."

"You mean you would follow me?"

"Certainly, for practice. And I'd like to see how you handle it."

He wasn't returning my grin. "I see you've earned your reputation, Goodwin. You'd be wasting your time, because this woman has no connection with this business, but I should have known better than to make this appointment. It's only three blocks from here. You might be willing to go and tell her I'm not coming. Yes?"

"Sure, if it's only three blocks. If you'll return the favor by calling on Nero Wolfe for a little talk. That's what I meant by reciprocating."

He considered it. "Not tonight. I'm all in."

"Tomorrow morning at eleven?"

"Yes, I can make it then."

"Okay." I gave him the address. "Now brief me."

He took a respectable roll of bills from his pocket and peeled off a twenty. "Since you're acting as my agent, you have a right to a fee."

I grinned again. "That's a neat idea, you being a lawyer, but I'm not acting as your agent. I'm doing you a favor on request and expecting one in return. Where's the appointment?"

He put the roll back. "Have it your way. The woman's name is Jewel Jones, and she's at the southeast corner of Christopher and Grove Streets, or will be." He looked at his wrist. "We were to meet there at midnight. She's medium height, slender, dark hair and eyes, very good-looking. Tell her why I'm not coming, and say she'll hear from me tomorrow."

"Right. You'd better take a walk in the other direction to keep the dick occupied, and don't look back."

He wanted to shake hands to show his appreciation, but that would have been just as bad as taking the twenty, since before another midnight Wolfe might be tagging him for murder, so I pretended not to notice. He headed east and I, west, moving right along.

I had to make sure that the dick didn't switch subjects, but I let that wait until I got to Christopher Street. Reaching it, I turned the corner, went twenty feet to a stoop, slid behind it with only my head out, and counted a slow hundred. There were passers-by—a couple and a guy in a hurry—but no dick. I went on a block to Grove Street, passed the intersection, saw no loitering female, continued for a distance, then turned and back-tracked. I was on the fifth lap, and it was eight minutes past twelve, when a taxi stopped at the corner, a woman got out, and the taxi rolled off.

I approached. The light could have been better, but she seemed to meet the specifications. I stopped and asked, "Jones?" She drew herself up. I said, "From Victor."

She tilted her head back to see my face. "Who are you?" She seemed a little out of breath.

"Victor sent me with a message, but naturally I have to be sure it reaches the right party. I've anted half of your name and half of his, so it's your turn."

"Who are you?"

I shook my head. "You go first, or no message from Victor."

"Where is he?"

"No. I'll count ten and go. One, two, three, four—"

"My name is Jewel Jones. His is Victor Talento."

"That's the girl. I'll tell you." I did so, giving a complete version of my encounter with Talento, and including, of course, my name and status. By the time I finished she had developed a healthy frown.

She put a hand on my arm. "Come and put me in a taxi."

I stayed planted. "I'll be glad to, and it will be on me. We're going to Nero Wolfe's place."

"We?" She removed the hand. "You're crazy."

"One will get you ten I'm not. Look at it. You and Talento made an appointment at a street corner, so you had some good reason for not wanting to be seen together tonight. It must have been something fairly urgent. I admit the urgency didn't have to be connected with the murder of Philip Kampf, but it could be. I don't want to be arbitrary. I can take you to a homicide sergeant named Stebbins and you can discuss it with him, or I'll take you to Mr. Wolfe.''

She had well-oiled gears. For a second, as I spoke, her eyes flashed like daggers, but then they went soft and appealing. She took my arm again, this time with both hands. ''I'll discuss it with you,'' she said, in a voice she could have used to defrost her refrigerator. ''I wouldn't mind that. We'll go somewhere.''

I said come on, and we moved, with her hand hooked cozily on my arm. We hadn't gone far, toward Seventh Avenue, when a taxi came along and I flagged it and we got in. I told the driver, ''Nine-sixteen West Thirty-fifth,'' and he started.

''What's that?'' Miss Jones demanded.

I told her, Nero Wolfe's house. The poor girl didn't know what to do. If she called me a rat, that wouldn't help her any. If she kicked and screamed, I would merely tell the hackie, Headquarters. Her best bet was to try to thaw me, and if she had had time for a real campaign—say four or five hours—she might have made some progress, because she had a knack for it.

There just wasn't time enough. The taxi rolled to the curb and I had a bill ready for the driver. I got out, gave her a hand, and escorted her up the seven steps of the stoop. I pushed the button, and in a moment the stoop light shone on us, the chain bolt was released, and the door opened. I motioned her in and followed. Fritz was there.

''Mr. Wolfe up?'' I asked.

''In the office.'' He was giving Miss Jones a look, the look he gives any strange female who enters that house. There is always in his mind the possibility, however remote, that she will bewitch Wolfe into a mania for a mate. I asked him to conduct her to the front room, put my hat and the raincoat on the rack, and went on down the hall to the office.

Wolfe was at his desk, reading; and curled up in the middle of the room, on the best rug in the house, was the dog. The dog greeted me by lifting his head and tapping the rug with his tail. Wolfe greeted me by grunting.

''I brought company,'' I told him. ''Before I introduce her I should—''

"Her? The tenants of the house are all men! I might have known you'd dig up a woman!"

"I can chase her if you don't want her. This is how I got her." I proceeded, not dragging it out, but including all the essentials. I ended up, "I could have grilled her myself, but it would have been risky. Just in a six-minute taxi ride she had me feeling—uh, brotherly. Do you want her or not?"

"Confound it." His eyes went to his book and stayed there long enough to finish a paragraph. "Very well, bring her."

I crossed to the connecting door to the front room, opened it, and requested, "Please come in, Miss Jones." She came, and as she passed through gave me a wistful smile that might have gone straight to my heart if there hadn't been a diversion. As she entered, the dog suddenly sprang to his feet and made for her, with sounds of unmistakable pleasure. He stopped in front of her, wagging his tail so fast it was only a blur.

"Indeed," Wolfe said. "How do you do, Miss Jones? I am Nero Wolfe. What's the dog's name?"

I claim she was good. The presence of the dog was a complete surprise to her. But without the slightest sign of fluster she put out a hand to give it a gentle pat, then went to the red-leather chair and sat down.

"That's a funny question right off," she said. "Asking me your dog's name."

"Pfui." Wolfe was disgusted. "I don't know what position you were going to take, but from what Mr. Goodwin tells me I would guess you were going to say that the purpose of your appointment with Mr. Talento was a personal matter that had nothing to do with Mr. Kampf or his death, and that you knew Mr. Kampf either slightly or not at all. Now the dog has made that untenable. Obviously, he knows you well, and he belonged to Mr. Kampf. So you knew Mr. Kampf well. If you try to deny that, you'll have Mr. Goodwin and other trained men digging all around you, your past and your present, and that will be extremely disagreeable, no matter how innocent you may be of murder or any other wrongdoing. You won't like that. What's the dog's name?"

She looked at me and I looked back. In good light I would have qualified Talento's specification of "very good-looking." Not that she was unsightly, but she caught the eye more by what she looked than how she looked. It wasn't just something she turned on as needed; it was there even now, when she must have been pretty busy deciding how to handle the situation.

It took her only a few seconds to decide. "His name is Bootsy," she said. The dog, at her feet, lifted his head and wagged his tail.

"Good heavens," Wolfe muttered. "No other name?"

"Not that I know of."

"Your name is Jewel Jones?"

"Yes. I sing in a night club, but I'm not working right now." She made a little gesture, very appealing, but it was Wolfe who had to resist it, not me. "Believe me, Mr. Wolfe, I don't know anything about that murder. If I knew anything that could help I'd be perfectly willing to tell you, because I'm sure you're the kind of man who understands, and you wouldn't want to hurt me if you didn't have to."

"I try to understand," Wolfe said dryly. "You knew Mr. Kampf intimately?"

"Yes, I guess so." She smiled, as one understander to another. "For a while I did. Not lately—not for the past two months."

"You met the dog at his apartment on Perry Street?"

"That's right. For nearly a year I was there quite often."

"You and Mr. Kampf quarreled?"

"Oh, no, we didn't quarrel. I just didn't see him any more. I had other—I was very busy."

"When did you see him last?"

"About two weeks ago, at the club. He came to the club once or twice and spoke to me there."

"But no quarrel?"

"No, there was nothing to quarrel about."

"You have no idea who killed him, or why?"

"I certainly haven't."

Wolfe leaned back. "Do you know Mr. Talento intimately?"

"No, not if you mean—of course, we're friends. I used to live there. I had the second-floor apartment."

"At Twenty-nine Arbor Street?"

"Yes."

"For how long? When?"

"For nearly a year. I left there—let's see—about three months ago. I have a little apartment on East Forty-ninth Street."

"Then you know the others, too? Mr. Meegan and Mr. Chaffee and Mr. Aland?"

"I know Ross Chaffee and Jerry Aland, but no Meegan. Who's he?"

"A tenant at Twenty-nine Arbor Street. Second floor."

She nodded. "Well, sure, that's the floor I had." She smiled. "I hope they fixed the rickety table for him. That was one reason I left. I hate furnished apartments, don't you?"

Wolfe made a face. "In principle, yes. I take it you now have your own furniture. Supplied by Mr. Kampf?"

She laughed—more of a chuckle—and her eyes danced. "I see you didn't know Phil Kampf."

"Not supplied by him, then?"

"A great big no."

"By Mr. Chaffee? Or Mr. Aland?"

"No and no." She went very earnest: "Look, Mr. Wolfe. A friend of mine was mighty nice about that furniture, and we'll just leave it. Mr. Goodwin told me what you're interested in is the murder, and I'm sure you wouldn't want to drag in a lot of stuff just to hurt me and a friend of mine, so we'll forget about the furniture."

Wolfe didn't press it. He took a hop. "Your appointment on a street corner with Mr. Talento. What was that about?"

She nodded. "I've been wondering about that—I mean, what I would say when you asked me—because I'd hate to have you think I'm a sap, and I guess it sounds like it. I phoned him when I heard on the radio that Phil was killed, there on Arbor Street. I knew Vic still lived there, and I simply wanted to ask him about it."

"You had him on the phone."

"He didn't seem to want to talk about it on the phone."

"But why a street corner?"

This time it was more like a laugh. "Now, Mr. Wolfe, *you're* not a sap. You asked about the furniture, didn't you? Well, a girl with furniture shouldn't be seen with Vic Talento."

"What is he like?"

She fluttered a hand. "Oh, he wants to get close."

Wolfe kept at her until after one o'clock, and I could report it all, but it wouldn't get you any farther than it did him. He couldn't trip her or back her into a corner. She hadn't been to Arbor Street for two months. She hadn't seen Chaffee or Aland or Talento for weeks, and of course not Meegan, since she had never heard of him before. She couldn't even try to guess who had killed Kampf.

The only thing remotely to be regarded as a return on Wolfe's investment of a full hour was her statement that, as far as she knew, there was no one who had both an attachment and a claim to Bootsy. If there were heirs, she had no idea who they were. When she left the chair to go, the dog got up, too. She patted him, and he want with us to the door. I took her to Tenth Avenue and put her in a taxi, and returned.

"Where's Bootsy?" I inquired.

"No," Wolfe said emphatically.

"Okay," I surrendered. "Where's Jet?"

"Down in Fritz's room. He'll sleep there. You don't like him."

"That's not true, but you can have it. It means you can't blame him on me. Anyhow, that will no longer be an issue after Homicide comes in the morning with a document and takes him away."

"They won't come."

"I offer twenty to one. Before noon."

He nodded. "That was, roughly, my own estimate of the probability, so while you were out I phoned Mr. Cramer. I suggested an arrangement, and I suppose he inferred that if he declined the arrangement the dog might be beyond his jurisdiction before tomorrow. I didn't say so, but I may have given him that impression."

"Yeah. You should be more careful."

"So the arrangement has been made. You are to be at Twenty-nine Arbor Street, with the dog, at nine o'clock in the morning. You are to be present throughout the fatuous performance the police have in mind, and keep the dog in view. The dog is to leave the premises with you, before noon, and you are to bring him back here. The police are to make no further effort to constrain the dog for twenty-four hours. While in that house you may find an opportunity to flush something or someone more contributive than Jewel Jones. . . ."

*   *   *

It was a fine, bright morning. I didn't take Meegan's raincoat, because I didn't need any pretext, and I doubted if the
program would offer a likely occasion for the exchange.

The law was there in front waiting for me. The plainclothes-
man who knew dogs was a stocky, middle-aged guy who wore
rimless glasses. Before he touched the dog he asked me its
name, and I told him Bootsy.

"A heck of a name," he observed. "Also, that's some leash
you've got."

"I agree. His was on the corpse, so I suppose it's in the lab."
I handed him my end of the heavy cord. "If he bites you it's not
on me."

"He won't bite me. Would you, Bootsy?" He squatted before the dog and started to get acquainted.

Sergeant Purley Stebbins growled a foot from my ear, "He
should have bit you when you kidnapped him."

I turned. Purley was half an inch taller than I am and two
inches broader. "You've got it twisted," I told him. "It's
women that bite me. I've often wondered what would bite
you."

We continued exchanging pleasantries, while the dog man,
whose name was Larkin, made friends with Bootsy. It wasn't
long before he announced that he was ready to proceed. He was
frowning. "In a way," he said, "it would be better to keep him
on leash after I go in, because Kampf probably did. . . . Or did
he? How much do we actually know?"

"To swear to," Purley told him, "very little. But putting it
all together from what we've collected, this is how it looks:
When Kampf and the dog entered, it was raining and the dog
was wet. Kampf removed the leash, either in the ground-floor
hall or one of the halls above. He had the leash in his hand
when he went to the door of one of the apartments. The tenant
of the apartment let him in and they talked. The tenant socked
him, probably from behind without warning, and used the leash
to finish him. The murderer stuffed the leash in the pocket of
the raincoat.

"It took nerve and muscle to carry the body out and down the
stairs to the lower hall, but he had to get it out of his place and
away from his door, and any of those four could have done it in

a pinch. Of course, the dog was already outside, out on the sidewalk. While Kampf was in one of the apartments getting killed, Talento had come into the lower hall and seen the dog and chased it out.''

"Then," Larkin objected, "Talento's clean."

"No. Nobody's clean. If it was Talento, after he killed Kampf he went out to the hall and put the dog in the vestibule, went back in his apartment and carried the body out and dumped it at the foot of the stairs, and then left the house, chasing the dog on out to the sidewalk. You're the dog expert. Is there anything wrong with that?''

"Not necessarily. It depends on the dog and how close he was to Kampf. There wasn't any blood."

"Then that's how I'm buying it. If you want it filled in you can spend the rest of the day with the reports of the other experts and the statements made by the tenants."

"Some other day. That'll do for now. You're going in first?"

"Yeah. Come on, Goodwin." Purley started for the door, but I objected: "I'm staying with the dog."

Purley looked disgusted. "Then keep behind Larkin."

I changed my mind. From behind Larkin the view wouldn't be good. So I went into the vestibule with Purley. The inner door was opened by a homicide colleague, and we crossed to the far side of the small lobby. The colleague closed the door. In a minute he pulled it open again, and Larkin and the dog entered.

Two steps in, Larkin stopped, and so did the dog. No one spoke. The leash hung limp. Bootsy looked around at Larkin. Larkin bent over and untied the cord from the collar, and held it up to show Bootsy he was free. Bootsy came over to me and stood, his head up, wagging his tail.

"Nuts," Purley said, disgusted.

"You know what I really expected," Larkin said. "I never thought he'd show us where Kampf went when they entered yesterday, but I did think he'd go to the foot of the stairs, where the body was found, and I thought he might go on to where the body came from—Talento's door, or upstairs. Take him by the collar, Goodwin, and ease him over to the front of the stairs."

I obliged. He came without urging, but gave no sign that the spot held any special interest for him. We all stood and watched him. He opened his mouth wide to yawn.

"Fine," Purley rumbled. "Just fine. You might as well go on with it."

Larkin came and fastened the leash to the collar, led Bootsy across the lobby to a door, and knocked. In a moment the door opened, and there was Victor Talento, in a fancy rainbow dressing gown.

"Hello, Boosty," he said, and reached down to pat.

Purley snapped, "I told you not to speak!"

Talento straightened up. "So you did." He was apologetic. "I'm sorry; I forgot. Do you want to try it again?"

No. That's all."

Talento backed in and closed the door.

"You must realize," Larkin told Purley, "that a Labrador can't be expected to go for a man's throat. They're not that kind of dog. The most you could expect would be an attitude, or possibly a growl."

"You can have 'em," Purley said. "Is it worth going on?"

"By all means. You'd better go first."

Purley started up the stairs, and I followed him. The upper hall was narrow and not very light, with a door at the rear end and another toward the front. We backed up against the wall opposite the front door to leave enough space for Larkin and Bootsy. They came, Bootsy tagging, and Larkin knocked. Ten seconds passed before footsteps sounded; and then the door was opened by the specimen who had dashed out of the Wolfe's place the day before and taken my coat with him. He was in his shirt sleeves and he hadn't combed his blond hair.

'This is Sergeant Larkin, Mr. Meegan," Purley said. "Take a look at the dog. Have you ever seen it before? Pat it."

Meegan snorted. "Pat it yourself."

"Have you ever seen it before?"

"No."

"Okay; thanks. Come on, Larkin."

As we started up the next flight the door slammed behind us, good and loud. Purley asked over his shoulder, "Well?"

"He didn't like him," Larkin replied from the rear, "but there are lots of people lots of dogs don't like."

The third-floor hall was a duplicate of the one below. Again Purley and I posted ourselves opposite the door, and Larkin came with Bootsy and knocked. Nothing happened. He knocked again, louder, and pretty soon the door opened to a two-inch crack and a squeaky voice came through:

"You've got the dog."

"Right here," Larkin told him.

"Are you there, Sergeant?"

"Right here," Purley answered.

"I told you that dog didn't like me. Once at a party at Phil Kampf's—I told you. I didn't mean to hurt it, but it thought I did. What are you trying to do—frame me?"

"Open the door. The dog's on a leash."

"I won't! I told you I wouldn't!"

Purley moved. His arm, out stiff, went over Larkin's shoulder, and his palm met the door and shoved hard. The door hesitated an instant, then swung open. Standing there, holding to its edge, was a skinny individual in red-and-green striped pajamas. The dog let out a low growl and backed up a little.

"We're making the rounds, Mr. Aland," Purley said, "and we couldn't leave you out. Now you can go back to sleep. As for trying to frame you—" He stopped because the door shut.

"You didn't tell me," Larkin complained, "that Aland had already fixed it for a reaction."

"No, I thought I'd wait and see. One to go." He headed for the stairs.

The top-floor hall had had someone's personal attention. It was no bigger than the others, but it had a nice, clean tan-colored runner, and the walls were painted the same shade and sported a few small pictures. Purley went to the rear door instead of the front, and we made room for Larkin and Bootsy. When Larkin knocked, footsteps responded at once, and the door swung wide open. This was the painter, Ross Chaffee, and he was dressed for it, in an old brown smock. He was by far the handsomest of the tenants—tall, erect, with features he must have enjoyed looking at in the mirror.

I had ample time to enjoy them, too, as he stood smiling at us, completely at ease, obeying Purley's prior instructions not to speak. Bootsy was also at ease. When it became quite clear that no blood was going to be shed, Purley asked, "You know the dog, don't you, Mr. Chaffee?"

"Certainly. He's a beautiful animal."

"Pat him."

"With pleasure." He bent gracefully. "Bootsy, do you know your master's gone?" He scratched behind the black ears. "Gone forever, Bootsy, and that's too bad." He straightened. "Anything else? I'm working. I like morning light."

"That's all, thanks." Purley turned to go, and I let Larkin and Bootsy by before following. On the way down the three flights no one had any remarks. As we hit the lower hall Victor Talento's door opened, and he emerged.

"The District Attorney's office telephoned," he said. "Are you through with me? They want me down there."

"We're through," Purley said. "We can run you down."

Talento said that would be fine and he would be ready in a minute. Purley told Larkin to give me Bootsy, and he handed me the leash.

I departed. Outside, the morning was still fine. The presence of two PD cars in front of the scene of a murder had attracted a small gathering, and Bootsy and I were objects of interest as we appeared and started off. We both ignored the stares. We moseyed along, in no hurry, stopping now and then to give Bootsy a chance to inspect something if he felt inclined. At the fourth or fifth stop, more than a block away, I saw the quartet leaving Number 29. Stebbins and Talento took one car, Larkin and the colleague the other, and they rolled off.

I shortened up on Bootsy a little, walked him west until an empty taxi appeared, stopped it, and got in. I took a five-dollar bill from my wallet and handed it to the hackie.

"Thanks," he said. "For what—down payment on the cab?"

"You'll earn it, brother," I assured him. "Is there somewhere within a block or so of Arbor and Court where you can park for anywhere from thirty minutes to three hours?"

"Not three hours for a finif."

"Of course not." I took out another five and gave it to him. "I doubt if it will be that long."

"There's a parking lot not too far. On the street without a passenger I'll be hailed."

"You'll have a passenger: the dog. I prefer the street. Let's see what we can find."

There are darned few legal parking spaces in all Manhattan at that time of day, and we cruised around several corners before we found one, on Court Street two blocks from Arbor. He backed into it and I got out, leaving the windows down three inches. I told him I'd be back when he saw me, and headed south, turning right at the second corner.

There was no police car at 29 Arbor, and no gathering. That was satisfactory. Entering the vestibule, I pushed the button under "Meegan" and put my hand on the knob. No click. Pushing twice more and still getting no response, I tried Aland's button and that worked. After a short wait the click came, and I entered, mounted two flights, and knocked with authority on Aland's door.

The squeaky voice came through: "Who is it?"

"Goodwin. I was just here with the others. I haven't got the dog."

The door swung slowly to a crack, and then wider. Jerome Aland was still in his gaudy pajamas. "What do you want now?" he asked. "I need some sleep!"

I didn't apologize. "I was going to ask you some questions when I was here before," I told him, "but the dog complicated it. It won't take long." Since he wasn't polite enough to move aside, I had to brush him, skinny as he was, as I went in.

He slid past me, and I followed him across the room to chairs. They were the kind of chairs that made Jewel Jones hate furnished apartments. He sat on the edge of one and demanded, "All right; what is it?"

It was a little tricky. Since he was assuming I was one of the homicide personnel, it wouldn't do for me to know either too much or too little. It would be risky to mention Jewel Jones, because the cops might not have got around to her at all.

"I'm checking some points," I told him. "'How long has Richard Meegan occupied the apartment below you?"

"I've told you that a dozen times."

"Not me. I said I'm checking. How long?"

"Nine days. He took it a week ago Tuesday."

'Who was the previous tenant? Just before him."

"There wasn't any. It was empty."

"Empty since you've been here?"

"No, I've told you, a girl had it, but she moved out about three months ago. Her name is Jewel Jones, and she's a fine artist, and she got me my job at the night club where I work now." His mouth worked. "I know what you're doing. You're trying to make it nasty and you're trying to catch me getting my facts twisted. Bringing that dog here to growl at me—Can I help it if I don't like dogs?"

He ran his fingers, both hands, through his hair. When the hair was messed good he gestured like the night-club comedian he was. "Die like a dog," he said. "That's what Phil did—died like a dog."

"You said," I ventured, "that you and he were good friends."

His head jerked up. "I did not!"

"Maybe not in those words. . . . Why? Weren't you?"

"We were not. I haven't got any good friends."

"You just said that the girl who used to live here got you a job. That sounds like a good friend. Or did she owe you something?"

"Of course not. Why do you keep bringing her up?"

"I didn't bring her up—you did. I only asked who was the former tenant in the apartment below you. Why? Would you rather keep her out of it?"

"I don't have to keep her out. She's not in it."

"Perhaps not. Did she know Philip Kampf?"

"I guess so. Sure, she did."

"How well did she know him?"

He shook his head. "If Phil was alive you could ask him, and he might tell you. Me, I don't know."

I smiled at him. "All that does, Mr. Aland, is make me curious. Somebody in this house murdered Kampf. So we ask you questions, and when we come to one you shy at, naturally we wonder why. If you don't like talking about Kampf and that girl, think what it could mean. For instance, it could mean that the girl was yours, and Kampf took her away from you, and that was why you killed him when he came here yesterday."

"She wasn't my girl!"

"Uh-huh. Or it could mean that although she wasn't yours, you were under a deep obligation to her, and Kampf had given her a dirty deal; or he was threatening her with something, and she wanted him disposed of, and you obliged. Or of course it could be merely that Kampf had something on you."

"You're in the wrong racket," he sneered. "You ought to be writing TV scripts."

I stuck with him only a few more minutes, having got all I

could hope for under the circumstances. Since I was letting him assume that I was a city employee, I couldn't very well try to pry him loose for a trip to Wolfe's place. Also, I had two more calls to make, and there was no telling when I might be interrupted by a phone call or a courier to one of them from downtown. So I left.

I went down a flight to Meegan's door, and knocked and waited. Just as I was raising a fist to make it louder and better, there were footsteps inside, and the door opened. Meegan was still in his shirt sleeves and still uncombed.

"Well?" he demanded.

"Back again," I said, firmly but not offensively. "With a few questions. If you don't mind?"

"I certainly do mind."

"Naturally. Mr. Talento has been called down to the District Attorney's office. This might possibly save you another trip there."

He side-stepped and I went in. The room was the same size and shape as Aland's, above, and the furniture, though different, was no more desirable. The table against a wall was lopsided, probably the one that Jewel Jones hoped they had fixed for him. I took a chair beside it, and he took another and sat frowning at me.

"Haven't I seen you before?" he wanted to know.

"Sure, we were here with the dog."

"I mean before that. Wasn't it you in Nero Wolfe's office yesterday?"

"That's right."

"How come?"

I raised my brows. "Haven't you got the lines crossed, Mr. Meegan? I'm here to ask questions, not to answer them. I was in Wolfe's office on business. I often am. Now—"

"He's a fat, arrogant half-wit!"

"You may be right. He's certainly arrogant. Now I'm here on business." I got out my notebook and pencil. "You moved into this place nine days ago. Please tell me exactly how you came to take this apartment."

He glared. "I've told it at least three times."

"I know. This is the way it's done. I'm not trying to catch you in some little discrepancy, but you could have omitted something important. Just assume I haven't heard it before. Go ahead.''

He groaned and dropped his head on his hands. Normally, he might not have been a bad-looking guy, with his blond hair and gray eyes and long, bony face; but now, having spent most of the night with Homicide and the D.A., he looked it, especially his eyes, which were red and puffy.

He lifted his head. "I'm a commercial photographer. In Pittsburgh. Two years ago I married a girl named Margaret Ryan. Seven months later she left me. I didn't know whether she went alone or with somebody. She just left. She left Pittsburgh, too—at least I couldn't find her there—and her family never saw her or heard from her. About five months later, about a year ago, a client of mine came back from a trip to New York and said he saw her in a theater here with a man. He spoke to her, but she claimed he was mistaken. He was sure it was her. I came to New York and spent a week looking around, but didn't find her. I didn't go to the police, because I didn't want to. You want a better reason, but that's mine.''

"I'll skip that." I was writing in the notebook. "Go ahead."

"Two weeks ago I went to look at a show of pictures at the Fillmore Gallery in Pittsburgh. There was a painting there—an oil—a big one. It was called *Three Young Mares at Pasture*, and it was an interior, a room, with three women in it. One of them was on a couch, and two of them were on a rug on the floor. They were eating apples. The one on the couch was my wife. I was sure of it the minute I saw her, and after I stood and studied it I was surer than ever. There was absolutely no doubt of it.''

"We're not challenging that," I assured him. "What did you do?''

"The artist's signature was Ross Chaffee. I went to the gallery office and asked about him. They thought he lived in New York. I had some work on hand I had to finish, and then I came to New York.

"I had no trouble finding Ross Chaffee; he was in the phone book. I went to see him at his studio, here in this house. First, I told him I was interested in that figure in his painting, that I thought she would be just right to model for some photographs I wanted to do, but he said that his opinion of photography as an art medium was such that he wouldn't care to supply models for it. He was bowing me out, so I told him how it was. I told him the whole thing. Then he was different. He sympathized with me and said he would be glad to help me if he could, but he had painted that picture more than a year ago, and he used so many different models for his pictures that it was impossible to remember which was which.''

Meegan stopped, and I looked up from the notebook. He said aggressively, ''I'm repeating that that sounded phony to me.''

''Go right ahead. You're telling it.''

''I say it was phony. A photographer might use hundreds of models in a year, and he might forget, but not a painter. Not a picture like that. I got a little tactless with him, and then I apologized. He said he might be able to refresh his memory and asked me to phone him the next day. Instead of phoning I went back the next day to see him, but he said he simply couldn't remember and doubted if he ever could. I didn't get tactless again. Coming in the house, I had noticed a sign that there was a furnished apartment to let, and when I left Chaffee I found the janitor and rented it, and moved in. I knew my wife had modeled for that picture, and I knew I could find her. I wanted to be as close as I could to Chaffee and the people who came to see him.''

I wanted something, too. I wanted to say that he must have had a photograph of his wife along and I would like to see it, but of course I didn't dare; it was a cinch that he had already either given it to the cops, or refused to, or claimed he didn't have one. So I merely asked, ''What kind of progress did you make?''

''Not much. I tried to get friendly with Chaffee, but I didn't get very far. I met the other two tenants, Talento and Aland, but that didn't get my anywhere. Finally I decided I would have to get some expert help, and that was why I went to see Nero Wolfe. You were there, so you know how that came out—that big blob!''

I nodded. ''He has dropsy of the ego. What did you want him to do?''

''I've told you.''

''Tell it again.''

''I was going to have him tap Chaffee's phone.''

"That's illegal," I said severely.

"All right; I didn't do it."

I flipped a page of the notebook. "Go back a little. During that week, besides the tenants here, how many of Chaffee's friends and acquaintances did you meet?"

"Just two, as I've told you. A young woman, a model, in his studio one day—I don't remember her name—and a man Chaffee said buys his pictures. His name was Braunstein."

"You're leaving out Philip Kampf."

Meegan leaned forward and put a fist on the table. "Yes, and I'm going on leaving him out. I never saw him or heard of him."

"What would you say if I said you were seen with him?"

"I'd say you were a dirty liar!" The red eyes looked redder. "As if I wasn't already having enough trouble, now you set on me about the murder of a man I never heard of! You bring a dog here and tell me to pat it!"

I nodded. "That's your hard luck. Mr. Meegan. You're not the first man who's had a murder for company without inviting it." I closed the notebook and put it in my pocket. I rose. "Stick around, please. You may be wanted downtown again."

I would have liked to get more details of his progress, or lack of progress, with Ross Chaffee, and his contacts with the other two tenants, but it seemed more important to have some words with Chaffee before I got interrupted. As I mounted the two flights to the top floor my wrist watch said twenty-eight minutes past ten.

"I know there's no use complaining," Ross Chaffee said, "about these interruptions to my work. Under the circumstances." He was being very gracious about it.

The top floor was quite different from the others. I don't know what his living quarters in front were like, but the studio in the rear was big and high and anything but crummy. There were pieces of sculpture around, big and little, and canvases of all sizes were stacked and propped against racks. The walls were covered with drapes, solid gray, with nothing on them. Each of two easels, one much larger than the other, held a canvas that had been worked on. There were several plain chairs and two upholstered ones, and an oversized divan.

I had been steered to one of the upholstered numbers, and Chaffee, still in his smock, moved a plain one to sit facing me.

"Only don't prolong it unnecessarily," he requested.

I said I wouldn't. "There are a couple of points," I told him, "that we wonder about a little. Of course, it could be merely a coincidence that Richard Meegan came to town looking for his wife, and came to see you, and rented an apartment here, just nine days before Kampf was murdered, but a coincidence like that will have to stand some going over. Frankly, Mr. Chaffee, there are those—and I happen to be one of them—who find it hard to believe that you couldn't remember who modeled for an important figure in a picture you painted."

Chaffee was smiling. "Then you must think I'm lying."

"I didn't say so."

"But you do, of course," He shrugged. "To what end? What deep design am I cherishing?"

"I wouldn't know. You say you wanted to help Meegan find his wife."

"No, not that I wanted. I was willing to. He is a horrible nuisance."

"It should be worth some effort to get rid of him. Have you made any?"

"I have explained what I did. In a statement, and signed it. I have nothing to add. I tried to refresh my memory. One of your colleagues suggested that I might have gone to Pittsburgh to look at the picture. I suppose he was being funny."

A flicker of annoyance in his fine dark eyes warned me that I was supposed to have read his statement.

I gave him an earnest eye. "Look, Mr. Chaffee. This thing is bad for all concerned. It will get worse instead of better until we find out who killed Kampf. You men in this house must know things about one another, and maybe some things connected with Kampf, that you're not telling. I don't expect a man like you to pass out dirt just for the fun of it, but any dirt that's connected with this murder is going to come out, and if you are keeping any to yourself you're a bigger fool than you look."

"Quite a speech." He was smiling again.

"Thanks. Now you make one."

"I'm not as eloquent as you are." He shook his head. "No, I

don't believe I can help you any. I can't say I'm a total stranger to dirt—that would be smug; but what you're after—no. You have my opinion of Kampf, whom I knew quite well; he was in some respects admirable, but he had his full share of faults. I would say approximately the same of Talento. I have known Aland only casually. I know no more of Meegan than you do. I haven't the slightest notion why any of them might have wanted to kill Philip Kampf. If you expect—''

A phone rang. Chaffee crossed to a table at the end of the divan and answered it. He told it ''Yes'' a couple of times, and then: ''But one of your men is here now. . . . I don't know his name; I didn't ask him. . . . He may be; I don't know. . . . very well. The District Attorney's office. . . . Yes, I can leave in a few minutes.''

He hung up and turned to me. I spoke first, on my feet: ''So they want you at the D.A.'s office. Don't tell them I said so, but they'd rather keep a murder in the file till the cows come home than have the squad crack it. If they want my name they know where to ask.''

I marched to the door, opened it, and was gone.

I was relieved to find the cab still waiting with its passenger perched on the seat looking out at the scenery. Jet seemed pleased to see me, and during the drive to 35th Street he sat with his rump braced against me for a buttress. The meter said only six dollars and something, but I didn't request any change from the ten I had given the driver. If Wolfe wanted to put me to work on a murder merely because he was infatuated with a dog, let it cost him something.

I noticed that when we entered the office Jet went over to Wolfe, behind his desk, without any sign of bashfulness or uncertainty, proving that the evening before, during my absence, Wolfe had made approaches; probably had fed him something, possibly had even patted him. Remarks occurred to me, but I saved them. I might be called on before long to spend some valuable time demonstrating that I had not been guilty of impersonating an officer, and that it wasn't my fault if the murder suspects mistook me for one.

Wolfe inquired, ''Well?''

I reported. The situation called for a full and detailed account, and I supplied it, while Wolfe leaned back with his eyes closed. When I came to the end he asked no questions. Instead, he opened his eyes, and began, "Call the—"

I cut him off: "Wait a minute. After a hard morning's work I claim the satisfaction of suggesting it myself. I thought of it long ago. I'll call the gallery in Pittsburgh where Chaffee's picture was shown."

"Indeed. It's a shot at random."

"I know it is but I'm calling anyway."

I reached for the phone on my desk and got through to the Fillmore Gallery in no time, but it took a quarter of an hour, with relays to three different people, to get what I was after. I hung up and turned to Wolfe:

"The show ended a week ago yesterday. And I won't have to go to Pittsburgh. The picture was lent by Mr. Herman Braunstein of New York, who owns it. It was shipped back to him by express four days ago. They wouldn't give me Braunstein's address."

"The phone book."

I had it and was flipping the pages. "Here we are. Business on Broad Street, residence on Park Avenue. There's only one Herman."

"Get him."

"I don't think so. It might take all day. Why don't I go to the residence without phoning? The picture's probably there, and if I can't get in you can fire me. I'm thinking of resigning anyhow."

He had his doubts, since it was my idea, but he bought it. After considering the problem a little, I went to the cabinet beneath the bookshelves, got out the Veblex camera, with accessories, and slung the strap of the case over my shoulder. Before going I dialed Talento's number, to tell him not to bother to keep his appointment, but there was no answer. Either he was still engaged at the D.A.'s office or he was on his way to 35th Street, and if he came during my absence that was all right, since Jet was there to protect Wolfe.

A taxi took me to the end of a sidewalk canopy in front of one of the palace hives on Park Avenue in the Seventies, and I undertook to walk past the doorman without giving him a glance, but he stopped me. I said professionally, "Braunstein, taking pictures, I'm late,'' and kept going, and got away with it. I crossed the luxurious lobby to the elevator, which luckily was there with the door open, said, "Braunstein, please," and the operator shut the door and pulled the lever. We stopped at the twelfth floor, and I stepped out. There was a door to the right and another to the left. I turned right without asking, on a fifty-fifty chance, listening for a possible correction from the elevator man, who was standing by with his door open.

It was one of the simplest chores I have ever performed. In answer to my ring, the door was opened by a middle-aged female husky, in uniform with apron, and when I told her I had come to take a picture she let me in, asked me to wait, and disappeared. In a couple of minutes a tall and dignified dame with white hair came through an arch and asked what I wanted. I apologized for disturbing her and said I would deeply appreciate it if she would let me take a picture of a painting which had recently been shown at a Pittsburgh gallery, on loan by Mr. Braunstein. It was called *Three Young Mares at Pasture*. A Pittsburgh client of mine had admired it, and had intended to go back and photograph it for his collection, but the picture was gone before he had got around to it.

She wanted some information, such as my name and address and the name of my Pittsburgh client, which I supplied gladly without a script, and then she led me through the arch into a room not quite as big as Madison Square Garden. It would have been a pleasure, and also instructive, to do a little glomming at the rugs and furniture and especially the dozen or more pictures on the walls, but that would have to wait.

She went across to a picture near the far end, said, "That's it," and lowered herself onto a chair.

It was a nice picture. I had half expected the mares to be without clothes, but they were fully dressed. Remarking that I didn't wonder that my client wanted a photograph of it, I got busy with my equipment, including the flash bulbs. She sat and watched. I took four shots from slightly different angles, acting and looking professional, I hoped. Then I thanked her warmly on behalf of my client, promised to send her some prints, and left.

That was all there was to it.

Out on the sidewalk again, I walked west to Madison, turned

downtown, and found a drug store. I went into the phone booth, and dialed a number.

Wolfe's voice came: "Yes? Whom do you want?"

I've told him a hundred times that's no way to answer the phone, but he's too pigheaded.

I spoke: "I want you. I've seen the picture, and it glows with color and life; the blood seems to pulsate under the warm skin. The shadows are transparent, with a harmonious blending—"

"Shut up! Yes or no?"

"Yes. You have met Mrs. Meegan. Would you like to meet her again?"

"I would. Get her."

I didn't have to look in the phone book for her address, having already done so.

I left the drug store and flagged a taxi.

There was no doorman problem at the number on East Forty-ninth Street. It was an old brick house that had been painted a bright yellow and modernized, but getting in was a little compli-cated. Pressing the button marked *Jewel Jones* in the vestibule was easy enough, but then it got more difficult.

A voice crackled from the grille: "Yes?"

"Miss Jones?"

"Yes. Who is it?"

"Archie Goodwin. I want to see you."

"What do you want?"

"Let me in and I'll tell you."

"No. What is it?"

"It's very personal. If you don't want to hear it from me I'll go and bring Richard Meegan, and maybe you'll tell him."

I heard the startled exclamation. After a pause: "Why do you say that? I told you I don't know any Meegan."

"You're 'way behind. I just saw a picture called *Three Young Mares at Pasture*. Let me in."

I turned and put my hand on the knob. There was a click, and I pushed the door and entered. I crossed the little lobby to the self-service elevator, pushed the button marked 5, and ascended. When it stopped, I opened the door and emerged into a tiny foyer. A door was standing open, and on the sill was Miss Jones in a giddy négligée. She started to say something, but I rudely ignored it.

"Listen," I said, "there's no sense in prolonging this. Last night I gave you your pick between Mr. Wolfe and Sergeant Stebbins; now it's either Mr. Wolfe or Meegan. I should think you'd prefer Mr. Wolfe, because he's the kind of man who understands; you said so yourself. I'll wait here while you change, but don't try phoning anybody, because you won't know where you are until you've talked with Mr. Wolfe—and also because their wires are probably tapped."

She stepped to me and put a hand on my arm. "Archie, where did you see the picture?"

"I'll tell you on the way down. Let's go."

She gave the arm a gentle tug. "You don't have to wait out here. Come in and sit down."

I patted her fingers, not wishing to be boorish. "Sorry," I told her, "but I'm afraid of young mares. One kicked me once."

She turned and disappeared into the apartment, leaving the door open.

"Don't call me Mrs. Meegan!" Jewel Jones cried.

Wolfe was in as bad a humor as she was. True, she had been hopelessly cornered, with no weapons within reach, but he had been compelled to tell Fritz to postpone lunch until further notice.

"I was only," he said crustily, "stressing the fact that your identity is not a matter for discussion. Legally, you are Mrs. Richard Meegan. That understood, I'll call you anything you say. Miss Jones?"

"Yes." She was on the red-leather chair, but not in it. Perched on its edge, she looked as if she were set to spring up and scoot any second.

"Very well," Wolfe regarded her. "You realize, madam, that everything you say will be received skeptically. You are a competent liar. Your offhand denial of acquaintance with Mr. Meegan last night was better than competent. Now. When did Mr. Chaffee tell you that your husband was in town looking for you?"

"I didn't say Mr. Chaffee told me."

"Someone did. Who and when?"

She was hanging on. "How do you know someone did?"

He waggled a finger at her. "I beg you, Miss Jones, to realize the pickle you're in. It is not credible that Mr. Chaffee couldn't remember the name of the model for that figure in his picture. The police don't believe it, and they haven't the advantage of knowing, as I do, that it was you and that you lived in that house for a year, and that you still see Mr. Chaffee occasionally. When your husband came and asked Mr. Chaffee for the name of the model, and Mr. Chaffee pleaded a faulty memory, and your husband rented an apartment there and made it plain that he intended to persevere, it is preposterous to suppose that Mr. Chaffee didn't tell you. I don't envy you your tussles with the police after they learn about you."

"They don't have to learn about me, do they?"

"Pfui. I'm surprised they haven't got to you already, though it's been only eighteen hours. They soon will, even if not through me. I know this is no frolic for you, here with me, but they will almost make it seem so."

She was thinking. Her brow was wrinkled and her eyes stared straight at Wolfe. "Do you know," she asked, "what I think would be the best thing? I don't know why I didn't think of it before. You're a detective, you're an expert at helping people in trouble, and I'm certainly in trouble. I'll pay you to help me. I could pay you a little now."

"Not now or ever, Miss Jones." Wolfe was blunt. "When did Mr. Chaffee tell you that your husband was looking for you?"

"You won't even listen to me," she complained.

"Talk sense and I will. When?"

She edged back on the chair an inch. "You don't know my husband. He was jealous about me even before we married, and then he was worse. It got so bad I couldn't stand it, and that was why I left him. I knew if I stayed in Pittsburgh he would find me and kill me, so I came to New York. A friend of mine had come here—I mean just a friend. I got a job at a modeling agency and made enough to live on, and I met a lot of people. Ross Chaffee was one of them, and he wanted to use me in a picture and I let him. Of course, he paid me, but that wasn't so important, because soon after that I met Phil Kampf, and he got me a tryout at a night club and I made it. About then I had a scare, though. A man from Pittsburgh saw me at a theater and spoke to me, but I told him he was wrong, that I had never been in Pittsburgh.''

"That was a year ago," Wolfe muttered.

"Yes. I was a little leery about the night club, appearing in public like that, but months went by and nothing happened. And then all of a sudden Ross Chaffee phoned me that my husband had come and asked about the picture. I begged him not to tell him who it was, and he promised he wouldn't. You see, you don't know my husband. I knew he was trying to find me so he could kill me.''

"You've said that twice. Has he ever killed anybody?''

"I didn't say anybody—I said me. I seem to have an effect on men." She gestured for understanding. "They just go for me. And Dick—well, I know him, that's all. I left him a year and a half ago, and he's still looking for me, and that's what he's like. When Ross told me he was here, I was scared stiff. I quit working at the club because he might happen to go there and see me, and I hardly left my apartment till last night.''

Wolfe nodded. "To meet Mr. Talento. What for?''

"I told you.''

"Yes, but then you were merely Miss Jones. Now you are also Mrs. Meegan. What for?''

"That doesn't change it any. I had heard on the radio about Phil being killed and I wanted to know about it. I rang Ross Chaffee and I rang Jerry Aland, but neither of them answered; so I rang Vic Talento. He wouldn't tell me anything on the phone, but he said he would meet me.''

"Did Mr. Aland and Mr. Talento know you had sat for that picture?''

"Sure they did.''

"And that Mr. Meegan had seen it and recognized you, and was here looking for you?''

"Yes, they knew all about it. Ross had to tell them, because he thought Dick might ask them if they knew who had modeled for the picture, and he had to warn them not to tell. They said they wouldn't, and they didn't. They're all good friends of mine.''

She stopped to open her black leather bag, took out a purse, and fingered its contents. She raised her eyes to Wolfe. "I can pay your forty dollars now, to start. I'm not just in trouble; I'm in danger of my life, really I am. I don't see how you can refuse— You're not listening!''

Apparently he wasn't. With his lips pursed, he was watching the tip of his forefinger make little circles on his desk blotter. Her reproach didn't stop him, but after a moment he moved his eyes to me and said abruptly, "Get Mr. Chaffee."

"No!" she cried. "I don't want him to know—"

"Nonsense," he snapped at her. "Everybody will have to know everything, so why drag it out? . . . Get him Archie, I'll speak to him."

I dialed Chaffee's number. I doubted if he would be back from his session with the D.A., but he was. I pitched my voice low so he wouldn't recognize it, and merely told him that Nero Wolfe wished to speak to him. Wolfe took it at his desk.

"Mr. Chaffee? This is Nero Wolfe. I've assumed interest in the murder of Philip Kampf and have done some investigating. . . . Just one moment, please; don't ring off. Sitting here in my office is Mrs. Richard Meegan, alias Miss Jewel Jones. . . . Please let me finish. I shall, of course, have to detain her and communicate with the police, since they will want her as a material witness in a murder case, but before I do that I would like to discuss the matter with you and the others who live in that house. Will you undertake to bring them here as soon as possible? . . . No, I'll say nothing further on the phone. I want you here, all of you. If Mr. Meegan is balky, you might as well tell him his wife is here—"

She was across to him in a leap that any young mare might have envied, grabbing for the phone and shrieking at it, "Don't tell him Ross! Don't bring him! Don't—"

My own leap and dash around the end of the desk was fairly good, too. I yanked her back with enough enthusiasm so that I landed in the red-leather chair with her on my lap, and since she was by no means through, I wrapped my arms around her, pinning her arms to her sides, whereupon she started kicking my shins with her heels. She kept on kicking until Wolfe had finished with Chaffee. When he hung up she suddenly went limp against me.

Wolfe scowled at us. "An affecting sight," he snorted.

*   *   *

There were various aspects of the situation. One was lunch. For Wolfe it was unthinkable to have company in the house at mealtime, without feeding him or her, but he certainly wasn't going to sit at table with a female who had just pounced on him and clawed at him. The solution was simple: she and I were served in the dining room and Wolfe ate in the kitchen with Fritz. We were served, but she didn't eat much. She kept listening and looking toward the hall, though I assured her that care would be taken to see that her husband didn't kill her on these premises.

A second aspect was the reaction of three of the Arbor Street tenants to their discovery of my identity. I handled that myself. When the doorbell rang and I admitted them, at a quarter past two, I told them I would be glad to discuss my split personality with any or all of them later, if they still wanted to, but they would have to file it until Wolfe was through. Victor Talento had another beef that he wouldn't file—that I had double-crossed him on the message he had asked me to take to Jewel Jones. He wanted to get nasty about it and demanded a private talk with Wolfe, but I told him to go climb a rope.

I also had to handle the third aspect, which had two angles. There was Miss Jones's theory that her husband would kill her on sight, which might or might not be well-founded; and there was the fact that one of them had killed Kampf and might go to extremes if pushed. On that I took three precautions: I showed them the Marley .38 I had put in my pocket and told them it was loaded; I insisted on patting them from shoulders to ankles; and I kept Miss Jones in the dining room until I had them seated in the office, on a row of chairs facing Wolfe's desk. When he was in his chair behind his desk I went across the hall for her and brought her in.

Meegan jumped up and started for us. I stiff-armed him, and made it good. His wife got behind me, Talento and Aland left their chairs, presumably to help protect her. Meegan was shouting, and so were they. I detoured with her around back of them and got her to a chair at the end of my desk, and when I sat down I was in an ideal spot to trip anyone headed for her. Talento and Aland had pulled Meegan down onto a chair between them, and he sat staring at her.

"With that hubub over," Wolfe said, "I want to be sure I have the names right." his eyes went from left to right. "Talento, Meegan, Aland, Chaffee. Is that correct?"

I told him yes.

"Then I'll proceed." He glanced up at the wall clock. "Twenty hours ago Philip Kampf was killed in the house where you gentlemen live. The circumstances indicate that one of you killed him. But I won't rehash the multifarious details which you have already discussed at length with the police; you are familiar with them. I have not been hired to work on this case; the only client I have is a dog, and he came to my office by chance. However—"

The doorbell rang. I asked myself if I had put the chain bolt on, and decided I had. Through the open door to the hall I saw Fritz passing to answer it. Wolfe started to go on, but was annoyed by the sound of voices, and stopped. He shut his eyes and compressed his lips, while the audience sat and looked at him.

Then Fritz appeared in the doorway and announced: "Inspector Cramer, sir."

Wolfe's eyes opened. "What does he want?"

"I told him you are engaged. He says he knows you are— that the four men were followed to your house and he was notified. He says he expected you to be trying some trick with the dog, and he knows that's what you are doing, and he intends to come in and see what it is. Sergeant. Stebbins is with him."

Wolfe grunted. "Archie, tell— No. You'd better stay where you are. Fritz, tell him he may see and hear what I'm doing, provided he gives me thirty minutes without interruptions or demands. If he agrees to that, bring them in."

"Wait!" Ross Chaffee was on his feet. "You said you would discuss it with us before you communicated with the police."

"I haven't communicated with them. They're here."

"You told them to come!"

"No. I would have preferred to deal with you men first, and then call them, but here they are, and they might as well join us. Bring them, Fritz, on that condition."

"Yes, sir."

Fritz went. Chaffee thought he had something more to say, decided he hadn't, and sat down. Talento said something to

him, and he shook his head. Jerry Aland, much more present-
able now that he was combed and dressed, kept his eyes fastened on Wolfe. For Meegan, apparently, there was no one in
the room but him and his wife.

Cramer and Stebbins marched in, halted three paces from the
door, and took a survey.

"Be seated," Wolfe invited them. "Luckily, Mr. Cramer,
your usual chair is unoccupied."

"Where's the dog?" Cramer demanded.

"In the kitchen. It's understood that you will be merely a
spectator for thirty minutes?"

"That's what I said."

"Then sit down. But you should have one piece of information. You know the gentlemen, of course, but not the lady. Her
current name is Miss Jewel Jones. Her legal name is Mrs.
Richard Meegan."

"Meegan?" Cramer stared. "The one in the picture Chaffee
painted?"

"That's right. Please be seated."

"Where did you get her?"

"That can wait. No interruptions and no demands. Confound
it, sit down!"

Cramer went and lowered himself onto the red-leather chair.
Purley Stebbins got one of the yellow ones and planted it behind
Chaffee and Aland.

Wolfe regarded the quartet. "I was about to say, gentlemen,
that it was something the dog did that pointed to the murderer
for me. But before—"

"What did it do?" Cramer cut in.

"You know all about it," Wolfe told him coldly. "Mr.
Goodwin related the events to you exactly as they happened. If
you interrupt again, by heaven, you can take them all down to
headquarters—not including the dog—and stew it out yourself!"

He went back to the four: "But before I come to the dog,
another thing or two. I offer no comment on your guile with
Mr. Meegan. You were all friends of Miss Jones's, and you
refused to disclose her to a husband whom she had abandoned
and professed to fear. I will even concede that there was a
flavor of gallantry in your conduct. But when Mr. Kampf was
murdered and the police swarmed in, it was idiotic to try to

keep her out of it. They were sure to get to her. I got to her first, only because of Mr. Goodwin's admirable enterprise and characteristic luck.''

He shook his head at them. "It was also idiotic of you to assume that Mr. Goodwin was a police officer, and admit him and answer his questions, merely because he had been present during the abortive experiment with the dog. You should have asked to see his credentials. None of you had any idea who he was. Even Mr. Meegan, who had seen him in this office in the morning, was bamboozled. I mention this to anticipate any possible official complaint that Mr. Goodwin impersonated an officer. You know he didn't. He merely took advantage of your unwarranted assumption.''

He shifted in his chair. "Another thing: Yesterday morning Mr. Meegan called here by appointment to ask me to do a job for him. With his first words I gathered that it was something about his wife. I don't take that kind of work, and I was blunt with him. He was offended. He rushed out in a temper, grabbing a hat and raincoat from the rack in the hall, and he took Mr. Goodwin's coat instead of his own. Late in the afternoon Mr. Goodwin went to Arbor Street with the coat that had been left in error, to exchange it. He saw that in front of Number Twenty-nine there were collected two police cars, a policeman on duty, some people, and a dog. He decided to postpone his errand and went on by, after a brief halt during which he patted the dog. He walked home, and had gone nearly two miles when he discovered that the dog was following him. He brought the dog in a cab the rest of the way, to his house and this room.''

He flattened a palm on his desk. "Now. Why did the dog follow Mr. Goodwin through the turmoil of the city? Mr. Cramer's notion that the dog was enticed is poppycock. Mr. Goodwin is willing to believe, as many men are, that he is irresistible both to dogs and to women, and doubtless his vanity impeded his intellect, or he would have reached the same conclusion I did. The dog didn't follow him; it followed the coat. You ask, as I did, how to account for Mr. Kampf's dog following Mr. Meegan's coat. I couldn't. I can't. Then since it was unquestionably Mr. Kampf's dog, it couldn't have been Mr. Meegan's coat. It is better than a conjecture—it is next thing to a certainty—*that it was Mr. Kampf's coat!*''

His gaze leveled at the deserted husband. "Mr. Meegan. Some two hours ago I learned from Mr. Goodwin that you maintain that you had never seen or heard of Mr. Kampf. That was fairly conclusive but before sending for you I had to verify my conjecture that the model who had sat for Mr. Chaffee's picture was your wife. I would like to hear it straight from you. Did you ever meet Philip Kampf alive?"

Meegan was meeting the gaze. "No."

"Don't you want to qualify that?"

"No."

"Then where did you get his raincoat?"

Meegan's jaw worked. He said, "I didn't have his raincoat, or if I did I didn't know it."

"That won't do. I warn you, you are in deadly peril. The raincoat that you brought into this house and left here is in the hall now, there on the rack. It can easily be established that it belonged to Mr. Kampf and was worn by him. Where did you get it?"

Meegan's jaw worked some more. "I never had it, if it belonged to Kampf. This is a dirty frame. You can't prove that's the coat I left here."

Wolfe's voice sharpened: "One more chance. Have you any explanation of how Kampf's coat came into your possession?"

"No, and I don't need any."

He may not have been pure boob. If he hadn't noticed that he wore the wrong coat home—and he probably hadn't, in his state of mind—this had hit him from a clear sky and he had no time to study it.

"Then you're done for," Wolfe told him. "For your own coat must be somewhere, and I think I know where. In the police laboratory. Mr. Kampf was wearing one when you killed him and pushed his body down the stairs—and that explains why, when they were making that experiment this morning, the dog showed no interest in the spot where the body had lain. It had been enveloped, not in his coat but in yours. If you won't explain how you got Mr. Kampf's coat, then explain how he got yours. Is that also a frame?"

Wolfe pointed a finger at him. "I note that flash of hope in your eye, and I think I know what it means. But your brain is lagging. If, after killing Kampf, you took your raincoat off of him and put on him the one that you thought was his, that won't help you any. For in that case the coat that was on the body is Mr. Goodwin's, and certainly that can be established, and how would you explain that? It looks hopeless, and—''

Meegan was springing up, but before he even got well started Purley's big hands were on his shoulders, pulling him back and down.

And Jewel Jones was babbling, ''I told you he would kill me! I knew he would! He killed Phil!''

Wolfe snapped at her, ''How do you know he did?''

Judging by her eyes and the way she was shaking, she would be hysterical in another two minutes. Meanwhile, she poured it out:

''Because Phil told me—he told me he knew Dick was here looking for me, and he knew how afraid I was of him, and he said if I wouldn't come back to him he would tell Dick where I was. I didn't think he really would—I didn't think Phil could be as mean as that—and I wouldn't promise.

''But yesterday morning he phoned me and told me he had seen Dick and told him he thought he knew who had posed for that picture. He said he was going to see him again in the afternoon and tell him about me if I didn't promise, and so I promised. I thought if I promised, it would give me time to decide what to do. But Phil must have gone to see Dick again, anyway.''

''Where had they met in the morning?''

''At Phil's apartment, he said. And he said—that's why I know Dick killed him—he said Dick had gone off with his raincoat, and he laughed about it and said he was willing for Dick to have his raincoat if he could have Dick's wife.'' She was shaking harder now. ''And I'll bet that's what he told Dick! I'll bet he said I was coming back and he thought that was a good trade—a raincoat for a wife! That was like Phil!''

She giggled. It started with a giggle, and then the valves burst open and here it came. When something happens in that office to smash a woman's nerves—as it has more than once—it usually falls to me to deal with it. But that time three other guys, led by Ross Chaffee, were on hand, and I was glad to leave Jewel Jones to them. As for Wolfe, he skedaddled. If there is one thing on earth he absolutely will not be in a room with, it's a woman in eruption. He got up and marched out. As for Meegan, Purley and Cramer had him. When they left with him, they didn't take the dog. To relieve the minds of any of you who have the notion, which I understand is widespread, that it makes a dog neurotic to change its name, I might add that he responds to "Jet" now as if his mother had started calling him that before he had his eyes open.

As for the raincoat, Wolfe had been right about the flash in Meegan's eye. Kampf had been wearing Meegan's raincoat when he was killed, and of course that wouldn't do, so after strangling him Meegan had taken it off and put on the one he thought was Kampf's. Only, it was mine. As a part of the D.A.'s case I went down to headquarters and identified it. At the trial it helped the jury to decide that Meegan deserved the big one. After that was over I suppose I could have claimed it, but the idea didn't appeal to me. My new coat is a different color.